The Scandalous Adventures of the Sister of the Bride

Center Point
Large Print

Also by Victoria Alexander and available from
Center Point Large Print:

My Wicked Little Lies
The Importance of Being Wicked

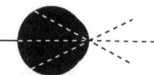

**This Large Print Book carries the
Seal of Approval of N.A.V.H.**

The Scandalous Adventures of the Sister of the Bride

Victoria Alexander

CENTER POINT LARGE PRINT
THORNDIKE, MAINE

This Center Point Large Print edition
is published in the year 2014 by arrangement with
Kensington Publishing Corp.

The text of this Large Print edition is unabridged.
In other aspects, this book may vary
from the original edition.
Printed in the United States of America
on permanent paper.
Set in 16-point Times New Roman type.

ISBN: 978-1-62899-102-4

Library of Congress Cataloging-in-Publication Data

Alexander, Victoria.
  The scandalous adventures of the sister of the bride / Victoria
Alexander.
    pages cm
  Summary: "Lady Delilah Hargate and Mr. Samuel Russell spent one
unforgettable night together in New York City. Now attending the
wedding of her sister and his friend at Millworth Manor, they pretend
they have never met before. But delightful grounds, lavish drawing
rooms, and secluded corners provide the chance to discover that one
night was only the beginning"—Provided by publisher.
  ISBN 978-1-62899-102-4 (library binding : alk. paper)
  1. Love stories. 2. Large type books. I. Title.
PS3551.L357713S33 2014
813′.54—dc23
                                                              2014011162

*The Scandalous Adventures of
the Sister of the Bride*
is my thirtieth novel.

So this book is for my family, and
for my old friends who were there at the
beginning and the new ones I've made along
the way, and for my readers.

I couldn't have done it without you.

This is dedicated to all of you
who gave me love and support.
Who held my hand and shared my stories.
Who believed.
Thank you.

The Scandalous Adventures of the Sister of the Bride

Prologue

New York, June 1887

"Do hurry with that." Delilah, Lady Hargate, cringed at the sharp note in her voice.

She did so hate to be rude especially after, well, after *everything* but she wasn't used to being in this position. She'd certainly never been in this position before, never imagined she would, and really had no idea how she now found herself here. Nor did she have any idea how to gracefully extricate herself, although she suspected graceful was no longer possible.

"If you would be so good," she added as politely as she could, even while knowing that minor attempt to atone for her impatience made no difference.

Behind her, he chuckled but thankfully continued to lace her corset. "Eager to be away, are you?"

Courtesy battled with honesty, although perhaps this was not the time to be polite.

"Well, yes, I am. It is almost dawn and . . . well . . ." Slipping out of his room in the fashionable Murray Hill Hotel and back to her own rooms without notice would be even more difficult once the sun was up. Not that it wasn't going to be awkward now. Still, the sooner she left, the better her chances of avoiding detection. "I do need to get back before my absence is noted."

"Of course," he murmured. "We wouldn't want that."

"No, we would not." Her jaw tightened. Discovery was the last thing she wanted.

Delilah shared a suite of rooms with her sister, Camille, Lady Lydingham. Camille's fiancé, Grayson Elliott, occupied the suite of rooms next to theirs. Fortunately, no doubt for both sisters, each bedroom had its own separate entry to the hotel corridor. Delilah didn't doubt for a moment that Camille took advantage of that door to join Grayson in his rooms on more than one occasion, if not nightly. But even though Delilah officially accompanied them in the role of chaperone, she did not feel it necessary to intrude on her sister and her fiancé. After all, Camille was a widow, older than Delilah, and was set to marry Grayson in just a few months. Besides, Grayson was the love of her sister's life even if it had taken years for the couple to realize they were meant to be together. But regardless of Delilah's feigned ignorance with respect to the goings-on between the engaged couple, she had no desire for Camille to discover Delilah's own indiscretions. Besides, Camille and Camille's twin, Beryl, Lady Dunwell, had a certain image of their younger sister that

Delilah preferred not to destroy. Whether that image was entirely accurate or not.

"If you could possibly be a little quicker. . . ."

"I'm doing the best I can. I am not a lady's maid, you know. And as surprising as it may sound given the circumstances, I have very little experience at this kind of thing."

"That is good to know," she said under her breath.

"Why?"

"Why what?"

"Why is that good to know?"

"I would hate to think I was merely another conquest."

"I would debate the term *conquest* and I would never call you mere." He chuckled again. "I don't do this sort of thing very often."

Why did he think this was so amusing?

"Yes, well, I don't do this sort of thing at all."

"And yet you did it remarkably well." His tone was mild but she could hear the smile in his voice.

She wasn't entirely sure if she should thank him for that or slap him. She decided to accept his comment as a compliment and not allow her own sense of impropriety, or possibly guilt, to make it something else. Not that she had anything to feel guilty about. It was not as if she was an innocent virgin who had escaped the notice of an unsuspecting chaperone to run amok amid the men of New York. She was an adult, a widow, and financially independent as well. If she wished to have a scandalous interlude in a hotel room in a city she fully planned never to visit again with a man she had barely met and planned as well never to see again it was her decision. Still, it wasn't at all like her and she wasn't certain what had come over her.

"There." A note of satisfaction sounded in his voice.

"Excellent." She glanced around and found the gown she had discarded last night.

When she had first decided to wear the costume of a Dresden shepherdess to last night's masked ball she had thought it charming, if perhaps a touch risqué. But then why not be a little risqué? It wasn't as if anyone knew her here. And it was a masked ball after all. Besides, it was time, past time really, to try something a little different in her life.

The costume was as much an effort to be someone other than Delilah, Lady Hargate, as was throwing caution to the winds and indulging in this intimate encounter with a man she scarcely knew. Now she realized it was a mistake. Not the costume, although that probably was a mistake as well, but this . . . this . . . this night of, well, *sin* for lack of a better word. She was who she was and one certainly couldn't change that sort of thing about a person even if one wished to. She was not the type of woman to wear risqué costumes and she was not the type of woman to join a virtual stranger in his bed. Not that it hadn't been most enjoyable and a great deal of fun. She pushed the thought aside. Now was not the time. Regardless of the mutual enjoyment of the last few hours, this wasn't something she would do again. Ever.

She'd had her moment of adventure. It was over and done with and best put behind her. Which she intended to do as soon as she could escape from his room. She turned away and stepped into the flounced and beribboned gown, pulled it up, slipped her arms into the puffed sleeves, and then tightened the laces on the bodice. As complicated as the gown appeared, it had been leased from an agency that provided costumes for theatrical productions and was constructed to be easily put on and taken off. Which had served her well last night. She groaned to herself. Too well, really.

"That's that then." She turned toward him and forced a smile. "Thank you for a lovely evening, Mr.—"

"Russell." A slight smile curved the corners of his lips. "Samuel Russell."

"Of course," she said with more than a little indignation. "I do know your name."

His brow quirked upward. "Forgive me, I thought perhaps you'd forgotten."

"I would not forget the name of the man I had just . . ." She glanced at the rumpled bed. "Well, I would not forget your name, that's all."

"Delilah." He stepped toward her. "I will never forget anything about last night." He smiled in an altogether too smug manner, his overall air of satisfaction heightened by the deep blue silk dressing gown he wore. If one had an image in one's mind of what a man would wear after a night of wild abandon, a dark blue silk dressing gown would certainly be included. As would a smug smile. "Or this morning for that matter."

This morning? Good Lord! "I must be going." She drew a deep breath. "I should thank you for a lovely evening."

"No." He took her hand and raised it to his lips. "It is I who should thank you."

She snatched her hand away. "Yes, well, be that as it may . . ."

She paused to marshal her senses. It was not at all easy. Mr. Russell—Samuel—was dashing in a rugged American sort of way and in many ways the kind of man she'd secretly found fascinating in her youth. Not now, of course. Still, there was an air of excitement about him, an air of adventure, although she might've been the only one who noticed. No doubt other women were too busy noticing how handsome the man was with his blond hair, somewhat unruly in spite of what she suspected were his best efforts, and dark brown eyes, that seemed at once intense and amused. His shoulders were broad, his body hard and muscled, he stood nearly a foot taller than she, and he looked every bit as delicious costumed tonight as a pirate as he had in his everyday clothes when they had first met. And looked even better without any clothing at all. Yet another thought she dashed from her mind. He was, in addition, charming and funny and she probably laughed more with him than she ever had with any man. There was something about this man and his laugh, free and unreserved, that caught at something deep within her. Silly of course—she'd heard men laugh before and she'd never found herself in their beds. Why she hadn't resisted this man had nothing to do with his laugh or his dark eyes or the shiver that ran down her spine when he so much as brushed her hand. No, this indiscretion was obviously due to the circumstances of her trip to America and an odd desire within herself to taste adventure the like of which she'd never known before. Unfortunately, Lady Hargate was ripe for adventure.

She wasn't entirely sure why that long-simmering desire had at last surfaced but she was fairly certain she knew when. It was the moment she realized that aside from Camille and Grayson, she knew no one in New York. No one would have any expectations of her. No one would judge her, no one would condemn her. She didn't have to be proper and perfect. She could be anyone she wanted to be here. She'd spent her entire life being who she was supposed to be and doing what she was supposed to do. Not that she didn't like being proper and perfect, and she was, for the most part, quite content with her well-ordered and well-planned life, but just once (and really, could anyone ask for more than just once?), just once she wanted to be anything but the eminently respectable Lady Hargate. It was wicked, she knew that from the start, but somehow now, in a place where she could be whomever she wished to be, if only for a few days, it did seem like a wickedness one could be forgiven for. It was just once after all.

It wasn't as if it had been her intention to fall into the bed of the first attractive man she'd met. No indeed. Such an idea hadn't even crossed her mind. Unfortunately, this was the sort of thing that happened when one didn't have a solid plan. She had simply decided to seize whatever opportunity for adventure presented itself, fully expecting that would be no more significant than an unescorted visit to a museum or a solitary walk in a park. Perhaps it would be nothing more than the purchase of a daring new hat or a gown that was more revealing than was approved of in London society. Or possibly her adventure might take the form of a dance with a gentleman she had not been properly introduced to or even a mild flirtation. Thoughts that had inevitably led directly to the Dresden shepherdess costume.

She would probably have come to her senses about this absurd desire for adventure if Samuel

Russell hadn't walked into her life and snatched all possibility of rational thought from her head. But apparently, when one has never had an adventure and is ripe for one, and one meets the handsome employee of a business associate of one's future brother-in-law, and one then willingly dons a revealing gown in the guise of a Dresden shepherdess for a masked ball, when one doesn't have a *plan* . . . well? Isn't a night of rather extraordinary passion with a stranger almost to be expected?

Now, however, with the clear-mindedness of the approaching dawn, she could see what a mistake she had made. What a horrifying mistake. Unlike her sisters, Beryl in particular, she was not, nor had she ever been, a woman prone to adventure. This was not the type of thing she did. Ever. She would return to England tomorrow and put this incident in the past where it belonged. And Mr. Samuel Russell along with it.

"Mr. Russell—"

Once again his brow rose.

"Mr. Russell," she repeated. In spite of their night together, use of his given name was entirely too, well, personal. "I don't wish to be rude. And I have no desire to offend you. Indeed, that is the furthest thing from my mind."

"Ah, yes, the only thing on your mind is leaving as quickly as possible." His eyes narrowed. "Why would I be offended by that?"

"You shouldn't be," she said quickly. "It really has nothing to do with you at all."

"Imagine my relief."

"I didn't mean—"

"That is interesting though, as I thought it had a great deal to do with me." His voice was a bit harder than was necessary.

Surely he wasn't annoyed with her? The man had no right to be annoyed but then the workings of the minds of men had never really made much sense to her.

"No, not at all. Believe me, I would be just as eager to leave if I were with someone else." She glanced past him, spotted her shepherdess bonnet on the other side of the room, and stepped around him to retrieve it. It was silly to put the hat on, but it would shield her face and perhaps prevent recognition. After all there had been no fewer than a dozen Dresden shepherdesses at the ball last night and who knew how many might still be wandering the corridors of the hotel. Even so, she had no idea how she would respond should she encounter her sister or Grayson. She slipped the bonnet on her head and then turned back to him. "I know that sounded dreadful and I do apologize but—"

"But the simple fact of the matter is you cannot wait to be on your way," he said in a wry manner. "Understandable, of course, as you do not do this sort of thing."

"And we scarcely know each other," she blurted

without thinking although it had occurred to her already. Precisely what made him as much an adventure as a mistake.

"I suspect we know each other better now than we did, oh, say, last night."

"Nonetheless, we—"

"Let me see." He paused for a moment. "I met you on Tuesday. Ran into you in the park on Wednesday—quite unexpectedly I might add. And again on Thursday our paths crossed. I was beginning to think it was fate."

"It wasn't fate," she said sharply. "The very idea is absurd."

"And then there you were last night." He stepped closer and gazed down into her eyes. "And I have always been fond of porcelain shepherdesses."

"Nonsense." She shrugged off his comment but couldn't tear her gaze from his. "No man is truly fond of frivolous knickknacks."

"Ah well then, perhaps I misspoke. Maybe I am simply fond of eighteenth-century portrayals. And as you chose to dress in that manner—"

"Nonetheless, it was not fate." She stepped back. "You may consider it whatever you wish I suppose, but it was really no more than coincidence. Fate had nothing to do with my choice of a costume nor did it have anything to do with our initial meeting and any subsequent meetings. Fate has not taken a hand here, Mr. Russell, and it would be best if you were to realize that."

His expression was somber but laughter danced in his brown eyes. "My mistake then."

"It is indeed a mistake if you think there is something more to this than what it is." She drew a deep breath and braced herself. "While it was indeed a lovely evening—"

"It was exceptional."

Heat swept up her face and she ignored it. "Regardless, it would be best to put this . . . this *incident* behind us."

"I'm not sure I can do that." He shook his head in a mournful manner. "It is not the sort of thing I am prone to forget. Indeed, I consider last night one of the more memorable nights of my life."

"What utter rubbish." She scoffed. "I don't believe that for a moment. I suspect you've had any number of unforgettable nights with women far more memorable than I."

"Do you?" A smile tugged at his lips. "And you base that on . . . what?"

"Well, you . . . you're very . . . well, good, I suppose and . . ." She met his gaze directly. "It is apparent you have done this before."

His brow furrowed with annoyance. "I have already said I am no more accustomed to—how did you put it? Ah yes—*this sort of thing* than you. And regardless of how many unforgettable nights I may or may not have had in the past, none of those women were you."

"Oh." Her breath caught and she stared at him. "I'm not sure what to say. I am most flattered."

"And I did say it to be flattering." It was impossible to miss the note of sarcasm in his voice.

"Then I thank you. Still, I am, for the most part, a most practical woman and it does seem extremely practical for us to go our separate ways."

He crossed his arms over his chest and stared at her. "Now, you mean?"

"Yes, now, of course." Why was the blasted man being so difficult? She was making her intentions perfectly clear in a calm, rational manner. Delilah forced a firm note to her voice. "Mr. Russell, I leave for home tomorrow. As there will be an ocean between us, I think it's best if we forget about this encounter altogether."

"Do you?"

"I think it would be wise if we pretended it never happened."

"As one does with mistakes?"

Had he been reading her mind? "I never used the word *mistake*."

"And yet it does seem apparent that is exactly what you're thinking." He paused. "So, this is not to be a beginning then?"

"Absolutely not." Surprise widened her eyes. "I do apologize if I gave you that impression."

He considered her for a moment. "You have

no intention of ever seeing me again, do you?"

She breathed a sigh of relief. "Oh, I'm so glad you understand."

"But I don't understand. And I have to say I am more than a little offended."

"Offended?" She stared at him. "Why on earth would you possibly be offended?"

"Why? Because you've had your way with me and now you are simply going to discard me."

"*I've* had my way with *you?*" She drew her brows together. It wasn't as if he hadn't had his way with her as well. Indeed, judging from the passion they'd shared throughout the night, passion shared more than once, he had had every bit as delightful a time as she had. Have her way with him indeed. "It's not like that at all."

"Then how is it?"

Dear Lord, she'd had no intention of explaining this all to him. Nor did it seem at all fair. She had fully expected him to be the kind of man who would be thrilled to hear her say good-bye with no fuss, no protests and no half-hearted promises. Of course, an annoying voice in the back of her head noted, if he had been that kind of man she probably would not have been attracted to him in the first place.

"Mr. Russell . . . Samuel." She chose her words with care. "As I have already said, falling into the bed of a man who is very much a stranger is not something I have ever done. Nor is it something I ever imagined I would do. And I certainly don't plan to ever do it again. I can attribute my actions to nothing more than a heretofore unknown adventurous streak within me."

"I'm an adventure, then?" A slow smile spread across his face. "That does take some of the sting out of it. I like being an adventure."

She ignored him and continued. "And, as the very nature of adventure is its uniqueness, this is something that will not be repeated. Nor is it an adventure I wish to be reminded of. I am not the kind of woman who has adventures. I am not an adventurous sort. Therefore . . ." She drew a steadying breath and squared her shoulders. "I do indeed think it would be best if we never saw each other again."

"I see." He nodded thoughtfully. "You really think that would be best?"

She nodded. "Oh I do, I truly, truly do."

"You leave me no choice then, do you?"

"No, I don't. Nor do I intend to. As I said it's for the best. Besides, as my ship sails tomorrow, there will be no more crossing one another's path unexpectedly and certainly no more . . ." She glanced at the rumpled bed. "Well, no more *anything*."

"Ah well." He shrugged. "If that's the way you want it."

"It is, Mr. Russell." She nodded with perhaps more enthusiasm than necessary. "Besides, this wasn't fate. It was only mere coincidence and nothing more significant than that."

"Are you certain?"

"Absolutely."

"And you would know fate when you saw it?"

"I would hope so. Although I will admit I have never especially believed in fate."

"Very well then." He nodded. "I have always thought that fate cannot be denied. But as you are leaving America, and the chances are indeed excellent that we will not see one another again, even in passing, I suppose you may be right. Besides, one can argue that if it was fate to be together, it is fate as well to part. Which does strike me as a terrible shame." He paused. "Shall I escort you back to your rooms?"

"No," she said quickly. "But I do thank you for offering. I might be able to explain why I am dressed like this if I am seen alone, but I should never be able to explain why you were accompanying me."

"Of course." He chuckled. "I should have thought of that myself."

"But then you do not do this sort of thing very often." Relief prompted her to cast him a teasing smile.

"I hope you're not disappointed that my reputation is not quite as tarnished as an adventure might require."

"I am not the least bit disappointed." She gazed

into his dark eyes and for no more than a fraction of a moment wondered what might have been between them had he been more than an adventure. Had he been the kind of man she planned to spend the rest of her life with. But he wasn't of course.

He took her hand and raised it to his lips, his gaze never leaving hers. "Thank you, Mrs. Hargate, for a most enjoyable evening. It was not merely my pleasure, it was my adventure as well."

"Thank you, Mr. Russell, for my adventure. It was indeed . . ." She smiled up at him and at that moment had never meant anything more. "Unforgettable."

Chapter One

*Eighteen days before the wedding of
Camille, Lady Lydingham,
To Mr. Grayson Elliott . . .*

Millworth Manor, October 1887

"You didn't need to come fetch me in person."
Samuel Russell smiled at his old friend. "I did
manage to get from one place to another in France
and Germany, you know, and I'd bet I could
have found my way from the train station to
Fairborough Hall. It's not as if you people don't
speak English."

"Yes, but you don't." Grayson Elliott grinned.
The differences between the American and British
forms of the same language had long been a
running joke between the two men.

"I say, old chap, do be so good as to shut your
mouth," Sam said in his best imitation of Gray's
accent.

Gray winced. "You have just made my point.
And whatever you do, don't attempt that again."

Sam laughed. He'd met the Englishman nine
or so years ago and the two had built their
respective fortunes in tandem. Sam grew his not
inconsequential empire from a small company

founded by his grandfather. Gray's success had begun with a loan from his family. They'd first met as competitors but soon discovered they shared a common work ethic, a similar way of looking at life and the possibilities the world presented for enterprising young men. Throughout it all, they'd formed a solid friendship. Now that Gray had returned to England after more than a decade spent in America, Sam missed the man who had been, at various times, confidant, cohort, partner, and friend.

"I must say I was surprised when I received your telegram." Gray slanted a casual look at the American.

Sam gasped in feigned dismay. "Surely you didn't think I would miss the wedding of one of my oldest friends as well as a valued business associate?"

"When I was in New York you said you wouldn't be able to attend the wedding."

"When you were in New York, I didn't think I would. But then I had no idea I would find myself in Europe. As I did, it seemed a shame to miss your wedding. And, every few years, it's wise to reacquaint myself with my London solicitors, as they oversee my international holdings."

"The firm I recommended."

"For which I will be forever in your debt. Besides, while I have been to England before, I have never had the time, or the inclination, to see anything beyond London. You have talked so much through the years about the idyllic world of Fairborough Hall and the English countryside, the opportunity to see it for myself just seemed too good to pass up." He glanced at the scenery passing by them in the open carriage. "I could use a few relaxing weeks in the country."

"A holiday?" Gray's brow rose in a skeptical manner. "You? I can't recall you ever taking a holiday."

"Past time then, don't you think?"

"I have thought exactly that for some time now." Gray paused. "Perhaps if you didn't devote every minute to work, we would be preparing for *your* wedding now."

"I believe we prepared for my wedding last year," Sam said mildly. There was a time when the mention of Sam's debacle of an engagement would have been met with annoyance. Not with Gray of course; the Englishman had stood by him when he had needed a friend even if Gray had had his suspicions about Sam's fiancée from the very beginning. Still, it was the mark of a good friend that Gray had not held over him the fact that he was right and Sam was so very wrong.

"She was never right for you." Although Gray couldn't resist mentioning it on occasion.

"And if I hadn't listened to you . . ."

"You would now be married to the wrong woman."

"Fortunately, I came to my senses and recognized the truth."

They both knew there was far more to it than merely recognizing the truth but now was not the time to discuss it. Although he suspected, given Gray's impending nuptials, the topic would raise its ugly head again in the days to come. "And now *you* have found the right woman."

"Indeed I have." Gray chuckled. "But as much as I am delighted to see you here, I doubt that it's the wedding that has lured you here. Nor do I believe that rubbish about a holiday."

"I am here to help celebrate your nuptials. There is nothing more to my presence here than that."

"No doubt." Suspicion sounded in Gray's voice. The problem with old friends was that they knew you entirely too well.

"And I am eager to see your family's home."

"I shall delight in showing you around but I'm afraid you won't be staying at Fairborough. It was severely damaged in a fire last winter."

"Good Lord." Sam stared at his friend. "How bad was it?"

"Very, but fortunately the repairs are nearly finished. While my family is residing there once again it's still not quite ready for guests. Those coming for the wedding will be staying at Millworth Manor, the country home of my fiancée's family."

"Ah yes, the lovely Lady Lydingham. How is she?"

"Busy bordering on frantic with a tiny touch of panic tossed in for good measure." Gray chuckled. "There is far more involved in a wedding of this sort than I had imagined. Camille wants everything to be perfect and even though she has been through this kind of thing before and has experienced help, as well as one of her sisters, there's a distinct touch of insanity about her."

Sam bit back a laugh. "Oh?"

"You know how women are. You have sisters."

"Yes, but my oldest sister's wedding was not as grand as I suspect yours will be and none of my other sisters are old enough to be planning a wedding. But I can imagine the chaos." Sam paused. "I know the wedding is still a few weeks away. I hope my early arrival isn't a problem. I have already spent several days in London. Since it's only an hour by train, I do plan on going into the city to take care of a few remaining matters while I'm here but I could certainly stay in London until—"

"Don't be absurd." Gray scoffed. "I'm delighted to have you here. Millworth Manor is more than large enough to house any number of guests. And I don't mind saying I do welcome another male presence in the house. Camille's parents have been traveling and we're not sure when they might arrive. And who knows where her uncle is but we hope he appears before the wedding. Although Uncle Basil is notoriously undependable."

Sam nodded. "We all have one or two relatives like that."

"Camille's twin sister's husband is a political sort and probably won't arrive until a day or two before the wedding although Beryl is expected any day now." He grimaced. "I can definitely use another man around once Beryl arrives. For protection if for no other reason. Beryl's not especially fond of me."

"Her twin sister?" Sam raised a brow. "That must make things interesting."

Gray chuckled. "You have no idea."

"And Mrs. Hargate?" Sam adopted a casual note. In spite of the fact that she had been adamant, almost rude really, about never wanting to see him again, he was looking forward to seeing her. It had been nearly four months since their tryst in New York. There was a chance she had changed her mind about renewing their acquaintance. A chance he had lingered just as much in her mind as she had in his. The woman did seem to be there every time he closed his eyes.

Gray's brows drew together in confusion. "Who?"

"The lady who accompanied you and your fiancée to New York? Your chaperone? I thought she was a relative of Lady Lydingham's."

"Oh, of course." Gray's expression cleared. "Delilah. *Lady* Hargate."

"*Lady* Hargate?" And wasn't that interesting.

"She's Camille's younger sister."

"Is she? I was under the impression she was a more distant relative."

"They haven't been close in the past, although Camille is trying to rectify that. That was one of the reasons why she asked Delilah to accompany us and probably why Delilah agreed to come. She'd have a fit if you addressed her as Mrs. Hargate by the way. She's very, oh, proper about that sort of thing." He cast Sam a curious look. "I wasn't aware you had met her."

"Only in passing," Sam said in an offhand manner. Only as her damned adventure. "I doubt that she even remembers my name." It was obvious now that while the woman hadn't actually lied to him, she had led him to believe she was someone she wasn't. Mrs. Hargate—ha!

"She arrived at the manor a few weeks ago along with Teddy, Lady Theodosia Winslow. Teddy's in charge of the wedding preparations. Her late father was an earl. She and her mother are among the most prestigious planners of weddings and social events in England. Camille says they're in high demand and agree to only the most important events. Fortunately, she is also Delilah's closest friend. Unfortunately, their services cost a small fortune," he said wryly. "Delilah claims they have to charge exorbitant fees because nothing free is truly valued."

Sam nodded. "She's right there."

"Aside from the soundness of their business practices . . ." Gray lowered his voice in a confidential manner. "I suspect the late earl might have squandered the family fortune but if so, it's not common knowledge."

"And yet you have your suspicions."

"I suppose my years away have changed the way I look at things. Anyone here who might have the same suspicions would never voice them aloud, at least not in public. It simply isn't done." He paused for a long moment. "Speaking of suspicions, why are you really here?"

"You wound me deeply, Gray." Sam adopted an indignant tone. "I'm here for your wedding of course. And to spend some time with an old friend. And reacquaint myself with the London firm that oversees my international holdings. If, in the course of that, conversation turns to some sort of, oh, I don't know, some sort of investment or opportunity or—"

"Aha!" Gray laughed. "I knew you had an ulterior motive."

"Not at all. I simply . . ." Sam grinned. "I don't think it's right to keep this to myself."

"Keep what to yourself?"

"Why, what kind of friend would I be if I didn't let you in on this?"

"In on what?"

"I know how you love anything that smacks of progress and the future."

"Progress?" Gray's eyes narrowed thoughtfully. "And the future, you say?"

"I should warn you, it's highly speculative."

"Is it?" A familiar glint sparked in Gray's eyes. "Then I suspect as well it's extremely interesting."

"Indeed it is." Sam leaned closer to his old friend. "What would you say to the idea of horseless carriages?"

"Horseless carriages?" Gray groaned. "Are you insane?"

"Shhh." Sam glanced at the carriage driver. "This is best discussed in private."

"Keech can be trusted. And I have no doubts as to his sanity."

"Even so."

"Still, I'd hate for him to think I was mad." Gray heaved a resigned sigh. "And I suspect this is one of the maddest ideas you've ever had."

"Or one of the most brilliant." Sam flashed another grin.

Gray studied him closely, then nodded. "Very well, then." He turned and called to the driver. "Keech, we'll get out here. Mr. Russell would prefer to walk the rest of the way and I wouldn't mind a bit of exercise myself. Who knows how long this grand autumn weather will last. Besides we are nearly to Millworth's drive now."

"Very well, sir." Keech reined the horses to a stop.

Sam and Gray got out of the carriage. Gray

nodded at the driver. "Please take Mr. Russell's bags to the house. We'll be there shortly."

"As you wish, Mr. Elliott." The driver tapped the rim of his hat and the carriage started off.

Gray waited until the vehicle was out of range. "Well, go on then. What is this nonsense about?"

"It's not nonsense and it might well be the way of the future."

"As might flying machines, but we've yet to see one that has managed to get an inch off the ground."

Sam cast his friend a smug smile. "I have."

Gray's brows shot upward. "You've seen a working flying machine?"

"Don't be silly. That would be absurd. I doubt man was meant to fly, although I'd never bet on that. After all, the world is changing every day." His grin widened. "But I have seen a horseless carriage."

"I too have seen a horseless carriage." Gray nodded and started off down the road, Sam by his side. "Rather useless things at the moment I'd say."

"Exactly."

Gray stopped and stared at Sam. "What do you mean exactly?"

"I mean that at the moment they are rather useless." Sam nonchalantly started walking again. "But only at the moment."

"I have always relished the way you enjoy being circumspect. What are you trying to say?"

"What is the biggest problem with horseless carriages?"

"I don't know. I really haven't been especially interested up to now." Gray thought for a moment. "An efficient, compact motor I suppose. Of course, there have been developments in recent years. Internal combustion and—"

Sam laughed. "I thought you said you weren't interested?"

"I'm not," Gray said staunchly then shrugged. "Although admittedly it is an intriguing proposition."

"I have an even better one. I have just come from meeting a German, a Mr. Benz, who has not only patented an internal combustion engine but has designed and constructed the vehicle to go along with it."

"As have others."

"Yes, but there's something about Benz I like. And he hasn't just slapped a motor on a carriage. He's designed a complete vehicle. Three wheels, tubular steel frame, differential gears, etcetera. Admittedly, the steering mechanisms still need work."

"And you want to invest in this horseless carriage?"

"Motorwagon," Sam said firmly. "He calls it a motorwagon."

"I believe the French are using the word *automobile*."

"Yes, I have heard that. *Automobile*." Sam considered the word. "I like it. It has a nice ring to it. Could be shorter, though. Something with a bit more snap to it—"

Gray halted and glared. "So are you or are you not planning to invest in this man's invention?"

"Yes. And no." Sam grinned and strolled down the road.

Gray hurried after him. "Yes and no?"

"That's what I said."

"If you would be so good as to explain straightaway rather than play this silly game—"

"Benz is starting to produce his motorwagons." Sam slanted a fast grin toward his friend. "I bought one."

"Imagine my surprise," Gray said wryly.

"I'm having it shipped here. You remember Jim?" James Moore had been Sam's right-hand man for the last four years. There were times when Sam wondered how he had ever gotten along without him.

"Of course."

"He's accompanying the motorwagon. Barring any unforeseen difficulties, it should be here within the week."

Gray's jaw tightened with impatience. "And what, dare I ask, do you intend to do with it?"

"I'm going to try it out. See how it . . . feels." He glanced at his friend. "See what the real potential is. I want to determine for myself if it really is the way of the future and if it is, I want to be at the beginning of it."

"And?"

"And, it seems to me that there is nothing rich Americans like better than anything liked by European aristocracy, particularly the British."

Gray nodded. "As evidenced by the grand mansions the newly rich are constructing in America with rapt abandon. Present company included, of course."

"It's really my mother and sisters, you know." Sam waved off the comment. The tendency toward excess of his mother and sisters was a source of constant irritation. "But they are exactly the type of people I'm talking about."

"And yet I still have no idea what you are trying to say."

"What I am trying to say is that if the British aristocracy embraces the motorwagon as a plaything of the wealthy, Americans won't be far behind. And once the upper crust in America latches on to something, everyone else wants a version of it. Eventually, there could be motor-wagons or *automobiles* all over the civilized world." Sam grinned. "And it all starts here."

"Here?"

"Benz expects to be producing and selling motorwagons within the next year, beyond the handful he has already sold."

"Once he gets that steering problem solved?"

"Exactly." Sam nodded. "He and I have reached an agreement whereby I will set up a small factory in England to produce his machines, with the finest materials, directed toward the upper class." Sam paused. He was fairly certain his friend would go along with his plan but this was Gray's wedding and the English had always struck Sam as being somewhat reserved about mixing business with social events. "I thought your wedding would be the perfect place to demonstrate it and gauge interest. Perhaps even solidify some advanced orders."

"We rarely make rash decisions in this country." Gray thought for a moment. "You'll have to begin your campaign well before the wedding." He cast his friend a knowing look. "Which is why you've come so early."

Sam grinned. "I was hoping you'd introduce me to some of the more influential among your lords."

"I would but I've been away too long and am sadly out of touch. Fortunately, Camille and her sisters probably know everyone there is to know, many of whom will be in attendance at the various social activities she has planned between now and the wedding. Dinner parties, picnics, and the like." A thoughtful note sounded in Gray's voice. "There will be any number of oppor-tunities to demonstrate the motorwagon and I wouldn't be at all surprised if we didn't get a great deal of interest. More than enough to set up production with a reasonable expectation of success."

"We?"

"I assumed you would be asking me to join you in this venture."

"I didn't know I had to ask."

Gray laughed.

Sam considered his friend. "I don't have to tell you how speculative this is. These motorwagons or automobiles might turn out to be nothing more than toys. There's a very great risk that we will lose whatever we invest in this endeavor."

"Risk has always been part of the game."

"And much of the fun. If nothing else, I think this will be fun. After all, we've both made significant fortunes. What good are they if we can't have a little fun?" Sam studied the other man. "So I can count you in?"

"Try to keep me out."

"Good." Sam nodded with satisfaction.

Sam hadn't doubted for a moment that Gray would want to be part of this venture. And risk was just part of the appeal. Neither man had gotten where he was by playing the safest card in the hand. Admittedly this was much more speculative than trains or steel or shipping had been. This was something completely new. And it would be a fun ride.

"But enough talk about business. Tell me more

about Camille and her sisters." Especially, *Lady* Hargate.

"And spoil the surprise? Best for you to draw your own conclusions. Besides, we're here now." Gray swept out his hand in a grand gesture. "Welcome to Millworth Manor."

Sam had been too busy laying out his plans for motorwagons to notice their approach. Now, he paused and considered the building looming before them.

Millworth was a grand enough house, built of stone in shades of muted gray. It wasn't of any one discernable style but rather looked as if it had grown through the years, evolved and changed with the whims of the owners. Even so, it was the epitome of what an English country manor should look like. Or it was to someone who had never seen one before.

So this was *Lady* Hargate's family home. Interesting and not what he'd expected. She'd given him the distinct impression that she was a relative of far less means than Lady Lydingham. A poor relation although admittedly she had never said that outright, crafty creature that she obviously was. Still, she hadn't struck him as such. No, she'd struck him as honest and forthright. Even so, he was much better at judging the character of men than women, which had proven his undoing in the past.

Now that he thought about it, she'd said very

little about herself although she was obviously educated and well versed in art and literature and even politics. She'd had the subtle sort of flirtatious manner he'd always found intriguing. That, coupled with the fact that she had assumed he was an employee of one of Gray's business associates when Sam had stopped by Gray's suite to drop off some papers, and had no idea of his wealth or position, had made her all the more interesting. He was damned tired of women who saw only his wealth and position.

Why she hadn't been honest with him about who she really was remained an unanswered question. And then there was that business about having an adventure. He smiled at the memory.

Gray's eyes narrowed. "Why are you smiling like that?"

"Like what?" Sam adopted an innocent air. "I'm simply glad to see my old friend again."

"Yes, I thought that was it." Gray started up the stairs to the house.

Sam followed his friend. Still, he hadn't been honest about who he was with her either. If you looked at it from the right angle, with one eye closed perhaps, one half-truth cancelled out the other. She had said she was a practical woman and that was a very practical way to view their previous encounter. Her *adventure*. Even so, it had been his experience that women who claimed to be practical very often weren't.

He'd find out soon enough he supposed. And find out, as well, which one she thought was truly unforgettable.

The adventure or the man.

Chapter Two

". . . and Grayson has gone off to fetch one of his American friends from the train." Camille sank down into the wrought-iron garden chair beside her sister's on the terrace overlooking the grounds and gardens of Millworth. A table had been set with tea out-of-doors to allow the ladies to enjoy the still delightful, late afternoon autumn day.

"Although Keech was perfectly capable of doing so without him." Camille drummed her fingers on the table. "Honestly, I think all those years spent in America have changed Grayson in ways that I don't understand."

"Good ways or bad ways?" Delilah poured a cup of tea and handed it to her sister.

"That is yet to be decided." Camille heaved a resigned sigh. "This American has come entirely too early. Why, the wedding is nearly three weeks away. But Grayson did mention the man might go into London on occasion. And, as I suspect Grayson could use some male companionship, it's probably for the best. It will keep him occupied and out of the way."

"Always a good idea," Teddy said absently, her gaze locked on the notebook in front of her on the table. She jotted a quick note then looked up. "Who is he?"

"Oh, I forget which one he is." Camille waved off the question. "Grayson has invited any number of American friends and quite a few have written that they plan to attend."

"But you can't remember any of their names," Delilah said in a casual manner as if she could not care less which of Grayson's American friends planned to attend the wedding. Not that she thought Mr. Russell would suddenly appear at Millworth Manor. No, his employer, a Mr. Moore she thought, might well travel to England for Camille and Grayson's nuptials but she doubted he would bring an employee along with him. It would be most inappropriate. Although one never knew what an American might do. Inappropriate was probably to be expected.

"It's right on the tip of my tongue." Camille's brows drew together. "I met several of Grayson's business associates when we were in New York and I'm fairly certain our new arrival was one of them. In fact, I think he and Grayson are very good friends as well as partners in any number of successful ventures. Which makes this even more annoying. What was his name?" She thought for a moment. "It scarcely matters now, I suppose. The man will be here at any minute."

"Which reminds me"—Teddy set down her pen and settled back in her chair—"we should go over the most recent responses to your invitations. I would hate to lose sight of how many people are actually coming to the wedding."

"I daresay there won't be many refusals." Camille smiled in a smug manner. "My wedding will be a social event to be remembered."

"As was the first," Delilah pointed out. Their mother would have had it no other way.

Camille laughed. "It was, wasn't it? Of course this time it's different."

"This time it's Grayson." Delilah smiled at her sister.

Camille's first husband, Harold, was considerably older and exactly the kind of man all three sisters were expected to marry: wealthy, with a respectable title and impeccable family connections. Camille was the first to admit she had indeed loved her husband and they had had a fine marriage. But if pressed, Camille would also confess that he was not the true love of her life. Which made her wedding at long last to Grayson Elliott even more special.

"That does make all the difference." A thoughtful smile curved Camille's lips. "You know, I never thought this would happen to me, to us rather. I really never thought I'd see him again after he left England. Never imagined we'd have a second chance at a life together."

"One does tend to give up hope after more than a decade passes." Delilah refilled her teacup.

"Grayson was gone for eleven years, wasn't he?" Teddy asked.

"Building a fortune in America," Delilah said. "Time well spent I would say."

"He shouldn't have been gone at all but I suppose, in many ways, that's as much my fault as it was his. Still, I would much rather he be rich than poor. I have my own fortune, of course, but I do think society tends to look askance when it's the woman who has the fortune as if it's somehow demeaning for the man in question. No one ever seems to mind when it's the man who has all the money."

"Although, no one queues up to marry a poor girl," Teddy pointed out.

"It doesn't seem fair, does it?" Camille shook her head. "A woman who marries for position and fortune, especially if she has no position or fortune herself, is often looked upon as a fortune hunter although it's the only way, even in this day and age, that a woman has to better herself. A man who marries for money is simply considered clever. And it does seem to me that a man dependent on his wife's money is more likely to stray." Camille shrugged. "Still, it is delightful that money is not a concern. We can put the past in the past where it belongs. I much prefer to look toward the future."

"I have no doubt you'll be blissful together." Teddy smiled then turned to her friend. "And what of you, Dee? Have you considered your future?"

Camille chuckled. "With her two older daughters now settled and happy with their second husbands, I daresay Mother has certainly considered the question of Delilah's future. I know a good portion of those invited to the wedding at Mother's urging are unattached gentlemen in need of a wife. I suspect she thinks it will be fertile hunting ground for you."

"I allowed Mother to direct my life the first time I married. I do not intend to allow her to do so the next time. However, I don't mind her assistance as I do intend to marry again. She is very good at this sort of thing. And as she, and you of course, have been so thoughtful as to gather potential husbands here for your wedding and my perusal, I further intend to begin my search in earnest among them." She turned toward her friend. "A bigger question than that of my intentions, Teddy, is what do you want?"

"I have always loved the way you manage to turn attention away from yourself when there is a question you don't wish to answer." A wry smile curved the corners of Teddy's lips.

"Not at all." Even to her own ears her objection did not ring true. "I simply can't imagine you wish to plan other people's social events for the rest of your life. I have no idea what your plans are. You've been so busy this past year organizing weddings and parties that I've scarcely seen you at all."

"Then you should have more parties." Teddy grinned.

"I shall certainly keep that in mind," Delilah said in a prim manner then returned her friend's smile.

She and Teddy had been as close as sisters since they had first met at Miss Bicklesham's Academy for Accomplished Young Ladies and had vowed to be good, true friends for the rest of their lives. While officially the purpose of the relatively new but already established academy was to prepare young women of the noble classes for the positions in life they were intended for, Miss Bicklesham's faculty had an unsuspected rebellious streak. Delilah and Teddy had both left school with a solid grasp of not only how to host a hundred people for dinner and manage a grand house but with a basic understanding as well of Latin, mathematics, astronomy, philosophy, and economics. None of which had come in particularly handy thus far in Delilah's life although she did credit her ability to handle any conversation with aplomb and confidence to Miss Bicklesham's unusual curriculum.

"Or a wedding," Teddy added.

Delilah sipped her tea. "I shall keep that in mind as well."

Teddy also knew most of Delilah's secrets just

as Delilah knew most of Teddy's. Others might suspect the truth of it but Delilah was certain she was the only one who actually knew Lady Theodosia and her mother, the Countess of Sallwick, were not merely amusing themselves with their wedding and party planning services but needed the income.

"I do intend to marry," Teddy said. "I just find it remarkably difficult to find the right man."

"Yes, there is that," Delilah said under her breath. A vision of Mr. Russell's enticing smile flashed through her mind. His face had an unnerving tendency to appear from nowhere whenever the topic turned toward desirable men and marriage, especially now.

Delilah had tried to put him completely out of her mind and indeed there had been days when she scarcely thought of him at all. Unfortunately, he was there very nearly every time she closed her eyes. It was both annoying and pointless. She would never see him again after all. But ever since her return to Millworth, recollections of him had stubbornly taken up residence in the back of her mind. It was due no doubt to the upcoming wedding and all those bloody Americans who would soon be invading.

It was certainly not because he was the right man. Far from it. Mr. Samuel Russell was the complete opposite of the type of man she planned on for her second husband. Aside from any number of other reasons, he was an American. That would never do. Besides which he was an adventure. Adventures were meant to be brief, enjoyable, and finite. And best kept to oneself. He was one secret she would never share even with her closest friend.

"Well then." A wicked gleam sparked in Camille's eyes. "We should indeed go over the guest list. We might be able to pick out your future husband as well as Delilah's."

Teddy laughed. "I would much rather pick him out in person than from a list, thank you very much."

"I wouldn't be at all surprised if you don't already know every single person on that list already." Camille tapped Teddy's notebook with a pointed finger.

"Nor would I." Teddy wrinkled her nose. "Which is no doubt part of the problem. I should like to meet someone new. Someone different." She thought for a moment. "Someone who, I don't know, doesn't know my family, my background. Someone I haven't known, who hasn't known me, for much of my life. Which I think is one of the problems of the society we live in. There's never any new blood. It's just the same people, the same families, it's just so . . . Well, I think *expected* is the right word. I would like something or rather someone *unexpected*."

"An adventure," Delilah said under her breath.

"Exactly." Teddy beamed at her friend. "I want a man to be an adventure. To be unknown and new and exciting."

"And make your heart race," Delilah said without thinking.

Camille and Teddy stared at her.

"Isn't that what an adventure does?" Delilah said quickly. "Make your heart race? Doesn't Grayson make your heart race?"

"He always has." Camille's satisfied smile had returned. "Perhaps one of Grayson's American friends would suit for your adventure, Teddy. They're not titled but I'm fairly certain they all have tidy fortunes."

"I'm not sure I wish to go all the way to America for a suitable match." Teddy sipped her tea thoughtfully. "Although that would certainly be unexpected and quite an adventure."

"You have no idea," Delilah said more to herself than the others. Especially if they were deliciously handsome with hard bodies and laughing brown eyes.

Camille studied the wedding planner for a moment. "Aside from the unexpected, Teddy, what do you want? What are you looking for in a prospective husband?"

"I don't know really. I do know I want someone who isn't looking for a debutante in her first season. I have, after all, reached the overly-ripe age of twenty-six." Teddy cast the others a rueful smile.

"As have we both," Delilah said mildly.

There was nothing she could do to alleviate Teddy's concern about age, a concern Delilah shared to a certain extent. But Teddy really had nothing to worry about. With her tall stature, rich red hair, and air of competence and intelligence, she was at once classic and unique. Delilah had long thought Teddy fit in far better in terms of appearance with Camille and Beryl than Delilah did. The twins were tall and blond and annoyingly perfect beauties. While the blue of Delilah's eyes did match her sisters, she was several inches shorter, her figure a bit fuller and her hair a definite, dark brown. Regardless, her mirror said she was quite lovely even if she had always felt rather plain when standing next to the goddess twins. As such, she could certainly understand Teddy's concern about a real or imagined flaw. "And I'm not the least bit worried."

"You're a widow. You've been married. If this was a game, you've already been chosen once. You're simply playing again. No one has ever chosen, or rather married, me." Teddy stirred sugar into her tea.

"That's not entirely true, is it?" Delilah pointed out.

"That was a dreadful mistake." Teddy's tone hardened. "I wasted nearly a year in an engagement to a man who was not at all right for me. I consider myself lucky that I did not marry him."

Camille's eyes widened. "What happened?"

Teddy sipped her tea, her manner matter-of-fact. "He died."

Camille winced. "Oh dear."

"You needn't look like that, Camille," Delilah said. "It's not as if she did away with him."

"Although I might have had to resort to that if we had actually married," Teddy said with a shrug and a sharp look at Delilah.

This was not something Teddy liked talking about and Delilah knew better than to bring it up. "But you have had other offers since then. None of which you've accepted."

"Fortunately I learn from my mistakes and I have very high standards." Teddy adopted a lofty tone. "And on the vine of matrimonial bliss, I have yet to be . . ." She rested the back of her hand against her forehead in a theatrical manner and heaved a dramatic sigh. "Plucked."

Delilah tried not to choke. That was one secret of Teddy's she'd take to her grave.

Camille laughed. "I wouldn't let my mother hear you say that. She claims she is not the type of mother to interfere in her children's lives but we know better. She simply can't resist meddling." Camille traded a long-suffering look with her sister. "Even though you're not her daughter, Teddy, she would take your comment as a challenge. She'd have you wed in no time regardless of your standards. But you have evaded my question. Unexpected is not a good answer."

"I suppose if I knew the answer to what I was looking for, I would know where to find it. Or him." Teddy thought for a moment. "I suppose all I want is what you and Grayson have found." She toyed absently with her spoon. "It's quite remarkable you know and terribly obvious to anyone around the two of you. I can't tell you how many weddings my mother and I have planned when neither the bride nor the groom looked especially happy about their union. What you have is exceedingly rare."

"No one is more aware of that than I am. And no one is more grateful." Camille smiled. "I hope the two of you find that one day." She glanced at Delilah. "If that's what you want of course."

"Well, I for one, have a plan," Delilah said. "I find things have always worked out quite nicely when I have a plan."

Camille and Teddy exchanged glances as if each knew Delilah well enough to know what she was thinking. Absurd of course. While Teddy probably knew Delilah better than anyone in the world, Camille scarcely knew her at all. Camille and Beryl were five years older than their younger sister, old enough that their lives had never particularly included her. Although admittedly all three sisters were making an effort to change that. Why, hadn't Delilah accompanied Camille and Grayson on their brief trip to the city of New

York for the exact purpose of getting to know her sister better?

And hadn't that worked out well? a little voice whispered in the back of her head.

She pushed the thought aside. She had come to know Camille, and even Beryl, much better in the months since Christmas when they had vowed to make an effort to be, well, sisters rather than merely blood relations.

"A plan?" Camille's brow rose. "What kind of plan?"

"Oh, Dee always has a plan of some sort." Teddy cast her friend an affectionate smile. "She's had plans for as long as I've known her about one thing or another."

"I've heard about your plans," Camille said slowly.

"From Mother I assume."

Camille nodded.

"Then you have heard the majority of them turn out most successfully."

"Well, yes, I have heard that as well." Camille nodded.

Teddy wisely held her tongue.

"Perhaps you have forgotten." Delilah ticked the points off on her fingers. "I had a plan for exactly the kind of man I intended to marry. No less than a viscount, a sizable income, and no previous wives or children to muck things up. I married exactly as I was expected to."

"I thought that was our mother's plan," Camille said in an aside to Teddy.

"Regardless it was an excellent plan," Delilah said. And exactly the same plan followed by her older sisters. "And proved to be exceptionally well thought out." Although admittedly she had not thought Phillip would die at such a young age. He had scarcely passed his forty-third year. Dashing, charming, unobtainable Phillip.

"After Phillip died, I decided upon a plan whereas I would actively begin looking for a new husband once he had been deceased for three years." She paused to collect her thoughts. "I must confess though it's not entirely my idea. Phillip left a letter along with his will in which he suggested I mourn no more than six months and remarry again after two to three years. That time has now passed."

"Wasn't that thoughtful of him," Teddy offered with a pleasant enough smile that wasn't the least bit genuine. It was the mark of a true friend that while Delilah might have forgiven Phillip, Teddy never would.

"It was thoughtful," Delilah said firmly. "But I haven't had a plan since Phillip's death and now I do."

"I see." Camille considered her sister thoughtfully. "And does your plan include the name of your future husband?"

"Don't be silly." Delilah scoffed. "I haven't

selected my next husband. I don't know that I've met him yet but it's possible that I have. I have more, oh, requirements, I suppose than an actual individual." Once again, she counted the points off on her fingers. "One, I want a title at least equal to my own."

"One would hate for you to have to give up being Viscountess Hargate for simply being Lady Whoever," Teddy said.

Delilah ignored the sarcasm in her friend's voice. "Exactly. One should always marry up. It defeats the purpose to marry down. Two, he should have a fortune again at least equal to my own. I agree that a woman should not be wealthier than her husband." She paused. "Although I shall follow Beryl's example in terms of legalities and make certain my funds remain mine."

"Very wise. One never knows what might happen in life." Camille nodded.

"I want him to be intelligent. Perhaps even of a scholarly nature."

"Scholarly?" Doubt rang in Teddy's voice.

"I cannot abide stupid men." Delilah shuddered. "I prefer a man who can carry on an interesting conversation. One who isn't overly amusing—"

"Can't have that," Camille said.

"Although I wouldn't mind a droll sort of wit. And above all, I want a gentleman of honor, of good English stock. A man who understands the value of tradition and heritage. One who treasures the symbols of that heritage like Millworth Manor and Hargate Hall." Delilah's gaze shifted between her sister and her friend. "Is that too much to ask?"

"Probably." Camille chuckled then sobered. "But what of love?"

Teddy shot Delilah a quick look.

"You haven't mentioned love or passion," Camille continued. "This time, Delilah, don't you want that?"

"Not necessarily. With the right match, love will surely come in time. Love is much more difficult to find than a suitable income and much less important." Delilah refilled her cup. "And a suitable income would come in handy at the moment."

"What do you mean?" Camille's eyes narrowed. "Phillip left you a fortune. Don't tell me you've gone through it."

"That's not all like you, Dee." Teddy stared at her friend.

"Of course it's not like me. And it's nothing of the sort. It's a . . . oh, a legal difficulty I would say." Delilah braced herself. She couldn't continue to hide the truth forever. Still, she had avoided it up till now and had hoped it would be resolved before she had to mention it to her family and her closest friend. She chose her words carefully and adopted a casual tone. As if this was of no importance whatsoever. "While I had always assumed Phillip had no heirs, indeed he thought the same, there seems to now be a claim on his— or rather my—properties and fortune and, well, everything from some scoundrel in Leister or somewhere thereabouts."

"Good Lord." Camille stared.

"My solicitors have assured me this is nothing more than a momentary annoyance. It should be resolved in no more than a few months although it does seem to be taking forever. Unfortunately, my assets are not available to me until this matter is settled. So you see . . ." Delilah cast them her brightest smile. "There is nothing to worry about at all."

"Nothing? Delilah." Camille leaned closer and put her hand on her sister's arm. "Nothing is exactly what you could end up with. And you are not the type of woman to survive long without money."

"I admit, it is a bit awkward. I have had to economize," Delilah said smoothly but then she had known she would have to reveal her predicament eventually and she had practiced. Why, the word *economize* scarcely stuck in her throat at all now. "I have closed Hargate Hall and the house in London for the immediate future. I intend to stay here at Millworth until this is settled. With any luck at all, it will be over before the wedding."

"And if it isn't resolved in your favor?"

"I shall cross that road when I come to it." That was a possibility Delilah tried not to consider even if it loomed in her mind nonetheless. "I am confident this is nothing more than a temporary inconvenience."

"When did you learn this?" Teddy asked.

"Oh, let me think." Delilah forced an offhand note to her voice. "Six weeks or so I believe, something like that." Six weeks, two days, and twenty-some hours but she couldn't be exact without looking at a clock.

"Delilah." Camille chose her words with obvious care. "I know we haven't been especially close in the past—"

Teddy choked then coughed and smiled apologetically.

"—but I shall of course provide you with whatever funding you need."

"Thank you, but it hasn't come to that yet. And I doubt that it will." Delilah had practiced that air of confidence as well.

"Are you sure?" Worry colored Camille's face.

"Quite. But I do appreciate the offer." She drew a deep breath. "And if you don't mind, I'd much prefer not to discuss it further. It does tend to make my head pound."

Teddy nodded. "Understandable."

"So you can see why a suitable income would be appreciated," Delilah said in hopes of steering the conversation in a different direction.

This was not something she wished to talk about, even with her sister and her dearest friend. It was bad enough that it was scarcely ever off her mind. Bad enough that a heavy weight that felt suspiciously like doom had settled in the pit of her stomach the moment she'd been informed about this difficulty, six weeks, two days, and twenty-some hours ago. She had never been an especially patient person and waiting to find out her financial fate was wearing on her nerves. The only time her finances were out of her mind was when her thoughts turned to Mr. Russell. Which was every bit as disconcerting.

"Even so." Camille studied her sister. "Don't you want to find what Beryl and I have found? Don't you want to be happy?"

"I fully intend to be happy. However, it's been my observation that love does not ensure happiness. One only has to look at the trials and tribulations you and Grayson have experienced to see that. No, I think life is much easier without allowing emotions to muck things up." Delilah shrugged. "I shall be quite happy with a man with a respectable title and impressive fortune."

"And should he be handsome as well?" Teddy teased. "Tall and broad-shouldered with a square jaw and a twinkle of amusement in his dark, smoldering eyes?"

"Goodness, Teddy. You've been reading romantic novels again. I am not so shallow as to judge a man on his appearance. Why, that would be the very definition of shallow."

The other women glanced at each other then burst into laughter.

"I know what you're thinking." Delilah huffed. "And choosing a man for his position and his fortune is not the least bit shallow. It's practical."

Teddy grinned. "So you wouldn't refuse to consider a man who was handsome?"

"That too would be silly, if he met all of my other requirements. This is absurd." She crossed her arms over her chest. "I will confess, I don't want a man whose visage would make small children run in fear. I will have to share his bed after all. He should be of acceptable appearance. And I would prefer that he not be more than ten years older than I. I would like my next marriage to last longer than the mere five years my first marriage did."

"I see." Camille glanced at Teddy's notebook. "Do you have the list of everyone we have invited?"

Teddy turned a page then slid the notebook across the table to Camille. "It starts here."

"Let me see." Camille studied the list.

Delilah didn't like the look of that. "What are you doing?"

"Helping you with your plan." Camille ran her finger down the page.

"Oh?" Delilah arched a brow. "I had the distinct

feeling you were not impressed with my plan."

"It's not a bad plan, as far as it goes, although I think there are any number of variables you have not considered. In truth, I have always believed in plans and in being prepared. I have had quite a few excellent plans myself in the past." Camille's voice was absent, her gaze on the list of names before her. "The weakness in my plans has always been that I was not fully prepared. Or perhaps they were not well thought-out," she added under her breath.

As evidenced by Camille's Christmas plan to substitute a theater troupe for her family to impress a prince into a marriage proposal, *not well thought-out* was something of an understatement.

"Here's an excellent possibility. In fact there are several." Camille glanced up. "Mother has done a very good job. Better than I would have thought." She looked back at the guest list. "Most of these gentlemen meet all your requirements including that of age. Let me see, there is Lord—"

"Goodness, Camille, that's enough." Delilah blew a long breath. "Any other time, I would quite relish this discussion and perhaps later we can look at every eligible gentleman on the guest list and debate the possibilities. But right now I would really rather discuss something, anything, else."

Teddy cast her a sympathetic look. But then Teddy, far more than Camille, could understand how the fear of becoming penniless might well take the fun out of debating the relative merits of one prospective husband over another.

"Of course." Camille smiled affectionately at her younger sister. "There's time enough for this later. Why, there's no hurry at all, really." She turned to Teddy. "And aren't we supposed to be discussing the flower arrangements?"

Teddy nodded, pulled her notebook closer, and flipped through the pages. "We've ordered nearly everything at this point but unfortunately, the . . ."

Perhaps Camille did understand, at least a little. After all, it was one thing to wish to marry a man with a suitable income and position and quite another to need to. Regardless, Delilah had no intention of leaping into an ill-advised marriage simply to save herself from poverty. She did hope for a certain amount of affection in a new match. If nothing else she wanted to like the next man she married. She intended to spend the rest of her life with him after all. But as much as she wanted to marry again, and there was no doubt as to the type of man she wished to wed, the idea of having to do so for financial reasons did indeed make her feel like a fortune hunter. Still, she had no intention of becoming a poor relation either.

No, Camille was right. There was no hurry at all. Besides, this claim on Phillip's estate was more than likely bogus and would be settled any day now. Once the sense of imminent disaster hanging over her like a black cloud had abated she could look for a new husband unfettered by the slightest doubt. Nonetheless, she fully intended to take advantage of the opportunity afforded by Camille's wedding and accompanying social events to inspect suitable candidates. It would be foolish to let this opportunity slip away. She would engage them in intelligent conversation. She would be charming and flirtatious, she had long enjoyed being flirtatious, and by the time Camille was wed, Delilah would be headed in the direction of the altar as well.

All things considered, and barring any unforeseen complications, it was an excellent plan.

"There you are, Camille," Grayson's voice sounded in the doorway behind Delilah. "Clement said I would find you on the terrace."

Her sister's eyes lit with pleasure at the sight of her fiancé and the slightest twinge of what might have been envy stabbed Delilah. She ignored it. It was all well and good that Camille and Grayson had found love, and Delilah wished them nothing but happiness, but she had no interest in love. Not this time.

"It's such a lovely day, it was a shame to stay indoors." Camille stood and moved toward him.

Delilah twisted in her chair to get a look at the newcomer. But he stood in the shadows of the doorway, a step behind Grayson. He was tall,

Delilah could tell that much. But then it did seem that all of Grayson's Americans were tall. Apparently, they grew them that way.

Grayson raised Camille's hand to his lips and gazed into her eyes in that manner he had that made Teddy and even Delilah want to sigh with the sheer romance of it. "And do you remember my good friend—"

"Of course I do." Camille pulled her hand from her fiancé's and stepped around him. "It hasn't been that long."

"Delighted to see you again, Lady Lydingham," the American said smoothly. Camille blocked her view and it was impossible to get a good look at him. His voice was vaguely familiar but then Americans did sound alike. "I must apologize for my early arrival. I hope it won't be too much of an inconvenience."

Delilah and Teddy exchanged skeptical looks.

"Not at all. Millworth is huge and there is more than enough room to spare," Camille said in her best gracious hostess voice. "But you must be famished from your travels. Do join us and I will ring for something for you to eat."

Delilah reached for her cup and drained the last of her tea.

"If it's no trouble," the American said.

"None whatsoever." Camille returned to the table. "Allow me to introduce Lady Theodosia Winslow. She is coordinating the wedding plans.

And I'm not sure if you met my sister when we were in New York."

Delilah affixed a pleasant smile, turned her head, and looked up.

And stared into the dark brown eyes of her grand adventure.

And worst nightmare.

Chapter Three

Her breath caught.

Her stomach lurched.

Her cup slipped from her hand.

"Dee!" Teddy jumped to her feet.

Delilah's gaze jerked from Mr. Russell—*Mr. Samuel Russell*—to the tabletop.

"Damnation," she muttered then winced. She never cursed. Never in front of others and rarely to herself. But if ever anything called for a reaction stronger than an *oh my* this was definitely it.

"Goodness, Delilah!" Camille gasped, whether at her sister's blasphemy or the dropped cup Delilah didn't know and didn't care. "It's a good thing your cup was empty or you would have drenched us all."

"Yes, of course. My apologies," Delilah said with a weak smile and was grateful she could manage that.

A footman hurried forward to tidy the table. In the back of her mind, Delilah noted how fortunate dropping her cup was as it gave her time to compose herself. Unfortunately, not nearly enough.

This was Grayson's friend? His *good* friend and occasional partner? Not the employee of one of his business associates? Obviously she was not the only one who had not been completely honest in New York. Why, the beast had practically lied to her!

"Delilah," Grayson said. "This is my good friend Mr. Samuel Russell. You might have met him in New York."

"One meets so many people." She could manage no more than a half-hearted smile. What in the name of all that was holy was he doing here? *Here?* In England? At Millworth Manor? Her family's home? *In her world?* Precisely where he didn't belong. Where she had never wanted to see him. Where she had never *expected* to see him. She drew a deep breath. "When one travels that is."

"And it is hard to remember one among so many," Mr. Russell said in an altogether too smooth manner.

"Indeed and I must apologize, I'm afraid I don't recall meeting you." Delilah adopted a pleasant tone and struggled to appear calm. The worst thing about lies and deception, no matter how relatively innocent, was that inevitably they returned to bite you when you were least prepared for them. And she certainly wasn't prepared for this. For *him*.

"But I believe we did meet. Briefly. At the ball if I remember correctly." He cast her an innocent smile that would have been most convincing to anyone watching but nonetheless spoke volumes to her. "*Lady* Hargate, isn't it?"

"It is." Delilah nodded, a million thoughts running through her mind, most of them dire and dreadful and quite beneath her.

Yes indeed, it would be best if she acted as if they had never met. Then there would be no speculation as to why she hadn't mentioned him before. It was highly suspicious when one thought about it. She raised her chin slightly. She could do this. Why, already the shock of Mr. Russell's appearance was shifting to irritation at his unexpected and unwanted presence. The man would ruin everything.

"Oh, you needn't stand on formality," Camille said. "We are all friends and family here. It would be most awkward if you were to refer to us all by our titles."

"And yet completely proper," Delilah said.

"Don't be silly." Camille shot her a sharp look then smiled at Mr. Russell. "You must forgive my sister. While she is the youngest in the family she is oddly enough rather stuffy when it comes to things like propriety."

"Someone has to be," Delilah murmured. It was at moments like this that she quite valued the importance of propriety, the barriers and the protection it provided.

Camille ignored her. "So please do call me Camille and this is Teddy."

"How delightful to meet you, Mr. Russell." Teddy extended a graceful hand to him. "I have always been fascinated by Americans, although I'm afraid you're the first that I have met."

Mr. Russell took her hand and gazed into Teddy's green eyes as if she was the only person present. "I hope you won't be disappointed then."

The man was obviously an outrageous and well-practiced flirt. Not at all surprising. He had certainly flirted in New York. Still, it was most annoying and could be added to a fast-growing list of complaints against him, although admittedly the most significant was simply that he was here. Nonetheless, Delilah had the absurd impulse to smack his hand away from her friend's.

Teddy tilted her head to one side in a flirtatious manner of her own. "I can't imagine that I would be."

He laughed, that deep, overly amused laugh that had burned itself into Delilah's memory. "I will do everything in my power to make certain of that. And my friends call me Sam."

"Sam it is then." Teddy smiled up at him.

Delilah's urge to smack Mr. Russell shifted to her friend. Which made no sense whatsoever. Teddy could certainly flirt with whomever she chose.

"As I do hope we will be friends." Did Teddy really just flutter her eyelashes?

"And apparently you remember Delilah," Grayson said.

Mr. Russell released Teddy's hand and turned to

Delilah. Without thinking, she offered her hand. It would have drawn attention had she not. "Mr. Russell."

He took her hand and gazed into her eyes. But then he would, wouldn't he? "Sam."

"Are we to be friends then as well?" she said in a tone sharper than she had intended.

"I do hope so." A slow, wicked smile curved his lips, although she might have been the only one who thought it wicked. But then she was the only one who knew just how wicked this man could be. And he was the only one who knew of her own wicked tendencies. "One can always use another friend."

"Yes, well, I suppose." She tugged surreptitiously at her hand but he held it fast. The man was not going to make this easy for her.

Laughter danced in his eyes. "I have to admit, I am disappointed that you do not remember our meeting. As I said, it was at the ball. But admittedly it was little more than an introduction."

"Was it?" she said lightly and tried again to pull her hand from his. "Surely you can forgive me for failing to remember. Everyone was in costume after all." She drew her brows together. "You were dressed as . . ."

"A pirate." His amused gaze bored into hers as if daring her to deny their meeting. The blasted man was playing some sort of game with her. Well, two could play at this game.

"A pirate, let me think." She paused as if trying to remember. Not that she had forgotten for a moment. Samuel Russell had worn the guise of a pirate as naturally as if he had just stepped off the deck of a marauding ship. Dashing and dangerous and altogether irresistible. Teddy wasn't the only one who read the occasional romantic novel. She shook her head regretfully. "There were so many pirates. It did seem there was a pirate lurking in every corner. So appropriate for Americans really."

His brow rose. "A compliment, Lady Hargate?"

"Delilah," Camille said.

"Yes, of course, you must call me Delilah." She forced a pleasant note to her voice. "I should think only an American would take being a pirate as a compliment. However"—she shrugged—"you may take it as you wish."

"And only a fool would prefer an insult to a compliment and I am no fool." The warning in his voice was so subtle again she was probably the only one to notice.

No, he might well be an annoying, deceitful beast of a man but he was definitely no fool. She wasn't sure she could say the same about herself.

"And so I thank you, *Delilah.*"

There was something about the way he said her name that was at once sensual and irritating. And unnerving. She tugged again at her hand.

"There were a number of Dresden shepherdesses

as well," he added. "And yet I'm fairly sure I remember you."

"A shepherdess?" Teddy's eyes widened with disbelief. "Dee?"

"I can't imagine anyone *not* remembering." Grayson chuckled.

"It wasn't the sort of thing I ever imagined my younger sister wearing. Beryl perhaps but not Delilah." Camille leaned toward Teddy and lowered her voice. "I daresay there were gentlemen who, upon seeing Delilah as a shepherdess, would have willingly volunteered to be sheep."

Delilah gasped. "Camille!"

"The bodice was exceptionally low in cut and the hem scandalously high," Camille said to Teddy. "Why, one could see her ankles."

"It was a costume." Delilah yanked her hand from Mr. Russell's. It wasn't bad enough that her mistake had appeared from out of nowhere but now her sister had to chastise her as well for her choice of costume. This day was not getting any better. "And as such, not the least bit inappropriate."

"But no less shocking," Camille added.

"And entirely out of character." Teddy studied her friend curiously.

"Perhaps you have forgotten, but it was a *masked* ball. Those attending were expected to remain anonymous, for the most part. It was, as well, in a country where I knew no one, a country

I do not expect to ever see again. Besides . . ." She considered the other women for a moment then drew a deep breath. "It does seem to me that on occasion in one's life, one should throw caution to the winds and do something completely unexpected."

Camille's eyes widened in surprise. "Well, yes, perhaps. I simply never expected you to throw caution anywhere."

"But you really don't know her very well," Grayson said. Camille turned an annoyed eye on him. "Although, you have been giving it a great deal of effort," he added quickly.

"She's right, of course." Teddy nodded. "It was a costume and perhaps if one has never thrown caution to the winds in any manner, starting with something as innocuous as a costume is the way to go about it." She cast Delilah a supportive smile. "A rather restrained way really."

Camille nodded. "Like dipping no more than one's toes in the pool of impropriety."

"It's not as if you did something truly scandalous like oh, dancing naked in a fountain," Teddy said.

A faint hint of discomfort washed across Camille's face. She or Beryl or perhaps both had probably done far worse. There were any number of things about her sisters' lives that Delilah didn't know and wasn't sure she wished to.

Teddy continued. "It was only a costume after

all, and not as if Dee's flinging of caution resulted in scandal."

"Or an untoward incident." Grayson nodded.

"Or an adventure," Mr. Russell offered, again in a deceptively innocent manner and again she wanted to smack him. The man was obviously intending to make a habit of twisting everything that was said into a reminder of their *adventure*.

"And well worth it, I'd say. She did make an exquisite Dresden shepherdess." Grayson grinned at her and gratitude toward her future brother-in-law washed through her. But then, even when her sisters had barely acknowledged her existence, Grayson had always been nice to her. There was a time when she had thought he was entirely too good for Camille. And not all that long ago.

"You did look lovely." Camille smiled.

"Even, dare I say . . ." Mr. Russell—Samuel—paused. She absolutely refused to think of him as *Sam*. "Unforgettable?"

Unforgettable? Ha!

"How very kind of you to say so," Delilah said politely. "Which makes it all the worse that I don't remember you. At all."

He gasped and clasped his hand over his heart in a dramatic manner. "I am wounded to the quick to have slipped the memory of so lovely a shepherdess. And yet"—he grinned—"I am certain I shall recover and bravely carry on." He paused for a moment. "Yes, yes, there you have it.

Completely recovered now and wondering if perhaps I mistook you for one of the other shepherdesses in attendance."

Delilah's jaw clenched but she managed a smile. "Perhaps."

"No, no. I'm certain of it now." Samuel nodded. "It was definitely another shepherdess I met. I never met you at all."

Grayson frowned at his friend. "But I thought you said—"

"My mistake, Gray." Samuel's voice was firm. "It must have been some other shepherdess. Someone who was indeed . . ." His gaze locked with Delilah's. "Unforgettable."

"No doubt," she said and pointedly looked away.

Camille's curious gaze slid between Samuel and her sister. "Well then, as we have this settled, do sit down, gentlemen, and join us."

The ladies retook their seats; Grayson pulled up a chair to sit beside Camille, Samuel selected another and seated himself between Grayson and Teddy. Delilah breathed a sigh of relief that he did not choose to sit beside her. Unfortunately, he was directly across the table where it was impossible to avoid his gaze. Blasted man. Why hadn't he stayed in America where he belonged?

Camille signaled to the butler and requested more cakes and tea and sandwiches for the gentlemen.

"Do tell me, Sam." Camille turned to the American. "We are delighted to have you here but I was under the impression you would not be able to join us for the wedding."

"I must confess, I did not plan on coming but business brought me to Europe and, as I have business in England as well, it seemed the hand of fate insisting that I attend your wedding." Samuel chuckled. "And I would hate to defy fate." His gaze met Delilah's briefly then moved on.

"Wouldn't we all," Teddy said.

"Then I am most grateful to fate." Grayson nodded. "I should hate to have one of my closest friends not be by my side on the most important day of my life." He cast an affectionate smile at his fiancée then returned his attention to his friend. "Besides, regardless of any plans I might have, *I* would never miss your wedding, should you venture down that path again."

"Again?" Teddy asked.

"Sorry." Grayson grimaced. "My apologies. I wasn't thinking. I shouldn't have brought it up."

"Nothing to apologize for, Gray," Samuel said in an offhand manner. "My ill-fated attempt to reach the altar is common knowledge at home. But, given the joyful circumstances of your impending nuptials, this is perhaps not the time to discuss it."

"How very thoughtful of you, Sam." Camille smiled. "Although I should warn you, there is nothing a group of women like better than to discuss scandal of any sort. Dare I hope there was scandal involved?"

"Camille." Delilah slanted her sister a quelling look. Regardless of whether she wished Samuel to be here or not, this was no doubt something he didn't want to talk about. At least not to virtual strangers. "I must agree with Mr.—Samuel, this is not the time."

"At this point, I can look back on it with a certain amount of amusement." Samuel offered a wry smile. "And yes, Camille, I imagine there is always scandal when a wedding does not occur as planned."

"Have you met Grayson's cousin yet?" A wicked twinkle shone in Camille's eyes. "I suspect you and Winfield might have a great deal in common."

Grayson chuckled. "He was engaged three times before he finally made it to the altar."

"Those are footsteps I do not intend to follow." Samuel shook his head. "No, I have learned my lesson and I try not to make the same mistake twice." His gaze briefly flicked to Delilah. "But we all make mistakes, don't we?"

"I know I have." Teddy wrinkled her nose.

"Once is a mistake," Delilah said primly. "Three times is nothing less than a habit."

"You strike me as the kind of woman who rarely makes mistakes," Samuel said.

"It is only human to make mistakes." Delilah

shrugged. And with any luck, those mistakes don't return to sit across the table and make comments with underlying meanings. Although, given the mess with Phillip's legacy, luck was apparently in short supply at the moment. "But I too never make the same mistake twice."

"I didn't say I haven't made the same mistake twice," Samuel continued. "I simply said I try."

"Perhaps you need to try harder." Delilah smiled pleasantly.

"The problem with mistakes is that one doesn't always realize they are mistakes at the time." Samuel's eyes narrowed slightly. "It isn't until later reflection that one realizes one might have made a mistake."

Grayson nodded. "True enough."

"And then, as it happens, what one person sees as a mistake another might see as a stroke of good fortune." Samuel's gaze pinned hers. "Don't you agree, *Delilah?*"

A shiver skated down her spine at his use of her name. She ignored it.

"Not at all," she said coolly.

"Nonsense, I agree completely," Camille said. "Why I should think that sort of thing happens all the time in business. One man's mistake is to another man's benefit." She refilled her cup. "You do realize, Sam, you may have made a grave mistake arriving when the wedding is still nearly three weeks away."

"Have I?" Samuel's brow rose.

"Indeed." Camille nodded. "You will most certainly be called upon to render your assistance should it be needed."

"There will be a great deal of decorating and rearranging to be accomplished." Teddy thought for a moment. "Of course, none of that will need to be done until the days just before the wedding and I do have workers arranged for but another hand is always useful. In addition, there will be errands to be run—"

"Quite a bit of fetching and delivering," Camille added. "From the village and from London as well."

"And, as Camille has planned several events before the wedding," Teddy began.

"It's not so much a wedding as a festival," Grayson said in an aside to his friend.

"You will be expected to do your part." Teddy smiled at Samuel. "There are never enough gentlemen at these things, so we will count on you to converse with the ladies and charm the dowagers."

"That should be no problem." Grayson chuckled. "I can attest to that."

"I'll do my best." Samuel grinned at Teddy. "I have been told I can be most charming."

Delilah choked on her tea.

Camille's forehead furrowed in concern. "Are you all right?"

"Quite." Delilah coughed. "I must have swallowed something that didn't go down well."

"Understandable," Samuel murmured.

Delilah resisted the urge to glare.

"Although, as Delilah does not remember you," Grayson said, "perhaps you should put more effort into your ability to charm and not depend entirely on those roguish American good looks of yours."

Samuel laughed.

"Nonsense, Grayson," Camille chided. "I find Sam most charming and I daresay I shall continue to do so the better I get to know him."

"I for one would never forget meeting you." Teddy flashed Samuel a brilliant smile. "Therefore, the fault must lie with Dee for doing so."

"As I said, it was probably another shepherdess I met. Therefore the mistake . . ." Samuel's gaze caught Delilah's. "Was mine."

"One of many, no doubt," Delilah said before she could stop herself.

"But rarely the same one twice." The look in Samuel's eyes belied the polite smile on his lips.

"Ah, well, rarely is not the same as never but the trick is in the rarely." Delilah smiled. "Isn't it?"

Samuel chuckled. "It usually is."

"Is this your first trip to England, Sam?" Camille said, steering the conversation in a far less dangerous direction.

"Actually, this is my third visit," Samuel said.

"Although I've never seen anything of the country outside of London."

"We shall have to change that," Teddy said. "You simply must see . . ."

The conversation erupted into a spirited debate on which of England's sights the American absolutely had to see from the ruins of Whitby Abbey to the ancient Stonehenge to the scenic lake district with Camille, Teddy, and Grayson each lobbying for their favorite. Good. Perhaps the man would spend these weeks before the wedding traveling the country.

There was nothing she could do about him really unless she intended to shove him out the door. And that would be rude. Tempting but rude. Still, as long as he was here, she would have to avoid him as much as possible. His presence might well ruin everything. The man seemed intent on baiting her. And it was exceptionally hard not to rise to that bait. Sooner or later, someone was bound to notice if they hadn't already. Why, every time she glanced in his direction, his gaze was on her.

The last thing she wanted was for anyone to know about her adventure or mistake or whatever it was. Teddy would keep her secret but Camille would never be able to resist telling Beryl. And if Beryl didn't tell anyone, although there was nothing Beryl loved more than being the bearer of juicy gossip, the simple fact that she knew was bad enough. Beryl would love knowing about

Delilah's indiscretion. Delilah could practically hear her chortling about it now. Camille would certainly tell Grayson as well, who would no doubt feel it his duty to say something to Samuel. And who knew what would happen then.

Besides, Delilah fully intended to narrow down the possibilities for her next husband in these last weeks before the wedding. It was her plan and an excellent plan at that. But it would not do for any of her candidates to think she was unsuitable. A woman of loose moral values. A tart. Her gaze met Samuel's once again and she'd had quite enough.

"If you will all excuse me, I have some pressing correspondence to attend to." Delilah rose to her feet, the men standing at once. "Grayson, I may need to call on you later for advice of a legal nature."

"Of course." Grayson nodded.

"If there is anything I can do," Samuel offered.

"You?" Delilah stared at him with as pleasant an expression as she could muster. "Are you well versed in the complexities of the legal system in this country then?"

"No, I'm afraid not." He shook his head. "However, I do have well-respected solicitors in London who are."

"I am certain Grayson can provide the assistance I need." She waved off his comment. "But I do thank you for the offer." She forced a polite smile. "Samuel."

"Sam." Again that annoying spark of amusement shone in his eye. The man was obviously trying to ruin her life.

"My apologies but I simply cannot call you *Sam,*" Delilah said. Let the others call him Sam and be his friend. She had no desire to do so. He did not belong here! "And I . . . I once had a dog named Sam."

"I don't remember a dog." Camille frowned.

"I daresay there are any number of things about my youth that you don't remember," Delilah said.

"Probably." Camille smiled apologetically.

It wasn't at all fair of Delilah to remind Camille how she and Beryl had behaved toward their younger sister in the past as Camille was sincerely trying to mend that rift. Still, Delilah had spent most of her life with sisters who barely acknowledged her existence and this effort of making amends and forging a new relationship was as difficult for Delilah as it was for Camille.

"I am sorry. It's all water under the bridge now really." Delilah smiled at her sister then turned to Samuel. "But my Sam was a loyal and faithful companion. I adored him and he adored me."

"Perhaps you simply need to prove to Delilah that you too can be a loyal and faithful companion," Grayson said mildly.

"I can indeed and even better." Samuel smirked. "I can't remember the last time I bit anyone and I hardly ever bark."

"You should be very proud." Delilah smiled politely, nodded at the others, and took her leave. Good Lord, that wasn't at all like her. What was she thinking?

"My apologies for my sister, Sam," Camille said behind her. "She is not usually so—"

"Rude?" Grayson said.

Rude? She cringed. She was never rude. It was his fault. Bloody American. Look at what he had done to her and he had only just arrived.

"I was going to say curt . . ."

Curt was the best Delilah could manage right now. Certainly, an hour from now or tonight or years from today she might be able to come face to face with her *adventure* without so much as twitching a brow. And indeed, she had wondered what her reaction might be should she ever encounter him. But as she had expected to never lay eyes on him again, she had not planned on how to handle such a meeting. As it turned out, she should have. And wasn't disaster to be expected when one didn't have a plan?

She drew a deep breath and continued toward the library. Writing to her solicitor would take her mind off the American, at least for a few minutes. She'd made every effort to curb her impatience at the incredibly slow manner in which her legal difficulties were being resolved. Why, she scarcely wrote for the latest news more than twice a week now.

"Dee!" Teddy's voice sounded behind her.

Delilah turned back. "Yes?"

"What was that all about?"

"What do you mean? What was what all about?" she asked as if she hadn't the faintest idea what Teddy was talking about.

"You know exactly what I mean." Teddy's brow furrowed in annoyance. "You were positively rude to Mr. Russell—Sam."

"Don't be absurd." She waved off the charge. "I wasn't at all rude. I might have been a bit, oh . . . sharp."

"You were far more than sharp."

"Just because you and Camille have taken to this American doesn't mean I have to." Delilah sighed. "Haven't you ever met someone you simply took an instant aversion to?"

"Outside of a villain in a melodrama, no. And never when the person in question is a guest. That's the most ridiculous thing I've ever heard you say. In truth, I've never seen you be less than unfailingly polite to someone you've just met." Teddy studied her closely then realization washed across her face. "Good Lord, of course. I should have realized it at once."

Delilah braced herself. No one knew her better than Teddy and if anyone could discern the truth it would be her oldest and dearest friend. "Realized what?"

"My dear friend, I do apologize. I should have

seen it sooner. It's obvious to me now why you're not being at all your usual self."

"Is it?" Delilah held her breath.

"You may be able to fool your sister, but then she doesn't know you as well as I do. And you've never been able to fool me."

"No, I suppose I haven't." Delilah sighed in surrender. She had never kept anything quite this significant from her friend before and Teddy had always seen right through her. "It's just so, well, awkward and embarrassing."

"Nonsense," Teddy said staunchly. "It's not your fault and you have nothing to feel awkward or embarrassed about."

"I don't?" Still, one might think it was at least partially her fault. The man hadn't forced himself on her after all. She had been a more than willing participant. Eager really.

"Of course not." Teddy laid her hand on Delilah's arm. "It's this business about the claim to Phillip's estates, isn't it? You're much more concerned than you're letting on, aren't you?"

Relief swept through Delilah. What a perfect excuse for her behavior. She should have thought of it herself. "Well, yes. I am worried."

"I know better than most how financial difficulties can make anyone a bit surly." Sympathy shone in Teddy's eyes. "You've been keeping it to yourself, and while I can understand that, it is always better to share your concerns."

"Perhaps," Delilah said in a weak voice.

"There is no perhaps about it. While there is nothing we can do to help, we can at the very least offer you our unflinching support and affection. And you do have that, you know. Besides, the load always seems a bit lighter when shared."

"Indeed it does." Delilah cast her friend a grateful smile.

"With all you have on your mind, it stands to reason that you might be a bit less than gracious."

"It does, doesn't it?" And really, when she thought about it, the feeling of doom in the pit of her stomach did seem much heavier now with Samuel's arrival.

"Still, I know it's hard, but you mustn't take it out on others. Sam is Grayson's good friend and the poor man has done nothing to deserve your being less than pleasant to him."

"You're right, of course. I was dreadful, simply dreadful." Delilah rubbed her forehead. "All that talk about my not remembering him, and, well . . . My head is pounding . . ." She sighed in a helpless manner. "I will apologize to him at the first opportunity."

Which wasn't a bad idea. She could apologize and then ask him to keep his mouth shut. And point out to him how it would be best if they avoided one another as much as possible. And perhaps suggest that he might want to spend the time before the wedding traveling England as it would be a pity to miss this opportunity.

"Excellent." Teddy paused. "You are certain you didn't meet him in New York?"

"Come now, Teddy." Delilah scoffed. "I don't doubt he was most memorable as a pirate. Can you imagine anyone would forget meeting him?"

"I know I never will." Teddy smiled in a wicked manner. "He's quite handsome and I found him most amusing."

"If you like that sort." She shrugged.

"Apparently, you're the only one who doesn't." Teddy thought for a moment. "You know, aside from the fact that apologizing is the proper thing to do, I suspect he has any number of resources, in addition to his London solicitors, that might be of assistance to you. He could prove to be a valuable friend."

"I hadn't thought of that but you're absolutely right." Delilah cast her friend a brilliant smile that belied a momentary stab of guilt. She'd rather lose everything she had before she asked the American for help. But she'd never lied to Teddy before nor had she ever practiced any kind of serious deception before. At least not until she had decided to experience adventure and had met Samuel Russell. "I shall make amends to Mr.— Samuel—at the first opportunity."

"I suspect he's a much more enjoyable friend than sparring partner."

"I don't know. I was rather enjoying myself." The moment the words left her mouth she realized they were true. Dear Lord! What a disturbing thought. "Now, I really must finish the letter that I started this morning. I'm not sure my letters make a difference but at least they remind my solicitors that I do want to know the moment this is resolved."

"Besides, your letters make you feel as if you are doing something rather than just waiting." Teddy wrinkled her nose. "I know how helpless that feeling can be."

It had taken nearly a year after the death of Teddy's father for her and her mother to learn the full extent of their loss. It wasn't bad enough that a distant cousin had inherited her father's title and most of their property but his debts had been far greater than they had imagined. While her mother did retain a house in London that had been part of an inheritance from her family, they'd been left with little else.

"I'll leave you to your correspondence and rejoin the others. You'll be finished by dinner?"

"I hope so." Delilah nodded. "And I will try to be in a much more pleasant mood, I promise."

"Good." Teddy turned to go then turned back. "I shall pray you have good news soon."

"I suspect it will take more than prayer but I do appreciate the thought."

"Sometimes prayer is all we have." Teddy

smiled in a supportive manner and started off.

Well, wasn't that an unexpected twist? Delilah bit back a grin and continued toward the library. She'd never expected to be grateful for her dreadful predicament but at this particular moment she was. Far better for her friend, and her sister, to attribute her curt manner toward *Samuel* to a symptom of her dismay over the prospect of losing everything she had than to know the truth.

If she apologized . . . She sighed. *After* she apologized she would point out that it would be just as unpleasant for him should the truth come out as it would be for her. No, it was best for both of them if their adventure remained their secret. Surely he would listen to reason. If nothing else, he had struck her as a reasonable sort. Why, hadn't he agreed with her that it would be best if they never saw each other again? Admittedly, upon reflection, he hadn't been especially pleased about that, which, again upon reflection, had been the tiniest bit gratifying, but he had agreed.

Good. Now she had a plan. Already her confidence had returned. Samuel Russell was a minor matter, in the scheme of the rest of her problems. In her head, her thoughts returned to composing the letter to her solicitor. Yes, indeed, things usually went well when she had a plan.

She refused to consider for so much as a moment the one time in her life when she hadn't.

Chapter Four

"So . . ." Gray swirled the whisky in his glass, his voice as nonchalant as his action. "Was she lying?"

"Was who lying?" Sam's tone matched his friend's even if he knew exactly whom Gray meant.

As the only two men in residence at the moment, he and Gray had taken the opportunity to meet in the Millworth library for a whisky before dinner. Sam figured he'd need it if he was going to do battle with Delilah again. Not that it hadn't been fun. Of course, only the two of them knew what their dispute was really about. He and Gray were to join the ladies in a half an hour or so. If Sam could pull himself away from the library.

He'd always loved libraries and this was a magnificent room. A massive fireplace was flanked on either side by shelves reaching upward to a wide, plaster frieze depicting what appeared to be Grecian-styled figures of the Fates or the arts. Ornate carved molding topped the plaster and framed a coffered ceiling. Walls not covered by shelves and hundreds of volumes of leather-bound books hosted portraits, probably family members going back generations. Dark wood gleamed with years of care and polish. The sofa and chairs positioned before the fireplace were well worn and comfortable. The impressive oak desk had an air of dignity about it, as if it was more important than anyone who sat at it. This was the sort of room a man could call his own. A retreat or a sanctuary from the world or, in Sam's case, a household of women.

He made a mental note to model the library in the new house his mother had been lobbying to build in Newport after this room. *If* he decided to build, which was still in question. But in his mind's eye, he could see himself sitting in a comfortable chair in a room like this, in front of a fire, reading the latest work of Mark Twain or Henry James with a dog lying on the floor by his side. A loyal and faithful companion. Maybe a greyhound. President Hayes had had a greyhound. Perhaps, he'd call her . . . Delilah.

"Delilah?"

"I can't think of a more appropriate . . ." Sam's attention jerked back to his friend. "What?"

"Pay attention, Sam." Gray rolled his gaze toward the wood-strapped ceiling. "I asked you if Delilah was lying."

"Delilah?" The vision of a long, lean, loyal beast shifted to that of a spaniel with a suspicious look in its eyes, a vile disposition, and a tendency to bite.

"Lady Hargate?" Gray eyed him curiously. "*Mrs.* Hargate."

"Are we on that again?"

"Until I get an answer I believe, yes."

"Come now, Gray," Sam said with a chastising smile. "If a lady says she has never met me, then she has never met me."

"Excellent answer. Very diplomatic. Nothing better than a response that does not answer a question."

Sam grinned. "My thoughts exactly."

"You knew she was costumed as a shepherdess."

"As were many others." He shrugged. "The place was littered with shepherdesses."

Gray studied his friend for a moment. "It's really none of my business though, is it?"

Sam sipped his drink. "I wouldn't think so."

"But you are sticking to your story?"

Sam laughed. "There is no story."

"Of course not. Because if Delilah says she has never met you, then she has never met you?"

Sam chuckled. "She doesn't impress me as the type of woman who would take well to being called a liar."

"Few women do," Gray said wryly.

As lies went, Delilah's struck Sam as relatively minor and completely understandable. Irritating but understandable. He could even understand her less-than-gracious manner toward him. Sam had never taken well to unexpected surprise himself.

This was, after all, her life, her world and if she, for her own reasons, didn't want anyone to know they had so much as met, well, far be it from him to say otherwise. Much simpler to deny they had met at all than to evade further questions such an admission might bring. No, he would keep her— their—secret. When it came down to it, while he had never considered denying they had met, he had never intended to tell anyone what else they had shared. He did not consider himself the sort of man who would reveal something like that about a lady. Regardless of what else Delilah might be, there was no doubt she was a proper lady. Unless, of course, she was in the midst of an adventure. He smiled at the memory.

"I don't believe you for a moment, you know."

"What?" Sam widened his eyes innocently. "You don't think she'd mind being called a liar?"

"That's not what I meant and you know it."

"I have no idea what you did mean."

"Then I shall let it go." Gray studied him closely. "But I do have my suspicions."

"What happened to this being none of your business?" Sam said mildly.

"The woman is going to be my sister-in-law. I have known her all of her life. Indeed, I have always thought of her as a younger sister. And I have certain . . ." Gray groped for the right words. "Brotherly feelings toward her."

"Oh?"

Gray nodded. "Delilah is five years younger than Camille and Beryl. While they have always been thick as thieves, their younger sister was never a part of their lives. When they weren't ignoring her, they weren't treating her especially well. They did the kinds of things that children tend to do to one another. Locking her in the attic, that sort of thing. It's my understanding that even as adults they scarcely ever saw her unless it was at a wedding or funeral or other family function. I don't think Camille realized how nasty they were until it was recently pointed out to her. This past Christmas they promised to work at being the kind of sisters they always should have been." He thought for a moment. "Camille and I were good friends in our youth and I was always nice to Delilah."

"The little sister you never had?"

"Exactly." Gray nodded. "I feel it's my duty to protect her."

"From me?"

"Don't be absurd. I've never seen you treat a woman ill, even when she deserved it."

"Tempting though it may have been," Sam said under his breath.

"You're a decent sort, Sam." Gray raised his glass to his friend. "I've always admired your sense of honor."

"I love it when I can live up to your high standards." Sam returned the toast and took a drink. "So, if you are not concerned with protecting your future sister-in-law from me, which is mildly irritating as I am reputed to be quite charming—"

Gray snorted.

"Who or what do you want to protect her from?"

"Everything." Concern washed across Gray's face. "Unfortunately, I can't."

"From what I saw this afternoon, she can take care of herself. At least verbally." The image of a snapping spaniel returned and he bit back a laugh. "She is an adult, Gray, not an innocent babe in the woods. She's been married after all."

"Her husband died three years ago." Gray finished the last of his drink then stood and crossed the room to retrieve the decanter the butler had placed on the desk. "Idiot."

"I'm assuming you mean her late husband and not me," Sam said when Gray returned with the whisky. "I didn't realize you knew him. Weren't you in America when he died? And when she married him for that matter."

Gray nodded and refilled their glasses. "You're right, I never met him." He sank back into his chair. "From what I've heard, through my cousin primarily, Delilah married exactly the kind of man she was expected to marry. She and her sisters were raised to marry well."

"Aren't all properly bred young women?"

"These sisters more so than most. Lady Briston, Camille's mother, encouraged—"

"Encouraged?"

"She did not force them into marriages but she did *strongly* encourage her daughters to marry older men with unblemished titles and significant fortunes. She had her reasons, which make sense when you know the family's history. Lord Briston was absent and believed dead for much of his daughters' lives. He only returned this past Christmas."

Sam raised a brow. "From the dead?"

Gray nodded.

"It must have been an interesting Christmas."

"You have no idea." Gray took a long, bracing swallow of his drink.

"So, if you didn't know the late Lord Hargate—"

"Why do I think him an idiot?"

Sam nodded.

"Don't misunderstand, from what I've been told, the man was quite skilled in matters of business. Indeed, his business interests supported his properties and estates. Land, you know, has long been the basis of wealth here. But even in England life is changing." Gray shook his head. "Management and the keeping up of these old estates is getting harder and harder. It takes more and more just to keep them from falling apart."

Gray's gaze scanned the library. "Millworth is no exception. The future of this bastion of tradition is uncertain. Decisions will have to be made about what to do with the place eventually. There's just Camille and her sisters. Lord and

Lady Briston never had a son and while they would never let Millworth go, I suspect when they pass on, the decision might be made to sell." He sipped his drink thoughtfully. "Both Camille and Beryl have the financial resources, thanks to their first husbands, to maintain the estate although the house is enormous and the grounds extensive. But I don't know if either of them wish to do so."

"I would imagine you'd have some say in what Camille decides."

Gray nodded. "I've always loved Millworth but I haven't given any consideration as to whether I wish to eventually own it. Camille and I have discussed selling the country house her late husband left her but we've not talked about the future of this place. Fortunately, as Lord Briston appears to be in excellent health—"

"For a man who used to be dead."

"For a man of his age, deciding Millworth's fate can be put off for now. Although eventually a decision will have to be made." Gray paused. "Regardless of whether one of them takes on the estate, the next generation will have some hard decisions to make."

"No doubt."

It was a pity really, all this tradition and heritage that might be lost. But the world was changing every day. The twentieth century was just around the corner. Progress was in the air. It was an exciting time to be alive and not the time to cling to the past. There might not be a place in the future for the Millworth Manors and Fairborough Halls and other antiquated symbols of a way of life that was fading away or being thrust aside. Or left behind.

Certainly, if Sam did decide to build a grand mansion of his own, he would model his library after Millworth's but his house would be a beacon of progress, not a relic of the past. His house would have all the conveniences modern life could provide including electricity, wiring for telephones, up-to-date plumbing, and an efficient heating system. His house would look toward tomorrow not yesterday. His house would reflect its owner.

"Interesting and quite a dilemma." Sam nodded. "Are you done with your tangent?"

"Probably, maybe, I don't know." Gray shook his head. "I see things differently now than I used to. It's all that time spent in America no doubt."

"We Americans are nothing if not a bad influence." Sam paused. "I still have no idea why you think Lord Hargate was an idiot."

"Ah well, that." Gray shrugged. "I simply think any man who is not aware that he might have an heir is an idiot."

"Misplacing something like that does seem stupid."

"Doesn't it though?" Gray sipped his drink. "I only heard about this a few hours ago. Camille told me. She didn't know anything about it until Delilah finally told her shortly before your arrival. Camille was a bit miffed Delilah didn't confess all to her before now especially as it appears this situation has been dragging on for a good six weeks or more."

"Delilah doesn't strike me as someone given to confession."

"You noticed that, did you?"

Sam shrugged.

Gray blew a long breath. "It seems there is now someone claiming to be Hargate's rightful heir."

"But you said he died three years ago. This alleged heir is just coming forward now?"

"Apparently. Camille doesn't have many details. Delilah is reluctant to talk about it and would just as soon avoid the issue entirely. Camille says her sister is putting a good face on it but she thinks Delilah is more worried than she is letting on."

"I can imagine," Sam said quietly.

Odd, she hadn't seemed like the type of woman who would keep something like that to herself but then he hadn't had an adventure with the wealthy *Lady* Hargate but rather with a poorer chaperone, *Mrs.* Hargate. He didn't really know Delilah at all. Even so, he could understand her reluctance to confide her problems. It wasn't easy to allow anyone, let alone those you knew best, to see how devastated you might be by matters over which you had no control.

"Delilah inherited all of Hargate's fortune and property. She's quite wealthy." Gray shook his head. "Or rather she was."

Sam drew his brows together. "Go on."

"Delilah and everyone else, including apparently, Lord Hargate himself, thought there was no heir, with the exception of Delilah of course. Now, some miscreant is claiming to be a blood relative."

"And the rightful heir?"

Gray grimaced. "Exactly."

"Where does that leave Delilah?"

Gray heaved a sigh. "As of this moment, penniless."

"I see." Given what Sam knew now, he couldn't imagine how he had ever assumed Delilah was a poor relation. "Isn't there something that can be done?"

"Camille says Delilah intends to marry again. She has a plan and will be husband hunting in earnest."

"Naturally." Delilah's intentions weren't the least bit surprising. Still, he noted the oddest twinge of what might well have been disappointment.

"You needn't take that tone." Gray eyed his friend in a chastising manner. "It's not as if she is a fortune hunter."

"Does she intend to marry for reasons other than money and social position this time?"

"I really don't know." Gray considered the

question. "But even as a girl, she was an extremely practical sort."

"And the practical thing to do is marry for money and position."

"You just said this is exactly what properly bred young women are supposed to do."

Sam shrugged. It shouldn't matter to him what she did. He scarcely knew her after all. The idea of Delilah marrying some old man, the Duke of Who Knows What, for his money and his title shouldn't be the least bit maddening. It shouldn't make his stomach twist and his jaw clench. She had made it perfectly clear in New York that she didn't want to ever see him again, that he was nothing more than a momentary adventure. Admittedly, he hadn't felt the same but he had agreed to her wishes.

And why not?

He certainly hadn't expected her to pop into his head at the most inopportune moments. Hadn't expected to see a familiar figure on the street and walk a little faster to approach her before she was out of sight only to discover it wasn't her. Hadn't expected their adventure to linger in his mind and perhaps even in his heart. But wasn't finding himself in England in time for Gray's wedding more than just coincidence?

No, he shouldn't care what she planned to do. But damn it all, he did.

Not that he would do anything about it. Giving

his heart to a woman who wanted him for his fortune and his status was one mistake he would never make again.

"She's not like Lenore," Gray said casually, as if bringing up the name of Sam's former fiancée wasn't at all significant. Which of course it wasn't.

"And just how is she different?"

"For one thing, Delilah's plans have nothing to do with whether she's lost her own fortune. She's not acting out of desperation. For another, she is honest about what she is looking for." Gray leaned closer and met his friend's gaze. "She'd never tell a man she loved him to get him to marry her."

"Ah, well then, that is different." Sam tossed back the remainder of his whisky.

"She just knows what she wants, that's all."

"My, that is practical."

Gray laughed. "You seem rather interested for a man who has never met her before."

"As well as a man the lovely Lady Hargate seems to have taken an instant dislike to." He grinned. "I'm not sure I've ever met anyone who has disliked me at first sight. Especially with such ill-concealed vehemence. I must confess, it's intriguing."

Gray's brow rose. "Like a challenge? A gauntlet thrown down?"

"I wouldn't go that far. I'm simply curious." Still, he had never backed down from a challenge. "Do you think this heir is legitimate?"

"I don't know." Gray shook his head. "Her solicitors are trying to get to the truth of the matter."

"Are they any good?"

"Camille says they're excellent. I hope so. I daresay it's harder to prove something isn't true than to prove it is."

"I've always thought that high-priced legal counsel, while very good at questions of law, was not nearly as good at ferreting out the truth. Maybe she should consider hiring a professional investigator."

"Not a bad idea." Gray paused. "This might well explain why she was so cross this afternoon. Understandable how one might be out of sorts with this kind of thing hanging over their head. Delilah has always been rather private. If there was a benefit to not being included by her sisters in her youth, it might well be her sense of independence. She has always kept her own counsel. I wouldn't be at all surprised if Delilah has any number of secrets she's never shared."

"One never knows."

"I beg your pardon, Mr. Elliott, Mr. Russell." The butler appeared in the open doorway. "Mr. Elliott, Lady Hargate has requested you join her before meeting the others for dinner. She said to tell you it was a financial matter of some importance."

"Very well." Gray glanced at Sam. "She might need your advice as well."

"Of course." Sam nodded.

"My apologies, sir," Clement said. "But Lady Hargate specifically asked that you come alone. She wants you to meet her in the garden on the far side of the maze."

"Does she? How odd." Gray frowned.

Clement lowered his voice in a confidential manner. "I believe, sir, that she wished to avoid the possibility of being overheard."

"Ah yes, I should have realized that." Gray nodded at the butler. "I'll go in a moment. Thank you, Clement."

"She also said, sir, if she was unavoidably delayed, as it is nearly time for dinner, you shouldn't wait more than fifteen minutes for her."

"Thank you, Clement," Gray said. The butler nodded and left the room.

"We're not expected by the ladies for nearly half an hour. We usually meet in the main parlor before going into dinner. Clement can show you the way."

"Oh, I'm sure I can find it on my own." Sam glanced around the room. "Until then, I think I'll see what I can find to read."

"Good." Gray rose to his feet. "The way I see it, if you and Delilah have met—"

Sam laughed. "You're like a dog with a bone, aren't you?"

Gray ignored him. "If you had met, then you did something that really offended her."

Sam gasped. "*I* did something?"

"If you didn't she thinks you did."

"Unless of course, as she has said, we have not met." He shrugged. "And she just doesn't like me."

"So hard to believe," Gray said and started toward the door.

"I know I'm shocked. I may never get over it." Sam heaved an overly dramatic sigh. "Women in particular usually find me charming. And amusing. And not unattractive."

"You forgot modest."

"No, I didn't." Sam grinned. "I was just being too modest to mention it."

"Yes, that's what I thought." Gray laughed then paused and studied his friend. "Have you given any consideration at all to the significance of your names?"

"Our names?" Sam drew his brows together in confusion then laughed. "You mean Samuel and Delilah?"

Gray nodded.

"Need I point out that my name is Samuel not Sampson."

"You may cling to that minor discrepancy but I doubt it makes much difference." Gray shook his head. "Do keep in mind what happened to him at her hands."

"I'm not worried."

"Neither was Sampson," Gray pointed out and left the room.

Sam chuckled and moved to the nearest bookshelf to survey the offerings, noting a set of several of Mr. Jules Verne's *Voyages Extraordinaires* novels. One couldn't ask for more in the way of adventure and progress and possibility inherent in the future than Jules Verne. He pulled out a volume of *Hector Servadac*. He'd read it, of course, but there was nothing better for enjoyable reading than Verne's tale of a group of strangers trapped on a comet sailing through the heavens.

"Perhaps you should be."

Chapter Five

Sam bit back a smile and continued paging through the novel. He didn't need to look to recognize that voice. "Perhaps I should be what?"

"Worried."

"What on earth do I have to be worried about?" He cast a casual glance toward the door.

Delilah stepped into the library looking as if she were ready to do battle. Or more likely, put him in his place. Either way, it would be fun.

"All sorts of things I would suspect." She shut the door behind her and moved closer to him. "But at the moment—me."

"You?"

She crossed her arms over her chest and glared at him.

"As much as that look might strike fear into the heart of any man, I'm not the least bit worried, *Delilah*." He snapped the book closed. "Or should I say *Mrs.* Hargate?"

She had the good grace to blush. "That was a mistaken assumption on your part."

"That's not how I remember it. I remember you distinctly said you were *Mrs.* Hargate."

"I might, possibly, have given you the impression . . ."

"There's no possibly about it." He replaced the

book on the shelf. "If I recall correctly, and I have an excellent memory, you led me to believe you were someone, or something, other than who and what you are."

"No more so than you led me to believe you were someone or something other than who you are."

Apparently, Delilah subscribed to the classic philosophy that the best defense was a good offense. Again, he stifled a smile. The woman might well be just as interesting when she was annoyed as when she was flirtatious. Although she had been delightful.

"That was indeed a mistake and might I add it was a mistake on your part." He shook his head. "I never said I was anyone other than who I am. I'm certainly not to blame for your incorrect assumption."

"It seems I made any number of mistakes when I was in New York." She paused. "I would prefer to forget them."

"All of them?"

"Yes, of course, all of them."

"Then we may have a problem."

"What kind of problem?"

"Whereas you may have made a mistake when last we met, I don't consider anything that passed between us a mistake."

"Come now, Mr. Russell—"

He held up his hand to stop her. "Although

admittedly, the moment I realized you thought I was an employee of Mr. Moore's and not the other way around, I should have corrected you."

"Yes," she said in a haughty manner. "You most certainly should have."

"Would it have made a difference?"

"I don't know. It might have, given your friendship with Grayson." She thought for a moment then sighed. "But probably not."

"Another mistake then?"

"A momentary error in judgment," she said firmly.

"A mistake," he said just as firmly.

"Yes, yes." She waved off his comment. "In hindsight, yes. But my intentions were noble."

"Pretending to be someone you're not is noble? Explain that logic to me."

"It really needs no explanation." She stared at him as if he were entirely too stupid to understand. "As I had incorrectly assumed that you were an employee of an associate of Grayson's, I thought you might be, well, intimidated—"

He laughed.

She glared. "What do you find so amusing?"

"That you thought I would be intimidated." He chuckled. "By what? By *Lady* Hargate rather than *Mrs.* Hargate?"

Her eyes narrowed.

"You're a snob, aren't you, *Lady* Hargate?"

"I most certainly . . ." Her lips curved upward in

a superior smile. "I simply know my place in the world. Do you?"

"*I* always have," he said in a mild manner he suspected might drive her mad. Her smile wavered a bit. He was right. "I don't need a title to prove it. We don't have titles in America."

She sniffed. "Pity."

He laughed again.

"This is not why I'm here," she said through clenched teeth then drew a deep breath. "I simply thought it would be more, oh, democratic to introduce myself as Mrs. Hargate rather than Lady Hargate as you were so very . . ." She squared her shoulders as if the admission was difficult for her. "Well, *friendly* and I will admit I was enjoying our encounter."

"I see." He circled around her, retrieved his glass from the table where he had left it, and moved to the desk. "Would you care for something?"

"I never drink hard spirits." She shrugged off the offer and stepped closer. "And then the second time we met, well, it was embarrassing to admit that I had not been entirely honest."

He filled his glass then filled a second. "Not entirely, no."

"I don't know what came over me really," she said more to herself than to him. "There are standards to be maintained and I have never veered from them. A certain model of behavior is expected and I do adhere to it. As should we all. I can't imagine what might happen if people didn't. If everyone went their own merry way without a thought as to honesty and principles and moral behavior."

"Anarchy I suspect." He handed her the glass and she sipped absently.

"The very thought is appalling." She sighed. "I do pride myself on my honesty, you know. Why, I never dissemble or prevaricate. And I've never been one to deal in falsehoods, no matter how minor, even when it might have made things a great deal easier."

"Then you are indeed meeting Gray near the maze even as we speak?" He cast her an innocent smile.

She stared at him for a moment. "Obviously not. But that was for a greater good and as such can be overlooked."

"I suspect there are any number of deceptions that are well meaning at the start." He studied her over the rim of his glass. "And what greater good is that?"

"Speaking to you privately of course." She raised her chin. "I wish to apologize to you."

"For which part?"

"What do you mean—which part?"

"For deceiving me in New York about who you really were or having your way with me and then throwing me out into the cold."

She gasped. "Mr. Russell!"

"Sam."

"Mr. Russell." She glared, anger sparking in her eyes. He noted how very similar it was to passion of another kind. "Please be so good as to watch what you say." Delilah shot a quick glance at the door, then stepped closer and lowered her voice. "The last thing I want is to be overheard. Goodness." She tossed back at least half of her drink. "I would think after this afternoon you would understand that."

"It was hard to miss."

"And that is what I wish to apologize for. My manner this afternoon was unacceptable. I was very nearly rude and I am never rude." She sighed in surrender. "My purpose in not being entirely forthright about my name really was well intentioned. But you do have my apologies for misleading you. As for the rest of it . . ." Her gaze hardened. "I did not have my way with you or at least no more so than you had your way with me."

He nodded slowly. "I can agree with that."

"Furthermore, I did not throw you out into the cold as, if I recall, we were in your room."

He shrugged. "A minor point."

"And . . ." She drew herself up in a haughty manner. "It was June and not the least bit cold."

He chuckled. "You have me there."

"Well?"

"Well what?"

Her jaw tightened. "Do you accept my apology or not?"

"For your less than gracious behavior this afternoon?" He nodded. "It was understandable, really, given my unexpected appearance. It does tend to be uncomfortable when one's adventure appears without warning on one's doorstep. So yes, I do accept your apology. As for the rest of it . . ." He sipped his drink. "I haven't decided yet."

"There's nothing to decide."

"It also seems to me that, as neither of us were completely honest when we first met, one deception cancels the other."

She studied him suspiciously then nodded. "That's fair enough, I suppose."

He laughed. "I never realized an apology was subject to negotiation."

"Neither did I." She paused. "Why are you here anyway?"

"I'm here for the wedding, of course. And I have business to attend to. And I met a charming woman in New York, who looked vaguely like you—"

She scoffed.

"That I did want to see again."

Her brow rose. "In spite of the fact that she did not want to see you again?"

"Or possibly because she was so vehement about not seeing me again." He grinned. "Her

117

protestations didn't ring quite true to me. I think thou dost protest too much, you know."

She stared in disbelief. "Are you trying to quote Shakespeare?"

"Sure. Why not?"

"Well, you're not doing it right. The quote is . . ." Her brows drew together and she thought for a moment. "Oh, for goodness' sake, I can't remember it now. Any other time it would spring to mind immediately."

He took another sip of his drink and tried not to laugh.

"It's simply not correct, that's all. And I did not protest too much. I daresay, I did not protest enough."

"You didn't want to be rude."

"I am never rude."

"Of course not."

"Admittedly, it is hard to be polite when you are trying to tell someone you never want to see them again."

"Without actually coming out and saying I never want to see you again."

"Yet another mistake on my part, although I thought I was quite clear. I should have simply said it." Her eyes narrowed. "I never wanted to see you again."

"Yes, that's probably what you should have said but what you did say was—oh, how did you put it?" He thought for a moment. "Ah yes, you said it would be *best* if we never saw each other again."

"It's the same thing." She fairly spit the words.

"No, it's not." He swirled the whisky in his glass. "What you said implied a mutual benefit on both sides. I saw absolutely no benefit to never seeing you again. I didn't think it would be the least bit *best*."

She glared.

"Although I can certainly see why it might be of benefit to you."

"Can you?" Suspicion colored her words.

"I understand you're looking for a new husband. It wouldn't do for any potential candidate to know you were the sort of woman to indulge in scandalous affairs at the drop of a hat."

She gasped in horror. "I am not!"

"Although I suppose it's not scandalous if no one knows about it," he said thoughtfully. "The scandal lies more in the telling and retelling and gossip and—"

"I have not told anyone!"

"Neither have I." He smiled.

She studied him closely. "Do you intend to?"

"Now *that* is rude, Delilah." He shook his head in a mournful manner. "Even in our short acquaintance, have I done anything to make you think that I am the kind of man who brags about something like this?"

A blush washed up her face. "No, you haven't."

"That I am not an honorable sort?"

"No, you were quite—"

"Gentlemen are not confined to England, you know."

"Of course, I didn't—"

"I might well be insulted."

"Well I didn't—"

"No, on second thought, I *am* insulted." He pinned her with the sort of hard look he usually reserved for business. "And offended."

She sighed. "Then apparently I owe you yet another apology."

"They are mounting up." He set his glass on a table, his tone as casual as his manner. "What do you intend to do about it?"

"Nothing." Her brow furrowed in annoyance. "I have apologized, more than once. What more would you have me do?"

"I'm not sure." He shook his head. "Perhaps if you sounded more sincere."

"Good Lord, you are an annoying beast." She downed the rest of her drink and set her glass down beside his with a thunk. "Very well then." She counted the points off on her fingers. "One, you have my heartfelt and sincere apologies for my rudeness this afternoon. Two, I apologize for not being completely honest with you in New York. And three, I am deeply sorry if I cast any aspersions as to the honorable nature of your character. There." She cast him an overly polite smile. "I do hope that was sincere enough for you."

"It wasn't bad." He shrugged. "It could use some practice. You're not used to apologizing, are you?"

"I rarely do anything that requires an apology."

"I find that hard to believe." He turned away from her and wandered around the perimeter of the room, stopping to study a large portrait of a woman and three young girls. He didn't need to look at Delilah to know she was debating whether to ignore his comment or take up the gauntlet. He'd bet on the latter.

A long moment drifted by in silence. Was he wrong?

"I'll have you know, I am usually quite pleasant."

It was all he could do to keep from laughing. Of course he wasn't wrong, he was rarely wrong.

"And amusing," she continued. "I'm excellent at conversing on any number of topics. People find me quite clever. And I'm polite, unfailingly polite. And I am never—"

"Rude," he said absently, bending closer to the painting to read the artist's signature. "You said that."

"Obviously, it bears repeating."

"You probably can't say that you're never rude often enough."

"Apparently!"

"One should always be clear about that sort of

thing." He glanced at her. "As one should always be clear about never seeing someone again."

"I thought I was clear."

"And yet, here I am." He smiled. "And here I intend to stay."

"No doubt." She considered him for a moment. "It might be frightfully dull for you here, though."

He chuckled. "I can't imagine that."

"And it does seem a shame, since you have never really seen anything outside of London, for you to be trapped here," she said, a sly note in her voice. "When you could be enjoying a bit of travel. Brighton is lovely this time of year."

"Brighton?"

"Oh, my yes." She bubbled with enthusiasm. "The crowds are gone now and it's quite a charming place."

"Nonetheless, I have no desire to travel to Brighton or anywhere else at the moment." He glanced around the library. "No, I am looking forward to enjoying the peace and quiet of the country here at Millworth."

"Yes, well, I suspected as much." She thought for a moment. "It might be awkward, you know. For the two of us to be in such close proximity."

"Because you never wanted to see me again?"

"There is that . . ."

"But then you told the others we have never met and I am not so lacking in chivalry that I would point out a lady's deceit."

"Thank you. That is most appreciated." The reluctant note in her voice belied her words. "I would appreciate as well if we did try to avoid one another. It would be easier to keep up the pretense of having just met."

"You needn't worry about that. I agree that avoiding one another is an excellent idea." He paused. "It won't be easy though as there are only five of us here at the moment and I imagine there will be any number of unavoidable instances when we are thrown together."

"Probably."

"However, allow me to relieve your mind on another matter, Lady Hargate."

"What matter?"

"Now that I have seen you again, I believe I have changed my mind."

"Changed your mind about what?" Caution edged her voice.

"About seeing you again." He shook his head. "Now, I think you're right. We should have gone our separate ways."

She stared at him. "I am usually right."

"So you have nothing to fear on that score." He strolled to the table where he had left his glass, picked it up, and drained the last of his whisky. "I have no interest in a woman who is looking for nothing more in a new husband than wealth and title."

She gasped. "I am looking for a great deal more!"

He cast her a skeptical look. "Love then?"

"Love is neither practical nor necessary. Love simply muddies the water and creates problems where none should exist. Regardless, what I want is none of your concern." Her blue eyes flashed. "But you have just made my point as to why I don't want anyone—anyone at all—to know we have met. It was only this afternoon that I mentioned my plans and already Camille has told Grayson. Who has obviously confided in you. You know about my financial difficulties as well, don't you?"

He nodded.

"Of course you do. There are no secrets to be kept in this house." She swiveled on her heel and paced the room. "Why, the very fact that I haven't mentioned you would be enough to have Camille and Teddy and probably Grayson as well wondering why I have kept that fact to myself. And why you went along with me." She paused and stared at him. "They would jump to all sorts of conclusions, you know."

"Some of them perilously close to the mark, I would imagine."

"Camille especially has quite a fertile imagination." She resumed pacing. "But whatever conclusion she might reach will pale in comparison to what Beryl will concoct. And once Beryl knows, or thinks she knows . . ." She shuddered.

"You don't get along with your sisters, do you?"

"Well, I haven't in the past but—" She threw her hands up in a gesture of surrender. "And you already know that, don't you?"

He winced. "Yes, I'm afraid I do."

"As I said, there are no secrets here." She shook her head in disgust.

"Except ours," he said slowly. "You may count on me to keep it."

"It would not be good for either of us." A warning rang in her voice. "If the truth came out, that is."

He chuckled. "Probably not."

"Very well then." She drew a deep breath. "We are agreed?"

"We are." He stepped close to her and held out his hand. "When I reach a verbal agreement, in matters of business, it's customary to shake a man's hand."

"I'm not a man."

"Then your word is less honorable than a man's?"

"What utter rubbish." She huffed. "Do you say things intended to annoy me or is it just part of your nature?"

He grinned. "Both."

She took his hand and met his gaze directly. "Has anyone ever told you that you are a most infuriating, annoying, bothersome creature?"

"Not to my knowledge and certainly not to my

face." He gazed down into her blue eyes, nearly the same color as Camille's. With the fair coloring of the older sister, blue was not a surprise. But with Delilah's deep, rich brown hair, the color of her eyes was unexpected and remarkable. He had noted their color when they had first met and now, gazing into the endless blue, he remembered as well how they had sparkled with the excitement of flirtation and glazed with the throes of passion. "Most people would hesitate making that sort of comment because it might be considered, oh, I don't know, rude?"

The corners of her mouth quirked as if she was trying to keep from smiling. "You do this to annoy me, don't you?"

"Shall I be honest?"

She shrugged. "We might as well try honesty."

"I do." He grinned. "I like annoying you."

"You do it very well."

She tried to draw her hand from his but he held fast and pulled her a little closer.

"It's your fault, you know." Close enough to bend down and kiss her should he be so inclined.

"What is?" She stared up at him but made no attempt to move. He suspected, in spite of herself, she would kiss him back.

"That I like annoying you."

"Oh?" There was a breathless quality to her voice. Intriguing and nearly irresistible.

"I like the way your eyes spark when you're

angry. And the way you say one thing and do something else entirely different. And I especially like the way you blush."

"Nonsense. I don't blush," she said even as a flush colored her cheeks.

"And you thought I would be bored here at Millworth?" He chuckled. "On the contrary, I expect to enjoy myself thoroughly."

She stared at him for another moment and something flashed in her eyes so quickly she probably didn't realize it herself. Something exciting and promising and intriguing.

She jerked her hand from his. "We meet in the main parlor before going into dinner. I'll go now and you should join us in a few minutes."

"Because we wouldn't want to be seen arriving together."

"Which would certainly arouse suspicion." She turned toward the door.

"You do realize you'll have to apologize again."

"What?" Delilah turned back and glared at him. "Why on earth would I apologize yet again? I believe I have apologized quite enough."

"You can do what you want, of course." He shrugged. "But it seems to me that unless you apologize in front of the others, they will continue to wonder why you haven't."

"I hadn't thought of that." She shook her head. "It can't be helped I suppose." Her gaze narrowed. "As long as you understand that apology won't be the least bit sincere as I have already sincerely apologized."

"You do want to make it look genuine and sound sincere."

"Oh, it will look sincere to the others." She favored him with a smug smile. "But it won't be." She nodded and swept from the room.

Sam grinned. This was going to be fun. She was going to be fun.

His smile faded. But fun was all it would be. She obviously had no interest in more. In picking up where they had left off. As much as that might have been a possibility in the back of his mind when he had arrived, now he had to agree with her. He had no interest in a woman whose sole purpose in life was to marry well.

He adjusted the simple gold buttons on his cuffs and considered the matter. While certainly some spark still lingered between them, on her side it was obviously nothing more than fear that his presence might ruin her plans. And anger that he'd had the nerve to show up at all. She could deny it all she wished, but it was apparent to him that whatever drew them together initially remained. Not that it mattered. Best to nip this in the bud now. Regardless of the attraction between them, he absolutely refused to give his heart to a woman who only wanted him for his money and his position. He'd been down that path before. He would not step foot upon it again. He flicked an invisible piece of lint from the arm of his evening coat and started toward the parlor.

And ignored the annoying thought that just possibly that step had already been taken.

Chapter Six

"Sam," Camille said with a gracious smile. "If you would be so good as to escort me into dinner, Grayson will accompany my sister and Teddy."

"There is nothing I like better than being entrusted with the escort of two such lovely ladies," Grayson said in a gallant manner, belying the chastising look in his eyes when his gaze met Delilah's.

She smiled weakly.

Clement announced dinner the moment Grayson had finally appeared in the parlor, leaving no time for Delilah to explain why she had failed to meet him. Yet another falsehood she should feel bad about but didn't. Dear Lord, what was happening to her? It was rather difficult to pride oneself on one's honesty if one wasn't, oh, honest.

As much as she hated to admit it, Samuel was right. Apologizing in front of everyone would prove she—they—had nothing to hide. Better to get it over and done with while she had the chance.

"I would be honored." Samuel smiled down at Camille.

He did have a nice smile. It was no wonder Camille and Teddy were taken with him. That smile in combination with his dark eyes and the wicked twinkle that perpetually lingered there, well, what woman wouldn't be taken with him? Not Delilah, of course. Not again anyway.

She drew a deep breath. "Before we go into dinner, there is something I should say. To Samuel."

Camille frowned and her anxious gaze shifted between her sister and the American. "This really isn't the time—"

"No, Camille, this is the perfect time." Delilah turned to Samuel and cast him her brightest smile. "Samuel." She braced herself. "*Sam,* I owe you my apologies. I was beastly to you this afternoon. I'm afraid my mind was, well, preoccupied I suppose. Still, that is no excuse. I am not usually so . . . *curt.* I don't know what came over me but I do hope you can find it in your heart to forgive me."

A look of relief passed over Camille's face. Goodness, what did her sister think Delilah was going to say to the man anyway?

"There is nothing to apologize for." He took her hand, raised it to his lips and gazed into her eyes.

Delilah swallowed. This was really not appropriate. Still, it would be most *curt* to say so. And what could one expect from an American anyway? It wasn't as if he wasn't doing it well. Indeed, the man was quite skilled at the kissing of hands. Still, he was probably just trying to be annoying.

"I can certainly understand how unexpected . . .

developments might affect one's manner." He smiled in an entirely too engaging way. "And I owe you an apology as well. For insisting we had met when I was so clearly mistaken."

"We all make mistakes on occasion." She pulled her hand from his without resistance and ignored a twinge of annoyance that he released her so easily. That was that then.

"Now that this is settled," Camille began. "We should go into dinner before Clement feels compelled to return and stare in an accusing manner. As though we personally destroyed Mrs. Dooley's fine cooking."

Teddy glanced at her and wrinkled her nose. The quality of Mrs. Dooley's cooking had been erratic of late.

"Shall we?" Samuel offered his arm.

Camille hooked her arm though his and they strolled into the dining room.

"Ladies." Grayson offered his arm to Teddy on one side, Delilah on the other. He inclined his head toward his future sister-in-law. "Very nicely done, Delilah. And most appreciated."

"I owe you an apology as well, I'm afraid. I'm sorry I didn't meet you. I was unavoidably detained."

Grayson studied her sharply then nodded. "I assumed as much."

Teddy peered around Grayson. "I thought your apology to Sam was nicely done as well."

"I do try," Delilah said under her breath. Now that she had apologized in front of everyone, hopefully she could get through the meal without being *curt*.

Or worse.

Dinner was far easier and far more pleasant than Delilah had expected. Samuel and Grayson entertained the ladies with stories of their exploits and misadventures during Grayson's years in America. Samuel was charming in a natural sort of way and mildly flirtatious with all three women but no more so than Grayson. American or not, one could scarcely find anything to criticize him for. He certainly paid Delilah no particular attention as if they had indeed just met. His gaze met hers no more often than it met Camille's or Teddy's. Exactly as she wanted. Still, why was it that she found very nearly everything he did so annoying?

Regardless, Delilah was startled to realize she was having quite a nice time. Somewhere between the fish and the fowl she nearly forgot that she and Samuel had shared an adventure. His fault entirely, much to his credit. Why, she was actually enjoying his company.

Not that she should be surprised by that. She had enjoyed his easy manner, so different from most gentlemen she knew, from nearly the first moment they'd met in New York. A moment that had, in many ways, changed her life. But then she was ripe for change. At least for a few days.

It had started innocently enough. Grayson had had some sort of luncheon meeting and as Camille was to accompany him, he had asked Delilah if she would wait in the parlor in his suite for an expected delivery of important papers regarding some matter of business. Delilah couldn't remember the details now and hadn't really paid attention then, she'd been entirely too busy planning her afternoon. Grayson did say the papers would likely be delivered by an employee or assistant of a business associate or something along those lines. Or at least that's what she'd thought he'd said. He did mention a Mr. Moore, but Grayson and Camille had been in a hurry to depart so that detail had slipped by Delilah. Upon reflection, she should have paid more attention but it had seemed a minor point. Not paying as much mind to details as she should had long been her greatest flaw.

So when Samuel arrived bearing those papers instead of Mr. Moore, and explaining Mr. Moore had some pressing problem to deal with, somehow Delilah had the distinct impression Samuel was the assistant and not the associate. It was a simple enough mistake and easily rectified but Samuel made no effort to do so at the time. Indeed, looking back on it, he had appeared oddly amused.

". . . and I would certainly never say that." Teddy's prim pronouncement belied the amusement in her eye. "Although, I'm not surprised Grayson would."

Samuel laughed. His gaze caught Delilah's and he grinned. Delilah returned his smile even though she had no idea what the others were discussing. From the snatches of conversation that did register, she thought it had something to do with an incident that occurred years ago regarding Grayson, a small dog, a lady's hat, and a train. Judging from the laughter around the table it was most amusing.

Samuel was indeed most amusing without being silly, she'd give him that. At their first meeting, she had said something—she couldn't recall what—and he had laughed. A laugh that struck her as genuine and quite contagious. Perhaps it was the setting, or the innate excitement of travel but before she knew it, they were engaged in a most lighthearted discussion over the trials and tribulations of travel. It was not at all like her to chat idly with a man she'd not been properly introduced to and yet it was a great deal of, well, fun. In truth, she hated to see it end. Which was probably why, in hindsight, she had introduced herself as Mrs. Hargate rather than Lady Hargate. She'd suspected tall, handsome, amusing strangers were far more likely to flirt with Mrs. Hargate than with Lady Hargate.

Although admittedly, when the falsehood had flowed from her lips she hadn't given the why of it any thought at all.

That lack of consideration probably explained as well why, the next day, when she was strolling in the park alone, which in and of itself was unusual for her, and she happened upon him, again she did nothing to dissuade him from concluding she was a poor relation acting as chaperone. She might even have encouraged that conclusion. Nor had she felt the tiniest bit of guilt about her relatively insignificant deception. What harm could it do? Besides, she would probably never see the man again.

They only spoke for a few minutes then and briefly encountered each other the next day in the hotel lobby, when she had explained away the bags and boxes a doorman carried as her sister's. Their meetings were surprisingly unsatisfying, as if she had been allowed to smell something delightful baking in an oven but would not be allowed to taste it. And she had wanted to taste it even if, at that moment, she had no clear idea what tasting it entailed. And why shouldn't she? Hadn't she planned on embracing whatever adventure came her way? Spending a few minutes alone with a handsome American was scarcely the stuff novels of adventure were written about.

". . . and quite an adventure as I understand," Camille said in a teasing manner.

Delilah's attention jerked to her sister, who continued without pause.

"Grayson." Camille pinned her fiancé with a firm look. "I suspect there is more to this story than you have revealed up to this point."

Grayson looked at Samuel, who was looking anywhere but at his friend. Then his gaze met Grayson's and both men burst into laughter.

"Oh come now," Teddy said with a laugh of her own. "You cannot let us hang like this. I can't imagine either of you dressed in such a manner. And certainly not at a ball. Neither of you are . . ."

It was the masked ball that was Delilah's ultimate undoing. Mask or not, she knew him at once and he recognized her. One might have said it was fate if one believed in such a thing. Although she had never been one to believe in magic either and yet . . . One dance led to a second, a second led to a third and before she had time to think, she was in his room and in his arms and in his bed. No. In retrospect, she could tell herself that all she wished now but it wasn't true. She'd had plenty of time to think, to consider what she was doing, to dwell on all the scandalous repercussions. She simply hadn't wanted to. Hadn't cared about anything beyond that night. It wasn't at all like her. *Lady* Hargate certainly would have cared. *Mrs.* Hargate was entirely too busy to care, too busy throwing caution to the winds. Along with her clothes.

She hadn't come to her senses until it was too late. And while she was mortified by her indiscretion, if she was being completely honest with herself, she had to admit it was a glorious night. She'd never imagined intimacies between a man and a woman could be quite so, well, delightful. She was no virgin, certainly, but the occasional rare relations with Phillip for the sake of a possible heir had always been brief and not particularly satisfying. And she had heard it mentioned by friends, it should be satisfying and even enjoyable. With Samuel it had been most enjoyable. Now, she could well understand why Beryl had once been so free with her favors.

Delilah had wanted adventure and adventure was what she had found. Pity, it had followed her home. His presence here now only reminded her of what an awful mistake she had made. It was most embarrassing to have a man—practically a stranger—who had seen her naked now staying in her family's home. Sitting across the dinner table. Flirting with her best friend! Surely some of the previous long-dead inhabitants of Millworth Manor were now turning over in their graves at this American invasion.

Regardless, she drew a deep breath, it was time to get on with her life and her plans. As long as Samuel cooperated, what happened at the Murray Hill Hotel would be left at the Murray

Hill Hotel. Her night of sin would be left in America where it belonged.

"Tell us, Sam, what kind of business brings you to England?" Teddy began. "If you don't mind my asking."

"Unless, of course, it's boring." Camille signaled to a footman to refill her wineglass. "I must say whenever Grayson speaks of business, I find it quite dull and uninteresting."

Grayson's brow quirked. "Do you?"

"Don't look at me that way, darling, of course I do. And you well know it." Camille scoffed. "You can't tell me you haven't noticed the way my eyes glaze when you go on and on about stocks and bonds and deals and whatever else it is you go on and on about."

"And I thought that look was one of sheer admiration for my business acumen," Grayson said mildly.

Camille stared at him for a moment then laughed. "You did not."

He chuckled. "Not for a moment. But I suspect you will find this interesting." He nodded at Samuel. "Go on, tell them why you're here."

"I'm here for your wedding of course."

"And," Grayson prompted.

"And to gauge interest among some of England's upper echelon for, well . . ." Samuel paused. "The future you might say."

"Oh dear, then you shall surely be disappointed."

Teddy heaved a dramatic sigh. "Unlike you Americans, we tend to ignore the future rather than embrace it. We are quite set in our ways, you know, mired in heritage and tradition and all that goes with it."

"As it should be," Delilah murmured.

Samuel turned toward her. "You can't possibly mean that."

"Oh, but I do." She cast him a pleasant smile. "There is nothing wrong with doing things the way they have always been done."

Samuel's smile matched hers. "Unless there is a better way to do them."

Curiosity sounded in Camille's voice. "What better way?"

"Horseless carriages." Samuel's tone was casual but an underlying current of excitement edged his words, as if he were announcing the way to salvation or the path to Nirvana or something equally preposterous. "Very possibly the way of the future."

Delilah stared for a moment then swallowed a laugh. Laughing would be rude.

"Really? How fascinating." Teddy fluttered her lashes at him but in the flickering candlelight Delilah might have been mistaken.

"Do you truly think they could ever replace horses?" Camille asked.

Better to keep her mouth shut entirely. Yes, that was an excellent plan.

Samuel nodded. "I do."

Surely he wasn't serious?

"That's rather far-fetched, isn't it?" Teddy's brow furrowed.

"Not at all." Samuel paused while a footman removed his empty plate.

How on earth did he become so successful? Was the man mad? He was so obviously wrong.

"Ultimately, I think a horseless carriage would be much more efficient than a horse," he continued.

Absolutely, completely, and without a doubt wrong.

"The cost of maintaining a horseless carriage would certainly be far less than that of a horse."

Someone should tell him how very wrong he was. Delilah glanced around the table. Teddy and Camille were staring with rapt attention and Grayson was studying his friend with approval. Good Lord, they were all mad! As well as wrong.

"And a horseless carriage can always be repaired." Samuel shrugged. "In theory, it can be repaired forever."

"That's absurd," Delilah said without thinking. "You can't possibly be serious."

He studied her. "Oh, but I am."

"The way of the future?" The words were out of Delilah's mouth before she could stop them. Apparently there was a fine line between rude and honest. "I've never heard anything so ridiculous."

Samuel studied her. "Why?"

"Why?" Delilah stared at him. "I'd say the why of it is obvious."

Samuel's eyes narrowed no more than a fraction. "Why do you think it's ridiculous?"

"I don't think it's ridiculous," Camille said quickly. "I think it sounds most exciting."

Delilah ignored her. "I don't *think* it's ridiculous either. It *is* ridiculous."

"Why?" Samuel asked again.

"We've all seen horseless carriages, at exhibitions and the like. Each and every one of us." Delilah gestured at the rest of the group. "Why, on occasion, one even sees one of those devices attempting to sputter its way down a road, at great inconvenience to the rest of us I might add."

"One would hate to see you inconvenienced," Camille murmured.

"They're nothing more than toys," Delilah continued without pause. "Playthings for men who refuse to give up being little boys."

Samuel's tone was cool. "Then I gather you have not been impressed?"

"I think they're most impressive." Teddy cast the group a bright smile.

"Impressed?" Delilah stared in disbelief. "Hardly. They'll never be practical. They're noisy. They're messy. They spew great fumes. They're not the least bit reliable. They look extraordinarily uncomfortable—"

"Have you ever ridden in one?" Samuel asked in a clipped tone.

"Absolutely not! Nor do I ever intend to."

"You'll get your chance soon enough," Grayson said under his breath.

"Admittedly, there is still work to be done." Sam's words were measured. "This is the beginning of an entirely new mode of transportation."

"Actually, Mr. Russell—*Sam*—it's not the beginning, is it?" Delilah asked.

Samuel's brow furrowed. "I'm not sure I understand."

"As far back as Leonardo da Vinci, man has been trying to develop a vehicle that would move under its own power. That was some four hundred years ago. Indeed, history is full of failed attempts to develop horseless carriages." Delilah reached for her wine. "I should think if someone was going to invent a vehicle that actually worked they would have done so by now."

Camille stared at her sister. "How did you know that?"

"I do read more than romantic novels, Camille." Apparently Camille not only thought her sister was unable to comport herself in polite society but she considered her uninformed as well. "I keep up on current events, politics and the like, even if I find some of it quite dull. And I am well versed in history."

"We had some very progressive instructors at

Miss Bicklesham's," Teddy said in a confidential manner. "One in particular was fascinated by mankind's history of invention."

"I should have attended Miss Bicklesham's," Camille murmured.

"And even that instructor accepted the basic fact that man will never be able to replace horses." Delilah smiled in triumph and sipped her wine.

"Until now," Sam said coolly.

"Horses are dependable, loyal, intelligent creatures," she said. "They have served man well for eons and will continue to do so far into the future."

"I'm not questioning the basic nature of the horse," Samuel said sharply. Obviously she was beginning to annoy him as much as he annoyed her. Good. "But I would much rather depend on something I control rather than something that has a mind of its own."

"Perhaps the fault lies in you for not being able to control a horse," Delilah said with a smug smile.

"I have no particular difficulties controlling horses." His manner was matter-of-fact but his hands flexed on the table. Apparently, Sam had no difficulties controlling himself as well. "I simply have more confidence in my own abilities than those of a dumb animal."

"I daresay, most of the horses I know are far

more intelligent than their riders," Delilah said pointedly.

Samuel smiled. "Friends of yours?"

Camille choked.

"Sam has just come from meeting with a gentleman in Germany," Grayson said. "A Mr. Benz who has made remarkable progress in the development of what he calls motorwagons."

"Motorwagons?" Delilah's brow rose. "What a silly word."

"No more so than telephone or photograph, when one thinks about it," Teddy said pleasantly.

"It doesn't matter what you call it." Samuel drummed his fingers on the table. "The fact of the matter is, given the progress being made in the development of new propulsion methods, the motorwagon is here to stay."

Delilah met his gaze directly. "Utter, complete, and total nonsense. A waste of time, money, effort, and energy."

Samuel's gaze didn't waver from hers. "I suspect the same thing was probably said about steam locomotives. History has proven those skeptics wrong. Today, we wouldn't think of a world without trains."

"That's an entirely different matter." Delilah adopted a lofty tone, although he did have a point.

"And time will prove those shortsighted cynics wrong as well." Samuel smiled.

She wanted to smack him but settled for

returning his smug smile. "Or, more likely, their refusal to be seduced by the lure of the impossible will be shown to be most intelligent."

"It's overcoming the impossible that has driven man since he first discovered the secret of fire." Samuel leaned forward slightly. "Mankind's greatest discoveries have come about in spite of naysayers who couldn't see past the nose on their faces. Impossible, Delilah, is merely improbable not yet accomplished."

For an endless moment, Samuel's gaze locked with hers. Silence fell around the table. The oddest thought struck Delilah that this man was as exciting as he was annoying. She'd forgotten that or perhaps simply ignored it.

"I'm so glad she apologized before dinner," Camille murmured.

Grayson choked back a laugh.

"What did you mean, Grayson?" Teddy said quickly, no doubt in an effort to divert the debate between Samuel and Delilah. Still debate was inevitable as she was right and he was so very wrong. "About Delilah having her chance to ride in a . . . a motorwagon?"

Grayson glanced at Samuel then shrugged. "Simply that Sam has purchased a vehicle that will be arriving any day."

"Arriving here?" Delilah stared. "You're bringing one of those things here? To Millworth Manor?"

"Goodness, Delilah." Teddy fixed her with a

curious glance. "It's not as if he's exposing us all to scandal. It's simply an intriguing new invention, that's all."

"Surely, you're not afraid it will scare the horses." Samuel took a sip of his wine. "Intelligent creatures that they are."

"Well I for one think it's most exciting," Camille said. "I cannot wait to take my first ride in it. Although I'm not sure why you're bringing it here."

"I want to try it for myself, evaluate its feasibility if you will, without Benz and his assistants hovering." Enthusiasm rang in Samuel's voice. "It's far easier to do that here than transport the motorwagon to America."

"This is only a first step." Grayson nodded. "We want to determine if there's enough interest here in England among those who can afford such a novelty—"

"It's only a novelty for now," Samuel said.

Camille's brow rose. "We?"

"And if so," Grayson continued, "produce motorwagons in England and then on to America."

"Grayson." Shock sounded in Delilah's voice. "Surely you're not a part of this absurd fiasco?"

"Oh, but I am," Grayson nodded. "And I consider it neither absurd nor do I expect it to be a fiasco."

"But it is highly speculative, is it not?" Camille studied her fiancé. "As well as costly?"

"Of course it is." Grayson chuckled.

Sam grinned. "That's part of the fun."

"Fun?" Delilah sniffed. "I don't think I would call risking a great deal of money on something so ridiculous *fun*."

"Oh?" Challenge twinkled in Samuel's eyes. "And what would you call fun?"

She shot him a scathing look.

"Sam and I have been partners on a number of ventures of an uncertain nature through the years," Grayson said. "Most of them have proved quite lucrative. I have no doubt this one will as well."

"And if it doesn't?" Delilah realized the sharp note in her voice might well be due more to her own financial plight than concern about Grayson's but she couldn't seem to help it.

"It will," Samuel said.

"Or it could be a dismal failure." Was Delilah the only one present who saw the perils in investing in something as ill-advised as *motor-wagons?*

"My dear Delilah." Grayson cast her an affectionate smile. "One of the joys of having made a great deal of money is being able to take a risk on something that, while seemingly far-fetched today, might indeed be the way of tomorrow."

"And while I am certain Grayson appreciates your caution on his behalf," Camille said in a chastising manner, "it really has nothing to do with you."

"Well, no, I suppose—"

"However, it does have something to do with me." Camille met her fiancé's gaze. "This is entirely your decision, Grayson. I trust you implicitly in matters of business and I would never think to question your decisions, but I am curious as to whether you intend to lose your entire fortune on this proposal?"

"That is a good question, let me think." Grayson frowned but there was a glimmer of amusement in his eyes. "I am about to marry an extremely wealthy woman, you know."

Camille nodded. "Indeed you are."

"Who would love me no less if I were penniless."

"Oh, perhaps a little less." Camille thought for a moment. "But not substantially less."

"However, I don't intend to risk my entire fortune. Nor does Sam."

"I have a very extravagant mother and sisters to support." Samuel chuckled.

"But you do still value my opinion?" Camille said to Grayson.

"As I value my life," he teased but there was something serious in his eyes. Delilah's heart caught at the look he gave her sister.

"Very well then, with apologies to Delilah who will certainly disagree with me." Camille paused, hopefully to come to her senses although Delilah suspected her sister was just as mad as her fiancé. "I think it's thrilling. It's so wonderfully progressive. I have no doubt it will ultimately be a huge success.

"And Sam." She turned an excited gaze toward him. "There are any number of gatherings planned between now and the wedding. You should take this opportunity to demonstrate the motorwagon."

Samuel and Grayson exchanged glances.

Camille continued without pause. "Which is no doubt exactly what the two of you have in mind." She looked at Teddy. "What do you think, Teddy?"

"I think it will be great fun." Teddy beamed. "*Most* people will be fascinated."

Camille thought for a moment. "A small group of friends and neighbors are joining us the day after tomorrow for a garden party, tennis and croquet, that sort of thing. It's to be very informal and the matches won't be at all serious. Do you play tennis, Sam?"

"I do. Not as well as I'd like I'm afraid."

"Delilah plays quite well," Teddy said.

"There is so much about you I don't know," Camille said to her sister. "Miss Bicklesham's, I presume?"

"A healthy body supports a healthy mind," Delilah said primly. "But, you may remember, even as a child I enjoyed tennis."

"Of course I remember," Camille said, although Delilah would have wagered she didn't recall that at all. Camille turned to Samuel. "With any luck, your motorwagon will be here by then."

"One can only hope."

"I can hardly wait to try it. I've never ridden in a horseless carriage." Camille's eyes lit with excitement. "I claim the first ride."

"And I shall be next." Teddy grinned. "I am quite looking forward to it."

Grayson smiled at Delilah. "When you see the fun the others are having, you'll want to ride in it as well."

"I wouldn't wager on that, Grayson," Delilah said. "I told you before, I have no intention of riding in some ill-conceived mechanical beast."

"Come now, Delilah," Samuel said. "Think of it . . ." His knowing gaze met hers. "As an adventure."

Chapter Seven

Sixteen days before the wedding . . .

"Will you be joining us for tennis today, Lord Fairborough?" Delilah smiled at Grayson's aunt and uncle.

Beside her husband, the Countess of Fairborough suppressed a laugh.

Her husband cast her an injured look. "I don't know what you find so amusing." He leaned toward Delilah in a confidential manner. "I'll have you know I was quite adept at the playing of squash in my youth. Similar to tennis but requiring much more skill and finesse." He huffed. "And I must say, I do prefer my tennis on an indoor court. That's the way the kings of England played and it's good enough for me."

"What he's trying to say is that he will not be playing tennis today," Lady Fairborough said with a firm look at her husband. "Nor, I'm afraid, will I. I don't play often anymore although I have always enjoyed it. There's little better than a hotly contested match played under the open sky in the fresh air."

Lord Fairborough snorted in derision.

"We have a croquet court laid out as well if

you'd prefer," Delilah offered. "If I recall correctly from my childhood, both Grayson and Winfield played a wicked game of croquet." She cast the older man a teasing smile. "And I suspect I know who taught them."

"Competition runs in the blood." Lord Fairborough chuckled.

Lady Fairborough sighed. "And blood was usually the end result." She shook her head. "One wouldn't think something as deceptively peaceful as croquet would be a blood sport but with my boys it was."

Grayson's parents had died when he was very young and he'd been raised beside his cousin Winfield, now Lord Stillwell.

Lady Fairborough peered around the terrace. "I saw Grayson when we first arrived but now I can't seem to find either my nephew or my son and daughter-in-law."

Twenty or so of Camille's friends together with neighbors Delilah hadn't seen in years milled about on the terrace, greeting each other and exchanging the sort of pleasantries people exchange when they haven't seen one another for far too long. Footmen navigated between the guests bearing trays of iced champagne and lemonade. Groups of two or three or more drifted toward the courts, a ten-minute walk from the terrace. Those who intended to play were overheard making rash statements as to their sporting prowess and Delilah suspected a few friendly wagers were made.

"Isn't that him?" Lord Fairborough squinted and pointed out a young man demonstrating how to swing a racket to an even younger woman.

"No dear," Lady Fairborough murmured. "Perhaps if you were to wear your spectacles . . ."

"Don't need them," he said in a gruff manner.

Lady Fairborough sighed. "Then keep looking."

Most of those under a certain age, men and women alike, carried rackets under their arm as did Delilah. The older guests would probably choose to play croquet. Teddy had said the courts were set up for both games. Her *mistake* was nowhere in sight, much to her relief.

She hadn't seen him at all yesterday except in passing. Samuel and Grayson had been ensconced in the library deep in discussion and plans for their motorized folly most of the day, going so far as to take their meals there. Delilah had noted any number of mechanical drawings strewn about when she'd happened to walk by the library door. As foolish as she thought this venture was, at least it kept Samuel occupied and out of her way.

With any luck at all, the American had decided to forgo today's activities as well. She hadn't encountered him at breakfast and wondered if he had decided to return to London after all. Her spirits brightened at the thought then just as quickly deflated. She certainly wouldn't count on that and someone probably would have mentioned his leaving to her. Samuel would no doubt appear when she least expected him if for no other reason than to be annoying. He derived entirely too much pleasure from annoying her. Which in and of itself was annoying.

Still, he had appeared on his best behavior at dinner the other night once the topic had turned to something less volatile than motorwagons. One could argue he was quite charming. Delilah too had tried very hard to be charming, or at least cordial, and thought she had succeeded nicely, all things considered. She still didn't understand why the others couldn't see that Samuel was wrong about the future of horseless carriages. He was wrong and she was right and there was no more to be said about it than that, even if she suspected there would a great deal more said once the blasted machine arrived.

Not encountering him yesterday had been a welcome respite. Now that the shock of his arrival had passed, Delilah vowed to do a better job of treating Samuel like a new acquaintance. It wasn't much of a plan but it was better than nothing. Especially as every time his name came up, Camille studied her with a speculative eye. Delilah wasn't sure why treating him as she would anyone else was so bloody hard to accomplish but then nothing seemed to be especially easy in her life at the moment.

Even today's garden party was awkward. Delilah was considered an accomplished hostess and it was decidedly odd today to be something less than a hostess and more than a guest. In truth she wasn't sure what her role was. This business of being a dutiful sister was new to her, although she had decided to simply be as pleasant and helpful as possible. As long as she avoided the American she might be able to manage that.

"Have you met Miranda?" Lady Fairborough asked.

"Briefly." Delilah smiled. "At the wedding."

"Yes, of course." The older woman shook her head in a disparaging manner. "You were there. I don't know where my head is some days."

Lady Miranda Garret had wed Winfield shortly after his cousin, Camille, and Delilah had returned from their trip to New York. Where, of course, she had made the biggest mistake of her life. Why was it that anything anyone said on very nearly any topic brought the blasted man to mind?

"Excellent choice on Winfield's part." Lord Fairborough nodded his approval. "I was beginning to lose hope."

"Nonsense." Confidence sounded in Lady Fairborough's voice. "I knew he'd find the right woman. Eventually." A triumphant smile graced the older lady's lips. "I like her a great deal. She's quite progressive you know and very modern."

"How nice." Delilah forced a weak smile. Why was everyone so concerned with progress all of a sudden? What was wrong with leaving things as they had always been?

"She talked Winfield into installing electricity when the hall was rebuilt." Lord Fairborough shook his head. "Can you imagine such a thing? Electricity at Fairborough Hall."

"Isn't it dangerous?" Delilah asked.

Certainly more and more areas of London were being electrified but her house had yet to be wired. This was another one of those *ways of the future* she thought one should be cautious about. Still, while she'd prefer not to admit it to certain parties, electricity was, well, intriguing. And if her house remained her house, perhaps it was time to take a tentative step forward. As long as that step was solidly on the ground and not into a self-propelled motorwagon.

"We are still getting adjusted to it but I like it." Lord Fairborough nodded. "It's certainly not without a few awkward problems—"

"That poor cat . . ." Lady Fairborough shuddered.

"But all in all, I think it's most exciting. I like being at the forefront of progress. Even Winfield is pleased and I don't mind telling you, he was adamantly against it in the beginning. It took a bit of convincing on Miranda's part to change his mind." Lord Fairborough nodded in a sage manner. "But I suspect that's when Winfield realized she was the woman for him."

"There's nothing more conducive for romance than argument or being on the opposing sides of an issue." Lady Fairborough smiled in a satisfied manner. Did all mothers smile that way or just the ones Delilah knew? "That was my advice to Miranda and needless to say I was right."

"Regardless, I doubt Delilah has need for your advice," her husband said.

"I am always grateful for words of wisdom." Delilah cast the lady a genuine smile even if she wasn't entirely certain of the validity of Lady Fairborough's advice. "And I shall certainly keep it in mind."

They chatted for a few moments more, then the couple headed down the terrace steps toward the playing fields. A light supper would be laid out on the terrace while the guests were playing croquet and tennis or cheering on those who were. Teddy mentioned there would also be music and perhaps even dancing if anyone was so inclined.

The crowd on the terrace had thinned. No doubt most of the guests had already made their way to the courts. She would have to hurry if she wished to play. Lady Fairborough was right. There was nothing like a well-fought game of tennis to make life look a bit brighter.

Perhaps Samuel was already at the courts. He was still nowhere in sight. For that matter, she didn't see Grayson and Camille or Winfield and his wife. Not that she cared where Samuel was but it would be convenient to know his location if she was to avoid him.

What on earth was wrong with her? Why couldn't she face being around him? And why did every word out of his mouth set her teeth on edge? Other people apparently found him quite likeable. Of course, he had never seen them in the throes of unexpected and unbridled passion. How did women like Beryl—who'd had any number of illicit affairs before she and her husband had fallen in love with each other—manage to function in public, where she might come face-to-face with a former paramour? Delilah shuddered at the thought. Why, Delilah couldn't face the one lover she'd had let alone the scores Beryl had left in her wake. If she and Beryl were closer, Delilah might turn to her for advice. Perhaps someday, not now of course and not in the foreseeable future, but someday when they were both old and gray and, at least for one of them, over the embarrassment of encountering one's mistakes. Although Beryl probably didn't consider them mistakes as much as adventures. For Delilah, it was one and the same.

"Where have you been?" Teddy appeared before her, her ever-present notebook in her hand and a touch of panic in her eyes. "I've been looking everywhere for you."

"Apparently not. I've been right here." She studied the other woman. "You, on the other hand, look as though you are quite done in."

"Not yet." The always efficient Teddy looked anything but competent at the moment. "I know we talked about this when we came to Millworth so much earlier than I have ever arrived to make certain a wedding goes smoothly. I agreed to take on all these other parties Camille had envisioned because you are my friend and Camille is spending an outrageous amount of money. And, admittedly I was grateful for the opportunity to escape my mother's house. Besides, I didn't think it would be at all difficult. And you said you would come early as well."

"I had nowhere else to go."

"Not that you mentioned that. And you should have, you know."

Delilah nodded. "I do. And if I am ever threatened with destitution again, you will be the very first one I will tell."

Teddy's lips twitched with a restrained smile. "I shall take that as a promise."

"As I meant it."

"Good." Teddy nodded. "As I was saying, my mother is not here to help, for which I am eternally grateful," she added quickly.

"As are we all."

Teddy's mother, while well meaning, had never been able to get over the fact of Teddy's failed engagement—apparently even death was not a legitimate excuse—or her daughter's refusal to marry the distant cousin who inherited her late husband's title and property. Just as Teddy had never been able to forgive Phillip for his transgressions against Delilah, Delilah had never been able to entirely see past Lady Sallwick's treatment of her only child.

"I need your help. Usually, my mother is with me for assistance along with several members of her household staff." She sighed. "I am only one woman and I cannot be everywhere at once. Why, even now I am expected at the tennis court to assign partners and, let me tell you, that will require the wisdom of Solomon as there will be those who wish and expect and have requested to play with their friends or relations and those who have specifically asked to play against them."

"Just tell me what you need and frankly I'm grateful to do it. I've felt a bit like a fish out of water myself not knowing quite what was expected of me."

It struck Delilah that perhaps this was what she might do for the rest of her life if she was indeed left penniless. Teddy's organization of weddings and various social events was not amassing her a fortune but it was keeping her financial head above water and allowing her to keep up the pretense that nothing had changed with the death of her father. If there was one thing Delilah knew how to do and do well it was host a party. Perhaps Delilah could join forces with Teddy and her mother. If they'd have her, of course. Still, that was a matter for the future, if the future turned out to be as dire as Delilah feared.

"Although I must say you are doing an excellent job thus far."

"Thus far." Teddy gave her a half-hearted smile. "Thank you but in ways too numerous to mention I am balancing a house of cards. Still . . ." She drew a deep breath. "All will be well momentarily, as soon as I herd everyone to their respective playing courts and the servants can begin setting up here. However . . ." Teddy glanced from side to side. "A fair number of the guests are not at the courts and seem to have disappeared."

Delilah drew her brows together. "What do you mean—disappeared?"

"I mean they've vanished. They're gone. Missing. I don't know what happened to them."

"Maybe they just went home?"

"They can't go home." Teddy glared. "This is home!"

Delilah stared in confusion. "What?"

"Camille and Grayson have vanished." Teddy counted the missing guests off on her fingers. "As have Lord Stillwell and his wife and a handful of others I think, including . . ." Teddy narrowed her eyes. "Sam."

"You needn't look at me like that. I haven't done away with the man."

"You obviously don't like him."

"Nonsense." She waved off the charge. "We simply have a difference of opinion that's all."

Teddy scoffed.

"Regardless, even if I detested him, I would not slit his throat and throw his lifeless body in the pond."

Suspicion glittered in Teddy's eyes.

Delilah huffed. "Clearly, you are overworked and it has affected your mind. I could never do something like that." The very idea that she could dispatch the American was absurd. Although, given her behavior around him, it was not entirely far-fetched. "Not without help anyway."

Teddy stared at her for a moment then smiled reluctantly. "And, as I am the only one here you would trust to help you with such a thing, I suppose he's safe enough." She paused. "Do you think you could find him and the others while I go on to the courts?"

"I think that's well within my abilities."

"And as quickly as possible would be appreciated." Teddy nodded and moved away, pausing at the first group of guests she encountered, appearing calm and smoothly efficient. Delilah doubted anyone she spoke to would so much as suspect she was not in complete control.

Delilah glanced around the terrace. There was

only one way to find her missing sister and the others. Delilah stopped a passing footman.

"William," she said with a pleasant smile. "Lady Theodosia is attempting to usher the guests toward the games but I fear we have misplaced Lady Lydingham and Mr. Elliott and a few others. Have you any idea where they might be?"

"I really am not certain, my lady." An uneasy look shaded William's eyes.

"Your best guess, then."

"Well." He shifted nervously from foot to foot.

Delilah studied the young man closely. There was no reason for him to wish to keep the whereabouts of Camille and Grayson and Sam from her. Unless . . . "It has arrived, hasn't it?"

"I'm afraid I don't . . ." He winced. "Yes, ma'am."

There was no need for further explanations. She didn't doubt for a moment that the servants were well aware of the debate at the dinner table. There were no secrets at Millworth.

"Where?"

For a moment, she felt sorry for the poor boy, torn as he was between answering her question and the avoidance of additional conflict in the household.

"I am not certain but I think, well . . ." He drew a deep breath. "The carriage house, Lady Hargate. It was put in the carriage house."

"Thank you, William." She nodded and turned to go, then turned back. "Did you see it?"

He nodded. "It arrived shortly before the first guests."

"And? What did you think of it?"

"It's not my place to say, ma'am."

"Come now, William, I'm simply asking your opinion." Goodness, did the poor boy think she would disembowel him if he disagreed with her? "I promise I will not hold it against you."

"Of course not, ma'am. I never imagined . . ." William drew a deep breath. "It's quite the most exciting thing I've ever seen. Smaller than I expected. I have not seen it run yet though and—"

She held up her hand to stop him. "I daresay you'll get your chance soon enough. Thank you, William."

"Yes, ma'am." He hesitated.

"Is there something else?"

"Begging your pardon, ma'am, for asking but . . ." The young man squared his shoulders. "Some of us were wondering, well, hoping that perhaps Mr. Russell's man, the one who arrived with the vehicle, might possibly give us rides in it. Not now, of course," he added quickly. "But when we're not otherwise engaged."

No doubt everyone in the household would want to ride in the blasted thing. Although that might well keep Samuel occupied. "I don't see why not."

"Thank you, Lady Hargate." He nodded and started to leave, then turned back to her. "And if I might ask another favor?"

"You don't want me to mention this request to Clement? Is that it?"

He nodded with relief. "He would see this as overstepping, my lady."

"He would be right of course but . . ." She sighed. "It's understandable that you and the rest of the staff, as well as my sister and everyone else in existence, would be curious about this piece of mechanical nonsense. I won't say a word to Clement."

"Thank you, my lady." William nodded and hurried off.

The carriage house and the adjoining stables were in the opposite direction of the tennis courts from the manor and no more than a five-minute walk. Delilah started toward it at a brisk pace. She would not allow Teddy's efforts to make this event a success go to waste simply because Samuel and his infernal machine were irresistible to some members of the company.

As soon as the carriage house was within sight she could see a small group clustered together. She drew a deep breath, plastered a friendly smile on her face, and started toward the others, determined to be pleasant no matter what feelings Samuel might provoke within her. She was nearly there when the gathering parted, as did the clouds above, allowing a shaft of sunlight to illuminate the vehicle. The *motorwagon,* for surely that's what it was, gleamed in metallic splendor. Good Lord. She cast an annoyed look heavenward. *You too?* Although it was more likely the American had positioned the contraption to its best advantage and not that it had any sort of celestial blessing. Why, she wouldn't be at all surprised if Samuel hadn't arranged as well for a heavenly choir to burst into a song of praise at any moment.

"Delilah." Camille caught sight of her sister. "What are you doing here?" She cast an uneasy glance at the machine.

"I haven't come to ruin your fun, if that's what you're thinking."

"She would never think that," Grayson said, although doubt lingered in his eyes as well.

Samuel and another man, tall, dark haired, and not unattractive, American by the sound of him, pointed out various parts of the vehicle to Winfield and Miranda, who appeared quite taken with the thing. They didn't notice her arrival, which gave her a moment to look at the machine.

"Why are you here?"

Delilah raised a brow. "Nervous, are you? As to my intentions?"

He studied her closely, then laughed. "No, of course not."

"I don't believe you but I shall give you the

benefit of the doubt." Delilah directed her words toward Grayson, but her gaze was on the vehicle. "Just because I think it's silly doesn't mean I'm not curious." She stepped closer.

William was right. It was smaller than she had expected, resembling a small phaeton with three wheels instead of two. The back wheels were considerably larger than the one in front. There was room for no more than two people on the leather bench seat. Something that was probably a steering mechanism, a lever of some sort, was affixed to wooden floorboards directly behind the front wheel. The motor was positioned behind the seat. It was at once the most absurd thing she had ever seen and just possibly one of the most intriguing. Not that she intended to admit that. Nor did she wish to ride in it but she was curious to see if it did indeed run.

"Well?" Sam said, without warning at her side.

"Well what?" She cast him a pleasant smile.

"Well, what do you think?"

She met his gaze directly. "Do you really want to know?"

He chuckled. "I'm afraid I do."

"In that case." She studied the vehicle for a moment. "I think it's . . . interesting."

He laughed. "That's better than I expected."

Her brow rose. "What did you expect?"

"Oh, I don't know." He grinned. "A scathing comment. A diatribe on the ills of progress. An impassioned speech about the joys of tradition. Something along those lines."

"I am sorry to disappoint you."

He leaned close and spoke softly, for her ears alone. "I doubt you could ever disappoint me, regardless of how hard you tried."

She struggled not to let her surprise show on her face. What on earth did he mean by that?

"I think it's fascinating." Lady Stillwell's eyes shone with eagerness. "Winfield should be the first to order one."

"I think we should wait to see if it works first," her husband said wryly.

"Oh, it definitely works," the other American said. "At least it did when it left Benz's hands."

"Jim, allow me to introduce Lady Hargate," Samuel said. "Delilah, this is Jim Moore, my assistant. Delilah is Lady Lydingham's sister."

"*The* sister?" Mr. Moore's eyes widened.

Samuel winced.

"One of them." Delilah refused to let his obvious wariness annoy her. What had the man been told? She cast him her brightest smile. "Delighted to have you at Millworth, Mr. Moore."

"My apologies, Lady Hargate." Mr. Moore grimaced. "I must have left my manners on that last train." He shook his head. "It's been a long journey."

"No need to apologize." Delilah shook her head. "I know all too well how wearing travel can be."

"While I was dealing with Benz," Samuel began, "Jim was learning all he could about the motorwagon. He's more in the business end of my projects now but he started as an engineer."

"I can't build one from scratch, not yet anyway. But it's not as complicated at it looks." Mr. Moore's gaze returned to the machine. "I should be able to keep it running."

"When can we see it run?" Lady Stillwell asked.

"More to the point." Camille grinned. "When can we ride in it?"

"You can't ride in it now," Delilah said, her voice a bit sharper than she had intended. She adopted a more congenial tone. "I was actually sent to fetch you. The games are about to begin and frankly, your absence is delaying everything. It is awkward, you know, when the hosts have abandoned their guests."

Camille wrinkled her nose. "You're right, of course. I simply lost my head in the excitement of seeing the motorwagon."

"And I would not want to do anything to delay the festivities," Samuel said. "We should be joining the others. Besides, we have had to send into the village for fuel so we can't start it up yet anyway."

"Something to look forward to then." Delilah gestured toward the road. "Shall we?"

Camille, Grayson, and Lord and Lady Stillwell

started off, chatting about the motorwagon, Delilah a step behind them. Samuel stayed to exchange a few words with Mr. Moore.

"I'm afraid I haven't played in a long time," Miranda said to Camille. "I'm quite out of practice. In truth, I stopped playing with anyone in my family years ago." She shuddered. "They all have a tendency to be quite cutthroat and it's no longer a game but warfare."

"Oh, this should be just a friendly game." Camille laughed. "And no one is expected to be very good."

Grayson chuckled. "There's no such thing as a friendly game when Winfield plays."

"I do intend to beat you into the ground," his cousin replied. "So tell me about this plan of yours and Russell's to market . . ."

Goodness, it was like herding recalcitrant sheep. Delilah was tempted to smack Camille's bustled backside with her racket to get them all to walk a bit quicker.

"I hope you're a good player." Sam caught up to Delilah.

"I am." She cast him a smug smile.

"Good." He chuckled. "As I requested you be my partner."

She stopped in mid-stride and stared at him. "Why on earth would you do that?"

"Because I am no fool, Delilah." He hooked his arm through hers and started after the others. "I am not stupid enough to allow you to be on the opposite side of the net with something as potentially lethal as a tennis ball at your disposal."

She tried and failed to stifle an amused smile. "Frightened, are you?"

"There are any number of emotions you invoke in me, my dear." Amusement curved his lips. "Fear is not one of them."

"Perhaps then you're not as clever as you think."

"Perhaps." He chuckled. "Besides, if we are attempting to act as if we have never met before, I don't think playing against one another is wise. Your irritation at my very existence is already proving harder to disguise than you expected." He glanced at her. "Or am I wrong?"

"No." She sighed. "You're right. It is hard to keep my feelings entirely to myself."

They walked on in silence for a few minutes.

"Why are you so angry with me?"

"I'm not . . ." Why deny it? He wouldn't believe her anyway. "Well, yes, I suppose I am."

"Why? What have I done?"

"Nothing, really. Nothing specific, that is. It's just . . ." She stopped and glared at him. "You're not supposed to be here."

He frowned. "Are you going to stamp your foot?"

"Of course not. That would be childish."

Although she had come very close to doing exactly that.

"Delilah." His voice softened and again he took her arm and they started after the others. "I am here and I don't intend to leave. I am sorry if that upsets your plans but we will both have to make the best of it."

"Now, you're being reasonable."

"You find it annoying, don't you?"

"Of course I do." She paused. "But then you know that."

"I do." He chuckled.

She sighed. "I do wish you wouldn't find everything I say quite so amusing."

"It's annoying, isn't it?"

"You know full well it is." She blew a long breath. "You probably wanted to be my partner because it would be easier to annoy me."

"Not at all." He paused. "Although it's not a bad reason."

"Hmph."

"But aside from the fact that I didn't think it was a good idea to be on opposing sides, you strike me as a competitive type of woman."

She glanced at him. "I'm not sure if that is a compliment or a criticism."

He shrugged. "I suppose it depends on how you look at it."

"I simply think if one is going to play a game, one should play to win."

"My sentiments exactly." He grinned. "And that, my dear Lady Hargate, is why I wanted you as my partner."

"Because you like to win."

"Because I too play to win." A wicked smile quirked his lips. "And I never accept defeat."

Chapter Eight

"Two more points and we win this game," Delilah said quietly to Sam, smiling at their opponents on the other side of the net.

Strands of her dark hair had escaped her pert straw hat to dance around her flushed face. Her blue eyes sparkled and her skin glowed. Sam tried not to remember the last time he had seen her chest heaving with every breath and her skin flushed with exertion. He had never thought of tennis as being particularly erotic but then he had never played with a woman he had known intimately before.

"And the set." He grinned down at her. "And the match."

"I probably should have told you before we started." A smug smile curved her lips. "I never accept defeat either."

"I expected nothing less." He handed her the ball. "Let's win this game, shall we?"

She flashed him a grin and moved to her serving position. Delilah employed an overhand serve, which had struck him as odd at first. His sisters all served underhanded. But she had excellent control and was an accomplished player. She hit her ball to Lord Stillwell as often as she did to his wife. While Sam would never admit it to her, she was probably better than he was especially as she had a handicap he did not. She played with the hindrance of a long skirt, corset, and bustle while he played in shirtsleeves. Nonetheless, she was good, very good. Unfortunately, so were their opponents.

They were matched against Lord and Lady Stillwell, although it took Lady Stillwell most of the first set to hit her stride. Fortunately for Sam. Delilah played closer to the net than he, and the sight of her loose bustle, bouncing behind her, emphasizing her lush curves, was nearly his undoing. Her dress was a white and off-white striped concoction and coupled with her blue eyes gave her the look of an angel come to earth. If one discounted the fierce look of a trained assassin in her eyes. Perhaps avenging angel was a more accurate description. And that too was most disconcerting.

He had to give her credit for not only her excellent play but also for not biting his head off when he made an error, as he had done more than once in the beginning. Delilah was just so damned distracting. Given her constant irritation with him, he had expected her to be less than patient with any mistake on his part. But she'd been cool and calm. He'd had to make a conscious effort to push all thoughts of her from his head and focus on the game. It was easier if he kept reminding himself that she wanted nothing more to do with him. And he was not interested in a fortune hunter.

Sam and Delilah easily won the first set, just lost the second, and now the last and final was being hard fought on both sides.

Delilah served a fast ball, barely in bounds, forcing Lady Stillwell to lunge for the return. Her shot was uncontrolled, nearly out of bounds.

"I have it," Sam yelled and made the shot.

The ball took an odd spin. Lord Stilwell swung at it, tipped the ball with the edge of his racket, and it shot out of bounds.

The ball was tossed back to Delilah. She caught Sam's eye, he nodded slightly, and she prepared to serve. Interesting, how quickly they'd learned to communicate and play to each other's strengths.

Between sets, he and Delilah had noted how a serve directed as close as possible to the center-line tended to be successful. It was apparent the newlyweds had not played together before. Delilah took careful aim, tossed the ball up, and hit it hard. It smacked the court just in Lady Stillwell's service box, almost perfectly between their opponents.

"Mine!" Lord and Lady Stillwell called at the same time, then both made the fatal mistake of hesitating. By the time they realized their error it was too late to fully recover. The ball hit the court and spun out of reach. Lady Stillwell did manage to connect with the ball but drove it into the net. And the game was over.

"Good job!" Sam beamed at his partner and moved to the net.

"Yes, well . . ." Delilah pushed a strand of hair out of her face and grinned back at him. "I had a more than adequate partner."

"Well done, Delilah." Lady Stillwell stepped to the net. "We must do it again while you're here at Millworth. I'd forgotten how much I enjoy tennis. I haven't had such an exhilarating time in longer than I can remember."

"It would have been much more fun if we had won." Lord Stillwell's smile belied his words. He shook Sam's hand over the net then turned his attention to Delilah. "Now I remember playing with you when you were a girl."

"And you didn't learn your lesson?" She gave him a saucy smile.

Saucy? This was a side Sam hadn't seen of her. It struck him that for the first time, even including their days in New York, she was completely unguarded.

"Excellent match." Gray strode onto the court. "On both sides."

Camille had chosen not to play in favor of her duties as hostess and Gray's game on the second court was long over. It was later than Sam had thought and their observers had abandoned them to return to the house. In fact, the sky had clouded over and the pleasantly warm autumn day had grown much cooler. They had been too busy to notice.

"I was told to give you no more than half an hour to finish then I was supposed to end the match if it wasn't over," Gray said. "But it was a very good match." He grinned. "It seemed wrong to end it."

"You just wanted to see me lose," Lord Stillwell grumbled.

"Yes, there was that." Gray turned toward the house. "Come on then." He and the others started off. "We should hurry, although I daresay it won't make much difference at this point."

Delilah shivered beside Sam. Now that they weren't playing, he felt the chill as well. He resisted the urge to put his arm around her. Instead, he picked up his jacket from a chair beside the court, thought about wrapping it around her shoulders, then discarded the idea. The gesture would be entirely too intimate for her and they'd had such a good time together, he hated to spoil it.

"Here." He thrust the jacket at her. "You're cold, you should put this on."

She hesitated then took the jacket. "Thank you." She shrugged into the jacket and tucked her racket under her arm.

"You're very attached to that, aren't you?"

"I've had this racket for years. I love tennis. I play as often as I can."

"Did your husband play?"

"No," she said and offered no further information. He had the distinct impression she didn't wish to speak of her late husband. "But aren't you cold? You're in your shirtsleeves after all."

"Ah, but we Americans are a hardy bunch." He tucked her hand in the crook of his arm. The others were already out of sight. Good. He wanted to spend a few minutes alone with her. The day had gone so well after all. "We scoff at minor inconveniences."

"Somehow, I didn't think of you as the type of man who would put up with minor inconveniences."

"I'm not." He glanced down at her and smiled. "Now."

"Now?"

"We're not all born to wealth and privilege, you know."

Her brow rose. "Yours is a rags to riches story, then?"

"I wouldn't say rags exactly." He paused. "My father owned a small foundry my grandfather had started. It was never overly successful but provided a decent enough living. He died shortly after my youngest sisters were born." He glanced at her. "Twins."

"But they're the youngest?"

"They are."

"They have each other then." She nodded. "Go on."

"I was studying law at the time but I took over the foundry, specialized, diversified, expanded, invested . . ." He shrugged. "I'm sure you're no more interested in the whys and wherefores of business than your sister."

"Yes, but I would never admit that to someone talking about his business," she said in a lofty manner.

"Because it would be rude?"

"Exactly." She bit back a smile. "And I am never rude. Please continue."

"Suffice it to say, I made intelligent and sometimes risky decisions. Most of which turned out to be quite profitable. A few of them proved to be . . ." He thought for a moment. "Oh, more falsely seductive I would say than successful. Luring me in with a promise of potential that did not materialize."

"And you think this motorwagon scheme will be more successful than seductive?"

"I think it's both." He paused. "Now that you've seen it, have you changed your mind about it?"

"Absolutely not."

"And you really have no desire to ride in it?"

"I do not." She paused. "Although I will admit it's a handsome looking device. In the manner in which the internal mechanism of a finely crafted clock is handsome."

"I'll take that admission as a sign that your attitude toward my machine is weakening."

"I wouldn't if I were you," she said in a firm manner. "I do not weaken."

"I don't believe you."

"Well you should. I never say anything I don't mean."

"Never?"

"Rarely then." She studied him. "Why don't you believe me? About the motorwagon, that is."

"Because you're an intelligent woman. Which is not merely a compliment but an observation," he added quickly. "And a person of intelligence does not take an unyielding stand but is open to logic and reason."

"Thank you, for part of that anyway. I'm not sure anyone has ever called me intelligent before." She thought for a moment. "At least not to my face. Beauty is usually the quality most men desire in a woman."

"And you have both intelligence and beauty."

"That's very kind of you to say but it scarcely matters." She shrugged. "Intelligence is rarely deemed important."

"And that is a very great shame." He shook his head. "I much prefer women who are clever and knowledgeable and can converse about subjects beyond the latest gossip and newest fashion. A woman who thinks. Regardless of a woman's appearance, I find women without a brain in their heads to be as boring as you find talk of business."

"Still you must admit most men rarely see beyond how a woman will look by their side."

"I am not most men."

"Apparently not."

"You should have no trouble finding a new husband," he said without thinking.

She cast him a startled look. "Oh?"

"We've already established you're both pretty and intelligent."

"And probably penniless as well," she said wryly. "That is always conducive to a good match."

"Any man who would allow the state of your finances to sway his affection would be a fool."

"Unless of course, the man in question wishes to avoid a woman who seeks nothing more in a new husband than wealth and a title."

"Ouch." He winced. "I did say that, didn't I?"

"Indeed you did." She thought for a moment. "I am a practical sort of woman, Samuel. If I do not marry, I don't know what I will do with the rest of my life. I do not have the temperament to become a teacher or a governess."

"You don't like children?"

"Oh, I suspect I shall like my own and I do hope to have them one day, but other people's children . . ." She shuddered. "No, I don't think I would do that at all well." She raised her chin slightly as if bracing herself against the winds of the future. There was a subtle strength about her and he suspected she was as unaware of that as she was the gesture. "I was trained to be the wife of a man with position and wealth. To be a perfect hostess, to run an efficient household, to look good on a man's arm, to be an asset. I don't really know how to do anything else." She uttered an uncomfortable laugh. She had obviously said more than she had intended.

"Be that as it may, you have forgotten to list your greatest skill," he said in an overly somber manner.

"Have I?"

"You play an excellent game of tennis." He grinned.

She stared at him for a moment then laughed and the moment lightened. "As do you, Samuel."

"Now, you're just being kind." He heaved a dramatic sigh. "A few minutes ago you said I was no more than adequate. And as you never say anything you don't mean . . ."

"Ah well there is that." She shook her head mournfully. "I'm sure with additional practice you can be more than adequate."

"I shall keep that in mind."

"I'm certain there are any number of other things you do quite well."

"Indeed there are." He cast her a wicked smile.

She stopped in midstep and glared at him. "Will you never let me forget that?"

He stared. "Forget what?"

"You know what," she snapped and started off without him.

He hurried to catch up. He hadn't intended to

remind her of their night together. It was completely inadvertent on his part. Not that she'd believe that. Sam caught her arm and spun her around to face him. "There's nothing to forget. Remember we've never met."

"I actually thought we could accomplish this . . . this farce!"

"It was not my idea."

She ignored him. "I've been doing my best to avoid you and then you request me as your partner!"

He drew his brows together. "We won, didn't we?"

"Yes, we won." She huffed. "That's beside the point."

"There is no other point. I certainly didn't want to play against you. I chose you as a partner because I thought we would play well together. And I was right."

"Well, we shall never play together again!"

"I'm talking about tennis." He stepped closer and stared down at her. It might have been a mistake. He was close enough to pull her into his arms and kiss her thoroughly, the way she was meant to be kissed. "What are *you* talking about?"

Anger flashed in her eyes. "Nothing!" She turned, started off, then turned back. "In my entire life, I have always done exactly what was expected of me. I married the man I was supposed to marry. I lived the life I was expected to live. The one time, the only time, I have deviated from what was expected of me was when I met you."

"Your *adventure.*"

"My mistake!" She shook her head. "You and I are not . . . you're not . . ."

"I'm not what?"

"You're not right. Not for me," she said more to herself than to him and he had to lean closer to hear. She ran her hand over her forehead in a weary manner then met his gaze. "You're not . . . *right*. You're not what I want." Her voice grew stronger with every word. "You're not what I have planned. We would never suit. Marriage between us—"

"Marriage?" Shock coursed through him. "I never said anything about marriage."

"Nonetheless . . ." Her eyes widened as if she had just now realized what she had said. "You were thinking it!"

"You have no idea what I was thinking but I never mentioned marriage. In fact, I haven't mentioned anything. You've given me no opportunity. The moment you saw me again, you began behaving like a lunatic—"

She sucked in a sharp breath. "I did not!"

"And . . ." He paused to emphasize his words. *"You were rude!"*

She gasped.

"You may well be the maddest woman I have

186

ever met!" He turned and stalked off. "Crazy, lunatic Englishwoman."

"Insufferable American!" she called after him.

He couldn't remember ever having been this infuriated by a female before. She was mad. Completely, utterly irrational. He stopped and turned back to her. "Do you want to know what I was thinking?"

"No!"

He ignored her. "Before I came to England, I was thinking a lot about a captivating, intriguing creature with whom I spent an interlude that was very nearly magical. An enchantress who disappeared from my life as surely as if she was never there. In fact, I couldn't get her out of my mind. Or for that matter my dreams. But that was when she was *Mrs.* Hargate. *Lady* Hargate is not to my liking."

"Good!" she snapped. "Because she would never marry you."

"I would never ask!" His tone hardened. "I want more in a wife than a woman who wants me only for my money and my position."

"I wish you well then because if you have anything else to offer it's not readily apparent."

"Interesting as *Mrs.* Hargate thought I had a great deal to offer."

"*Mrs.* Hargate does not exist!"

"Obviously, that is my loss." He scowled at her. "And hers!"

"Hmph." She huffed and started off again, but he grabbed her and pulled her back. "Unhand me at once!"

"One more thing," he said in a hard tone. In the back of his mind he noted there was only anger in her eyes, not fear. No matter what else passed between them, he would hate to scare her. "If I remember correctly, the terrace will be in sight just over this rise. If you want to continue this little charade you've embroiled me in, you'll calm down."

"I am calm!" She wrenched out of his grasp.

"Don't forget, it's not my reputation at stake. I'm not the one trying to find the perfect husband."

"I am calm," she said through clenched teeth, then pulled off his jacket and flung it at him.

He snorted and released her.

She stared at him for a long moment. She might not be afraid of *him,* but only a fool wouldn't be uneasy at the look in *her* eye. A lesser man might well be terrified. He was grateful she was only armed with a tennis racket.

She cast him a last scathing look, drew a deep breath, then started toward the manor. He stepped up beside her. The moment the terrace was in sight, she adopted a polite smile.

"Do not be fooled by my pleasant demeanor, Mr. Russell."

"I haven't been thus far, Lady Hargate."

"I think you're a beast."

"Then perhaps we are well suited after all." His smile matched hers. "I think you're a bitch."

She sucked in a hard breath. "I should slap your face for that." Her eyes narrowed but her smile remained.

As did his. "Try it."

Neither said another word until they reached the terrace then each went their own way. Sam made it a point to avoid her for the rest of the evening. Much to Camille and Teddy's disappointment, the day grew colder with the setting sun and most of the guests preferred to take their leave rather than wait for the musicians to move from the terrace to inside the house. Sam took the first available opportunity to slip away. He needed to talk to Jim about the motorwagon. That was what should be foremost in his mind, not an irrational little termagant with a bouncing bustle and endless blue eyes.

Why did he have to keep reminding himself he did not want this woman?

And why did it feel like a lie?

Chapter Nine

Delilah Hargate was not the sort of woman to be confused. Of course, she was never rude either and that no longer seemed to be true.

She paced the floor of her room, the same rooms she'd occupied as a girl. She refused to consider that in many ways, she had come full circle, back to where she began. Hopefully, the years had taught her much. Unfortunately, not enough. Apparently, when one made one mistake, it was impossible to avoid another. And another. And so on.

The rest of the day had been a blur after she'd left Samuel. But then what could one expect after having had a revelation of epic proportions? Or perhaps it wasn't a revelation as much as a realization. As much as an acceptance of a truth she'd prefer not to face.

She'd gone through the motions of enjoying the rest of the party. She'd been pleasant and polite and even laughed at the occasional joke but she'd been more than a little relieved when the gathering had ended earlier than expected and everyone had departed. Fortunately, both her sister and her friend had been too busy attending to the guests and preoccupied with future plans to note any difference in Delilah's demeanor. Teddy would surely have noticed otherwise and Camille was proving to be far more perceptive than her sister had expected. Nor had she eaten; she hadn't been the least bit hungry, which in and of itself was something Teddy would have remarked upon if her attention had not been otherwise occupied. Delilah rarely passed up food. She was relieved as well to notice Samuel too had taken his leave. Delilah was simply not up to pretending they had just met.

She'd gone to her rooms as soon as she could gracefully escape, pleading a headache. The housemaid who'd come to turn down her bed told her Camille and Teddy had also retired. Good. Neither would be seeking her out and she wasn't up to pretense with them either.

She had gone to bed far earlier than was her custom but after a day of tennis and emotional turmoil, a good night's sleep was called for. Things always did look better in the morning.

Still, morning was very far away and she couldn't sleep a wink. Every time she closed her eyes he was there. Every moment they'd shared filled her head. From their first meeting and the vague hint of confusion in the eyes of a tall, blond American to the wicked smile of a pirate at a masked ball. From the pride in his voice today when he'd explained the intricacies of his horseless carriage to his look of triumph at their tennis victory to the justifiable anger in his dark eyes at her irrational fury. When she closed her eyes she saw the look on his face before he'd kissed her for the first time. And when he'd kissed her for the last.

After hours of tossing and turning she'd given up the attempt entirely. She'd been pacing the floor for a good hour now, hashing and rehashing everything that had passed between them. Everything she now understood and everything he didn't know.

Rational thought was certainly called for even if it was as elusive as sleep. She never should have responded to Samuel today the way she did. She could have ignored the way he smiled when she'd asked what else he was good at. But God help her, that was the only thing on her mind when he was around. It had been bloody hard to concentrate on the game when he was behind her, watching her every move. Even when they were arguing, she was all too aware of the passion that emanated from the man. His presence was not merely a constant reminder of what had passed between them, but more and more it was a temptation. And a warning.

It was time, past time really, to face the truth at least to herself. She hadn't up to now. Hadn't dared to accept the truth even in her own mind.

Samuel Russell had terrified her from the moment his laugh had wrapped around her heart.

She wasn't used to being afraid. It was as if she

were standing at the edge of an endless precipice and it would take no more than a nudge to push her over. And she would be lost. She had no idea how to deal with such fear. But as long as she never saw him again, she wouldn't have to. He could remain her secret. Like a treasure hidden away only to be taken out on occasion when one needed a measure of comfort from a memory and the thought of what might have been.

She pulled her lace-trimmed wrapper tighter around herself and continued to pace. He was wrong though. He was wrong about all of it.

It wasn't the possibility of scandal that concerned her. Her life had always been scandal free. One misadvised adventure certainly wouldn't ruin her. And she was a widow after all. It wasn't how gossip might affect her prospects for a second marriage that worried her either. Even as much of a stickler for propriety as she was, she had no intention of marrying anyone who would allow gossip to influence his choice of wife.

She'd been appalled not so much by her behavior in New York but because she had let her guard down. But she'd felt so, well, free in those few days. Not at all constrained by the rules she lived by. She could have stopped what happened between them at any time. But she hadn't wanted to. From the moment his hand had brushed hers, she hadn't wanted anything but him. She had quite simply been swept away. For the first time she had known what even the most practical woman would acknowledge as magic. And in that had violated the one rule she'd set for herself.

Then she'd come to her senses. They were completely different people. They wanted different things. They saw the world in different ways. If she couldn't find love with a perfect match, one so completely imperfect, so utterly wrong, would ultimately end in disaster. She'd vowed long ago, she would never allow her heart to be broken again.

And he would break her heart. She'd known it from the start and knew it as surely as she knew the sun would rise in the east. Still, for a few days in New York, she hadn't cared. It hadn't mattered. But then she'd thought she would never see him again. Planned never to see him again. It was for the best. Why didn't he see that?

And now he was here. He'd never understand that her unpleasantness toward him had little to do with him and everything to do with her. She hadn't really understood it herself until today. She'd only known she was angry and frustrated and, yes, scared.

She glanced at the clock on the mantel. It was past two. There was nothing to be done about it. She had to talk to him. Apologize again, of course, attempt some sort of explanation and ask him, again, to leave. Surely after today he would see the wisdom of that.

He had to leave before it was too late.

It was probably foolish to go to him now. In the wee hours of the morning. Dressed in her nightclothes. But better now than during the day when everyone was about. Besides, she had summoned up at least a small measure of courage and she wasn't going to be able to sleep until she spoke to him.

She opened her door, glanced up and down the corridor, and started down the hall. A gas sconce burned low, filling the corridor with dim light and shadows. His rooms were at the far end of the hall, away from those occupied by the others. Her footfalls echoed quietly in the night. A light shone under his door. Good, he wasn't yet asleep.

She stood before his door and hesitated, trying to sort out in her head what she'd say, searching for the right words. She had no idea really what to say but she did know, the one thing she wouldn't tell him, was the one thing she knew firsthand from bitter experience.

Love did not conquer all.

She drew a deep breath and knocked softly. Without warning, panic swelled within her. It was all she could do to keep from turning and fleeing back down the corridor. What was she doing? What was she thinking? Or was she thinking at all? This was not the least bit wise. Surely it could wait until—

The door opened and he stared at her. "What do you want?"

What did she want? "May I come in?"

His hair was tousled and he wore dark striped pajamas under that blasted blue silk dressing gown. At once she remembered the feel of that silk against her skin and a shiver ran down her spine. She ignored it. That was not why she was here.

His eyes narrowed. "Did you come to berate me again?"

"No, I came to apologize."

"Did you?"

"Yes, I did and I would prefer not to do so standing here in the hall."

He studied her closely then nodded. "Very well then." He stood aside and she slipped into his room. "You seem to be making a habit of apologizing to me."

"When one is a lunatic." She forced an offhand note to her voice. "One tends to say things one shouldn't."

He closed the door behind her. "As one does when one is dealing with a lunatic. I have apologies of my own to make."

"Accepted."

He frowned. "I haven't made them yet." He ran a hand through his hair. "I have never in my life called a woman a—"

"No need to say more," she said quickly.

"It was coarse and crude. I don't know what came over me."

"You were provoked and I was . . ."

"Rude?" he said with a hint of a smile.

"No, Samuel." She straightened her shoulders. "Rude is something of an understatement. I was beyond rude and for that I am truly sorry."

"You're getting better at this, you know."

"At apologizing?"

He nodded.

"I am getting a great deal of practice." She glanced around his room. The covers on his bed were disheveled and papers were scattered on the writing desk. "I see you couldn't sleep either."

"Either?"

He was obviously not going to make this easy for her. She sighed. "I'm afraid my ill manners have weighed on my mind." She nodded at the desk. "Were you working?"

"I was trying but I don't seem to be accomplishing anything." He moved to the desk and straightened the papers. "Gray and I had a long talk tonight about our plans for manufacturing the motorwagon. Unfortunately, his business contacts are primarily in America."

"I thought Winfield was involved in business. Can't he help?"

"Possibly." He nodded. "But Gray says he's fairly conservative and not as progressive as one would hope. Still, Lord and Lady Stillwell's interest is a good beginning. Of course they haven't seen it run yet."

"I'm sure that will only increase their enthusiasm."

"With luck." He crossed his arms over his chest and rested his hip on the desk. "If that's all, you should probably go."

She drew a deep breath. "I'm not quite finished."

"Go on then."

"Very well. It seems to me, along with my apologies I owe you some sort of explanation or perhaps it's a confession, I'm not sure." She wasn't about to tell him she feared she had found her soul mate, if one believed in such things, and he was the wrong man. Nor had she said she'd be completely honest but part of the truth was surely better than no truth at all. She sighed. "For one thing, I am so very tired of being angry with you."

"Imagine it from my side," he said wryly.

"It's not merely that you are here . . ."

"No?"

"Or that I was surprised, well, shocked really, to see you again."

"And?"

"And I was, well, this doesn't seem to have as much to do with you as it does with me."

"I never thought otherwise," he said coolly.

She drew her brows together. "This is not easy for me and you aren't being very helpful."

"Oh, well, my apologies then."

She ignored the sarcastic note in his voice. "As I was saying, it really has as much to do with me as it does with you I think. More so probably. I mean you could be anyone."

"Anyone?" His brow rose. "That is flattering."

"That's not what I meant." She wrung her hands together. "This is so confusing and it's not coming out at all as I intended it."

"Just tell me what you have to say."

"I am trying. I'm, well, every time I see you . . ." *I'm terrified that you will break my heart.* "I'm embarrassed." Yes, that was good and not a complete lie either. "After all, you and I . . . Horribly, horribly embarrassed."

"Embarrassed?"

"Well, yes. You . . ." She drew a deep breath. "You have seen me . . . *naked.*"

"I'm not embarrassed."

"Goodness, Samuel, I would think not, you're a man. No doubt many women have seen you . . . *naked.*"

"I wouldn't say many but some."

"I've never been seen completely *naked* by anyone." Indeed, it was decidedly awkward even to say the word aloud. "And therefore every time I look at you—"

"Not even by your husband?" Surprise widened his eyes.

"That's really none of your concern."

"I believe you've made it my concern."

"Yes, I suppose I have." She paused. "My husband was a very proper man."

"I see." He studied her for a moment. "And something of a fool as well. A smart man would have your clothes off at every opportunity."

"Nonsense." She tried to ignore the heat that washed up her face. "My husband was . . ." She struggled to find the right word. "Perfect." Yes, that was it. "He was perfect. Exactly the type of man I had always planned to marry."

"And I am not."

"No, you're not." She shook her head. "We don't suit at all."

"Then it's fortunate I have not asked you to marry me."

"I never should have raised the subject of marriage with you. I have no idea why I did, although I suppose marriage has been on my mind of late."

"Probably because you are determined to find another perfect husband."

"Yes, well that would explain it."

"Which has nothing to do with me."

"No, it doesn't." She shook her head. "It seems the one thing we do agree on is that we don't agree on anything. It's in our natures really. You're American, so very American, and I'm British. You believe in progress and I am rooted in tradition. You are nouveau riche and I am—"

"Penniless?"

"Only at the moment," she said sharply, then drew a calming breath. "When you look at it in a practical, rational way, we have nothing in common."

"I wouldn't say nothing," he said under his breath.

She was not going to rise to that bait, not again. "And obviously, as whenever we're together, I am not disciplined enough to pretend nothing has ever happened between us."

"Because I've seen you naked."

"Well, yes."

"Or maybe it's because you've seen me naked."

She stared. "Possibly."

He studied her closely. "Do you think every time I look at you I see you naked?"

"No, of course not." She drew her brows together. "Do you?"

His gaze skimmed over her and he shrugged.

She gasped. "Do you?"

"More to the point, do you see me naked every time you look at me?"

"I don't think that's the point at all and don't be absurd." She huffed. "Not every time." The words were out of her mouth before she could stop them.

A slight smile played on his lips. "Then I would say we have a problem."

"We wouldn't if you would do the . . . the gentlemanly thing and leave."

"I have already said I have no intention of leaving before the wedding."

"But as an intelligent man surely you're open to logic and reason."

"I do love having my own words thrown back at me."

"They were very good words," she said quickly.

"I will be at the wedding, however . . ." He thought for a moment. "Gray and I talked about spending some time taking the motorwagon around the country, visiting friends of his family's, to gauge interest. If we decide to do so, we will be gone most days, probably until late in the evening. He says he's really not needed here."

"Oh, he isn't," she said eagerly.

"Which means there will be days when you and I don't see each other at all." He met her gaze directly. "Will that do?"

"Yes." She breathed a sigh of relief. "It's something of a compromise and I've never been good at compromise—"

He snorted.

"But the fact that you are willing to make a concession in view of my feelings, it's very gallant of you. That will do quite nicely, thank you."

"Then we are agreed." He straightened. "I will determine a schedule with Gray in the morning."

"Excellent." She thrust her hand out toward him. "Isn't it customary to shake hands now?"

"It is." He stepped closer, took her hand, and gazed into her eyes. A shiver ran through her at his touch. "As this seems to be a night of confessions, might I make one of my own?"

"Don't you think there's been enough confession for one night?"

"Probably, but I may never get another opportunity." He pulled her closer, his gaze never leaving hers. "I wasn't entirely truthful with you earlier."

"Oh?" She swallowed hard. Why, the man practically radiated heat. Not that she had forgotten.

"When I said I had been thinking about you a lot, that wasn't quite true."

"No?"

"A lot was not entirely accurate. I never forgot so much as a moment with you." He raised her hand to his lips and kissed her palm. "I thought about you nearly every day and dreamed of you almost every night."

"That does sound like a lot," she said weakly.

"It seemed pointless, though." His lips moved to her wrist and her breath caught. "You said you never wanted to see me again."

"I said it would be . . . best." She could barely choke out the words. What was he doing to her?

"That's right, it would be best, I remember." His lips whispered across her wrist. His free arm encircled her waist. "And so I did nothing but dream."

"Did you?" She should push him away, right now, and end this. Only a fool would fail to see what was happening.

"I did." His gaze bored into hers. "Did you?"

Or perhaps only a fool would push him away. "I might have. Possibly. Once. Or twice." *Or every night.*

"And in your dreams, were my lips on yours?" He leaned in and brushed his lips across hers and she wondered that she didn't melt at his feet.

"Perhaps," she whispered.

He dropped her hand and wrapped his other arm around her. "And were you in my arms?"

"Possibly." Her heart thudded hard in her chest.

"Was your body pressed against mine?"

"It might have been . . ." As if of their own accord, her arms slipped around his neck and she gazed up at him.

"Could you feel my heart beating against yours?"

"I thought it was my heart. Oh, God." She gazed into his eyes. "You're seducing me again, aren't you?"

"I thought we agreed that it was a mutual seduction."

"In New York but now . . ."

"I was not the one who came to your room."

"I only came to talk."

"Did you?" His gaze locked with hers.

"That was my plan." She didn't sound the least bit convincing even to her own ears. She wasn't a fool. Somewhere in the back of her mind hadn't she known how their talk would end? Hadn't she wanted this to end in his bed?

"And you are one for plans."

She nodded. "Excellent plans for the most part."

"But even the best plans don't always work as expected."

"Apparently."

"Did you plan this?" He pressed his lips to hers, softly but insistently.

"No," her lips murmured against his. For a moment, a dozen reasons why this would be yet another mistake raced through her mind. She discarded them all. "Perhaps."

His kiss deepened, her mouth opened to his. He tasted as she remembered. Of heat and desire and wonder. Lord help her, she was indeed a fool. This was another mistake. Or maybe it was simply . . . right. Or fate. Or magic. She didn't know. Didn't care. It didn't matter. Nothing mattered save the heat of him, the feel of him pressed against her, the passion in his kiss. The desire in her own.

His arms tightened around her. Her breasts pressed against his chest. The beat of his heart echoed the beat of her own. Hunger surged within her. Desire. Need. Truth. And fear. She'd lost herself in him once before and she would again.

Whether it was wrong or right or simply mad, she wanted him. And had from the moment she'd left him. She angled her head, reveling in the feel of his tongue dueling with hers. The heat of his body wrapped around her. How could something so obviously wrong be so very right?

She pulled her lips from his and gazed into his eyes. "Not a plan but . . . dear Lord, Sam, yes." She swallowed hard. "I haven't forgotten anything." Her lips again met his. "Not for a moment. . . ."

His mouth crushed hers and every doubt, every fear vanished in the feel of his mouth pillaging hers. She responded in kind, her kiss as hard, as hungry as his. Months of denying the magic between them vanished, swept aside by aching desire and frantic need. She tugged at the sash of his dressing grown and pushed the cool silk off his shoulders. Her mouth still clung to his, his hands roamed over her shoulders, her back, her derriere. Her wrapper slipped to the floor followed almost at once by her nightclothes. She hadn't noticed his clothes were gone as well until she felt the hard, hot muscles of his chest against her breasts. And she shivered with the heat of his naked body pressed against hers. No, she hadn't forgotten so much as a moment. . . .

The instant the hotel door closed behind them, a dam of restraint between them burst. Her lips crushed to his. His hands, her hands were everywhere at once. They undressed one another with an urgency born of desire and need. She scarcely noticed when the shepherdess costume crumpled at her feet or when his pirate attire joined her discarded clothes. All she knew was the heat of him pressed against her, escalating her desire, searing her soul. . . .

She wrenched her lips from his and ran kisses down the slope of his neck and lower. His head fell back and he moaned. She rained kisses on his chest, catching a hard nipple in her mouth to tease and toy. He sucked in a sharp breath, his hands skimming over her heated flesh, over her back and lower to cup her buttocks and pull her tighter against him. She couldn't touch him enough. Couldn't get enough of the taste of him. . . .

He tasted of heat and desire and man. She explored him with her tongue and her mouth and her hands, reveling in the hard, strong planes and valleys of his chest and his shoulders and his legs. Aching for more. . . .

Her body pressed against his and she wanted more. So much more. She raised her leg and hooked it around his, and the hard length of his arousal slipped between her legs. She felt the strength of him, demanding and insistent, and gloried in the feel of her own slick desire on him. . . .

They tumbled together onto the bed, a tangle of

lips and limbs and passion. She'd never known, never so much as suspected, such unrelenting need could claim her and wondered in a small part of her mind not clouded by desire how something so intense, so all consuming could happen with a stranger. A man she scarcely knew. It was wrong, certainly a sin. And nothing in her life had ever felt so right. . . .

Together they twisted and stumbled toward the bed, her body and his, her mouth and his, her hands, his hands never losing the contact between them. As if parting for so much as an instant would drive them both mad. They fell onto the bed, frantic with the need to touch and taste and feel. The need for more. His hands, his lips were everywhere at once. He sucked at her breast and she heard an odd, whimpering sound and realized it was her. She tunneled her fingers through his hair. Her legs wrapped around him and he slid down her body, his mouth blazing a trail between her breasts and lower to her stomach and lower still. . . .

He buried his head between her legs and she held her breath, resisting the urge to push him away. This was not . . . She had never . . . Phillip had never . . . Panic welled within her. She couldn't possibly . . . She gasped. He tasted her and all hesitation fled, washed away by exquisite sensation and the deepest intimacy. Surely she would die of the sweet torture he inflicted with his tongue and his teeth. And she knew as well it would be a glorious way to die. . . .

Her breath came faster and she writhed beneath him, urging him on. She distinctly recalled a moment of shock at this sinful intimacy in New York. Now, she ached for his touch. Ached for him. She raised her hips. His fingers parted her, his breath whispered over her. She cried out at the first touch of his tongue, dissolving onto a being of sheer sensation. Knowing nothing but his caress. Existing only in the feel of his touch. The touch that threatened to be her undoing. Her hands fisted in the bedclothes. His tongue teased and stroked and carried her closer and closer to that place only he had brought her. . . .

Tension coiled tighter and tighter within her, straining and reaching until at last her body shook in waves of unexpected, unimagined pure pleasure. For no more than a fleeting instant, Phillip flashed through her mind and she hated him for never sharing this and never caring. The thought vanished at once, dashed aside by rising need. And she wanted more. . . .

"No," she murmured and shifted beneath him, sliding lower until his erection nudged her. She wrapped her legs around his waist and gazed into his dark eyes, glazed with passion, reflecting her own. "I want . . ."

"You," he said, his voice hoarse with passion. "Always, only you . . ."

Her hand slipped between them and her fingers curled around the hot length of him and he moaned. She arched her hips upward and guided him into her. He gasped and slid deeper, stretching her, filling her, claiming her once again as his. . . .

"Delilah," he murmured against her ear. "Oh, God."

"Samuel . . ." She struggled for breath. "Please, now . . ."

He positioned himself between her legs and entered her slowly, carefully. As if she were fragile and precious and valued. Until he filled her and she knew with blinding clarity, for this moment, she was his. And he was hers. . . .

She rocked her hips against him, urging him on. Faster and harder. He thrust into her again and again, burying himself deeper and deeper. Hard and hot, and slick and wet. Pleasure and the joy of being one with him gripped her, filled her, devoured her. With every stroke, the past and the present, the dreams and the memories twisted, entwining together like vines of desire and passion and wonder. Had it been months? Or forever? Or only yesterday? His slick body slid against hers, every movement urging her on, taking her higher. Her blood pounded in her ears. His heart thudded in tandem with her own. Her body throbbed around him, aching, yearning, reaching for more. Always, ever more . . .

And when release again caught her unawares,

she wondered if this was the stuff adventures were made of. Or dreams . . .

He groaned and his muscles tightened and he shuddered against her. He stroked into her once more and again until she cried out and her back arched and her body exploded. And ecstasy washed through her and curled her toes and caught at her soul.

When at last she could breathe again, she propped herself up on her elbow, gazed into his brown eyes, and smiled in a most sinful, wicked manner.

His brow rose. "Why, Mrs. Hargate, if I didn't know better I'd think you have another plan."

"My dear American." Her hand drifted over his stomach and lower to his still hard erection. "I believe I do."

He laughed and caught her hand, drawing her palm to his lips. "Good."

He pulled her back into his arms and in that moment before she lost herself again in the joy of being with him, a tiny voice whispered in the back of her head.

Perhaps one adventure was not nearly enough.

Chapter Ten

Sam rolled over on his side, bunched the pillow under his head, and studied her. What did it say about a man who couldn't get a woman out of his head? Especially a woman who was interested only in what a man had rather than what a man was. The kind of woman he had sworn never to lose his heart to again.

"Well." She stared up at the ceiling. "That was certainly . . ."

He chuckled. "Worth waiting for?"

"One could say that." She smiled. "One could definitely say that."

"Welcome back, Mrs. Hargate."

She glanced at him. "I do hope you understand this was not my intention in coming to your room."

"Wasn't it?"

"Don't be absurd." Her objection didn't quite ring true, especially as she'd made no effort to avoid ending up in his bed.

"My apologies then. I have must have misunderstood." He shook his head thoughtfully. "You did not knock on my door, dressed only in a lace robe and nearly transparent nightgown—"

"It's not the least bit transparent."

"It is when you stand in front of the light."

"It's really quite practical." She propped herself up on her elbows and glanced around the room. "Wherever it is."

"It seemed practical to me." He grinned. "Especially when you stand in front of the light."

"I shall keep that in mind the next time I come to a man's door in the middle of the night," she said in a prim manner.

He laughed. "Oh, but you don't do this sort of thing."

"I don't. Except for that once." A smug smile creased her lips. "And now."

He studied her for a long moment. How had he ever let her go? "I missed you, Dee."

"Teddy's the only one who calls me Dee."

"Not anymore. I like it. Besides, Samuel and Delilah are entirely too biblical for me."

"Good Lord, Sam." She sat up, pulled a pillow behind her, and drew the covers up around her. "We're not a couple. This is not what I want—"

"No?" he chuckled.

"No. And it certainly isn't what I've planned. I thought you understood that."

"Plans change."

"Not mine." She shook her head. "I did not plan on you."

"You're being practical and rational now, aren't you?" He took her hand.

"I am trying." She glanced pointedly at his hand on hers. "You're not making it easy."

"Good." He leaned forward and kissed the crook of her elbow. "If I were Lord Stickinthemud, and my money had come from King Arthur himself—"

"You do realize he was only a legend?"

"You'd be trying right now to think of how you could get me to propose."

She started to deny it, then smiled. "Possibly."

He chuckled softly. "Is this where you tell me it would be best if we never saw each other again?"

"No." She sighed. "I daresay it would be pointless."

"Then you do want to see me again?"

"Perhaps we should more clearly define *see*."

"I will define it however you wish."

"There's that unexpected gallantry of yours again." She smiled. "Marred only by the fact that you know full well what I mean by *see*."

"Unfortunately." He trailed kisses up her arm to her shoulder.

"It can't be helped. Seeing one another, that is. We are both residing at Millworth. You insist on staying for the wedding and beyond that you're one of my future brother-in-law's closest friends." She paused. "However, I suspect we can now be on friendlier terms with one another."

"I doubt we can get much friendlier," he murmured against her shoulder.

"Now that we have eased this, well, this tension between us."

"Yes, that's what I thought it was." Tension seemed as good a word as any. Although magic was better.

She plucked absently at the covers with her free hand. "I must say I have never felt this comfortable with a man. Oh, perhaps with Grayson and Winfield but I've known them all of my life."

"That's what happens when one eases tensions." He nibbled at the curve where her shoulder met her neck and she shivered beneath his lips.

"Now that I think about it . . ." That breathless quality he had found so irresistible was back and his stomach tightened. "I can't recall ever feeling this relaxed before. Certainly never in the company of a man," she added thoughtfully.

He drew back and stared at her. "And you want to talk about it? Now?"

She shrugged. "I just find it interesting that's all."

He frowned. "Why?"

"Because one should always be on one's guard around men. Men are generally not to be trusted."

"That's a scathing indictment of an entire gender."

"Oh, I'm certain there are a few worthy of trust. But I daresay that's why men and women are rarely, truly friends."

"Because we can't be trusted?"

She slanted him a chastising smile. "You needn't take it as a personal affront. We're not talking about you specifically."

"But about me in general as, oh, specifically, I am a man."

"And an easily insulted one at that."

"Actually, given some of the things you've said to me since my arrival, I thought I had a fairly thick skin."

She smiled.

"So men are not trustworthy?"

"When it comes to women, no."

"Not even husbands?"

"Oh, especially not husbands."

"I see."

Her brow furrowed. "Don't read more into my words than what I am saying."

"Then we're not talking about your husband?"

She paused for no more than a heartbeat but it was enough. "We are not."

Again he noted her reluctance to talk about her husband. He suspected Lord Hargate hadn't been nearly as perfect as she claimed. "Because he was perfect?"

"Exactly."

"I see."

"You see far less than you think you do," she said mildly.

"And I thought I was most astute."

She ignored him. "For the most part, one should never count on men to do what they are supposed to do."

"I had no idea we were so unreliable."

"That's because you deal with men in matters of business. That's a different thing altogether. I'm speaking of man in his domestic dealings. In his dealings with women." She shook her head. "Men have to be guided. Directed as it were."

"Manipulated?"

Her brow furrowed. "That's entirely too harsh a word."

"But accurate nonetheless."

"I suppose it's not completely inaccurate."

He heaved a heartfelt sigh. "I know I feel manipulated. However . . ." He paused. "I enjoyed it."

She cast him a startled look. He grinned wickedly and she laughed. "You do realize there will be no more of this."

He considered her for a long moment. She was a difficult woman to decipher. "If that's what you want."

"It is."

He didn't believe her or maybe he just didn't want to believe her. Nonetheless, if this was the game she wanted to play, he'd play along. "All right. We'll be friends from this point forward." He held out his hand. "Agreed?"

She cast him a suspicious look. "Oh, no. I know what happened the last time I shook your hand."

He laughed, grabbed her hand, pulled her close and kissed her hard, then released her.

"Nor shall we ever shake hands again," she said with a breathless catch in her voice.

He wasn't sure he could simply be her friend nor was he sure he wanted to. In fact, he wasn't actually certain about anything at the moment let alone what he really wanted. Was she a pleasant interlude or something more? Perhaps he needed to sort out his own desires before he tried to address hers.

"Now then, if you would be so kind . . ." She fluttered her hand at him. "If you could find my night things."

"I'll have to get out of bed to do that."

"Yes, I know."

He lifted the covers, glanced beneath them, then looked back at her. "I am naked, you know."

"I am well aware of that."

"I wouldn't want you to be embarrassed."

"It's a risk I am willing to take."

"And I don't want the thought of my naked body to haunt you every time you looked at me."

"I shall endeavor to bravely carry on."

He sat up, swung his legs over the side of the bed, and grabbed the crumpled blue silk heap that was his dressing gown off the floor. He threw it on, stood up, and spotted her nightgown. He grabbed it and presented it to her with a flourish.

"Thank you." She pulled the covers tighter and her brow furrowed. "Would you be so good as to turn around or avert your eyes so that I might dress?"

"Ah modesty has reasserted itself."

"I find it hard to believe it ever wavered." She gestured again. "Go on then."

He chuckled and turned away. Behind him, he could hear the rustle of fabric.

"I have a, well, a proposal for you."

"Oh?" He arched a brow. "I thought you said we wouldn't suit?"

"Not that kind of proposal. While I have not changed my opinion on the absurdity of your motorwagon, as you are willing to absent yourself from Millworth, I should like to show my appreciation."

"I thought you just did." He turned toward her and grinned wickedly.

"Good Lord, Sam, do you think of nothing else?" She pulled her wrapper around her and tied the ribbons tight.

Did she have any idea how delicious she looked? With her dark hair disheveled around her face, a sparkle in her blue eyes, and a flush coloring her creamy skin? As he remembered her from New York. As she was in his dreams.

"At the moment it's difficult."

"Well, do your best." Her tone was firm but a smile shone in her eyes. "My late husband was very involved in business. I can't tell you anything more specific because I don't really know specifics. He never discussed matters of business with me." She shrugged. "But I do know that he and his oldest and closest friend were partners in any number of business endeavors. I was thinking of going to London tomorrow, primarily to meet with my solicitor. If you would like to accompany me, I would be happy to arrange a meeting. Mr. Tate might be able to offer some assistance or make some suggestions. It might be, oh, beneficial."

"It might at that." He studied her for a moment. "You would do that for me?"

"I would simply like to make amends for my bad behavior."

"Again, I thought you just had."

She ignored him. "Besides, we are friends, aren't we?"

For now. Where did that come from? He chuckled. "We are at that."

"I should be getting back to my room." She moved to the door, opened it carefully, and peered down the hall.

"And there will be no more of this?"

"Absolutely not," she said absently, still perusing the hallway.

"In that case . . ." He stepped to the door, closed it quietly, and pulled her into his arms.

"What are you doing?"

"Kissing you." His lips claimed hers. For a brief moment she hesitated then wrapped her arms around his neck and met his passion with her own. This is what he had dreamed of since he had last kissed her in New York. Her lips warm and supple and welcoming beneath his. The curves of her body melding so perfectly with his. The beat of her heart echoing the rush of blood through his veins. But this was better than any dream. This was real.

At last she pulled away and gazed up at him, her blue eyes glazed with desire and resolve.

"I do need to go."

He smiled down at her. "If that's what you want."

"I'm not sure what I want I'm afraid." She smiled in a wry manner. "Your fault entirely, I might add."

"And for that I am more than willing to accept the blame." He kissed her again then reluctantly released her.

She opened the door, glanced down the hall, then looked back at him. "You are right though, you know, about one thing."

"And what might that be?"

"There are indeed activities beyond tennis that you do quite well." She cast him a wicked grin. "Quite well indeed." She nodded and slipped into the hallway.

He chuckled and closed the door. This was not at all what he had expected when she'd knocked on his door tonight. In fact, after their argument today, he would have bet serious money that she would never speak to him again. Not that he was complaining. But he was certainly confused. And not merely about the lovely Lady Hargate.

He crossed to the desk and absently straightened

his notes. He wasn't used to being confused and couldn't remember the last time he had been. Doubt was simply not part of his nature. No, he was a man of confidence in the decisions he made and the paths he chose to take. He was clear-headed and decisive and never uncertain about anything.

But when it came to this annoying, maddening, infuriating woman, he had no idea what he wanted. Which in and of itself was odd. He always knew what he wanted. Always had a goal in mind, a destination at the end of a road. Abruptly, the thought struck him that while tonight was delightful, it was not enough.

Nor did he want it to be enough. Which was a much more startling revelation. One would assume that after having thought and dreamed about her for these many months, he would now be satisfied. The question, as it were, of *her* should now be settled. Instead, there were more questions in his head than before.

It was damned difficult to reconcile that he obviously felt something for this woman who was not at all the kind of woman he wanted. He couldn't have chosen a woman more exactly the type he intended to avoid. She saw marriage as little more than a . . . a business transaction. It might not be entirely accurate to call her a fortune hunter but she was raised to see marriage as a way to improve her lot in life and nothing beyond that.

He wanted more than a good bargain or a beneficial arrangement. When he decided upon a woman to spend the rest of his days with, he wanted someone who didn't care if he had money or power. Who wanted him for who he was not what he had. He wanted a partner. And he wanted love.

No, Delilah Hargate was entirely wrong for him. There wasn't the least doubt in his mind about that.

He wasn't sure he could say the same about his heart.

Chapter Eleven

Fifteen days before the wedding . . .

"Good morning, Clement." Delilah sailed into the breakfast room.

"Good morning, Lady Hargate," the butler said. "Coffee?"

"You know me so well." She grinned at the older man. Clement had been with their family since she was a child. She suspected it wouldn't be long now before he handed in his notice and gave up the life of loyal family retainer to spend the rest of his days living with a relative, a niece if she was correct, in Wales or somewhere thereabouts. And while last night the acknowledgment that she was back where she had begun had been disheartening, this morning it was wonderful to be home at Millworth where she had always belonged.

"Good morning, Teddy."

Her friend sat at the table, perusing papers spread out before her, the pen in her hand hovering over her notebook. She glanced up briefly then returned her attention to her work. "Good morning."

"Beautiful day, don't you think?"

"Very nice," Teddy said absently.

It was a brilliant autumn day. The sun was shining. Sam had agreed to absent himself from the manor. Delilah was going into London to see her solicitor, who might actually have good news for her, and possibly contact an investigator Camille had insisted she hire at Camille's expense. To borrow from Mr. Browning, God was in His heaven and all was right with the world. Although, admittedly, God might look askance at her much-improved demeanor given its source was sin.

Teddy glanced up. "You are certainly in a better mood today."

"I couldn't be out of sorts forever." Delilah cast her friend her brightest smile and moved to the sideboard. Mrs. Dooley had outdone herself this morning and laid out a virtual feast. But then didn't the dear woman outdo herself nearly every day? And never was it appreciated as much as today.

"One could only hope," Teddy murmured and returned her attention to the work in front of her.

Delilah laughed. It was nothing short of amazing what a good night's sleep would do for one's appetite. Delilah was famished. She'd slept shockingly well after leaving Sam's room. Indeed, she'd slept better than she had since Sam had arrived at Millworth. No, upon reflection she'd slept better than she had since she'd returned from New York months ago. Why, this was the best sleep she'd had in longer than she could remember.

She selected sausage, a coddled egg, kippers, and debated over a slice of a tasty looking pheasant pie. Possibly later.

Astonishing how indulging in a bit of unanticipated sin brightened one's outlook on life. She felt like a completely new woman. Perhaps when one threw caution to the winds once, one couldn't rest until one did so again. As if, only in doing so, would the adventure truly be put in the past. Now, it need never happen again.

It was as though she had been reborn. Fresh and new and unsullied. New York no longer hung over her head like a dark cloud. No, that wasn't it exactly. She put a slice of bacon on her plate then took a second. Her ebullient mood was more akin to how, when one has been allowed to sample something delightful, like chocolate, but hasn't been completely satisfied, the desire for more chocolate will grow and grow until one simply has to have chocolate. It's inevitable really. Once one has had one's fill, why, one can then easily ignore chocolate.

She took a piece of the pie and joined Teddy at the table.

"I see your appetite has returned." Teddy jotted something in the notebook.

"My appetite never left." Delilah accepted her coffee from Clement, topped it with cream, and dropped a few cubes of sugar in her cup. Phillip had drunk coffee and she'd picked up the habit from him.

"You weren't hungry last night," Teddy said mildly.

"I was very tired last night." Delilah selected a piece of toast from the rack on the table and slathered on marmalade. "But today I am ravenous." She took a bite and savored the sweet tart orange flavor of the spread. "Where is everyone?"

"I'm not sure where Camille is. Clement said Grayson and Sam are at the carriage house with Mr. Moore."

Delilah started on her egg. "Ah, little boys and their toys."

Teddy glanced up and frowned. "You're being surprisingly pleasant today."

"Nonsense," she said between bites. "I am pleasant every day."

"You haven't been the least bit pleasant since Sam arrived."

"I've been preoccupied." She dabbed at her mouth with a serviette and took a sip of coffee. "With my dire financial future."

Teddy's eyes narrowed.

"Why are you looking at me like that?" She glanced down. "Have I spilled something?"

"No."

"Then—"

"Because I don't believe you."

"I don't know why not." Delilah picked up her bacon. "The threat of my dire financial future occupies very nearly my every waking thought." She took a bite. "Excellent bacon, by the way."

"Nonetheless, there's something decidedly different about you today."

"Beyond the fact that I am being pleasant?" Delilah took another large bite of toast. Really, she couldn't remember the last time she had been quite this hungry. "Goodness, I would think you would be grateful."

"I am but . . ." Teddy studied her closely. "You're hiding something, aren't you?"

"What on earth would I be hiding?"

"I don't know. But you are."

"Nonsense." Delilah sampled the sausage and resisted the urge to moan with pleasure. "Have you tried the sausage? It's very good. Perhaps the best I've ever tasted."

"I had some earlier."

"I wish you would stop looking at me as if I were an insect under glass."

"And I wish you would tell me what's going on in that head of yours."

"I am simply optimistic, that's all." Which really was more or less true. "It's a perfect day and I am confident all will turn out . . . perfectly." She smiled and sipped her coffee.

"That in itself is suspect."

"What?"

"Your optimism," Teddy said and returned to her work.

Delilah laughed and dipped into her egg.

Sam strode into the room, said something to Clement, then took a seat across from Delilah.

"Good morning," he said in a clipped tone.

"Good morning." Something odd fluttered in her chest. She ignored it and cast him a smile that was no more than polite.

"How are you this morning, Sam?" Teddy glanced up from her papers and favored him with a smile.

"Fine." He drummed his fingers on the table. Clement set a cup before him and he nodded his thanks.

Delilah traded glances with Teddy.

"Forgive me for saying so but . . ." Delilah chose her words with care. "You sound anything but fine."

"Admittedly, things aren't quite as fine as I would like." Sam blew a long breath. "The motor-wagon isn't working."

"Oh, dear," Teddy murmured.

Before last night, Delilah might have pointed out that she knew it all along, that she was not the least bit surprised. Today, however, she was not inclined to do so. She might even feel a bit sorry for the man. Remarkable how a refreshing night's sleep could improve one's demeanor. "Can't your Mr. Moore fix it?"

"I hope so." Sam nodded. "He is working on it. He thinks it's just a part that has shaken loose in transit. Unfortunately there are any number of parts it could be." He looked at Teddy. "I'm afraid your ride is going to have to wait."

"Ah well." Teddy smiled, as gracious and charming as ever. "I will simply continue to enjoy the anticipation then."

He glanced at Delilah. "Have you changed your mind? About riding in my motorwagon."

"Not really." She shrugged apologetically. "Although I do hope you manage to get it running."

"Why?" Suspicion rang in his voice.

"Goodness, Sam." Delilah stared at him. "As much as I might think it's utter foolishness, I am not an idiot. You did not make a success of your life by taking exceptionally stupid risks. If you think horseless carriages are the way of the future, it seems to me, I would indeed be an idiot in not acknowledging that I know nothing whatsoever about business and that you probably know what you are doing. And that there is the possibility that you might be right and I might be wrong." She popped the last bite of toast into her mouth and smiled. "Slim but it exists."

Teddy's mouth dropped open in shock.

"Thank you." Sam's tone was cautious.

"You're quite welcome." She waved at the toast rack. "Toast?"

"I've eaten but again thank you."

"Did you try the sausage?" She lowered her voice in a confidential manner. "It was exceptional."

Teddy choked.

"I did." He nodded, a smile in his eyes. "It was very good."

"I thought so." She wiped a tiny bit of marmalade from the corner of her mouth with her finger. His gaze flicked to her mouth then to her eyes. She hesitated then deliberately licked the jam from her finger. Oh, dear. Hadn't she just said she wasn't an idiot? Apparently she was wrong about that, too. "Possibly the best sausage I've ever had."

He swallowed hard. "It was very good."

She'd never had a man mesmerized before. "Are you sure you don't want a bit more?"

"No, thank you." His voice had the tiniest strangled quality to it.

"Did you try the marmalade as well?"

"Yes, um, very good . . ." he said weakly.

Delilah met his gaze, took a bite of toast, and chewed it slowly. The man couldn't take his eyes off of her. Perhaps Delilah had more in common with Beryl than she had imagined. This was great fun. She swallowed and sighed with pleasure. "Mmmm. There is something about orange marmalade, especially in cooler weather, that brings to mind the heat of the summer sun and—"

"I'll have some," Teddy said abruptly, grabbing a piece of toast and smearing it with marmalade.

Delilah choked back a laugh. Sam cleared his throat and his amused gaze met hers.

"Teddy." Delilah turned to her friend, still busy savoring her toast and whatever else might have been brought to mind. "I've decided to go into London today and pay a call on my solicitors. I've not received any word from them and I fear I'm dreadfully impatient."

"There are a few matters I need to attend to in London as well. Would you mind if I accompanied you?" Sam said with just the right touch of offhandedness followed by the merest hint of hesitation as if he had only now thought of it and wasn't entirely sure how she'd take the idea. It was very good. The man must be brilliant in matters of business.

"Well." Delilah drew her brows together thoughtfully. "I suppose I wouldn't mind company on the train. London is only an hour away but one never knows what one might encounter on the way." She nodded. "I shall quite appreciate having you along for . . ."

"Safety?" Teddy's gaze shifted from Delilah to Sam and back. "Protection?"

"Yes, safety." Sam nodded with perhaps a shade too much enthusiasm.

"Exactly what I was thinking," Delilah said at the same time.

"Yes, that's what I thought," Teddy said.

"I need to have a few words with Gray before we go," Sam said. "It should take me no more than a quarter of an hour."

"Excellent." Delilah nodded. "We should be able to take the next train."

"In a few minutes then." He smiled at Teddy, nodded at Delilah, and left the room.

Delilah tasted the pie, decided it was every bit as good as it looked, and took another bite. She glanced at Teddy and paused. "You're staring at me again. Why?"

"Oh, I don't know. No reason really."

"And yet you continue to stare."

"Imagine that. Perhaps it was the marmalade? Tasty but not extraordinarily so."

"Really?" Delilah widened her eyes. "And I thought it was indeed extraordinary."

"Possibly the country air has sharpened your senses."

"I suppose that's it." Delilah took another forkful of her pie but it was impossible to enjoy with Teddy staring at her. "You know, if you have something you wish to say, it might be best if you simply said it."

"I'm just trying to sort something out."

"Oh?" Delilah set down her fork, pushed her plate away, and folded her hands on the table in front of her. "Go on then."

"What was that about?" Teddy gestured at the

pot of orange preserves. "With the marmalade and the sausage."

"They were very good and I thought it would be a shame if Sam failed to taste them." She stifled a grin. "I considered it, oh, my duty as a loyal subject of Her Majesty to make certain our American visitor had the opportunity to partake of our fine English sausages and excellent Scottish marmalade."

"How very gracious of you."

"I thought so."

Teddy aimed an accusing finger. "You were flirting with him."

"Was I?" Delilah widened her eyes innocently. "I thought I was just being pleasant."

"Well you were, flirting that is. And you were more than pleasant." Suspicion shaded Teddy's face. "You're being exceptionally nice to him."

"I wouldn't say exceptionally nice." Delilah searched for the right word. "I would say cordial is more accurate."

"Yesterday you weren't even cordial."

"That's not entirely true. We did play tennis together."

"Yes, I know but—"

"And won."

"I know that too."

"I doubt that we could have won if we hadn't been cordial to one another."

"I suppose but—"

234

"So I really have no idea why you are so suspicious." Delilah cast her friend a pleasant smile. "First you chastise me for not being nice to the man and now you think I'm being too nice."

"I don't think you're being too nice. I think you're being . . ." Teddy shook her head. "I don't know. There's something I can't quite put my finger on. . . ."

"I would certainly like to hear it, whatever that something might be."

"It's obvious to me—" Teddy sucked in a sharp breath. "You called him Sam!"

"So did you."

"Yes, but you refused to do so as you once had a dog named Sam. A faithful and loyal companion you said."

"And indeed he was."

"Have you decided Sam—Mr. Russell—is faithful and loyal as well?"

"He does play a fine game of tennis."

Teddy stared. "What has come over you?"

"Nothing really. I simply decided I needed to stop being so . . . unpleasant." Delilah heaved a heartfelt sigh. "It's not at all like me and frankly I was tired of it."

"Perhaps but, I know you, Dee, and . . ." Teddy blew a frustrated breath. "You've been odd in recent months. Decidedly odd."

"Threat of financial disaster, remember?" Delilah

shook her head mournfully. "It's like the sword of Damocles hanging over my head."

"You said this threat appeared six weeks ago."

"Give or take a few days."

"Ah-ha!" Triumph sounded in Teddy's voice. "I first noticed a change in you when you returned from New York. I thought perhaps travel did not agree with you."

Delilah rested the back of her hand against her forehead. "Travel is so dreadfully—"

"Stop it, Dee. Stop it at once." Teddy's brow furrowed and she glared at her friend. "You're keeping something from me and I want to know what it is."

"May I point out, until we arrived here, you and I had barely seen one another at all since my return from New York."

"Even so—"

"Don't you think if something truly significant had happened in my life I would tell you?"

"I have always thought so until I discovered you were hiding this threat of a new heir from me."

"I wasn't hiding." Delilah shrugged. "I suppose as long as I didn't have to admit it, it wasn't real. I could ignore it completely. Surely you understand that?"

"Of course I do but—"

"There's really nothing more to it than that." She cast her friend her brightest smile, rose to her feet, and started toward the door. "Now then I must gather my things if we are to make our train."

"I still think there's something you're hiding."

"My dear sweet friend." Delilah paused in the doorway. "You've become entirely too suspicious. Looking for things that don't exist." Delilah shook her head in a sympathetic manner. "It's not at all becoming." She smiled and took her leave.

"Dee!" Teddy called behind. "This discussion is not over!"

Delilah grinned and continued toward her rooms. It was rather remarkable how, when one dipped one's toes in the pool of deceit, one did seem to be pulled farther and farther in. At this point revealing the truth about Sam to Teddy would do more harm than good. She'd always shared everything with her friend. That she hadn't shared this would no doubt injure Teddy terribly. Why, it was in the other woman's best interest to continue to keep this from her.

Besides, she still had no desire for anyone to know about her adventure—*adventures*—with Sam. It would be different if she intended to, well, keep him. As she didn't, it would still be best if no one knew. There would be no explanations to make and no recriminations.

No, Sam Russell was her secret and hers alone.

And wasn't that every bit as delicious as the sausage?

". . . and if you'll look down that street you'll see . . ."

Now this was the Delilah Sam had met in New York. This delightful woman sitting beside him in a hansom cab pointed out the various sights of London with unrestrained enthusiasm.

". . . and then of course that particular gallery is where . . ."

No, that wasn't entirely accurate. The woman he'd met in New York had been enjoying the sights of his city but had been more reserved than the one sitting next to him now. This Delilah was in her element. This Delilah was home.

". . . and yet, I must confess, I am not at all fond . . ."

Regardless, she was a far cry from the Lady Hargate he'd recently met at Millworth Manor. He was not so arrogant as to take credit for her change in demeanor but he was not so humble as to think it had nothing to do with him. Still, it was confusing.

"Who are you?" he said without thinking.

She laughed. "Many things to many people I suspect. Let me think." She paused and her brow furrowed. "I am, of course, Lady Hargate, Delilah Channing Hargate, widow of the late Lord Phillip Hargate. I am the younger sister of Ladies Lydingham and Dunwell and the youngest daughter of the Earl and Countess of Briston. There, that should cover it all."

"It doesn't." He shook his head. "You're not the same woman I met in New York, although you bear much more of a resemblance to her than to the Lady Hargate I met a few days ago."

"Dare I ask how I am different? From the woman in New York that is."

"*Mrs*. Hargate was charming and engaging but somewhat more subdued than you are today."

"Ah, well, in New York I was a visitor. A bit out of place really. But here . . ." She swept a wide gesture at the city around them. "Here is where I belong."

"You love London, don't you?"

"I can't imagine living anywhere else. Much of London is not at all pleasant, as I suspect is true of most cities. There is entirely too much poverty and crime and more should be done to solve those problems. It's the responsibility of those of us who have more to do what we can to assist those who have nothing."

"Do you?"

"Of course I do." She raised a brow. "You sound surprised."

"My apologies. I don't mean to."

"I may not have the skills needed to be a teacher or governess, but I have organized several charitable events that have been most successful."

"I don't doubt that for a moment."

"Excellent. The next time I am engaged in such an endeavor I shall expect a sizable donation."

She cast him a firm look. "Even from the other side of the ocean."

He grinned. "You can count on it."

"Oh, I shall." She nodded and continued. "Any number of people I know prefer living in the country. I do like the country but, well, London is the most exciting place in the world." Pride colored her words. "It's the heart of the empire, the largest empire man has ever known. London is the center of theater and art, intellect and literature, politics and history. It has been a community for nearly two thousand years. And . . ." She smiled in a teasing manner. "The shopping is excellent."

He laughed. "It suits you. London that is."

"Do you think so?" She arched a brow. "Why? A moment ago you asked me who I was. You scarcely know me."

"On the contrary, my dear Lady Hargate. I know you better than you think."

"Oh?" She studied him with amusement. "Then tell me what you know."

"Everything?"

She blushed. "Perhaps not everything."

"All right. Let me think." He considered her for a moment. "I know even while you say you are a stickler for tradition, you find a great deal of enjoyment in something new."

"You mean like a motorwagon?"

"No, I mean you like seeing something new to

you. Unless I'm mistaken, you very much enjoyed the sights of New York."

"True." She nodded. "I suppose I haven't traveled enough to be nonchalant about seeing somewhere I have never been before. I've never been outside of England except to accompany Camille and Grayson to New York. Oh, and I have been to Paris, of course." She bit back a smile. "The shopping is excellent there too."

"I have heard that." He chuckled. "As have my mother and sisters. I doubt that I can avoid accompanying them to Paris for too much longer." He grinned. "But I am trying."

"You've mentioned your sisters before. How many do you have?"

"It seems like dozens." He blew a long breath. "But only five, one of whom is married. The others are still too young." He drew his brows together. "And growing up entirely too fast."

She laughed. "The next years should be interesting for you."

"I am not looking forward to it." He shuddered. Of all the tasks he had taken on in the wake of his father's death, watching over his younger sisters was already proving to be the most difficult.

"What else do you know about me?"

"I know you have never been close to your own sisters but you are all making efforts to improve your relationship."

She scoffed. "That scarcely counts. Grayson told you that."

"He did but he didn't need to. You and Camille aren't completely comfortable in each other's presence. There's a tentative undercurrent between you, as if you are both carefully feeling your way along. It's apparent to anyone the least bit observant." He shrugged. "Or maybe it's just apparent to someone with sisters."

"That's very good." She studied him coolly. "And I think that's quite enough. I'm not sure I want you to know everything about me and I'm a bit concerned about what you already think you know."

He grinned. "Scared, Lady Hargate?"

Something akin to acknowledgment flashed through her eyes so quickly he might have been mistaken. "Of you? An arrogant American? Don't be absurd."

"I see I have improved in your eyes." He smiled. "I used to be an insufferable American."

"Perhaps I know *you* better than you think."

He laughed and glanced at the passing scenery. "How long have you been staying at the manor?"

"Just a few weeks." She paused. "I assume you know I closed my house here in town and the country house."

"Gray mentioned that."

"I would have come to Millworth even without the excuse of Camille's wedding. I had nowhere else to go. It's not at all pleasant to be without funds when one has never had to be concerned with money before."

"I can imagine," Sam said. He suspected Delilah's offhand manner hid a much deeper fear. His family had always had an adequate income, not the vast fortune he had amassed now. He could live a simpler life but his mother and sisters would not do well without money. Nor, no doubt, would Delilah.

"Oh, I could have thrown myself on the mercy of friends but the only thing worse than being a poor relation is being an impoverished friend." She wrinkled her nose. "There is nothing that makes others more uncomfortable than having a friend in their midst who has fallen upon difficult financial times."

"And these are friends?"

"One does wonder." She smiled. "I imagine it's because it could happen to anyone. There but for the grace of God, you understand."

He nodded.

"Precisely why it's best to keep such difficulties quiet. No one would talk about it to your face anyway. Everyone usually pretends life is as it always has been."

"Isn't that when you discover your true friends?"

"Perhaps, but I'm not sure I wish to test that theory," she said wryly.

"You remained friends with Teddy when her family lost its money."

She cast him a sharp glance. "Grayson again?"

He shrugged. "He has his suspicions."

"I'm not surprised. I imagine Camille has her suspicions as well. One doesn't go from throwing the kind of elaborate soirees Teddy and her mother did to managing weddings and parties for other people simply on a whim. Although they want people to believe they're simply bored and this is a way to fill their time." She gazed at the passing scenery for a moment. "Teddy is as close to me as any sister, closer than my own have been in the past. She has built a new life for herself. I'm not sure I can do the same."

"I suspect you are stronger than you think."

"And you suspect that because you know me so well?"

"Perhaps I suspect it because I don't."

"As much as I hate to disappoint you, strength is not my forte. I find the unknown nothing short of terrifying. I like life to be planned and expected." She shook her head. "I certainly didn't have the courage to tell my family about my financial quandary until I had no other choice. If not for Camille's wedding, and everyone gathering at Millworth, I probably would have hidden that as long as necessary." She sighed. "It's not easy to explain, even to those who know you best, that your world has been upended. There's an inherent failure in it, as if what has befallen you is your fault."

"That's ridiculous." He drew his brows together. "The fact that your late husband might have an unknown heir has nothing to do with you."

"You're looking at this rationally, Sam, and I am speaking of perceptions." She thought for a moment. "One does what one is supposed to do in life, you know, with certain expectations."

"That things will turn out as they should?"

She nodded.

"And if they don't?"

"If they don't, well, somehow, you've failed." She smiled. "And that is the twist, isn't it?"

"What is?"

Her gaze met his. "Regardless of expectations, even if one does exactly what one should, plays the game according to the rules if you will, life does not always turn out as planned."

"That's the problem with plans. The best laid plans and all."

"Still . . ." She set her jaw in a stubborn manner. "They do give one something to cling to in the midst of chaos and uncertainty."

"Does your plan to marry someone with wealth and position give you something to cling to now?"

"Yes, Sam, it does," she said and turned her attention toward the streets passing by.

Well, that was certainly stupid. He had pushed her entirely too far. Delilah's lighthearted manner had sobered. The least he could do now was try to brighten her spirits. After all, she was introducing him to her husband's associate, a Mr. Julian Tate if he recalled correctly, for no other reason than to help him. Besides, they had agreed to be friends. As her friend, he should do something.

"What is your favorite place in London?" It was the first thing that popped into his mind.

"My favorite?" She studied him cautiously. "Why do you want to know?"

"I thought you might like to show me."

Her eyes narrowed. "Why would I want to do that?"

"My God, you're a stubborn woman." He shook his head. "I'm trying to be friends."

"Oh, well." She waved her hand at him. "Go on then."

"I want to see your favorite place in London because I'm a visitor and everyone else has very definite opinions about what I should see. This is your city, you're proud of it, and you probably know it well. Besides, if we're going to be friends, I'd like to see what my friend likes. We are going to be friends, aren't we?"

"Yes." A slow smile creased her lips. "I believe we are." She paused. "You're certain you want to see my favorite place?"

"I do," he said staunchly.

"It's not terribly exciting."

"Some of my favorite places are not especially

exciting but they have meaning to me. Of course . . ." He heaved an overly dramatic sigh. "If you would prefer not to show your friend . . ."

"Oh for goodness' sake." She leaned forward and called an address to the driver. "It's not far from Julian's so it won't take us out of the way."

A few minutes later they pulled up before an imposing redbrick house. Tall and narrow, it was a good five stories high.

"This is it," she said with pride. "This is my house." She glanced at him with a half-hearted smile. "For the moment anyway."

"Very nice." He nodded. "Should we get out?"

"It's not necessary." She studied the building with obvious affection. "It's closed up and I'd prefer not to go inside right now. There are dust-covers over everything and I find it altogether too melancholy. Besides we should be going."

"Maybe another time, then?"

"Perhaps." Her gaze stayed on her house. "I know what you're thinking."

"What am I thinking?"

"You're surprised it isn't as grand as you expected a house of mine to be. Given that I am such a snob."

"I would never think such a thing." He grinned.

She cast him a skeptical look then returned her attention to the house. "Phillip's father bought this house as a future wedding gift for his son long before Phillip and I actually met. He had died by the time we married. I love it. I have had a hand in the decoration of each and every room. Of course Phillip had a say as well. He had excellent taste. But this is, well, mine or I feel it's mine. It's as close to a sanctuary as I have ever had. Unfortunately, Phillip preferred the country and solitude. I preferred the city. So I spent much of my time here."

"Alone?"

"Usually."

He stared for a long moment. Gray was right. Hargate was an idiot.

"Stop staring at me. It's rude you know, even for an ill-mannered American."

"Sorry," he murmured.

"What? No clever quip? No sarcastic barb? No response designed to put me in my place?"

"No," he said simply. "You were right, I was rude."

"I am usually right." She slanted him a quick smile. "Well?"

"Not that I've noticed," he said coolly.

She laughed. "Much better."

Good. He had made her laugh. That was something anyway.

"We weren't separated, we simply had different interests, that's all. And we were wise enough to accept those differences between us." She paused. "Don't think alone is the same as lonely. It's not, you know."

"I would never think that."

"I was never lonely. I have a great number of friends and acquaintances, aside from Teddy. I entertained quite a lot, musical evenings and soirees and literary salons and the like. I am—was—active in charitable endeavors. My husband gave me the freedom to pursue my own path as it were. Our life together was quite—"

"Perfect?"

"Exactly." She nodded. "And my life will be again."

"With another perfect husband."

She hesitated for no more than a fraction of a second. "That is the plan. Now then." She turned to him and smiled. "We should be off if you wish to meet with Julian. And I have a great deal to accomplish today."

"That's right, you want to meet with your solicitor."

"Among other things." She gave the driver the address and they started off.

A few minutes later the cab pulled up in front of a grand mansion at least three times the size of Delilah's. He helped her out of the carriage and they approached the house.

"Julian's family is quite well connected. He is the nephew of a marquess, although dozens would have to perish before he inherited a title of any kind. Still, do try not to be too American."

He chuckled. "I shall do my best."

"That will have to do I suppose." She considered him with a critical eye. "I will say one thing for you, Sam, you do know how to dress properly."

"Is that a compliment, Lady Hargate?"

"No, Mr. Russell, it's an observation." She nodded and started toward the door.

"I would hate for you to be embarrassed." He grinned.

"My dear, Mr. Russell, you're quite an attractive man and you well know it. It's not your appearance clothed that I find embarrassing." A wicked twinkle gleamed in her eye. "It's the most distracting memory of when you aren't."

Chapter Twelve

"Delilah, my dear, it's been entirely too long." Julian Tate stepped into his library, his eyes lit with apparent delight. But then Julian had always been good at appearances. He took her hands and kissed her on each cheek. "I have missed you."

"You needn't have, you know," Delilah said with a smile. "I am quite cross that you have never accepted one of my invitations."

She'd scarcely seen him at all in the three years since Phillip's death even though she had dutifully issued him invitations to various social and charitable functions. He'd been Phillip's lifelong friend but Delilah had never quite taken to him. Or he to her for that matter. Still, they were always cordial to one another, even friendly. It would have been difficult otherwise. In many ways, he had been the third person in her marriage.

"Oh, I've become something of a hermit I'm afraid." He chuckled. "Health problems and that sort of thing."

"You look well," she lied. Julian had been quite a handsome man when she'd first met him. Indeed, he and Phillip could have passed for brothers. He was the same age as her husband, who would have been forty-six this past May, but

Julian appeared far older. These last years had not been kind to him.

He laughed. "You never did lie well."

"Perhaps because I don't lie at all." She studied him closely. "You should get out more, Julian. It would do you good."

"Nonsense, I have everything I need right here and I can do everything I want to do from right here. And what I can't, can be arranged." He leaned toward her and lowered his voice. "One of the benefits of having a tidy fortune and a measure of financial power is that I can hire people to do what I need done."

"Of course." She pulled her hands from his and nodded at Sam. "I was hoping you might spare some time to have a few words with my friend, Mr. Russell."

"Ah yes, the American." Julian eyed Sam curiously. "My butler said you were accompanied by an American. I found it most surprising."

"Life is full of surprises, Julian."

"It's a pleasure to meet you, Mr. Tate." Sam nodded a greeting. "I hope we haven't come at an inconvenient time."

"Not at all. My schedule is my own." He glanced at Delilah. "There's something to be said for living a solitary life."

"Mr. Russell is engaged in a business pursuit with my sister Camille's fiancé and I thought perhaps you might give him the benefit of your wisdom. Phillip always said no one had a better head for business than you."

"I daresay Phillip said a lot of things about me and that might well have been the kindest." He smiled, took her arm, and led her to the sofa. "But first, let's talk about you, shall we? How are you, my dear?"

She took a seat on the sofa and Julian sat down beside her. Sam settled in a nearby chair. The American was subtle enough, and Julian probably didn't notice, but Delilah did wish Sam would stop studying them as if he were trying to work out some sort of puzzle. Given his observation about the undercurrents between her and Camille, he was much more astute than one might expect.

"I am well enough. My life is rather uneventful really." *Aside from the threat of losing all I have to an alleged heir.*

"I doubt that." His gaze met hers. "Phillip has been gone for three years now."

"I am well aware of that."

"It was Phillip's wish that after no more than three years—"

"I am aware of that too," she said in a sharper tone than she had intended. It had never sat well with her that this man had always been closer to her husband than she was. Julian was Phillip's confidant. She was merely his wife. "However, I was not aware that you knew of his wishes."

"We discussed it when he had his will drawn

up." Julian paused, obviously choosing his words. "We thought, rather, he thought, if he were to die while you were still a young woman, it wouldn't be at all fair for you to be tied to him for the rest of your life." He shook his head. "It seemed like such a waste."

"And yet, as he is gone, shouldn't what I do with the rest of my life be my decision?"

He ignored her and addressed Sam. "My apologies, Mr. Russell, for speaking of something you know nothing about. I'm afraid my social skills have become rather rusty."

"Understandable." Sam's pleasant smile did nothing to hide the curiosity in his eyes.

"This is really a private matter, Julian," she said in a hard tone. "I'm certain Mr. Russell has no interest in it."

"You introduced him as your friend, Delilah. And you brought him to see me, which indicates you do indeed consider him your friend. As your friend, I'm certain he has only your best interests at heart." He looked at Sam. "Am I wrong, Mr. Russell?"

"Not at all, Mr. Tate," Sam said smoothly. "I haven't known Lady Hargate for long but, especially as she is soon to be related to one of my closest friends, I do indeed want nothing but the best for her."

"Fine." Delilah shrugged in surrender. Apparently it didn't matter what she wished; Julian was determined to reveal Phillip's *plan* for her future. For the first time she wondered whether it might not be better to be poor but able to manage your own life than to be married. At the moment, poverty did not seem quite as dreadful a fate as marriage. And she had never in her life thought of marriage as dreadful. Indeed, Phillip's last wishes hadn't bothered her at all until this moment.

"Good." Julian nodded and addressed Sam. "Phillip—Lord Hargate—left a letter detailing his wishes along with his will. It was his desire that his wife remarry after he had been gone for no more than three years. He did not wish her to mourn for the rest of her days. To that end, he instructed me to do what I could to ensure that his wishes were carried out."

Delilah stared in surprise. "What are you supposed to do? Find me a husband?"

Julian glanced at Sam then shook his head. "I'm afraid he was not that specific."

"How thoughtful of him to encourage her to go on with her life." Sam's tone was as neutral as if he had been discussing something of no importance rather than her dead husband's direction for the rest of her life. "That does lead one to wonder though . . ."

Julian's brow rose. "Yes?"

"Yes?" she snapped. What was it now?

"Well . . ." Sam's brow furrowed. "This letter was not actually part of his will?"

Julian shook his head. "No."

"Then it's not legally binding? There is no penalty if she does not remarry in the allocated amount of time? She does not lose her property or her fortune if she fails to marry? No dire fate befalls her?"

"I fear you've been reading too many novels, Mr. Russell." Julian chuckled. "It was Phillip's wish, not his command. So no, of course not."

"Then I assume as well, there is no particular benefit to remarrying? She does not stand to gain from it? There is no additional inheritance dependent upon her remarriage?"

"Other than the fact that she will be content and secure and fulfilled in her proper role in life?" Julian asked as if the answer was obvious. "No."

"Then it seems to me that, while it might have been considerate of Lord Hargate to want his widow to move on with her life, she is under no obligation to adhere to his wishes." Sam smiled pleasantly. "And she can do as she damn well pleases." He shot an amused glance at Delilah. "Which I suspect she intends to do anyway."

She stared at him. The loveliest feeling washed through her. Had the annoying man just defended her right to live her life as she wished? How very . . . *American* of him.

"Quite right, Mr. Russell." Julian laughed. "And clever of you to point that out." He smiled at

Delilah. "He simply wanted you to be happy, you know."

"I would be happy if this discussion was at an end," she said. "Besides we are not here to discuss me. We are here to discuss . . ." She paused in the manner of a master storyteller. "Horseless carriages."

"Are we now?" Julian's gaze slid to Sam. "You know, some are saying they're the way of the future."

"Good Lord," she muttered.

"I think so." Sam cast her a smug look. "I have recently come from a meeting in Germany with a man who has developed a new internal combustion engine."

"Ah yes, Mr. Benz." Julian nodded.

Surprise colored Sam's face. "You know of him?"

"I am not as stodgy or as old-fashioned as I may appear, Mr. Russell." Julian smiled. "Just because I prefer not to leave my house doesn't mean I'm not well informed. So you have seen his motor-wagon?"

"Better than that." Sam grinned. "I bought one."

"I see." Julian's eyes narrowed thoughtfully. "And what do you intend to do with it? I assume you have some sort of plan in mind."

"I do indeed." Sam leaned forward and addressed the other man. "Gray—Mr. Elliott— and I are confident motorwagons can be . . ."

Delilah's mind wandered almost at once. She had heard all this before and saw no need to pay close attention now.

It was decidedly odd being once again in the room that had served more as an office than a library for both Julian and Phillip when they were engaged in some sort of financial enterprise. Phillip had said a true gentleman did not have an office outside of his home, although apparently it was acceptable to have an office in another man's home. At least in the city. The library at Hargate Hall had served a similar purpose for the two men.

Nothing had changed here since the last time she'd been in this room or the first for that matter. She distinctly recalled Julian had hosted a small dinner party in the first year of her marriage to Phillip in their honor. Then as now the same sofa and chairs were positioned in front of the fireplace. Portraits of Julian's father and grandfather still hung over the mantel. An elaborately carved library table separated the halves of the room. A partners' desk, identical to the one at Hargate Hall, dominated the far end of the room as it always had. No, nothing had changed, as if Phillip would walk back into the room at any moment. She wondered what he would say to find her here. She'd never felt particularly welcome in this room. Even though Julian had been gracious and welcoming today, the feeling of being out of place remained.

Sam and Julian were deep in discussion and there was no need for her to stay. She could probably call on her solicitor and be back before they were finished. Whether or not she also called on the investigator Camille had recommended depended on what she learned at her solicitor's office.

"Gentlemen." She rose to her feet. Sam stood at once, Julian a bit slower. "I do apologize for the interruption, but I have a matter to attend to and if I stay much longer it shall be too late. So if you will forgive me, I shall be off."

"Do you want me to come with you?" Sam's gaze met hers.

"Thank you but I much prefer to go alone." She smiled and nodded at Julian. "The two of you are obviously nowhere near finished. I daresay I'll be back before you even notice I'm gone. Besides, if we are to catch the last train, it's simply practical for me to go alone."

"If you're sure." Sam smiled and something odd happened in the pit of her stomach. When had he become such a very nice man? Or more to the point, when had she finally noticed?

"I am." She nodded. "Julian, we must get you out of this house. Perhaps you can join me for dinner one evening."

Julian smiled. "Perhaps."

"Excellent. Good day, gentlemen." She smiled and took her leave.

A footman hailed a cab for her and she was on her way in a matter of moments. In spite of the heavy traffic, she was soon at her solicitor's. And had scarcely any time at all to consider the ramifications of being friends with Sam but it was all she could think of.

She liked the blasted man. It was shocking to realize but there you had it. He was, well, a good man. A nice man. It wasn't enough that she had wanted him in a purely sinful way although that appetite had been sated.

For the moment, an annoying voice that sounded suspiciously like his said in the back of her head. She ignored it.

Sam was the sort of man one could possibly trust. Not with her heart, of course, but with her friendship. She hadn't lied when she'd told him she had a great many friends but aside from Teddy she didn't know how many, if any, of those she could turn to if she were in dire need.

She could indeed be his friend but there it would end. He would go back to America after the wedding. She would find a new husband. He would do whatever it was he was doing with his horseless carriages and no doubt, vastly increase his wealth. They would go on with their respective lives exactly as planned. For the first time, her plans didn't sound quite as perfect as they usually did.

Not that today's plans were going well. Her

solicitor was ill, his partners were otherwise engaged and out of the offices. Annoying but no matter really. He probably had no news for her anyway. She'd write to him tomorrow and arrange a specific appointment for next week. For now, she'd return to Julian's, collect Sam, and they would have to hurry if they wanted to catch the last train back to the country.

"I'm afraid they are still closeted in the library, Lady Hargate," Julian's butler said upon her return. "Shall I—" A crash sounded from the direction of the back stairs and he winced. "Announce you?"

"Oh, that's not necessary, Mr. Bender. I am more than capable of announcing myself and I can certainly find the library. Besides, it appears you may have something else you need to attend to."

"Thank you, my lady," Mr. Bender said with relief. "We've been in the midst of an upheaval here. Half the staff is new and not as well trained as one would expect." He shook his head in despair at the lack of quality of today's servants. "Good day then, Lady Hargate." He nodded, turned sharply, and hurried out of sight.

Delilah resisted the urge to grin. If there was one thing she knew about Julian, he did not tolerate a poorly run household. Of course, neither had Phillip.

She circled the center gallery to the library door. It was already open a crack. Poor Mr.

Bender. The turmoil belowstairs was obviously taking its toll on him. The well-trained butler would never leave a door partially opened when privacy was called for.

". . . and most impressive," Julian's voice drifted from the doorway. She raised her hand to knock. "Now then, before Delilah returns, I was wondering if I might have a word with you."

She paused.

"Of course," Sam said.

This was eavesdropping and not the sort of thing she did. Although admittedly, she didn't seem to have any particular qualms about it. And they were talking about her.

What on earth did Julian wish to say to Sam without her?

And why?

"It has recently come to my attention that there is a new claim to Lord Hargate's estate," Tate said.

"I was under the impression that was a well-kept secret," Sam said cautiously.

"It is for the most part. I only learned of this a few days ago and only because I have made it my business to keep a close eye on Delilah's welfare. At least, her financial well-being. I owe her that much," Tate said, a faint hint of regret in his voice. "I knew all of Lord Hargate's secrets. Phillip and I were very close. Indeed, I was the executor of his estate after his death."

"Go on."

"Phillip could not have an undisclosed heir." He shrugged in an offhand manner that belied his words. "He was unable to have children."

"Oh?"

"A childhood illness rendered him incapable of siring children."

Sam drew his brows together. "Does Lady Hargate know this?"

"No." Tate shook his head. "Phillip didn't want her to know."

"I don't understand."

"No, I'm sure you don't." Tate blew a long resigned breath. "Appearances, Mr. Russell, are everything in this world. Phillip needed a wife and he chose Delilah for the usual reasons. She was a young woman of good family, well educated, unblemished by scandal, and quite attractive as you may have noticed."

"She's lovely."

"Indeed she is. She was, for all intents and purposes, the perfect wife for him. And he had hoped, that possibly, with the right wife, the doctors might have been wrong."

"But they weren't?"

"No. Perhaps if he had been more, I don't know . . . enthusiastic is as good a word as any I suppose." Tate considered Sam carefully. "You see, there was another difficulty as well."

Sam raised a brow. "Oh?"

"Phillip was not . . ." Tate looked off into the distance as if gathering his strength then drew a deep breath. His gaze met Sam's. "Phillip did not, well, he did not especially like women. They were not his . . . preference, shall we say. He understood his duty to his family and his title but . . . This is awkward, Mr. Russell. Please tell me I do not need to be more explicit."

Sam stared at the older man. "Probably not."

"This is not the sort of thing one speaks of, certainly not openly."

"And Delilah knows nothing of this? Of her husband's . . ." Sam hesitated. "Preferences?"

"Absolutely not," Tate said. "Nor did he intend for her ever to know. Although, if he hadn't died, as the years went on, she might well have surmised the truth. They were only married for five years. Still, one tends not to see what one is not looking for."

"But she is an intelligent woman."

"That she is." Tate chuckled. "It came as something of a surprise to Phillip. He did not expect intelligence, nor do I think he particularly wanted it."

"I'm sure that made life more difficult for him."

"You have no idea." Tate scoffed. "But even if she had suspected, I doubt that she would have said anything. It's usually easier to keep up a pretense than to face the truth."

"I suppose." Sam considered the other man for a

long moment. "It wasn't fair, though, was it? To Lady Hargate I mean."

"It wasn't especially fair to anyone. Not to Phillip or to me and certainly not to his wife. But I'm sure you know as well as I that life is rarely fair."

"Even so—"

"You must understand, Mr. Russell." Tate leaned forward in his chair. "Phillip had reached the age of thirty-eight when he decided it would be prudent to marry. The world is a dangerous place for an unmarried man of a certain age who has never been married or does not have a scandalous reputation for having indiscriminate affairs with any number of amenable women.

"Delilah's mother was looking for a suitable match. Phillip was eminently suitable. He had the fortune, he had the title, and he was a handsome devil. He was twenty years older than she, which was not at all considered too old. After all, her sisters had both married men considerably older. And Delilah and Phillip got on well together. In fact, Phillip was quite taken with her. In every way, it did appear to be an excellent match." His voice hardened. "But make no mistake about it, this was as much a business arrangement as anything else. Most marriages are, you know. Phillip was fond of her, of course, but . . ." He shook his head. "For the most part, theirs was a marriage like many others. He provided Delilah with wealth and a prominent position in the world. She gave him an excellent wife."

"But you're certain she didn't know the truth about her husband?" Sam hesitated. These were uncharted waters for him. "About his . . . preferences?"

"How did I come up with that term?" Tate cast Sam a wry smile. "It will do as good as any, and better than most I suppose. No, as I have already said, I am sure she never knew. If she had, she wouldn't have . . ."

"Wouldn't have what?"

"I've never told anyone any of this." He grimaced. "I have probably said entirely too much already."

Sam studied the other man closely. "Why have you told me anything at all?"

"As I said, I only heard of Delilah's difficulties a few days ago. Since then I have been debating how best to reveal this information without going directly to Delilah. I would prefer not to be involved." He shook his head. "I have no desire to unduly upset her. Coming from me, this information would only bring up more questions. The situation is no doubt trying enough as it is. To find out Phillip lied to her about his ability to have children—admittedly it was by omission but a lie nonetheless—would not help anyone now. There's no need for her to know that or any of the rest."

"Why not go to one of her sisters?"

"I don't know either of her sisters past a nodding acquaintance. It's my understanding that Lady Lydingham is residing in the country at the moment. As for her other sister . . ." A pained expression crossed his face. "Have you met Lady Dunwell?"

"Not yet."

"I only know her by reputation, not as sterling as one might hope," he said in a wry manner. "Phillip had an innate distrust of her but then admittedly Delilah rarely saw her sisters. Besides Lord Dunwell is actively engaged in politics." He shuddered as if the very word was distasteful.

"You could have sent the information anonymously to her solicitors."

"I considered that and might well have taken that step eventually. But anonymous information is often discredited unless delivered by a creditable messenger."

"Me?"

Tate nodded.

"I still don't see—"

"One seizes opportunity when it presents itself, Mr. Russell. You are an opportunity that I do not intend to squander. As a man of business I am certain you understand that."

"Yes, of course but—"

"Delilah brought you here, which indicates she thinks very highly of you. She would not have done so otherwise."

"Perhaps." Sam nodded slowly. He hadn't quite thought of it that way but it was a nice idea.

"That said, I suspect you have earned her trust as well." Tate pinned Sam with a hard look. "And you now have mine."

"So you're asking me to lie to her?"

"Not at all. I am simply entrusting you with the means to ensure she receives everything she should. Everything that is rightfully hers. It's up to you to decide when or if she receives this information. I would suggest, however, that you might wait until this matter is resolved and in the past before you tell her everything."

Sam stared at him for a long moment. The man was right. There was no need for Delilah to know this. Any of it. At least, not at the moment. He ignored the thought that, regardless of how Tate chose to phrase it, Sam would indeed be lying to her.

"What do you want me to do?"

"Nothing especially difficult. Simply contact Delilah's solicitor and give him this information." Tate stood and moved to the large desk. "This will only take a moment." He sat down, selected a piece of paper, and threw Sam a quick glance. "Do pour yourself a brandy, Mr. Russell. My apologies for not offering earlier."

"Thank you." Sam spotted a decanter and a tray of glasses on the library table and headed toward it. He poured a glass and took a much-appreciated sip. When Delilah had offered to introduce him to her late husband's friend and partner, he had hoped for a bit of insight, perhaps some advice or suggestions. He certainly hadn't expected to have Delilah's fate put in his hands.

"This is the name and address of Delilah's solicitor as well as the name and address of the doctor Phillip regularly consulted here in London. That too he kept secret from her."

"He had a lot of secrets," Sam said under his breath.

"Don't we all in one way or another, Mr. Russell." Tate finished writing, slipped the page into an envelope, then stood and joined Sam. "I shall send a note round to the doctor in the morning, instructing him in my capacity as Lord Hargate's executor, to confide Phillip's condition to Delilah's solicitor upon request."

He accepted the envelope from the older man and slipped it into his breast coat pocket. "So I'm simply to instruct Lady Hargate's solicitor to contact the doctor?"

"Discreetly of course." Tate nodded. "But yes, that should do it."

"How should I say I came by this information?"

"Come now, Mr. Russell, you're an intelligent man. I daresay you can come up with something plausible." Tate poured a glass of brandy. "I know it seems silly to you, my desire to keep my distance. As much as I feel obligated to assist

Delilah, Phillip would expect no less, I have my own life to be concerned with."

"She is following his advice." Sam sipped his brandy. "She is looking for a new husband."

"Good." Tate nodded. "I wish her nothing but happiness. I was married once, years ago. Lovely woman. She died entirely too young." He paused. "I owe it to Phillip and to Delilah as well to help her. I'd marry her myself but she'd never have me."

"Nor is she your preference?" Sam said slowly.

"I'm afraid Phillip was the great love of my life. I only hope he wasn't the great love of hers." Tate sipped his brandy thoughtfully and said nothing for a few moments. "Love was not expected to enter into their marriage, you see. Oh, Phillip felt a certain measure of affection for her but he never anticipated that she would fall in love with him. He feared he had broken her heart. He felt dreadful about it."

Sam's heart twisted for her. "But not dreadful enough?"

Tate's gaze met his. "No." He shrugged. "As I said before, life is not fair. And matters of the heart are often the most unfair of all."

And didn't Sam know that from experience? "True enough."

"I don't know why I have told you all this. Although I suppose if I am asking you to help her, you deserve to know everything." He blew a long breath. "Now that that is settled, let us go back to consideration of your motorwagon. It seems to me the best way to reach our upper ten-thousand . . ."

Tate continued with a few further suggestions but Sam was hard-pressed to put these new revelations about Delilah out of his mind. Not simply the information about her husband, interesting though it was, but Tate's revelations put Delilah's comments about love with regard to marriage in an entirely new light. It made perfect sense that she was not interested in love when love had failed her before.

A knock sounded at the door and the butler entered at once. "I beg your pardon, sir, but I thought perhaps Lady Hargate might like some refreshment."

"Lady Hargate hasn't returned yet," Tate said with a quizzical frown.

"My apologies, sir, but she returned some time ago." The butler paused. "She said she was joining you."

Tate and Sam exchanged glances.

"I see," Tate said slowly. "That will be all, Bender."

"Yes, sir." The butler nodded and took his leave.

Tate waited until the door closed behind the servant. "Do you think she heard us?"

"If she hadn't, she would have come in." Sam downed the rest of his brandy and set the glass on the table.

"Good Lord, I didn't want her to know any of this." Tate rubbed a weary hand over his forehead. "Now what?"

"Now, I have to find her." Urgency sharpened his tone. Sam considered the other man. "You know her better than I; where do you think she would go?"

"I have no idea." His gaze met Sam's. "Do you think she heard all of it?"

"I suspect she heard enough," Sam said. Tate was right. Delilah would be devastated. How could she not be?

"We can only hope she didn't hear everything I suppose."

"If she didn't, she's either going to guess the rest or she'll be back to demand answers. The problem, Mr. Tate, with secrets of this magnitude, is that their revelation is often worse than the secret itself." He shook his head slowly. "The betrayal is in the not knowing."

Tate heaved a heartfelt sigh. "You're right of course."

"A more pressing question at the moment isn't so much what she heard." Sam's tone hardened. "The question is, where is she now?"

Chapter Thirteen

Sam tore up the steps to Delilah's front door. The sun was already setting and if she wasn't here he had no idea where to find her. He debated whether to pound on the door or ring the bell or just try to get in. The house was closed so there wouldn't be servants to answer the bell and Delilah might well ignore the door.

A crash sounded from somewhere inside just as he reached the door and urgency made the decision for him. He tried the door, found it unlocked, pushed it open, and strode into the spacious foyer. Her mantle had been dropped in a heap on an upholstered bench against the wall, her hat and the bag she had carried carelessly thrown on top. He tossed his hat aside to join hers and looked around. On one side of the foyer, a door was opened to a dining room. A second door—

Another crash rang out. He sprinted up a broad stairway, following the sound to the next floor and a parlor to the right. The furniture was shrouded in yards of fabric sheeting, the room itself shadowed and dim in spite of two lit gas lamps. Delilah stood by an open glass-front cabinet, a porcelain box in her hand. Similar boxes sat on the shelves in front of her. A rumpled pile of sheeting that had probably covered the cabinet had been tossed to one side. The remains of another box were scattered at her feet.

"Dee?"

She glanced at him, her brow furrowed. "Don't you have any manners? Surely even in America it's customary to knock before barging into someone's house."

"My apologies," he said cautiously and stepped farther into the room. She appeared remarkably calm. "I heard a crash and thought you might need help."

"Well, I don't." She studied the box in her hand. "I'm doing quite well by myself, thank you."

Entirely too calm. "What is that?"

"Phillip had a collection of antique porcelain snuffboxes. He was very fond of them." She hefted the box in her hand.

"I see." He wasn't sure exactly what he expected; the woman had sustained quite a shock after all. But calm, even serene, was definitely not it.

"Unfortunately, I seem to have broken one." She held the box at arm's length and released it. It shattered at her feet. She didn't so much as flinch. "Or two."

He glanced around the room. Shards of broken porcelain were on the floor by the fireplace, as well as by the far wall. "Or four?"

"Five I think." Her tone hardened and she reached for another box. "Thus far."

"They're very valuable, aren't they?" He'd certainly seen her lose her temper before but this was different. This was more than a little frightening.

"They were to him."

He cautiously moved closer to her. "Do you think this is a good idea?"

"What?" She stared at him. "This you mean?" She flung the box in her hand toward the fireplace. It hit the mantel and exploded into pieces. "Probably not." She drew a deep breath. "But it is most satisfying."

"Still, it doesn't do any good, does it?"

"Not in the scheme of things, I suppose." She selected another box. "But, oddly enough, with each one I shatter, I feel better."

The boxes were her property after all. If she wished to destroy them, she had that right. He shrugged. "Well then continue."

"I intend to." She cast him a wry glance. "But thank you for your permission."

"You don't need my permission although it does seem a shame."

"Because they're so lovely?" She looked at the one in her hand with contempt. "The craftsmanship so exquisite? The colors so vivid?"

"No, because I imagine they're worth a lot. You could sell them and use the proceeds for something completely frivolous and totally impractical."

"And yet I am enjoying this thoroughly."

"Ah well then." He gestured toward the collection. "Proceed."

"Besides, if I were to sell them, they'd no doubt go to someone who would love and cherish them. They've been loved quite enough." She hurled the box with a vengeance. It flew past him entirely too close to his head and he jerked to the side. The delicate porcelain shattered on the wall behind him. Fortunately, her aim was excellent.

"I see your point. However, if you are going to continue to do that, allow me to get out of your way." He pulled the dustcover off a sofa and sank into it. "Now, go on."

She stared at him. "You're really not going to stop me?"

He shook his head. "Absolutely not."

"Good." She turned back to the cabinet and considered the rows of remaining boxes. "Camille gave me the name of an investigator. I think the wisest course would be to give him the information Julian gave you and allow him to bring it to my solicitors."

Sam winced. "You heard it all then, didn't you?"

"I left at the point at which Julian said how very dreadful Phillip felt that he had broken my heart." She paused for a long moment. "Did I miss any-thing after that?"

"No."

"If I hadn't heard what Julian confided in you . . ." She looked at him. "Would you have told me?"

Now was not the time for games. "I don't know," he said simply. "On one hand, you deserve to know the truth. It is your life after all. On the other, does it do you any good to know?"

"I'm not sure I like your answer but it is honest. I'll give you that." She returned to her perusal of the boxes. "I married Phillip when I was eighteen. Aside from the obvious qualifications—"

"Fortune and title?"

She nodded. "Aside from those practicalities, he was handsome and dashing and charming. He was considered quite a catch. Julian was right, love was not expected. But I was young and not nearly as sensible as I am now. I suspect I was a little in love with him right from the beginning." She picked up a claret-colored box, her hand trembling slightly, and stared at it. "We did get on well together. We were perfectly suited after all." She cast him a hard look. "Aren't you going to say anything about that?"

"About how perfectly matched you were?" He shook his head. "Not a word."

"Very wise of you." She shifted the box from hand to hand. "We enjoyed much the same things. Entertaining, attending parties, going to the theater, art, fine clothes and fine furnishings. He liked chess and we would spend long hours playing together. He was very good and, after a while, so was I."

"Did you let him win?"

"No."

"Good, for a moment I thought I was talking to someone I'd never met."

"You'll have to do better than that if you're trying to annoy me." The barest hint of a reluctant smile played over her lips. "I was probably expected to let him win being the proper, perfect wife that I was. The proper, perfect wife he had, oh, purchased for lack of a better word." She threw the maroon box toward the fireplace to shatter and join the others. "Although that's not quite fair, is it?"

Sam wisely held his tongue.

"Trade is probably a more accurate word than purchase. I received a title and a fortune and he received the wife who had been brought up to be exactly what was expected. But then that is marriage, isn't it? It's a practical arrangement all in all. We both got exactly what we bargained for, really. For the most part.

"It didn't take me long to fall completely head over heels for him." She met Sam's gaze directly. "You have to understand, he was—"

"Perfect?"

"Yes. And all I had ever wanted. Or thought I wanted. Or had been trained to want." Her expression tightened. "We had been married nearly two years when I finally told him of my feelings. I poured out my heart to him. I thought, foolishly as it turned out, that it was only his natural reserve that had kept him from declaring his love for me. Because surely something that intense and wonderful was meant to be shared."

She stared at the remaining boxes neatly displayed on the shelves but made no effort to take one. For a long time she said nothing, then she drew a deep breath. "He was surprised, of course. Really rather shocked. He'd had no idea of my feelings. While he expressed affection for me, indeed he said he was quite fond of me, he told me in a kind but firm manner he was flattered but love was not what he wished for in marriage. He said companionship and a shared stewardship of his family heritage was what he wanted from a wife. Aside from all those other sterling qualities of mine of course, that all well-bred young women are expected to have."

Sam had no idea what to say. But he did have an irrational desire to fling one of the snuffboxes himself.

"I didn't believe him. I thought he was simply set in his ways. He had never been married before after all. So I set out to make him love me." She shook her head in disbelief. "I know, it sounds absurd."

His heart twisted for her. "Not at all."

"I was flirtatious with him and strived to be as

charming and delightful and enticing as possible. I kept up with current events and the latest gossip and everything that might interest him so that he would not be bored by my conversation. I became an accomplished hostess and I always looked my very best and, well, I did all I could to be . . ."

"Perfect?"

"Exactly. I even talked of plans for the children we would have. Can you imagine?"

"You had no idea—"

"And shouldn't I? Shouldn't I have suspected at least part of it?" She grabbed the closest box and flung it at the wall. "What a fool I was. I allowed myself to love him and I let him break my heart. I should have known. I should have been smarter." She clenched her hands by her side. She was visibly shaking now. "It wasn't long before he started spending more time at Hargate Hall than he did here, claiming he preferred the peace and solitude of the country and insisting that I stay in London. He said on more than one occasion that it would be unfair of him to demand I rusticate with him in the country as I so clearly loved all that London offered. It seemed so generous and thoughtful of him. Even then I hadn't quite given up hope of more than fondness between us.

"In the beginning, he came to London frequently and I went to the country just as often. But as time passed, it seemed harder and harder for him to manage to come into the city and I felt more and more out of place at Hargate Hall. Silly, as I am Lady Hargate. Of course . . ." The corners of her lips curved up in a mirthless smile. "Julian was usually with him." She paused. "He was there on the day Phillip died."

He studied her closely. Her air of calm was crumbling. "You're shaking, you know."

"Am I?" She held her trembling hands out in front of her and stared at them as if she had never seen them before. "Isn't that odd."

"Aside from that"—he nodded at her hands—"you don't appear nearly as angry as I thought you would be."

"Well, I've always been one for appearances. But make no mistake." Her eyes narrowed. "I am angry. I am furious." She turned on her heel and stalked from the room.

Sam jumped to his feet to follow her but she returned almost at once with a bottle in one hand and two glasses in the other.

"Scottish whisky. Excellent stuff." She thrust the bottle and glasses at him. "You should probably pour. I'm not sure I can do it."

"I know I would welcome a drink." He pulled a cover off a table, took the whisky and glasses from her, set them down, then poured a glass. "I'm not sure this is the best thing for you, however." He handed her the glass.

"On the contrary, my dear Samuel, I suspect this

is the very best thing for me." She accepted the glass and took a healthy swallow.

"I thought you didn't drink hard liquor?"

"Good Scottish whisky is scarcely hard liquor." She sniffed.

"It is in the rest of the world."

"Well, not in this house." She took another sip. "Phillip introduced me to it. We used to drink whisky while we played chess so I made certain there was always some kept here."

His brow rose. "He's been gone for three years and yet the whisky is still here?"

"Don't be absurd. It's not the same bottle." She took a long sip. "I don't drink it often but I like the way it burns my throat and warms my soul."

"I don't think it's your soul it's warming."

"My soul could use some warming." She stared into her glass. "I don't think I've ever been so angry with anyone. He should have told me."

"Yes, he should have."

"I don't understand why he didn't, really." A thoughtful note sounded in her voice as if she were looking into the past. "At least about not being able to have children. I could have understood that. I suspect it was pride more than anything that kept him silent on that score. But the rest of it . . ." She shook her head. "I never would have allowed myself to fall in love with him, you see, if I had known that he couldn't return my love." She lifted her glass to Sam. "I have always been a practical sort."

He smiled. "Not the type to be swept away by foolish emotions like love?"

"Not anymore. I do learn my lessons well." She raised her chin slightly. "I am as angry with myself I suppose as I am with him. I should have known or at least suspected. There were any number of clues but the thought never even crossed my mind. If I had known . . ."

"Would you have divorced him?"

"I don't know."

He shrugged. "His inability to have children would have been grounds enough I would think. Nothing else would have had to enter into it."

"Probably." She nodded. "It scarcely matters now. He's gone and I am . . . free." She took another long drink.

He studied her for a moment. "Do you feel better?"

"No." Her gaze met Sam's. "I am very nearly as sad as I am angry. Perhaps more so. Horribly, horribly sad." Her voice caught.

He set down his glass, took hers from her, and placed it beside his. "You need to sit down."

"I don't need—"

"Yes, you do," he said in a hard tone. "Your hands are still shaking and you look like your knees are going to collapse at any minute." He wrapped his arm around her and led her to the sofa.

"Nonsense," she muttered but sank down into the sofa nonetheless.

He returned her glass to her, took his, and sat down beside her.

"Is this what betrayal feels like, Sam?" An awful look of pain shone in her eyes and he resisted the urge to take her in his arms and comfort her. Now was not the time. "This dreadful overwhelming sorrow? This feeling of complete and utter loss?"

"I'm afraid so."

She drew a deep breath. "Might I confide something in you?" She smiled in a wry manner. "Although at this point, given all I've already said, asking might seem silly."

He smiled. "I am at your command."

She met his gaze directly. "I should like nothing better at this moment than to fling myself onto your very kind shoulder and weep."

"You can if you wish," he said gently.

"I'm afraid if I start I will never stop."

He paused. "It gets better, you know. The way you're feeling now. With time, the pain of betrayal fades although admittedly, the anger might linger."

"And you speak from experience?"

"Unfortunately."

"Ah yes." She took another sip and studied him curiously. "The former fiancée?"

He nodded.

"Tell me." She slumped back in the sofa, an

obvious indication that the emotion of the day coupled with the whisky was taking its toll.

"It's not all that interesting."

"Nonetheless, you now know all the most devastating secrets of my life." She wagged her finger at him. "It seems only fair that I know yours."

"All right." His story might help take her mind off hers. He gathered his thoughts. "Miss Lenore Stanley was, for all intents and purposes, well . . ." He slanted Delilah a quick smile. "Perfect."

She grimaced.

"Or I thought she was. She was beautiful and intelligent and exactly what I wanted in the woman I intended to spend the rest of my life with. My mother and hers were involved in the same social and cultural and charitable activities. Her family was well off. It was an excellent match according to the way the world views such things." He paused. "And I fell hard for her."

Delilah's eyes widened. "You loved her?"

"I did." He nodded.

"And therein lay your mistake," she said in a sage manner.

"Apparently." He thought for a moment. "As it turned out she was more interested in becoming Mrs. Samuel Russell than being my wife." He chuckled. "Which came to light when I discovered her in the arms of another man."

Delilah winced. "That is awkward."

"This was a few weeks before the wedding." He shrugged. "I allowed her to call it off, to save her embarrassment."

"How very gallant of you."

He glanced at her. "Sarcasm?"

"No, I mean it. If there is one thing I have noticed about you is that you're very gallant, like a knight of old. I didn't expect that."

"In an American?"

"No, in any man." Delilah raised her glass to him. "It's most appealing."

"Thank you," he said wryly.

"So, she broke your heart?"

"She did at that." He nodded. "Like you, I should have known. I should have seen the signs. Gray knew what kind of woman she was. He tried to warn me but I ignored him."

"I suppose we don't often see what we aren't looking for," she said softly, more to herself than to him. "Or perhaps what we don't want to see."

"It wouldn't have been so bad if she hadn't claimed that she loved me." He sipped his whisky. "So you see, I too have known betrayal. And, while it did take time, I recovered and I have learned my lesson. No more fortune hunters for me although admittedly, they aren't always easy to recognize."

"At least now you know what to look for."

"Hopefully." He nodded. "But I shall be smarter in the future."

"You don't just want a wife though, do you?" She studied him curiously.

"What do you mean?"

"You want love?" It was as much an accusation as a question.

He smiled. "Yes, I suppose I do."

"You want to fall in love?" She sat up and stared at him as if he had just grown another head. "Again?"

"It was quite wonderful while it lasted," he said mildly.

"Until your heart was left crushed and mangled beneath her fashionably shod heel."

"Admittedly, that was somewhat less than wonderful."

"Good Lord." She shook her head in disgust. "You're one of those romantic types, aren't you?"

"I suppose I am."

She rose unsteadily to her feet, accusation sounding in her voice. "Do you write poetry as well?"

He laughed and stood up. "I haven't yet. Nor have I ever felt the need to."

"That's something at any rate." Her brow furrowed and she took another swallow. "This is yet another area in which we differ."

"Oh?" He bit back a smile. "You write poetry then?"

"No, of course not. But you wish for love and I

intend to avoid it." She straightened her shoulders. "I will never make that mistake again."

"That's right, you never make the same mistake twice."

"Never." Resolve rang in her voice.

"I think you use the word *never* entirely too much. Never is an absolute and leaves no room for the unexpected." Without thinking, he grabbed her free hand, and pulled it palm-up to his lips. "And as you said today—life is full of surprises."

Her gaze met his. "Do you realize we have missed the last train?"

"Have we?" He lowered her hand but kept it held in his.

"We shall have to spend the night here." A challenge gleamed in her eyes. "Will you be sharing my bed?"

"My dear Dee, I would like nothing better." He took her glass and set it on the table. Then took her other hand in his. "But you're still distraught and more than a little tipsy, aren't you?"

She thought for a moment then nodded. "Possibly."

"Well then we do have a problem." He raised her hands to his lips and kissed them. "There is nothing I would like more than to spend the night with you by my side but unfortunately . . ." He heaved a reluctant sigh. "What kind of gallant knight would I be if I were to take advantage of you in this state?"

"Well, yes there is that. And we did agree not to. Still, I might be willing to ignore that." A wicked twinkle sparked in her eyes. "What if I were to take advantage of you?"

He laughed. "As tempting as that is, and you have no idea how tempting, I think it would be best if we retired separately tonight. And, as you said, we did agree that there would be no more of that sort of thing."

"Lord save me from men of honor," she said in a lofty manner and started for the doorway. She stopped and swiveled back to him. "The house is not closed up because I was off on a holiday. All the furniture upstairs is covered but there are blankets and sheets in chests." She aimed a pointed finger at him. "You shall have to make up your own bed, you know; there are no servants."

"I shall do my best," he said in a solemn manner. Now that she was standing, she was obviously more tipsy than he had thought. The whisky probably hadn't hit her until she got to her feet. Still, this would help her sleep, and didn't things always look better in the morning?

"You might have to make mine too. I'm not sure I have ever made up a bed." She made her way through the doorway and paused at the foot of the stairs. "I had to economize"—she shuddered at the word—"when my funds were cut off but I only closed the house right before I went to Millworth, a few weeks ago." She cast him a sly smile. "I had a secret cache of money I always kept for emergencies. My mother says one should always keep a hidden reserve because, as you know, men—"

"Are not to be trusted?"

"Exactly." She nodded. "And as much as I hate to admit it, my mother was right. And my secret fund allowed me to keep the house running as long as I could. When I couldn't, my bags were packed, and I let my servants go while assuring them I would take them back as soon as I could. Before they left, they threw dustcovers over everything." She sighed. "Everything is almost exactly as it was on the day I left."

"Then we should have no difficulty." He gestured at the stairs. "Shall we?"

She considered the stairway and frowned. "Odd, I don't remember it being quite this steep."

"Allow me to assist you." He swept her into his arms.

"My, you are gallant," she said with a grin.

"Not really." He flipped her over his shoulder, anchored her with one hand, and grabbed a lamp with the other. "But I do need to see where I'm going."

She giggled. He wasn't sure he'd ever heard her giggle before. It was shockingly delightful. Damnation, this woman was going to be his undoing.

"Which room?" he asked when he reached the top of the stairs.

"The second on the right," she murmured as if she could barely get out the words. He'd seen this kind of exhaustion before. The upheaval of intense emotion sapped the strength of even the strongest. That coupled with the whisky and he was surprised she had lasted this long.

"Here we are." He nudged open the door with his foot, set the lamp on a dresser, then stood her on her feet. "Good night, Dee."

"You can't leave yet." She huffed.

"Well, I'm not staying," he said in a sharper tone than he had intended.

She frowned at him. "Of course not. That would be . . . exceptionally improper. But a great deal of fun."

He clenched his teeth. "You're making this very difficult for me."

"Oh for goodness' sake, Sam." She rolled her gaze toward the ceiling. "I'm not going to accost you. Rip your clothes off with my teeth or something of that sort." She paused. "Interesting idea though."

"Dee!"

"Oh, don't be so stuffy. I'm the stuffy one, mired in tradition, remember? You're a proponent of progress and the future and all that nonsense. Why you're probably a great supporter of free love and that sort of thing."

He sucked in a sharp breath. "Lady Hargate!"

"I've shocked you, haven't I?"

"Free love?" He could barely choke out the words. "Where did you—"

"I read a great deal. All sorts of things that I should and any number of things that I probably shouldn't." She smirked. "I am exceptionally well informed."

He stared. "Apparently."

She smiled as if she knew a secret he did not. It was most unnerving. She turned her back to him. "Now then, if you would be so good as to unbutton my bodice and loosen my corset—"

"Delilah, I said I am not going to take advantage of you."

"Nor are you going to allow me to take advantage of you. As disappointing as that is, for both of us I might add, I don't have a maid here and if I am going to get any rest at all, I cannot do it in these clothes." She glanced at him over her shoulder. "Are you going to help me or not?"

"Yes, of course." He fumbled with her buttons then loosened the laces on her corset. "Done," he said with relief and stepped back.

She shrugged out of her sleeves, let her dress fall to the floor, and stepped out of it. Then she removed her corset and dropped it. He swallowed hard. How could any man still breathing possibly have resisted this?

She turned, now wearing nothing but a lace trimmed, sheer chemise, and matching drawers in a faint blush color. Or perhaps that was her. God, she was exquisite. A goddess come to life. She stepped toward him.

Sam had always prided himself on his willpower but right this very moment he had no idea where it might be. Nor did he care. He should leave. Right now. Before he lost his head. Before he started something they might both regret. Before she wrapped her arms around his and pressed her warm, supple body close to his. Before—

"Sam," she said softly and placed her hand in the middle of his chest. She pushed gently and he took a step back. "Good evening." She smiled and closed the door firmly in his face.

He drew a deep breath and ran his hand through his hair. Well, that was close. He wanted her but it was a mistake. At least tonight.

Without warning the door opened and she thrust the lamp at him. "You'll need this to find a room for yourself. Any one along this hallway should do." She nodded. "Sleep well." And the door closed once again.

What was the woman doing to him? He crossed the hall and pushed open the door directly across from hers. This would do well enough. Not that he imagined he'd manage to sleep. And if he did, no doubt, his dreams would be filled with her.

Dee, a goddess concealed by the barest whisper of a blush-colored chemise.

Delilah, Sampson's downfall.

It was going to be a long night.

Chapter Fourteen

Fourteen days before the wedding . . .

Tea. There would be tea in the kitchen. Surely she could figure out how to boil water for tea. And she desperately needed tea.

Delilah made her way carefully down the stairs, clinging to the handrail. She was not at all confident of her ability to descend the stairs without assistance. She hadn't had nearly enough whisky last night to make her feel this bad this morning and yet she felt dreadful. Her head throbbed and her stomach churned. Of course, she'd had a very large glass and nothing to eat either.

She'd certainly had enough whisky to loosen her tongue. Although admittedly most of what she had confided had been said before she'd had so much as a drop of liquor. Good Lord, the things she had said to Sam. She groaned. The personal, private, intimate things she had revealed. That might be at least partially to blame for how she felt this morning. That and all she had learned about Phillip. She rubbed her hand over her forehead. How had she been such a fool? Phillip's betrayal alone was certainly enough to make her head pound and her stomach lurch.

The faintest aroma of coffee drifted up from the ground floor. *Coffee?* Coffee would be so much better than tea. Had one of the servants returned?

She reached the first floor and glanced into the parlor. Pieces of broken snuffboxes littered the floor by the cabinet, more lay by the fireplace and by the far wall. Her housekeeper was not going to be at all pleased to return to the house and discover this mess. At least she would now have a job to return to thanks to Julian's revelations. It did seem a pity though. A good two-thirds of Phillip's collection remained untouched. Still, the day was young.

"You did do a good job in there," Sam said behind her.

"Not good enough." She turned around. He was dressed and obviously ready for the day. Indeed, the man looked astonishingly well rested and composed. It was most annoying. He held two steaming cups of coffee.

"I noticed you drank coffee." He offered her a cup. "I thought you could use this."

"Thank you." She accepted the cup gratefully and took a sip. It was strong and hot and bitter. She wrinkled her nose. "I prefer it with cream and sugar."

"I beg your pardon, Lady Hargate, but one works with what one has," he said in a passable imitation of a proper English butler.

"Don't let Clement hear you talk like that."

He chuckled. "There might be sugar but there are no perishables in the kitchen."

"Of course not." She took another sip. It was more bracing than it was bad. "You made this?"

"I told you, I was not born to great wealth. There have been times in my life when I have had to do for myself." He shrugged. "I lit a fire in the stove, found a pot, and brewed coffee. It wasn't hard."

"Hmph." She certainly couldn't have done it. Indeed, she'd have no idea where to begin.

His brow furrowed. "Have you ever been in your kitchen?"

"Of course I have." She scoffed. "Once or twice. It's scarcely necessary. I do have a cook, you know. Or at least I did."

"Well, you'll have her again, now that we have the information needed to resolve the problem of your inheritance." He studied her closely. "I think it would be a good idea if I brought that to your investigator while you . . ." His gaze skimmed over her. "Pulled yourself together. Then we can take the next train."

"Thank you, that would be . . ." She frowned. "What do you mean pull myself together?" She had managed to dress unassisted after all and thought she had done a fine job of it.

"Nothing," he said quickly. "Not a thing really but . . ."

"What?"

"Have you looked in a mirror?"

"Yes," she snapped. Actually the mirror in her room had been covered and she hadn't had the strength to pull off the sheeting but she had glanced in its general direction.

"You might wish to look again."

She patted her hair with her free hand. She hadn't taken it down before going to bed and it felt more than a little disheveled. Still, it was most annoying, even rude, for him to mention it. Although perhaps it was better for him to say something now than allow her to leave the house looking unkempt.

She clenched her teeth. "Thank you." She took another sip of the coffee. It really did improve her spirits and settle her stomach. Even so, she did need something to eat. "On your way back, should you run across a tea shop or even a baker's where you could perhaps procure a few biscuits or buns or anything at all, it would be most appreciated."

"Hungry, are we?"

"Very much so. Aren't you?"

"It was a long night."

She set her cup on a cloth-covered table and started down the stairs. "Did you have trouble sleeping?"

Behind her he paused. "I had a great deal on my mind."

Much better. He probably did not feel as good as he looked. It was vile of her, she knew, but that idea lifted her spirits a bit. And he did look delicious although she was probably just hungry. He no doubt regretted what he had told her about his past every bit as much as she regretted what she had said to him. And then there was the matter of her overly flirtatious manner toward him. She winced. If she had thought putting New York out of her mind had been next to impossible, forgetting about last night would be worse.

She found her bag, retrieved the note Camille had given her, and handed it to him. "This is the name and address of the investigator my sister recommended."

"Good." He nodded. "I'll be back as soon as possible." He smiled. "With food."

"One always does feel better without the ravages of hunger to contend with."

"My thoughts exactly."

She met his gaze and, without warning, the fear was back. Her heart skipped a beat. She had let him get entirely too close. She had revealed too much. She had opened herself up to him and that was a first step.

She would not go down that path.

Delilah drew a deep breath. "Before you go, you should know I was not inebriated last night and you shouldn't think I was."

"Oh, I would never think such a thing." His tone was solemn but laughter danced in his eyes.

She ignored it. "Admittedly, the whisky might have loosened my reserve and my tongue, but I clearly remember every word that was said. And everything that happened."

"And everything that didn't?"

"Yes," she said sharply. *Especially everything that didn't!* "And I think it would be best, for both of us I might add, if we, well, pretend it never happened."

"Nothing did happen," he said slowly.

"Yes, yes, I know." She waved off his comment. "I mean we should pretend that nothing was said."

"Because pretending has worked so well for us thus far?"

She glared at him. "You do insist on being stubborn, don't you?"

"I'm not being stubborn." His brows drew together. "I am being realistic. Practical, if you will."

"The practical thing is to forget everything you heard about my life last night. And I shall forget everything I learned about yours."

He stared at her for a long moment. "No."

"What do you mean—no?"

"I mean no. I will not forget anything about last night."

"Why on earth not?"

"I'm being honest with you, Dee." He met her gaze. "Oh, I can promise to pretend or forget or however you wish to phrase it but there is absolutely nothing on heaven or earth that will make me forget what you said or how devastated you were or how helpless that made me feel. Or how you trusted me enough to confide in me." He leaned closer and his gaze bored into hers. "Do you understand?"

She resisted the urge to step back. "Not really, no."

His eyes narrowed. "I won't make that promise to you because it would be a lie. It seems to me you have been lied to enough. The only promise I am willing to make is that I won't lie to you. If we are to be friends, that is the condition of my friendship."

"Oh." She stared at him. "Well . . ."

"At a loss for words?"

"So it would appear," she said under her breath. The man was an enigma. How could a man so gallant and charming one minute be so bloody annoying the next?

"Good." He nodded. "Then do something to yourself and I will be back shortly."

"Do you talk to your sisters that way?"

"Yes."

"I'm surprised one of them hasn't smothered you in your sleep by now," she said under her breath.

"*They* like me." He glanced at the note in his hand. "You do realize this means you can marry whomever you want."

"I've always intended to marry whomever I wanted."

"But you'll have your fortune back and you'll have no need to marry for money and a title or whatever."

She stared at him. Did he understand nothing? "One has nothing to do with the other."

His brow furrowed in confusion. "What?"

"Seeking an appropriate match has nothing to do with my own financial status. My plan as to what kind of man I will marry has been in place long before this difficulty arose. Regardless of the circumstances, I would never think of marrying anyone who did not meet my . . . my requirements."

Disbelief washed across his face. "So you still want another perfect husband?"

"Of course I do."

"Because that worked out so well for you the first time?" Sarcasm fairly dripped from his words.

She waved off his comment. "Phillip was unique. I can't imagine something like that happening again."

"And you never make the same mistake twice?"

"Yes!" She glared. "Never!"

His brow arched upward in a sarcastic manner.

"Well, never again!"

"So you don't intend to fall in love with this one?"

"Of course not. But I certainly don't intend to marry anyone I don't like. I do expect to feel a certain affection for him. After all, we will have a great deal in common. And ultimately, love is not a necessary ingredient for a good match."

"There are those who think it's the only necessary ingredient."

"Romantics." She snorted in disdain. "And you're one to talk to me about mistakes? You are actively seeking to make the same mistake again."

"Because I have not dismissed love out of hand? Because I realize there is more to life than money and position?"

"No, because you let your heart be broken once before and you're willing to take that risk again." Her voice rose. "Well, I am not!"

"No, you'd rather live in a dying world of manors and castles and pointless titles where tradition triumphs over progress and intelligence and committing one's life to someone for the rest of your days is completely devoid of all human emotion!"

She sucked in a hard breath. "That's not fair!"

"But it is accurate!" His voice grew louder.

"It is not! I said I intended to like him!"

"Well then, Lady Hargate, my apologies!" He glared. "I wish you the very best in your endeavors. Your fortune-hunting endeavors!"

"My, my." A familiar voice sounded from the front entry. "Look who has veered from the straight and narrow."

"What are you doing here?" Delilah snapped.

Her sister surveyed her from the open doorway. "I might ask you the same thing."

"Good morning, Camille," Sam said with a brusque nod.

"Not exactly." Beryl's gaze ran over Sam like a lioness appraising a fresh kill. "An American? How very interesting." Her gaze slid to her sister. "Who would have imagined."

"Does no one knock anymore?" Delilah glared.

"The door was unlocked," Beryl said mildly and closed the door behind her. "Foolish of you to be so forgetful."

"Probably my fault," Sam said under his breath.

"I would wager on it." Beryl cast him a knowing look.

And wasn't this just the perfect addition to the day? Beryl was the last person Delilah wanted to see at the moment. Or most moments for that matter. While she had grown closer to Camille in recent months, she and Beryl were still treading cautiously around each other.

Delilah drew a deep breath. "Sam, allow me to introduce my sister, Lady Dunwell. Beryl, this is Mr. Samuel Russell."

"Oh." Realization washed across his face. "Camille's twin. Yes, of course." Sam nodded. "Forgive me, Lady Dunwell, for my confusion. The resemblance to Lady Lydingham is remarkable."

"Mr. Russell is a business associate of Grayson's," Delilah said quickly, "as well as a good friend."

"I see." Beryl studied him with an appraising eye. "And has Grayson mentioned me?"

"Once or twice," Sam said, caution in his voice.

"Well, Grayson and I are not the best of friends so I won't be so foolish as to ask exactly what he has said." Beryl's gaze shifted to her sister. "Nor will I ask any of the other numerous questions that have sprung to mind. At least, not yet."

"But if you would be so good as to answer mine." Delilah crossed her arms over her chest. "Why are you here?"

"I'm here in my capacity as a loving and concerned older sister." Beryl coolly removed a glove and glanced around the foyer. "It has come to my attention that your house has been closed for several weeks. Not that you saw fit to confide that fact to me."

"I've been in the country." Delilah shrugged. "With Camille. Preparing for the wedding."

"Have you indeed?" Beryl raised a disbelieving brow. "Putting aside the fact that you've been gone several weeks by my estimate, which does seem rather a long time to prepare for a wedding that is still two weeks away, one does not routinely close up one's house and dismiss one's servants for a sojourn in the country."

"One might," Delilah said in a lofty manner. "On occasion."

"No, one doesn't, ever," Beryl said in a no-nonsense tone. "And, as much as I would like an explanation, that can wait for the moment." She pulled off her other glove. "As soon as I discovered that your house was closed, I made it a point to drive by daily to make certain the place had not been ransacked or burned to the ground. Which I did out of the goodness of my heart, I might add."

"And not rampant curiosity?" Delilah would wager all of Phillip's fortune on the latter.

"Oh, don't underestimate me, little sister. I could have pursued it further but I assumed if something dreadful had happened someone, probably Camille, possibly Mother, would have informed me. As you did not find it necessary to inform me yourself, I further assumed it was a private matter that you wished to keep private. I respect that, more or less. However . . ." Beryl's gaze pinned her sister's. "Your failure to take me into your confidence is not at all in the spirit of our efforts to become closer."

"Probably not," Delilah muttered.

"So you can see why, when in passing today, I noted a figure at one of the windows, I was compelled to investigate." She glanced at Sam. "At some risk to myself, I might add."

Sam nodded. "Very courageous of you."

"I thought so." She turned back to her sister. "Imagine my surprise when I approached the door and heard raised voices. One of which obviously belonged to you."

"It was a simple misunderstanding," Delilah said with a shrug.

Sam coughed.

"And I was worried that you were being attacked by an intruder." Beryl's speculative gaze shifted from her sister to Sam and back. "In spite of your less than presentable appearance I assume in that I was wrong."

Without thinking Delilah tried to smooth her hair back into place. "Yes, of course, nothing of the sort."

Beryl's gaze slid to Sam. "Pity."

Sam's expression remained noncommittal but there was a definite twinkle in his eye. Why the blasted man found Beryl amusing! How very . . . *male* of him!

"Now." Beryl adopted a pleasant, sisterly sort of smile. "Perhaps this would be a good time to confess all. Or . . ." Again her gaze settled on Sam. "I can leave and draw my own conclusions."

"Fine." It would be the height of stupidity to allow Beryl to draw her own conclusions. Delilah sighed. "I closed the house because of a financial problem. An unexpected difficulty."

"Obviously, the two of you have much to discuss and I have an errand." Sam picked up his hat and stepped to the door, glancing back at Delilah. "I'll return as quickly as possible and we can take the next train."

Delilah paused. "Thank you."

"Oh, and Mr. Russell, on your way, would you be so kind as to inform my driver that there is no need for alarm. He was prepared to come to my rescue if I found it necessary to scream for assistance." Beryl lowered her voice in a confidential manner. "Although the dear man is getting on in age and I daresay by the time he managed to so much as get out of the carriage, I would have been dead at the hands of some miscreant."

"I shall assure him that you are quite all right." That blasted twinkle was back in his eye. "Delighted to meet you, Lady Dunwell. No doubt we will be seeing each other again soon."

"You may count on that, Mr. Russell." Beryl smiled. "And I am quite looking forward to it."

Sam bit back a grin, nodded, and took his leave.

The moment the door closed behind him Delilah glared at her sister. "He meant at the wedding."

"Oh, I know what he meant."

"You were flirting with him."

"Why, yes, I suppose I was."

"I thought you didn't do that sort of thing anymore. I thought you were in love with your husband. I thought you and he had given up your . . . your *dalliances* and were now completely faithful to one another."

"Dear Lord." Beryl's brow furrowed. "It sounds dreadfully dull when you say it that way."

"Well?"

"Well what?"

"Well, you were flirting."

"Goodness, Delilah, I'm reformed not dead. A few flirtatious words are nothing to get in a snit about. It's not as if I threw him on the floor and had my way with him." She met her sister's gaze directly. "And you're scarcely one to talk. I've certainly seen you flirt. Why, if I recall correctly, you flirted quite a bit with Grayson this past Christmas."

Delilah ignored her. "I suppose you can't help yourself."

"Nor do I wish to." Beryl considered the other woman. "Now that we have thoroughly dissected my character or lack of it, do you care to tell me what is going on here?"

"Not especially." *Not at all!* "Can I avoid it?"

"Why, certainly you can, dear, if you want us to go back to being the kind of sisters who only see each other at weddings or funerals. Oh, Camille will be dreadfully upset and annoyed with both of us." She raised a shoulder in a nonchalant shrug. "And I have to admit I rather enjoy having a sister who seems to be a bit more like me in character than my identical twin."

Delilah started to protest then thought better of it. She blew a resigned breath. "What do you want to know?"

"All of it of course."

"Very well. But I do need to fix my hair."

"At the very least."

Delilah turned and started up the stairs, her sister at her heels. "I suppose I should start at the beginning."

"The beginning is always an excellent place to start although, on occasion, the end might be more interesting."

"The end?"

"The argument I interrupted sounded most interesting. Nearly as interesting as your some-what disheveled appearance and the fact that your bodice is misbuttoned."

Delilah reached her hand around to feel her buttons and winced. "That's how they're wearing them in Paris."

"Odd, I hadn't heard that."

"I don't have a maid here," Delilah added. "I had to do it myself."

Behind her, Beryl heaved a long-suffering sigh. "My dear little sister, one must always insist a gentleman assist in re-dressing. It's a cardinal rule of indiscretion."

"There was no indiscretion," she said sharply. At least not last night. "Nothing happened."

"Perhaps that's why you were both in such a

309

foul mood." They reached the first floor and Beryl glanced at the doorway into the parlor then drew up short and stared. "What on earth happened here?"

"A minor accident." Delilah waved off the question. "Nothing of significance."

"An accident?" Beryl stepped into the parlor and scanned the room. "It doesn't look like an accident." She crossed the room to the cabinet, bent down, and picked up a large piece of porcelain. Her gaze shifted from the piece in her hand to the remaining snuffboxes. "Indeed, I would suspect it was more in the manner of . . ." She met her sister's gaze. "Vengeance?"

Delilah shrugged.

"This financial difficulty of yours. If I had to guess, as apparently I do since you are not being nearly as forthcoming as you should, I would surmise that it had something to do with a late husband. A late husband who was perhaps fond of very expensive antique snuffboxes. How accurate would that supposition be?"

"Fairly."

Beryl's brow rose.

"Very accurate then." Delilah sighed.

She didn't know why she resisted telling Beryl everything. Camille would surely tell her after all. But when she had revealed her financial problem to Camille, she hadn't felt like quite as much of an idiot as she felt today. And, even though she and

Beryl still weren't particularly close, she did hate for this sister to think poorly of her. Regardless, it appeared she had no choice. She drew a deep breath.

"About six weeks ago a claim was made against Phillip's estate by a man who claimed to be his heir. My accounts were unavailable to me until a determination as to the validity of the claim could be ascertained." She shrugged. "That's it, really."

"I see." Beryl gestured with the piece in her hand. "And this is because your late husband had an heir you knew nothing about?"

"No, this is because I learned Phillip couldn't have an heir because Phillip was unable to have children at all." There was no need to tell Beryl the rest of it.

"And you didn't know?"

"I had no idea."

"But this does solve the problem of the claim against the estate?"

"I hope so."

"That's something anyway." Beryl placed the broken piece on the shelf. "I must say, though, I admire your restraint."

"My restraint?"

"Indeed." Understanding glimmered in Beryl's eyes. "I would have broken them all."

Delilah smiled reluctantly. "I may not be finished."

"That explains the mess but not the American."

"He is much easier to explain." She shrugged. "Mr. Russell accompanied me from Millworth. He had business to attend to here and I needed to meet with my solicitor."

"And?"

"And, that's all there is to it."

Beryl's brow rose in a skeptical manner.

"Good Lord, Beryl, there's really nothing more to it than that." She heaved a frustrated sigh. "I was upset over learning the truth about Phillip even though it does mean my life will soon be back to normal. We stayed here longer than we should have and missed the last train so we spent the night. In separate rooms," she added.

"Excellent explanation, dear, as far as it goes." Beryl settled on the sofa and smiled pleasantly, as if they were about to take tea or something equally innocuous. "Yet nothing you have said explains why he was accusing you of marrying for financial gain and why you think he's a foolish romantic who is bound to have his heart broken. Again apparently."

Delilah stared. "How much did you hear?"

"Quite a lot." Beryl shook her head. "It seemed rude to interrupt as you were both so passionate. And I do hate to be rude."

"Then you know everything," Delilah snapped.

"Oh, I don't believe I do." Beryl studied her sister closely. "There's more between you and the ever so dashing Mr. Russell than you are letting on."

"Not really." Delilah sat down beside her sister. "We simply clashed upon our initial meeting, that's all. Now we have agreed to be friends."

"My dear, dear little sister." Beryl shook her head in a mournful manner. "I don't believe a word of that. One does not discuss reasons for marriage at the top of one's lungs with a mere friend. And certainly not a male friend. There's more to it than you're saying."

"Don't be absurd."

"I'm not. I am shockingly perceptive. And very persistent. I do not give up easily." She paused. "And while I do enjoy a juicy tidbit of gossip, when it comes to something very important, popular opinion aside, I can keep a secret."

"There isn't . . ." Delilah studied her sister. "Can you really?"

"It has always seemed to me that the first step to a solid relationship be that with a man or a woman or a sister, is trust." She leaned toward Delilah and met her gaze directly. "You've had no reason to trust me in the past but no reason not to trust me either as we have never shared confidences before. As your sister, I'm asking you to trust me now." She smiled. "If one only has two sisters it does seem a pity to squander one." A gleam of amusement sparked in her blue eyes. "And the more interesting one at that."

Delilah stared at her for a long moment. Why not? "Oh, very well then." Besides, she was tired of having no one to talk to about Sam other than herself. "You do understand I have told no one this."

"Those are the very best kind of secrets."

Delilah drew a deep breath. "I first met him in New York. We had a . . . an adventure together, if you will."

"You?" Surprise rang in Beryl's voice.

"This is not going to go well if you're going to be shocked by everything I say," Delilah said sharply.

"I daresay I won't be shocked by everything now that the initial shock is over." Beryl shook her head. "I simply didn't expect this sort of revelation from you." Her brow furrowed. "I am assuming when you say *adventure* you mean of the amorous kind?"

Delilah nodded. "I'd never been with anyone besides Phillip before so it was quite, well, a revelation."

"A revelation?"

"Are you shocked again?"

"Not yet but do go on." Beryl cleared her throat. "A revelation, you say?"

Delilah continued, the words coming faster almost of their own accord. "Well, yes. But that was certainly not the sort of thing I do. Of course, I expected never to see him again. After all an adventure should be finite. And indeed, I told him I had no desire to see him again. Surely you understand?"

"I suppose. But never when the adventure was a revelation."

"Although admittedly, he didn't appear to feel the same but he did agree. So you can imagine my shock when he appeared at Millworth without warning for Camille's wedding with an absurd business proposal about horseless carriages and a very, well, smug attitude. The man can be most annoying."

"He does seem to have that potential," Beryl said thoughtfully. "It's the amused look in his eye I think."

"But he is awfully nice as well, which is also oddly annoying." Delilah leaned closer to her sister. "I was dreadful to him at Millworth, very nearly rude most of the time. And I thought I should apologize and try to be nicer. So I went to his room and . . ."

Beryl's eyes widened. "Oh my."

"Oh my is something of an understatement I'm afraid." She sighed. "You and I have much more in common than I had ever dreamed."

"My apologies," Beryl murmured.

"It's not your fault." Delilah waved off her sister's comment. "It must run in the blood. But we did agree, Sam and I, that it would not happen again. Which does seem best, all in all."

"And last night?"

"I said nothing happened. But . . ." She buried her face in her hands. "I wanted it to."

"And he didn't?"

"Oh no, he did." Her words were muffled by her hands but she wasn't quite ready to see the knowing look in her sister's eyes. "But I had had a bit too much to drink and he said he would not take advantage . . ."

"The beast," Beryl murmured.

"He was a perfect gentleman."

"One could say that was good and bad news, I suppose."

Delilah lifted her head. "He is a decent sort, really, for an American."

"Will wonders never cease?"

"And he is proving to be an excellent friend."

"That's something."

"I suppose."

"One more thing—" Beryl paused. "You said you and Mr. Russell—"

"Sam." She sighed. "His friends call him Sam."

"Didn't you have a dog named Sam?"

"I did." She stared at her sister. "I can't believe you remembered."

"No one ever gives me credit for being thoughtful." Beryl sniffed. "As I was saying, you and Sam agreed that it would never happen again. So the question is—is that what you want?"

"Absolutely." Delilah paused. "Why would you think otherwise?"

"Just idle curiosity. There does seem to be something between you."

"There isn't, not really," she said firmly. "Admittedly, I have not been able to get him out of my mind since New York but . . . ."

"But?"

"I find him frightening."

Beryl frowned. "Because you can't get him out of your head?"

"Partially. And he makes me feel . . . things." She absently picked at a bit of lint on her dress. "You see, I fell in love with Phillip and he, well, it sounds so trite and rather pathetic really."

"Go on."

"He didn't share my feelings. And he broke my heart." She raised her chin. "I will not allow that to happen again."

"I see." A sage note sounded in Beryl's voice.

"What do you see?"

"Well, from what you have said, and from what I overheard, your Mr. Russell thinks the main reason for marriage should be love. And you have a more practical view of the matter."

"Indeed I do." She drew a deep breath. "It simply seems to me that if two people who are completely perfect for each other cannot find love then love between two people who have nothing in common is out of the question. And one if not both hearts will surely be broken."

"My, that is practical of you."

"Thank you."

"Although, one of the difficulties with love is that it tends not to be the least bit practical." Beryl studied her closely. "Are you in love with him?"

"No, of course not. That would be absurd and foolish and an enormous mistake."

"We wouldn't want that," Beryl murmured.

"Exactly." Delilah shook her head. "Good Lord, Beryl I have never met any man who was so completely wrong for me. Love does not conquer all, you know."

"I suppose not." Beryl considered her sister for a moment. "I may not be one to talk given that neither of my marriages were for love. When I married my first husband, I married for the reasons we were all expected to marry. But Charles was a charming man and I did love him even if I was not in love with him. Do you understand the difference?"

Delilah nodded.

"I married Lionel for similar reasons. Title, money, ambition. He will be prime minister one day, you know."

"Yes, you've mentioned that." Over and over and over again. Beryl's ambition for her husband matched his own.

"We were both living our own lives really,

having any number of well, adventures, and then the oddest thing happened." A smile that might well be called sweet on anyone else curved Beryl's lips. "One minute were we amicable companions and the next . . ." Her gaze met Delilah's. "We realized we couldn't live without each other. We further discovered we preferred adventure with each other rather than with other people. It was shocking and utterly wonderful. Love caught us entirely unawares." She shrugged, as if somewhat embarrassed by the revelation.

"But you and Lionel are not from completely different worlds," Delilah pointed out. "Why, if any two people were expected to find love one would anticipate it would be the two of you."

"Perhaps." Beryl chose her words with care. "Still, one of the most marvelous things about love is that it is completely unexpected."

"Nonetheless, I am neither in love with Sam, nor do I intend to allow that to happen."

"If you aren't already?"

"I'm most definitely not." Delilah ignored a stab of doubt and set her chin. "My plan is to marry again for practical reasons. Precisely as you did."

"I'm not sure I would advise following in my footsteps, although my life has turned out to be better than I could have imagined. We all have to tread our own paths, Delilah."

"Exactly as I am doing."

"Very well then, you certainly don't need advice

from me." She reached out and patted her sister's hand. "However, I do so love giving advice and I am very good at it, so don't hesitate to come to me again. I plan on being at Millworth within the week. Perhaps sooner now that I can see how very much I am needed." She cast her sister a smug smile. "You can't get this kind of advice from Camille, you know."

"And you won't tell her about this?"

"Absolutely not." Beryl huffed with indignation. "I gave you my word after all not to repeat any of this to anyone. Although admittedly, if Camille were to say to me directly, 'Did you know that Delilah is in love with Mr. Russell?' why I would hate to lie to her."

"I never said that," Delilah said quickly, then realized her mistake. "I mean I'm not in love with him."

"Of course not. That would be foolish."

"It would indeed."

Beryl nodded. "And absurd."

"Completely."

"Not to mention an enormous mistake."

"Without question."

"Still, you have made other mistakes," Beryl said thoughtfully.

"Who hasn't?"

"Falling in love with him isn't your worst."

"No, of course not. It's . . ."

Beryl arched a knowing brow.

"That was a . . ." Delilah searched for the right word.

"Let's just call it something you did not intend to admit, shall we? Not to me and certainly not to yourself." Beryl studied her sister for a long moment. "There is one thing you should keep in mind, however."

Delilah sighed. "And what is that?"

"The very best adventures, my dear sister." Beryl smiled. "Are those that never end."

Chapter Fifteen

"Good day, Lady Hargate, Mr. Russell." William greeted Delilah and Sam at Millworth's front door. The young footman had a definite harried air about him. "Welcome home."

"Good day, William." Sam nodded a greeting. It wasn't the most he'd said all day but it was close.

His visit to the investigator's had been uneventful but, aside from telling her that, he'd had very little to say on the trip back from London. She'd made no effort to converse with him either; there was entirely too much on her mind. Her conversation with Beryl kept repeating itself in her head. All she'd said and all she'd almost said and what any of it meant. If indeed it meant anything at all. And she was more confused than ever.

Not that she had time to dwell on that. First, she had to come up with a plausible explanation as to why she and Sam had stayed the night in London.

"Thank you, William." Delilah handed him her mantle and glanced around the grand foyer. The house struck her as oddly quiet. "Where is Clement?"

William chose his words with care. "I'm afraid there has been a bit of a mishap, my lady."

Her breath caught. "Has something happened to Clement?"

"Something has happened to nearly everyone." William winced. "Except for myself of course, and three of the maids and Mr. Moore seems fine but then he isn't staying at the manor and he did eat in the village yesterday. The grooms and gardeners are unaffected as well but they rarely take their meals at the house—"

"When you say mishap, what exactly do you mean?" Sam said cautiously.

"It was something they ate last night, sir," William said. "All of them. We're not entirely sure what it was but it seems to have affected everyone including most of the house staff. It was a bad night, sir." He grimaced. "A very bad night for all of them. As I said, only three of the housemaids and myself were unaffected, or we didn't eat whatever caused the problem, we're not sure, but then my mother always said I had a constitution made of iron and it does appear—"

"What about my sister? And Lady Theodosia and Mr. Elliott?" Delilah stared at the footman. "Are they all right?"

"They will be." William nodded. "The doctor came from the village last night. He said the worst was over and once everything was out of their systems, they should all be fine. And I believe everything is." He grimaced. "While they all seem much better today, he said they'd probably sleep through today and most of tomorrow—getting their strength back and all—but they should be able to be up and about by the day after. He left a note with instructions and he will be round later today.

"When last we checked, everyone was asleep." He lowered his voice. "It has been an exceptionally long night, Lady Hargate. Especially with only myself, Jenny, Mildred, and Margaret to attend to everyone. But we have made it through." He squared his shoulders. "Clement issued some instructions from his bed—"

"I don't recall Clement ever taking to his bed before," Delilah murmured. "He must have felt dreadful."

"You have no idea, my lady." William shuddered. "He directed me to get some girls in from the village to assist us and they were here all morning but unfortunately they could not stay. Although they might be able to come back tomorrow should we need them."

"I suspect we will need them, given that everyone else is abed." She paused. "I assume Mrs. Dooley was stricken as well."

William nodded. "I'm afraid so."

"So there is no one to cook?"

Sam leaned close and spoke into her ear. "You've never been in this kitchen either, have you?"

"Of course I have." She huffed. "Not since I was a child but I have been there."

"Mrs. Dooley had us dispose of anything left

from last night's meals. Deliveries are not expected until tomorrow. However, there are cold meats and breads in the pantry and larder. We have eaten from those stores with no ill effects," William added.

"That's something anyway." Sam looked at her. "I assume you're hungry."

"We've scarcely eaten anything at all today, in case you've forgotten," she said in as cool a manner as she could muster. Of course she was hungry but he needn't say it as if there were something wrong with being hungry. Although she could be reading more into his comment than was really there. She did tend to do that with him. She drew a deep breath. "I should look in on them, my sister and Lady Theodosia and Mr. Elliott, that is."

"Jenny and Mildred have been attending to the ladies, I have been seeing to Mr. Elliott's needs," William said. "And we have all been caring for the rest of the staff."

"No wonder you look so tired." Delilah cast the footman a sympathetic smile.

"It appears that you've done an excellent job of managing this crisis, William," Sam said.

"I was recently promoted to underbutler," the young man said with pride. "I hope to be a butler some day, sir."

"I'm sure you'll be more than up to the job." Sam smiled. "Especially given how well you're surviving this trial by fire."

"It has been challenging, sir."

"I shall also look in on Clement and Mrs. Dooley and Mrs. Carter of course." She glanced at Sam. "The housekeeper."

He nodded then turned to the footman.

"I beg your pardon, Lady Hargate," William began. "But Mr. Clement, well, he wouldn't, that is . . ."

"He would be embarrassed, wouldn't he?" She should have realized it herself.

"Yes, my lady." The footman nodded with relief.

"Then we shall leave care of the staff in your capable hands, at least for today. Mr. Russell and I will see to the needs of the others."

He nodded. "Yes, my lady."

"William, if you will direct me to the kitchen, I'll see what I can find for Lady Hargate and myself to eat."

"Oh no, sir. I couldn't possibly permit that." William paled. "I shall see to it myself."

"Don't be absurd," Sam said. "You're obviously exhausted and Lady Hargate and I are more than capable of fending for ourselves." He glanced at her. "Aren't we?"

"Absolutely." Although when had she ever fended for herself? She forced a note of resolve to her voice. "It is a crisis after all and we should all do our part."

"I knew you'd agree." A distinct challenge shone in Sam's eyes. It was most annoying.

She squared her shoulders. "Then I shall check on the others and join you shortly."

Sam nodded at the footman. "Would you give us a minute, William?"

"Of course, sir," William said. "I shall wait for you in the dining room."

"Thank you." Sam smiled and waited until William took his leave. "How many servants are there at Millworth? On the house staff, that is."

"I have no idea. I don't really live here, you know." She thought for a moment then counted the numbers off on her fingers. "There's Clement, Mrs. Dooley and her assistant, Mrs. Carter and the under-housekeeper, a kitchen maid, five housemaids I think, three footmen not including William, my personal maid as well as Teddy's and Camille's, Grayson's valet . . . That's all I can think of but I may have missed someone."

"So, by my count that means there are at least twenty people in the house who have been stricken." He pinned her with a firm look. "And only six of us to see to their needs."

"That does seem insurmountable." *Insurmountable?* Ha! Why, she'd never had to take care of anyone who was ill before in her entire life. The very idea was as foreign to her as, well, the making of coffee. Even so, she absolutely refused to give him the satisfaction of knowing how completely useless she was at this sort of thing. "And yet, there is no choice." She started for the stairs. "I shall check on Camille, Teddy, and Grayson while you find something for us to eat."

"You know, there is a good side to this."

"Good Lord, are you always so optimistic?" She turned and glared at him. "It's incredibly annoying."

"Good," he snapped. "I'm not being optimistic, I'm being realistic."

"Well then please, do go on."

"If everyone was stricken last night, then they probably have no idea that we were not here. Which means there will be no questions about why we didn't return until today. And no speculation as to what we might have done."

"We didn't *do* anything!" She huffed. "But you're right." She nodded. "I hadn't thought of that. There's really no one to say when we did or did not arrive."

"It's not as if we planned this." He shrugged. "But it does work to our advantage."

"I do appreciate you pointing it out. Thank you." She nodded and started up the stairs.

"Delilah?"

She paused in midstep and looked at him. "What is it now?"

"Do you have any idea what you're doing?"

"Absolutely not." She lifted her chin and continued up the stairway. "But, I daresay, we didn't get to be the greatest empire the world has ever seen by knowing what we were doing every minute. Goodness, Sam, where would be the adventure in that?"

She didn't have to look back to know that infectious grin of his was back on his handsome face. She bit back a grin of her own. No matter what other feelings she might have about the man she did indeed like him. And he did make her laugh. There was something to be said for that.

Delilah reached Camille's door and paused to gather her courage. She'd never been around people who were ill. Her family had always been remarkably healthy. Indeed, she couldn't remember the last time she had been indisposed. The whole idea of illness struck her as unpleasant and rather messy. Still, there was nothing to be done about it but bravely carry on. She drew a deep breath and opened the door.

William was right. Camille was sleeping and quite soundly judging from the faint snorting sounds coming from her bed. Delilah quietly moved to her sister's bedside then rested her hand gently on her forehead. She was a bit clammy but not hot. It seemed like a good sign.

Teddy felt much the same but her eyes fluttered open at Delilah's touch.

"Where have you been?" she croaked.

"London, of course."

Teddy waved in the direction of the pitcher on the table beside her bed. "Thirsty."

Delilah poured her a glass then helped her sit up.

Teddy took a few sips then slid back down. "All night?"

"All night what?"

"You were in London all night?"

"Don't be absurd." Delilah replaced the glass on the nightstand. "What would I be doing in London all night? You were probably dreaming." When she looked again, her friend was fortunately already back to sleep.

Checking on Grayson proved a bit more awkward. The man was obviously a restless sleeper. One foot was flung over the side of the bed, his covers were bunched around his waist exposing his bare chest. Oh my, did the man sleep in anything at all? Not that it wasn't an attractive sight although she much preferred Sam's naked chest. Why, she had no desire at all to run her hand over Grayson's naked chest. If it had been Sam lying here—

Dear Lord! The thought jerked her upright. Sam wasn't the only one with only one thing on his mind. She had other matters to attend to at the moment and the thought of Sam naked and hot and . . . Well, this simply wasn't the time. Besides, they'd agreed it would not happen again.

Delilah carefully straightened Grayson's covers, felt his forehead, and decided it would be wise for Sam to be the one to check on his friend from now on. She and the three unaffected maids would see to Camille and Teddy and the female staff. It was decidedly improper otherwise. She heaved a heartfelt sigh. Why she continued to concern herself with propriety at all made no sense. She was beginning to suspect she had a heretofore unknown penchant for impropriety that had somehow been released by a voyage to America and, of course, the American who had shared her thoroughly improper adventure.

By the time Delilah joined Sam in the kitchen, she had a fair measure of confidence. Why, she could pat foreheads and dispense sips of water with the best of them. She would certainly never become a nurse of course. Indeed, she sent a silent prayer of thanks heavenward that she had not been here last night. She didn't think she could have handled last night.

She pulled a stool up to the large kitchen worktable and sat down. The kitchen was smaller than she remembered but warm and cozy. And oddly comforting.

"Coffee." Sam set a cup before her.

"Thank you." She took a sip. Her brow rose. "With cream and sugar?"

"That's how you take it," he said coolly. "William says everyone is asleep and I told him he and Jenny, Mildred, and Margaret should take this opportunity to get some rest."

She nodded. "I would hate to lose them to exhaustion."

"How would we bear up?" He picked up two

plates from a side counter and sat them down on the table. "And I made sandwiches."

She stared at the enormous slices of bread blanketing equally large pieces of cold roast beef. He plunked a mustard pot on the table, pulled up another stool, sat down, and slathered mustard on his sandwich. Delilah wasn't sure she'd ever seen sandwiches quite this huge. She was more used to the delicate little things her cook made for tea with watercress and cucumbers. This was obviously a man's sandwich. And an American man's at that.

Sam picked up his sandwich, started to take a bite, then hesitated and stared at her. "Is it all right?"

"Well, yes, it looks wonderful. I'm simply not sure where to start." She stared at the massive offering. "It's so . . . big."

"I thought you were hungry?"

"I am but . . ." Her stomach chose that moment to growl in a most embarrassing manner.

"But?"

"But . . . nothing." She shook her head, picked up the top piece of bread, and spread it with mustard. "It looks wonderful. Thank you." She took a bite and wondered that she didn't moan out loud. "Oh my, that is delicious."

"Probably because you were so hungry." He took a bite and nodded. "But I do make a fine sandwich."

They ate in silence for a few minutes.

"There's something we should talk about," he said at last.

"No, there isn't," she said quickly. "I see no need to discuss last night or this morning for that matter. We simply see things differently. We have different plans for our lives. There's really nothing to discuss." She took a sip of coffee. "I am sorry that I raised my voice this morning but then so did you. And I am sorry that I allowed things to get out of hand but again, so did you and it does seem to me that you and I are equally at fault. Furthermore"—she drew a deep breath—"I really wish you would stop being so, well, angry with me. I find I miss your admittedly interesting conversation and even your sarcasm and I'm not at all enjoying the decidedly cool manner you've had toward me since this morning."

He stared at her.

"Well?"

"Well what?"

"Well, say something."

"I'm sorry?" He shook his head. "As interesting as your confession was, it's not what I wanted to discuss."

"Oh." She nodded slowly. "Well, that's good then."

"Although I would like to talk about it all at some point."

"I really don't—"

"Because as your *friend,* I think it's my responsibility to convince you of the error of your ways."

"Oh, come now, I scarcely think—"

"A *friend* would not stand idly by and watch his *friend* throw herself over a cliff without trying to stop her."

"You have no—"

"A cliff she had thrown herself off once before."

"This is not—"

"However." He held up his hand to quiet her. "At the moment, we have more pressing matters."

"We do?" What was more pressing than his arrogant attitude about her life?

"Given that everyone has been, well, poisoned for lack of a better word, yes, we have a great deal to discuss."

"Yes, of course." Now was certainly not the time to discuss the differences between them. Actually, never seemed like the best time.

"William suggested we send a note to Fairborough Hall and see if they could spare their cook's assistant or any of their servants for the next few days."

"That's a brilliant idea." William was going to make an excellent butler one day. "I shall write a note as soon as we're finished eating and one of the grooms can take it at once."

"Hopefully, we can get some help." He shook his head. "In spite of your admiration of my culinary prowess, I'm afraid coffee and sandwiches are the limits of my skills in the kitchen. And everyone here is going to need sustenance tomorrow. According to the doctor's note, they'll need tea and toast, which I can probably manage but then they'll want real food. Broth and then a light soup he said to start with." Sam grimaced. "I have no idea how to make that." He eyed her skeptically. "Do you?"

"Come now, Sam, you know the answer to that." She took another bite of her sandwich and chewed thoughtfully. "I've never really given much thought to what goes on in the kitchen. Only to what comes out of it." She smirked. "I have an excellent cook. Or I did."

"And you will again." He smiled.

She sighed. "I do hope so."

"And while we're on the subject of cooks, William mentioned something about a party?"

"Good Lord, I had forgotten." She wrinkled her nose. "There's something, dinner and cards I think, planned for the day after tomorrow. Even if everyone is back to normal by then they certainly won't be up to having guests. We'll have to cancel it." She thought for a moment. "When Teddy awakens, I'll get a list of who has been invited. We'll have to send out notes, we can have the grooms and gardeners deliver them." She drew her brows together. "I imagine there might be a few people from London invited, we shall have to contact them as well. You might need to run back into town for that."

He nodded.

"I do wish we had a telephone here." She drummed her fingers on the table. "It would make this much easier."

He stared at her. "A what?"

"A telephone." She should have known he would catch that.

"But that's so . . . so progressive."

"Yes, well, it's also terribly convenient. A number of people I know in London have them. Why, the queen herself has a telephone." She met his gaze directly. "I'm not completely opposed to progress, Sam."

"Imagine that." He studied her closely. "And here I thought you were."

"Well you were wrong. Indeed there are some areas in which I not only see certain benefits but I quite welcome them."

"Areas which do not include motorwagons."

"Of course not." She shrugged. "I am not taking my life in my hands when I use a telephone. Nor am I relegating a noble beast to certain extinction. I'll tell you something else, Mr. Russell."

He gestured in a magnanimous manner. "Please do. I can hardly wait."

"I have given serious consideration to the installation in my house in London of . . ." She cast him a smug smile. "Electricity."

He gasped and clapped his hand over his heart. "Oh no, not that! What will the neighbors say?"

"The neighbors are interested in it as well. It's not necessary to completely abandon tradition and all that one holds dear in order to embrace the conveniences offered by modern life. We are nearing the twentieth century after all."

"My, my, how very forward thinking of them."

"You needn't be sarcastic," she said coolly. "It's most unbecoming."

"You like my sarcasm."

"Not always."

"But that wasn't sarcasm." He grinned. "That was nothing less than smug superiority."

"Enjoy it while you can." She pushed her plate aside—she couldn't eat another bite—folded her hands on the table, and smiled in as pleasant a manner as she could muster. "And how is your motorwagon?"

His expression fell. The tiniest twinge of guilt stabbed her. She tried to ignore it; after all the man had deserved what he had gotten. Still, this was important to him and she suspected the motorwagon's failure to run weighed on his mind. It wasn't at all nice and really beneath her to use his vehicle's problems as a weapon against him.

Sam shook his head, his manner abruptly serious. "I don't know. I haven't had a chance to talk to Jim yet."

"Why don't you find Mr. Moore and see if the problem has been resolved."

"Are you sure?"

"Absolutely." She nodded. "Everything seems to be well in hand for the moment, although I daresay that will change when everyone starts feeling better. Hopefully we'll have more help by then. So you should take this opportunity to check on your motorwagon." She cast him an encouraging smile. "I shall write a note to Lady Fairborough and begin the notes cancelling the party. I'll add the names later."

"That sounds like a plan."

"It is," she said smugly. "There is nothing like a plan to make one feel life is once again under control."

He chuckled and got to his feet. "I won't be long." He started to leave then stopped and studied her. "You are the most confusing woman I have ever known."

"Why thank you, Sam. How very kind of you to say so."

"It's not really a compliment."

She smiled. "I didn't think it was."

"But it's not a criticism either."

"Simply an observation?"

He nodded. "One minute you're completely helpless and the next you have the entire world under control."

She sipped her coffee and smiled. "Again, thank you."

"What I don't understand, well, one of the many things I don't understand about you is why someone as intelligent as you are and as willing to accept progress—"

"In certain areas," she pointed out.

"Yes, when it might make your life easier."

"Exactly."

"And yet you are unrelenting on the subject of my motorwagon."

"I can see why you're confused." The man was right, her attitude might well be construed as confusing. "I simply think some things are beneficial and others absurd."

His eyes narrowed. "It's pointless to argue with you on this, isn't it?"

"My goodness, Sam, you do know me after all." She grinned.

"I said I did."

"Still . . ." She considered him thoughtfully. "I'm not sure I don't prefer you confused."

"Imagine my surprise," he said dryly.

She studied him for a long moment then nodded. "Very well then."

"Congratulations, Dee, once again you have me confused." His brows drew together. "Very well then what?"

"Very well then." She shrugged. "I shall ride in your motorwagon. But only once," she added quickly.

He stared for a moment then grinned. "I knew you were weakening."

"Not at all," she said in a lofty manner. "You

have simply shown me that my tendency to pick and choose only those advancements of this modern age we live in that appeal to me might be a bit shortsighted." She shrugged. "There's nothing more to it than that. You needn't think of this as some sort of victory."

He grinned. "Oh, but it is."

"Enjoy it for the moment." She smiled pleasantly. "It won't be quite so enjoyable if your infernal machine doesn't work."

He chuckled. "You have me there."

She raised a shoulder in a casual shrug. "Yes, I know."

"If we're lucky, you can have your ride today."

"Oh that would be lucky," she murmured.

He laughed. "And then tonight . . ." He smiled in an altogether too wicked manner and she held her breath.

"Tonight?"

"Tonight, for dinner, I'll show you how to make a sandwich."

Relief and the oddest sense of disappointment washed through her. She suspected even she could slap some meat between two slices of bread. "I'll count the hours until then."

"If you like that, next . . ." He met her gaze and lowered his voice. Excitement shivered up her spine. Good Lord, the bloody man was addictive.

Without thinking, she leaned forward. "Yes? Next?"

"I'll teach you to make coffee."

"My heart is positively fluttering at the thought."

He laughed and she joined him. A moment later he had taken his leave. She sipped her coffee thoughtfully. He made her laugh and she did like that. The funny thing about their exchange though wasn't so much in their laughter or their witty banter.

But when she'd said her heart was fluttering, it was.

Chapter Sixteen

Thirteen days before the wedding . . .

"How on earth have you been managing?" Camille studied her sister with a fair amount of concern and more than a little doubt.

"I'm not entirely sure really." Delilah sat by her sister's bedside and debated the merits of complete honesty versus something a bit more fictional.

Her initial impulse had been to tell Camille everything was perfectly fine, that she and Sam had been more than up for the challenge of dealing with a house full of the indisposed. And indeed they had been, thanks to the very gracious Lady Fairborough who had sent over a small army of her own servants as soon as she'd received Delilah's note yesterday and this morning had sent someone to cook as well. Still, Delilah didn't want it to sound as if she and Sam had had it too easy. They had been willing to do much more after all.

"But we have managed to muddle through somehow."

"Are you sure?"

"Quite."

"I daresay it was fortunate that you and Sam were delayed in London and missed dinner."

Camille sighed. "Otherwise you would probably be in the same state as the rest of us."

"That was lucky."

"You haven't, well . . ." Camille winced. "Killed him or anything, have you?"

"No." Delilah bit back a smile. "He is quite well."

"And you haven't been rude to him?"

"I've been most pleasant." She ignored a twinge of annoyance at her sister's comment. Although one could scarcely blame Camille for her concern given Delilah's behavior when Sam had first arrived. "In fact, we've been getting along quite nicely."

They'd had sandwiches again last night for dinner and afterward had played chess together, although she had forgone any whisky with their game. It did seem wise given how she had thrown herself at him the night before. Besides there was that pesky vow of hers that she would not share his bed again.

He was a better than average player and as competitive at chess as he had been at tennis. But then, so was she. It had been an easy and delightful evening. She wasn't sure when she had laughed quite so much. Sam was amusing and intelligent and well read. Their conversation had ranged from music and art and history to more personal matters. He'd confided that his mother wasn't at all pleased by his broken engagement, which he found most disloyal. She'd confessed that while forging a new relationship with her sisters wasn't especially easy she was rather pleased with their progress thus far. Even when it came to Beryl. They prudently stayed away from the topics of her plans for marriage and his horseless carriage. By the time they retired, they were both weary from the long day. Even so, she had wondered what she would do if he were to take her in his arms again. And was a bit disappointed when he had made no effort to do so but had instead warmly bid her a good evening. Exactly as she had said she wanted.

She was asleep very nearly the moment she laid her head on her pillow and had slept quite soundly. Her slumber marred only by a strange yet lovely dream of flying along in a carriage pulled by a mechanical horse with a laughing American by her side.

"Delilah?" Camille frowned. "Are you listening to me?"

"Of course." She paused. "What did you say?"

"I said I'm glad that you and Sam have put aside your differences." Camille's brow furrowed. "Not that I knew what those differences were other than the fact that you think his motorwagon is absurd."

"To be perfectly honest, neither did I. He simply struck me the wrong way upon our initial meeting, I suppose. Probably because my mind was occupied with my financial difficulties. It was

foolish of me, of course, but there you have it."
Interesting how very easy it was to embellish a
mistruth although, if one thought about it
correctly, he had indeed struck her the wrong way
as she had planned never to see him again. "But
that's all behind us now. Indeed, Sam and I have
become friends."

"Have you now?" Camille's brow rose. "Who
would have imagined?"

"Not me." Delilah grinned. "But, as it turns out,
he's very nice. And intelligent. He's quite good at
chess. He very nearly beat me last night. Only the
fact that we ended the game when we were both
too tired to continue saved me from defeat."

"Did it?"

"Yes, but don't tell him that. He thinks he was
about to lose." She grinned. "He can be most
amusing as well and has a sort of wry sense of
humor. And he's quite dedicated to his family,
which I find most admirable. Did you know he
has five sisters?"

Camille stared. "I had no idea."

"The oldest is closest to him in age. She's
married and has children. Boys, I think. He's very
fond of them." She thought for a moment. "He
does seem to like children."

"Always good to know," Camille murmured.

"The rest of his sisters range in age from
sixteen to twelve," Delilah continued. "The two
youngest are twins. But they have each other so I

daresay they'll always have someone to confide in."

Camille winced.

"Apparently, it's not easy being a practical sort of man in a house full of women. He's worried about their futures and whether he's capable of providing them with the steady hand he's certain they'll need." She leaned forward confidentially. "He's not sure his mother is up to the task. She sounds a bit flighty."

"Not unlike our mother."

Delilah nodded. "That's what I told him. Did I mention that he's intelligent?"

"I believe so."

"It bears repeating." She nodded. "You should hear him talk about his ideas for promoting his vehicle. I suspect if anyone can make this motor-wagon nonsense successful it will be Sam. With Grayson's help of course."

"I don't think it's help so much as a partner-ship," Camille said with a frown.

"Yes, well, whatever." She waved off her sister's comment. "The man is really quite brilliant and terribly successful. Why, he built a business started by his grandfather into something of an empire."

"Did he?"

"He didn't use those exact words but it was evident. He's entirely too modest to proclaim his own accomplishments and yet he is extremely arrogant as well." She shook her head. "One of those men who thinks he knows what's best for everyone. I feel rather sorry for his sisters."

"Do you?"

"I do indeed. I can't begin to imagine the battles they'll have with him when they attempt to make their own choices in life." She bit back a laugh. "He is certainly in for a time of it."

"No doubt."

"He wants only the best for them and as his father is dead, he takes that responsibility very seriously. He has a great sense of responsibility. He is, well, a good man."

"How very interesting." Camille studied her curiously. "Why the man sounds practically perfect."

"Oh no, not at all. He's not the least bit perfect."

"What's wrong with him?"

"Well . . ." Delilah thought for a moment. "He's quite arrogant."

"You mentioned that."

"He thinks his way is right and everyone else's way is wrong."

"That is the very definition of arrogant," Camille said slowly.

"Beyond that . . ." What was wrong with him? Certainly there were basic and insurmountable differences between them but other than those questions of background and heritage and their opposing views on progress, she couldn't really put her finger on anything specific. Aside from his arrogance of course. Still, what man didn't think he was always right? And what woman didn't know he was wrong? "Admittedly, I can't think of anything at the moment but I can assure you, he is not perfect."

"Few men are." Camille chose her words with care. "And you like him."

"He is a most likable sort." She shrugged. "It's very hard not to like him."

"As a . . . friend?"

"He is an excellent friend. And he knows how to make coffee."

"That is good to know." Camille studied her sister for a long moment.

"You're staring at me." Delilah narrowed her eyes. "Why?"

"No reason really." Camille shrugged. "I just find it interesting that you and Sam have become civil, let alone friends. I would not have wagered on that."

"Life is full of surprises. This is neither the first I've experienced in recent months nor do I think it shall be the last." Her tone hardened. "One can either let the unexpected twists of life devastate you or one can carry on. I have chosen to carry on."

Camille's brows drew together. "Are we still talking about Sam?"

"We're talking about everything," Delilah said. "And as we are, we should probably discuss the wedding." She picked up Teddy's notebook from the bedside table where she had placed it earlier.

Camille's eyes widened. "Teddy relinquished her notebook to you? She must be feeling horrid for her to do that."

"Even so, it wasn't easy to pry it from her hands. But I managed." She cast her sister a smug smile. "She is feeling better though—"

"As am I."

"Regardless, you are both to remain in bed today." She adopted a no-nonsense manner. "The wedding is less than two weeks away and you do need to recover your strength. Especially since Beryl and Mother and Father and who knows who else will be arriving any day and then there will be no chance to rest at all."

"Very well then. I shall refrain from futile protesting and enjoy being taken care of." Camille leaned toward her sister and lowered her voice. "Was I dreaming or was there a new maid here this morning?"

"Lady Fairborough sent some of her staff to assist us."

"Including a cook?"

Delilah nodded.

"I see." Camille nodded in a knowing manner. "Well, that explains why you have managed so well. The broth, by the way, was excellent."

"Then you should have realized I didn't make it." Delilah flipped open the notebook. "Now then, we have cancelled the dinner scheduled for tomorrow night."

"Oh, but by tomorrow—"

Delilah leveled her the same look a long-ago governess had perfected.

Camille paused then nodded. "Very wise."

"I thought so." Delilah glanced at the notebook. "You should be aware that Mrs. Gilbert, the seamstress, is expected for your final dress fitting tomorrow. And . . ." She flipped through a few pages although the moment she had wrestled the book from Teddy she had thoroughly gone through it. Partially out of curiosity as to just how efficient her friend really was. The answer was very. But then Teddy had always been resourceful and well organized. "Aside from that, there really isn't anything that can't wait until Teddy can give it her full attention." She snapped the notebook closed. "And that is that for the moment."

"Can you believe in less than two weeks I will finally marry Grayson?"

"Well, less than two weeks plus the nearly twelve years it took the two of you to get to this point."

"All in the past now, my dear sister." Camille breathed a sigh of pure happiness. "I shall soon be Mrs. Grayson Elliott and nothing else really matters."

"You won't mind being Mrs. Elliott rather than Lady Lydingham?"

"Not in the least," she said in a lofty manner. "Indeed I think being Mrs. Elliott is far superior to any title I can imagine."

"Do you?" Delilah bit back a grin. "And yet just this past Christmas your goal was to win the hand of a prince and thereby become Princess Camille."

"Oh, I was much younger then." Camille grinned. "And quite, quite foolish. And I had no idea Grayson would come back into my life. I am eternally grateful I came to my senses before it was too late."

"As are we all."

"I will admit that I'd be lying if I said I wouldn't miss being Lady Lydingham at all. But it seems a minor trade."

Delilah tossed the notebook onto the bed, then stood and picked up Camille's tray, setting it on a table by the door. She'd have one of the maids bring it down to the kitchen. It was a huge relief to have enough servants to see to everyone's needs. Delilah was under no illusion as to her own abilities in that regard and was grateful she wasn't put to the test. "I still have things I need to accomplish today so I should be off. I must say I am most grateful everyone invited for your next party lives fairly close. Otherwise, I would have had to send Sam back into London."

"And you'd miss him."

"Of course I would. There's no one else to occupy my time with here except for him."

"Yes, that's what I thought."

She heaved a resigned sigh. "Don't read more into this than there is, Camille."

Her sister gasped. "I would never."

"You would and you are."

"I've been very ill." Camille slid down her pillows and pulled her covers up to her chin.

Delilah laughed. "You are obviously feeling better."

"Yes, I am. And as I am, there are things I should say." She sat up and addressed her sister in an earnest manner. "In spite of what Mother has said, in spite of what we were all brought up to believe, there are more important things than position and even wealth. Although wealth would be terribly hard to live without," Camille added under her breath.

"Yes, I suppose there are."

"Love, Delilah, is much more important."

"Is it?"

Camille nodded. "Without question."

"For you."

"For all of us," Camille said. "You should keep that in mind, my dear sister, as you continue your quest for your next husband. Regardless of your financial state, it's not—"

"Oh, the problem of Phillip's alleged heir should be resolved any day now," Delilah said with a casual shrug. "We gathered a bit of information while we were in London that should settle the matter." She paused. "I must admit Sam was most helpful in that regard."

"Was he? How very interesting," Camille murmured.

"I said we have become friends and he is proving to be an excellent friend."

"One can always use another friend."

"I've always thought so."

"Still . . ." Camille began in an offhand manner. "There is more to life than friendship."

"Still," Delilah said in a hard tone, "friendship will not break your heart. At least not in the manner that love will."

"I suppose not."

"Tell me this, Camille." She met her sister's gaze directly. "Are you so certain that Grayson will never break your heart?"

"Yes," she said without hesitation. "I am. There's a great deal to be said for second chances, Camille. Grayson and I both were wrong in the past and we paid a price for that. We both hurt each other. Now, we have a second chance. Given that Mother has taken Father back, even she would agree with that.

"Trust and faith and all of that goes hand in hand with love. You cannot have love without the rest of it." Certainty rang in her voice. "Admittedly, I would be a fool to think that the rest of our lives will be blissful. There are no assurances in life. Life is not perfect. I'm certainly not perfect, nor is

Grayson. There are bound to be difficulties and problems and even tragedy in the years ahead. My heart may well be broken by any number of things as the years go on but we shall have each other to see us through. You may call it blind faith if you will. There isn't a doubt in my mind, or in my heart, that he will be exactly where I need him to be, by my side, as I will be by his until the day I breathe my last. And the one thing I am utterly and completely confident of is that Grayson will not break my heart."

"That's . . ." Delilah hesitated. It was hard not to envy her older sister for having found the very thing that Delilah wished to avoid. But Camille was absolutely right. Love and trust did go hand in hand. One could not have one without the other. Delilah wasn't sure she could trust anyone enough to allow herself to love him. She had trusted Phillip after all. "That's remarkable and quite wonderful."

"I know," Camille said with a smug smile then sobered. "It's not just words, you understand. It's how I feel. Grayson would never hurt me." She hesitated. "Love, Delilah, is much more important than anything else."

"And much harder to find."

Camille grinned. "But half the fun is finding it."

Delilah laughed. "I'll give you that."

"It's magic, Delilah. Simply magic."

"I've never been one for magic. I'm entirely

too practical." Still, hadn't the thought of magic already occurred to her? "But it is something to consider, I suppose."

"Have you changed your mind then?" Camille's brow rose. "Have I given you something to think about?"

"Not really." She shrugged. "But you've been ill and I thought I would humor you."

"I would just hate for you to miss something that might be everything you've ever wanted."

"I have every intention of getting everything I want." She cast her sister an affectionate smile, picked up Teddy's notebook, and started for the door. "So you needn't bother worrying about me."

"I believe worrying about my younger sister is part and parcel of being a better sister."

"And it's most appreciated." Genuine affection for Camille washed through her. Who would have imagined a year ago that she and Camille and Beryl would truly become sisters?

"I will give you this," Delilah said. "It was recently pointed out to me that an intelligent woman does not close her mind to possibilities."

"You're not talking about love though, are you?"

"No, but as an intelligent woman I am willing to admit I may, on occasion, have been too hasty in my convictions. Therefore, Camille, in the interest of being open-minded . . ." She grinned. "I am about to take my first ride in a horseless carriage."

• • •

Sam stood in the drive by the carriage house studying his motorwagon and going over a checklist in his head. He was no engineer but he knew nearly as much about the vehicle as Jim did. When he'd checked on Jim yesterday, he had the motorwagon sputtering but it hadn't actually run. This morning, however, Jim had managed to get it going. He and Sam had spent the last few hours checking and double-checking the machine's parts. They'd driven the vehicle up and down the drive in a halting fashion with Jim muttering about incomprehensible connections and damned foreigners and stopping every few feet to make adjustments. Until at last, with a satisfied grin, Jim had pronounced it fit. Sam had sent him back to the village for more fuel but there was enough left in the small tank for a decent ride. If, of course, his passenger would ever make an appearance.

Sam grinned. Delilah could deny it all she wanted, but she was weakening. Definitely about the motorwagon and certainly about never seeing him again. After all, they were friends now even if he wasn't sure friendship was enough. She was without a doubt the most confusing woman he'd ever met although perhaps much of his confusion was in his own mind. Or possibly his heart. One minute he wanted to take her over his knee and thrash her and the next he had to resist taking her into his arms and never letting her go.

Adding to his confusion was the simple fact that he liked her. He genuinely liked her. His gaze wandered along the intricate gears and belts and mechanicals of the motorwagon. He couldn't recall ever simply liking a woman before. Surely he had liked Lenore but, in hindsight, maybe not. At least not in the same way he liked Delilah. Lenore had never shared confidences with him as Delilah had. They'd never had a quiet evening of chess and conversation. They'd never simply enjoyed one another's company. Of course, she'd never argued with him either, which now struck him as odd.

Lenore was an intelligent woman. And as much as he liked to think he was always right, in truth he wasn't. No one was right all the time, not even him. But Lenore had never argued or questioned, although she did seem to get whatever she wanted. She had been, in very many ways, simply perfect. Good Lord. If one looked at it in the right way, couldn't one say he had been ready to marry her for many of the same reasons Delilah intended to marry?

Was he in love with Delilah? He bent down and checked the gear chain tension. As complicated as the vehicle was, it was child's play in comparison to that question. This wasn't the first time the idea of love had raised its disturbing head. He had wondered right from the beginning although, as much as Delilah claimed he was a romantic sort, he was not so foolish as to believe in something as absurd as love at first sight. Still, he hadn't been able to get her out of his thoughts since the moment they'd met. Which did seem to indicate something even if he had no idea what. Was it nothing at all? Or was it magic?

Nor did he have any idea of her feelings for him, if indeed she had any feelings at all. One minute she was flirtatious and seductive, the next cool and distant. She'd been quite explicit about there not being any additional *adventures* between them. And as much as he wasn't sure he believed that was what she wanted—the night they stayed in London being a case in point—it did seem a good idea to abide by her decision. At least for now. But God help him, it was becoming more and more difficult. Was this the end result of being friends with a woman? Or, more likely, being friends with this one particular woman.

That it had not been easy for Sam and Delilah to get to this point only made it more significant. Perhaps friendship between a man and a woman was the beginning of trust, and who knew where that might lead?

"Are you willing it to start simply by staring at it?" an amused voice said behind him.

"I am invoking the gods of progress and forward thinking." He grinned and turned toward her.

"You'd best hope they're not armed with thunderbolts and lightning," Delilah said wryly.

"Ah, but my gods are wise and beneficent." He bowed in an overly dramatic manner. "Even to those who do not believe."

"I am here, aren't I?" She cast a skeptical look at the motorwagon. "Taking my life in my hands no doubt."

"Your life is as safe as if you were lying in your own bed."

"My, yes." She circled the vehicle. "That is safe."

"Not by my choice," he said without thinking.

She stopped on the other side of the motor-wagon. "You have been a perfect gentleman these past few nights."

He sighed. "Yes, I know."

"Why?"

He stared in surprise. "Because that's what you said you wanted."

"Then your restraint is appreciated," she murmured. Once again, he had no idea what was going on in that lovely head of hers. Did she?

"Your carriage awaits, my lady." He waved his arm in a grand gesture.

She hesitated, studying the vehicle with more than a little apprehension.

He stifled a grin. "Scared?"

"Prudent," she said, her gaze still locked on the motorwagon. "Cautious, if you will, and not so foolish as to blindly risk my life." She looked at him. "Is it very fast?"

"Nine or ten miles an hour I think." He shrugged in an offhand manner. "Not much faster than a trotting horse."

"Well then I would think a horse—"

"But much more reliable. Or at least it will be one day."

"Maybe I should wait until then," she said weakly.

He studied her curiously. "You really are concerned about this, aren't you?"

"Wary is perhaps a better word than concerned."

"I've ridden in it any number of times and lived to tell the tale." He cast her a confident smile. "It's really quite safe." Now was not the time to mention the lingering problems with the steering mechanism. "Why don't I demonstrate it for you?"

"Would you?"

"Absolutely." He nodded. "And once I've shown you how very safe and enjoyable the motor-wagon is, you can join me." He stepped to the back of the vehicle. "That will give you a few minutes to work up your courage unless you've changed your mind."

"I said I would ride in it and I will." Her eyes narrowed. "And courage has nothing to do with it. I'm simply being—"

"Cautious, wary, prudent? You said all that." He grabbed the flywheel and spun it. The motor sputtered but did not catch.

"There's nothing wrong with being cautious you know. It's really quite sensible."

He spun the flywheel again. Again the motor failed to catch. "I'd wager you weren't especially cautious the first time you put a phone to your ear."

"That's an entirely different matter," she said in a lofty manner. "Besides, while the queen herself has a telephone I suspect she would never step foot in something like that . . . that contraption."

"Fortunately, she is not the one who has agreed to do so. You are." It routinely took three or more tries to get the motor running but this certainly wasn't helping his case. He gritted his teeth and tried again.

"I daresay, we'd be on our way by now if that was a horse," she said pleasantly.

"Well, it's not a horse," he said through clenched teeth. "It's better than a horse." He spun the flywheel again.

"And anything this new and this remarkable"—the motor coughed—"is bound to have a few minor problems"—and sputtered—"nothing to be concerned about"—and finally caught. He cast her a triumphant smile. "As I said, nothing to be concerned about at all."

"It's very loud." Her voice rose over the sound of the engine. Sam would never admit it to her, but it was hard to hear over the noisy chugging of the motor.

"A minor problem that will be resolved eventually." He climbed into the motorwagon and settled on one side of the leather bench. He grinned at her. "Are you ready?"

"The real question is, are you?" She cast the vehicle another skeptical look then stepped back. "Do be careful."

"I've driven it before, Dee." He nodded in a reassuring manner then turned his attention to the vehicle. He gripped the brake handle with one hand and the steering lever with the other. It did need to be finessed a bit. He turned the knob that fed the fuel to the engine, slowly released the brake, and then was moving off down the drive. He looked back at her and waved.

She tentatively waved back but the expression on her face was more intrigued than concerned.

He circled around her on the broad drive and she laughed.

"I told you it was safe," he called.

"All right then, Sam," she called back. "You convinced me. I'll try it."

"Good." He turned the steering lever but it was unaccountably stiff and difficult to move. Before he could correct for the problem, the motorwagon lurched off the drive and was picking up speed on a slight downhill slope, a slope he hadn't even noticed. The machine was moving faster and faster. Damnation. This would certainly not impress her. He jerked the brake handle at the same moment the front wheel dropped into a hidden hole and the vehicle pitched forward, throwing him into the air.

Dimly he heard a scream and the moment before he hit the ground the oddest thoughts flashed through his mind:

What a terrible waste never holding her again would be.

And the blasted woman was going to think she was right all along.

Chapter Seventeen

"Sam!" The scream ripped from her lips.

Oh, God no!

Realization struck her with the force of a physical blow. Compounded by fear. And terror. And an unrelenting sense of loss. Without thinking, she ran toward him. The world slowed as if in a dream. Her legs wouldn't move fast enough.

She couldn't lose him. Not now. Now that she knew. Her heart caught in her throat. She choked back a sob and raced toward Sam's lifeless body, sending a prayer heavenward with every step.

Dear Lord, please don't let him be dead.

The damnable motorwagon had tumbled and rolled over and over at least three times and now sat at an odd, twisted angle, the front wheel lower than the back two, the merciless motor still chugging away, the whole thing listing heavily to one side. It resembled nothing so much as a wounded mechanical beast. A deadly, vile beast. Sam had been thrown some feet away.

Dear Lord, he wasn't moving. What if he was dead? What if she had lost him? What if his stupid machine had killed him? She dropped down on her knees beside him.

"Sam! Oh God, please!"

Was he breathing? A pulse, she should feel for a

pulse. Frantically, she grabbed his wrist and tried to find some semblance of life. He wasn't dead. He couldn't be. Surely she would know if he were dead.

"Please, Sam, please stay with me."

She couldn't feel anything. She should feel something. The beat of his heart, the throb of his blood in his veins. Panic gripped her. She needed help but she couldn't leave him lying here. Alone. What if he died and she wasn't here? What if he came to and had no idea where he was or who he was or anything?

"Please, please don't die. Come back, Sam, please." She patted his cheeks briskly, hoping to get some reaction, some color back into his face. "There's so much you don't know." He was so pale, ghastly, deathly pale. She slapped his face harder. "So much I didn't realize. What a fool I've been. Please, Sam, please come back. Don't leave me. Not now."

Surely his lashes flickered against his cheek. She bent over him, leaning closer, hoping to feel his breath. "Sam?"

Without warning his arms wrapped around her, pulling her down on top of him, and his lips met hers in a kiss hard and firm. Joy and relief swept through her. He was alive! *Thank God.* He was . . . Her eyes widened. This was not at all the kiss of a dying man. Nor was it the kiss of a man who was less than perfectly all right. At least thus far.

She pulled away and stared down at him. "You're alive."

He grinned up at her. "Disappointed?"

"Yes! No, of course not." She swallowed hard. "I thought you were dead."

"Not today."

"You looked dead," she said slowly. "You weren't moving."

"Just the wind knocked out of me."

"Your eyes were closed."

"I needed a moment."

She sat back and studied him closely. "You're fine, aren't you?"

"Fine might not be entirely accurate but I seem to be in one piece." He struggled to sit up then rubbed his face and cringed. "Ouch." He stared at her. "You hit me."

"I was patting your cheeks in an effort to revive you."

"With undue enthusiasm, I would say," he said, still rubbing his cheeks. "My face is stinging."

"Come now, Sam. I was just trying to, well, bring you back to life as it were. Which does call for more than a half-hearted attempt. And I did a fine job of it as you are so clearly alive."

"I was never dead." He scrambled to his feet and groaned at the movement. "Holy mother of . . ." He gently felt the back of his head and grimaced. "Did you smack me on the back of the head as well?"

"Don't be absurd. That would have been stupid." His cheeks were fairly red. "Admittedly, your face does look a little pink but I didn't know what else to do. And you are such a stubborn man it seemed necessary to . . . to attract your attention. To bring you back from the brink of death." She stared up at him. "One might say I saved your life. It seems to me a little gratitude is called for."

"Had it actually needed saving I'd be extremely grateful." He extended a hand to help her up.

"I didn't know that. You certainly looked dead."

"I wasn't." The moment she was on her feet he released her hand and headed toward the motorwagon.

"You kissed me!"

"You noticed that, did you?" He reached his vehicle and grimaced. "Damn it all. Look at that."

She hurried after him. "You let me think you were dead."

"I didn't let you think I was dead. I had nothing to do with what you thought." He circled the motorwagon, found whatever it was he was looking for, and turned off the still-chugging motor. "I certainly could have been dead, I suppose."

"But you kissed me."

"You said that." His tone was absent, his gaze fixed on his vehicle. "Probably because I wasn't dead."

"You took advantage of me!"

"You're not the one who was dead. One might

say you took advantage of me. And I'm pretty sure you kissed me back. With a great deal of enthusiasm."

"I was simply glad you were alive."

"You kissed me back." He squatted down and studied the front wheel. "And you hit me."

She glared. "I wish you would stop saying that. I did not hit you, I . . . I *patted* your cheeks. Briskly. In a manner designed to stimulate the flow of blood."

"You did not pat me, you *hit* me. Hard." He tugged at a metal bracket. "And you kissed me."

Her eyes narrowed. "*You* kissed *me.* I was simply trying to determine if you were breathing."

"I was." He blew a frustrated breath. "Look at that."

She eyed the vehicle. "Look at what?"

"Right there." He ran his hand over the front wheel. "Some of the spokes are broken or bent. And here." He pointed to a part of the metal tubing underneath the floorboards. "That's bent." He straightened and continued to move around the vehicle. "The damn thing did roll over—"

"More than once," she murmured.

"But you wouldn't think it would do that much damage. And there's probably more here that I'm not seeing."

"I knew that thing wasn't safe." She crossed her arms over her chest. "I told you it could kill you."

"No, you said I was taking my life in my hands." He bent forward and examined the motor.

She huffed. "It's the same thing."

"Not really." He glanced at her. "It was the fall that would have killed me." His attention returned to his wounded beast. "Jim is not going to be happy about this."

"It can't be that bad. The motor still ran."

"It's not enough." He ran his hand through his hair. "Repairs are going to be significant."

"It doesn't look bad." She studied his vehicle. "A few scratches perhaps."

"It's more than a few scratches." He worked his way slowly around the motorwagon. "There are things that are bent that shouldn't be. It's an innovation, Dee. You don't want something like this not to be in perfect condition. Not if you want people to commit to buy one in the future." His jaw tightened. "Jim's going to need a real workshop for this, not just the tools he has with him. And this is going to set everything back. Just the damage I can see is problematic enough. Who knows what Jim will find when he starts working on it. What did you mean by 'don't leave me'?"

Her breath caught. "What?"

He straightened and looked at her. "What did you mean when you said don't leave me?"

"I don't recall saying anything of the sort," she said quickly. Now that he wasn't dying or dead there was no need to say anything. At least not until she decided what if anything she wanted to say. Or do. "You must have imagined it. When you hit your head. Head injuries will do that sort of thing, you know."

"I didn't imagine anything."

"You could have. You were flying through the air, after all. That alone would probably be enough to make you hear things that weren't said. I for one have never seen a man fly before." She shuddered. "I don't mind telling you, I found it most disturbing."

"You were devastated at the thought of my death."

"Well, of course I was devastated." She scoffed. "You're a guest at Millworth, and not being distraught at your death would be—"

"Rude?"

"Exactly."

"And you are never rude."

"Never."

"And that's all there is to it, then."

"Absolutely." She nodded. It was obvious that he didn't believe her. "Goodness, Sam, why wouldn't I be upset? We are friends, after all."

He studied her for a moment then smiled in a knowing manner and turned back to the inspection of his machine. "Yes, that's what I thought."

"And that's exactly what you should think."

"All right." He turned back to his perusal. "Then that's what I think."

"Because that's all there is."

"If you say so."

"There's nothing more to it than that."

"The lady doth protest too much, methinks," he murmured.

She rolled her gaze toward the sky. "Not again."

"It's the right quotation this time. I checked," he said in a hard tone. "I do like to be prepared."

"I know it's right." She shrugged. "I wasn't going to say anything."

"I am usually right."

"Not that I've noticed."

"What don't I know?" he said abruptly.

"What do you mean?"

"You said there was so much I didn't know. So much you didn't realize. What don't I know?"

"I have no idea. You certainly think you know everything."

"For God's sake, Delilah." Before she could protest, he moved closer and pulled her into his arms. "You didn't want me to die because you're in love with me."

"Don't be absurd." Even to her own ears her protest sounded weak. "I would have been concerned about anyone's death."

"You're lying."

"I am not!" She tried to push out of his arms but he held her fast. "I wouldn't have wanted anyone to die at the hands of that mechanical beast of yours. Especially not a friend."

His gaze bored into hers. "Why won't you admit there's something remarkable between us?"

"Of course there is," she said, still pushing against him. "Why, we're friends."

"We're more than friends and you know it."

"I know nothing of the sort. Obviously, you're suffering from some sort of delusion brought on by a hit to your head."

He stared at her for a long moment. "Yes, that must be it."

"Now, unhand me." She wasn't sure if he believed her or not. There were moments when the man was truly difficult to decipher. Regardless, she certainly couldn't think with his arms around her and she did need her wits about her. "At once."

"My apologies, Lady Hargate." He released her and stepped back. "I don't know what came over me. My injuries must be more significant than I had thought."

"Well, you're not dead," she said helpfully.

"There is that."

"And you realize your mistake."

"Oh, I've made no mistake."

"But you said—"

"I know exactly what I said." His unflinching gaze met hers.

"But you are wrong."

He raised a brow.

"You are." She glared at him.

He shrugged.

She threw up her hands in frustration. "You are the most arrogant man I have ever met."

"And you are the most confusing woman I have ever met." He paused. "And stubborn. My God you're stubborn. Have I mentioned that?"

"I can't recall. Possibly."

"Well, it certainly bears repeating." He studied her closely. "It's also worth noting that in spite of your feigned indignation—"

"It's not the least bit feigned. I am indignant!"

"In spite of that, you have not denied what I said."

"It doesn't warrant a denial," she said in a lofty manner.

"Of course not." He cast her an annoyingly smug smile.

"It's entirely too absurd to deny."

He shrugged. "If you say so."

She stared at him. "And you claim I am stubborn."

"If the fashionably shod shoe fits," he said under his breath and turned back to his machine.

"As there is no possibility of riding in that beast of yours today I am going back to the house." She turned on her heel and started off. "I didn't want to ride in it anyway. I was just trying to be polite."

"Because you're never rude?" He called behind her.

"Never!"

"Hah!"

"What an annoying, irritating, arrogant beast you are!"

"One more thing before you go stalking off."

"You're too late, I am already stalking off!" She stopped in midstep and swiveled to face him. "What is it?"

"I would never leave you." His eyes narrowed. "All you ever have to do is ask."

Her heart thudded. She deliberately misunderstood him. "What I have asked, what I've wanted, is for you to leave."

"That's the problem then, isn't it? I've never believed you."

"One of many problems!"

He smiled in a slow, annoying manner. "And I find it interesting that when you thought I was dead, you begged me not to leave you when all you've been trying to do since I arrived is get me to leave."

She stared at him. "Ironic, isn't it?" She turned and started off again.

"I wouldn't call it ironic. I'd call it just deserts." He called after her. "Or fate."

If one believed in such things as previous lives, one might, at the moment, have decided one did something quite terrible in a previous incarnation. Delilah must have been very bad indeed to find herself now in this situation.

Blast it all, she was indeed in love with the man. Of course she was. For an intelligent woman she'd been fairly stupid. She should have known it from the beginning. And perhaps she did. Perhaps she'd known somewhere, in the dim recesses of her heart, the moment she'd looked into his brown eyes. The moment he first made her laugh. The moment he first touched her hand. And perhaps that was why she'd told him she never—no—*it would be best*—if they never saw each other again.

She'd fallen in love with the arrogant, annoying American. The man who was totally and completely wrong for her. Because falling in love with a man who was all wrong would be every bit as heartbreaking as falling in love with one who was supposed to be entirely right.

And even worse, he knew she loved him. Bloody hell. What was she going to do now? The man would surely break her heart.

But only if she let him.

It wasn't at all difficult to avoid Sam for the rest of the day. Delilah had people still in bed to attend to after all. Not that there was much attending necessary given Lady Fairborough's generous loan of servants.

Sam and Mr. Moore were occupied with the damage to the motorwagon and had practically barricaded themselves at the carriage house. William did mention that Sam had conferred with Grayson who had then insisted he was feeling too good to remain abed. He too was now at the carriage house. William had also mentioned all three gentlemen wished to take their meals there for the foreseeable future.

Camille insisted she was bored and tired of being by herself so she commandeered a large, comfortable, overstuffed chair in Teddy's room and the three women spent much of the evening going over plans for the approaching wedding.

Delilah had paid scant attention to the mundane details of her own wedding, leaving it in her mother's capable hands. And while the details of Camille's might well be fascinating any other time, at the moment Delilah had entirely too much on her mind to pay any attention at all. Fortunately, between Camille and Teddy, Delilah couldn't have wedged a word of her own in even if she'd wanted to. Still, she did smile and nod when it seemed appropriate or in those rare moments when her sister or her friend looked at her for agreement.

"Although the chapel really is rather small," Teddy said thoughtfully. "I was wondering if perhaps . . ."

It was to be an elegant affair, admittedly a bit grander than Grayson had preferred and not as extravagant as Camille had wished. Still, it was to be quite festive with an evening ceremony followed by dinner and a wedding ball.

It did seem to Delilah that there was very little

left to discuss although Camille and Teddy did go on and on about any number of things completely out of their control. The interesting thing about a grand wedding was that once everything was selected and arranged for, one could do nothing more until the event was very nearly at hand. That was when disaster would strike or all would be well. Either the flowers that had been ordered arrived as expected—which wouldn't be until the day before the wedding itself—or they did not. Either the pastry chef, whose arrival was expected in the next few days, would prove worthy of his reputation and expense and create an unforgettable wedding cake as well as confections for the wedding dinner or he would not. Either the pale blue Worth gown Camille had ordered from Paris months ago, now in the hands of an expert London seamstress approved by Mr. Worth himself, would either be absolutely perfect or it would not.

"Why the flowers alone will be enough . . ."

As important as all this was to Camille, Delilah simply could not get her mind off the question of what to do about Sam. There was no getting away from the truth of the matter: Delilah had fallen in love with the man and he knew it. If she hadn't been terrified that he was dead, she would have kept her mouth shut and that would have been that. She probably never would have acknowledged her own feelings and he never would have known. It struck her that there was some flaw in her reasoning that she couldn't quite put her finger on but at the moment it scarcely mattered. All that mattered now was what was she going to do about it? Her choices seemed relatively slim. Indeed, only two came to mind.

She could certainly accept how she felt, acknowledge her feelings to Sam, and hope they were mutual. And what then? He had never mentioned marriage and even if he had, marriage between them would be impossible. They were such completely different people and they wanted completely different things in life. Oh, certainly, she liked him and yes, she did enjoy his company but beyond that they had little in common. Why, they probably wouldn't even be able to agree where they might live. She had no desire to live in America and she certainly couldn't imagine he would be willing to live in England. He was so very American after all. And that was one of their minor differences. What if they did marry? Could they truly spend the rest of their lives together?

"I think that's an excellent idea. Beyond that, we could certainly . . ."

Oh, they might well be quite blissful in the beginning but sooner or later the differences between them would prove their undoing. Each would grow to resent whatever compromises they had originally agreed to. Everything good they shared would wither and die. Bitterness would surely replace love. Hearts would break eventually. Hers or his or both.

The second choice was the most obvious and made the most sense, all things considered. Certainly, there would be some pain involved but better now rather than when there was nothing left of her heart at all. It was a small enough price to pay to avoid sure and certain heartbreak. There was no choice really. It was best for both of them.

Delilah had to do exactly what she had attempted when he first arrived at Millworth. She had to get rid of the man once and for all. She ignored the odd way her heart twisted in her chest at the thought.

But this time she would be successful.

This time she would have help.

Chapter Eighteen

Twelve days before the wedding...

"You were remarkably quiet last night," Camille said in an entirely too casual manner and tore off a piece of lightly buttered toast.

"It's really not at all like you." Teddy sat across the table from Camille.

"I'm glad to see the two of you are back to your usual selves." Delilah moved to the sideboard and perused Mrs. Dooley's breakfast offerings. Nothing looked particularly inviting today. Still, she heaped her plate with eggs and sausages and a bit of everything available. "I must say, I'm surprised to see the two of you at this hour."

"It is rather late," Teddy admitted.

"It's nearly eleven and you are usually an early riser." It was later than usual for Delilah as well but then she'd had no sleep to speak of. And no idea if doing the practical thing, the intelligent thing, was doing the right thing.

"Or are you surprised because we managed to bravely rise from our sickbeds even though we are still exceptionally weak?" Camille popped the toast in her mouth. "And exceptionally hungry."

"Yes, I can see that." Delilah took her place at

the table and at once realized what was different. "Good Lord, it's all back to normal today, isn't it?"

"Why yes, I believe it is." Camille smiled. "The servants are back at their usual stations, performing their usual duties. Clement said Lady Fairborough's servants left the first thing this morning. And Grayson is with Sam at the carriage house. Apparently there's a problem with the motorwagon. There was an accident yesterday."

Delilah sipped her coffee.

"Oh, I'm sure Sam and Mr. Moore will put it right." Confidence rang in Teddy's voice.

"I don't know." Camille shook her head. "Grayson didn't sound optimistic. The vehicle sustained a lot of damage."

Teddy's brows pulled together. "How bad is it?"

"Bad enough that their plans have been set back. And it appears Sam will have to extend his stay in England." She slanted a quick glance at her sister. "Fortunately, Grayson and I weren't planning on a wedding trip until spring. I suspect he would feel inclined to cancel a more immediate trip at this point. Although I can't imagine he'd be of much help. As far as I know he's not the mechanical sort." She paused. "Although it's entirely possible he knows much more about such things than I'm aware of."

"When did you talk to Grayson?" Delilah asked.

"Last night." Camille smiled innocently. "He too is feeling much better. He popped in to see how I was getting on."

"Good," Delilah said with a half-hearted smile, ignoring the thought of exactly what *popping in* might entail.

Camille studied her sister casually. "Grayson said Sam hit his head in the accident."

"He's fine," Delilah said shortly.

"That's right," Camille said slowly. "He said you were there."

Delilah nodded.

"Grayson said Sam was thrown out of the vehicle."

"Good Lord." Teddy's eyes widened. "That must have been dreadful."

The horror that had twisted Delilah's heart at the sight of Sam flying through the air again stabbed her. She ignored it. "He's fine."

Teddy and Camille traded glances.

"Yes, you said that." Camille stared at her.

Delilah shrugged.

"I understand you and Sam are getting along much better," Teddy said in an offhand manner.

Delilah nodded and pushed the food around on her plate. She really wasn't hungry.

"Camille told me you and Sam have become friends," Teddy began. "She says you've been spending a great deal of time together."

"The rest of you were indisposed."

"I also mentioned that you like him," Camille said.

"Of course I like him." Delilah forced a light note to her voice. "There's really no reason not to like him. He's a very nice man. Intelligent, amusing, well read—"

"Charming, dashing," Teddy added.

"And quite handsome." Camille grinned. "I find his dark eyes coupled with his blond hair to be nothing short of delicious."

"Why, I certainly wouldn't have minded being the one forced to spend a great deal of time with him." Teddy smirked.

"It wasn't by choice," Delilah said in a sharper tone than she had intended.

Camille's eyes narrowed. "What is wrong with you? Yesterday afternoon you were positively lighthearted. But last night you scarcely said two words."

"You were preoccupied and obviously concerned about something. And today . . ." Teddy pinned her with a firm look. "You're not eating. That's not like you." She glanced at Camille. "The one sure way to know when something is bothering Dee is to watch whether or not she eats." She nodded at Delilah's plate. "You haven't taken a bite."

Delilah could deny it but it was pointless. Besides, she needed their help. Unfortunately, the price for their assistance would no doubt be complete honesty. She set down her fork and sighed. "You're right."

"It has something to do with Sam, doesn't it?" Camille said.

Delilah's gaze shifted between her friend and her sister. "I need to talk to you both. I have a, oh, a problem and I need your help."

"What kind of problem?" Camille asked.

"What kind of help?" Caution edged Teddy's voice.

Delilah huffed. "Does it matter?"

"No. Of course not," Camille said. "It doesn't matter in the least. However, if this help was of an illegal or immoral nature I would have to think twice." She smiled slowly. "But I would still help you."

Teddy nodded. "As would I."

"Still, I would prefer not to be arrested or jailed before the wedding." Camille wrinkled her nose. "That would be most awkward so I do hope it's not terribly illegal. However, I have no qualms whatsoever about immoral. Although Beryl is much better at that sort of thing."

"It's neither illegal nor immoral." Delilah pushed her plate away and drew a deep breath. "And I have a plan . . . of sorts."

"A plan of sorts? Oh dear." Teddy grimaced. "Your plans are even worse when they're not well thought out."

"Nonetheless, it is a plan. Or at least the

beginning of a plan," Delilah said. "Life is always so much better when one has a plan."

"I've always been fond of plans myself." Camille smiled. "Are you going to tell us or are we going to have to guess? I have a very fertile imagination and there are any number of things that would come to mind if I had to guess."

"Of course I'm going to tell you. But not here where we could be overheard by anyone coming in for breakfast." Delilah stood. "I'd much prefer to have this discussion in Mother's parlor."

Camille's eyes widened. "This is serious, then."

Delilah nodded. "Quite serious."

Teddy looked from sister to sister. "I don't understand."

"Whenever we had discussions of a serious nature, Mother would always call us into the small ladies' parlor," Camille said. "It's much more conducive to revelation and confession and has been the site of all manner of unexpected disclosures in the past. At least among the female members of the household."

"Serious matters involving Father or Uncle Basil are usually conducted here in the dining room," Delilah added.

"Mother told us Father was dead in the ladies' parlor," Camille said.

"And we learned he was alive in the dining room." Delilah shrugged.

"I see." Teddy nodded.

"I beg your pardon, Lady Lydingham, Lady Hargate, Lady Theodosia," Clement said, stepping into the room. He looked fully recovered but he did appear older to Delilah's eyes than he had only a few days ago. Millworth Manor would not be the same when the dear man finally decided to pass the mantle of authority to a new butler. "Lady Lydingham, Mrs. Gilbert and her assistant have arrived with your gown."

"Oh, how wonderful." Camille jumped to her feet. "Would you see them to the upstairs sitting room please and tell them I'll be there in a moment."

"As you wish, my lady." Clement nodded and took his leave.

Teddy started toward the door. "I can scarcely wait to see—" She stopped and looked at Delilah. "Oh, but you—"

"The gown can wait," Camille said with a nod. "Delilah's problem is much more pressing."

"Don't be absurd." Delilah waved off the comment. "Besides, I am just as eager for you to try on your gown as you are. Teddy and I have only seen a drawing of it after all."

"If you're certain." Doubt battled with eagerness in Camille's eyes.

"Of course I am." Delilah was in no great hurry to reveal everything she had kept secret up to now. She hooked her arm through her sister's elbow and started for the door. "Disclosure of my plan can wait a few hours."

"Well, if you insist." Camille practically dragged her to the door.

A scant half an hour later, Camille stood in the sitting room all three sisters had shared in their youth. A tall mirror had been brought in from a dressing room and reflected Camille in the gown she would wear when she promised to share Grayson's life forever. The seamstress and her assistant stood off to one side beaming. Teddy and Delilah perched on a settee and stared. The gown fit like a kid glove and the overall effect was one of perfection itself.

Mr. Worth had outdone himself. The gown was magnificent, trimmed with ecru-colored lace and edged with tiny pearls. Peach-colored satin rosettes, as perfectly crafted as if they were real roses, were gathered on either side of the waist and trailed down the back of the gown. As a widow, Camille would never wear white but the blue silk was perfect for her. The color was a pale version of the blue of Camille's eyes. A small diamond brooch that Mother had worn when she had married Father was pinned to the center of the bodice. With the fair color of Camille's hair and the deep blue of her eyes, her sister was every bit as magnificent as the gown.

"Well?" Camille studied herself in the mirror. "What do you think?"

"It's quite simply stunning." Teddy stared. "It's perfect, Camille. Absolutely perfect."

"Delilah?" Camille pulled her gaze from the mirror and glanced at her sister. "Will it do, do you think?"

For a moment, Delilah was again a young girl staring at a beautiful older sister in a glorious ball gown who, on those rare occasions, didn't mind the presence of a younger sister. Then, she never would have cared what Delilah thought. Now, well, now was different.

A lump lodged in Delilah's throat and she swallowed hard. "You look like a princess in a fairy tale."

"I do, don't I?" Camille laughed with delight and her gaze met her sister's. "Thank you."

Delilah cleared her throat. "Thank you for . . . for letting me be part of this."

"You're my only younger sister and you should be part of my life. That you haven't been in the past is nearly unforgivable. This is long overdue and I am so sorry."

Delilah nodded and choked back what felt suspiciously like a tear.

"Goodness, I've never seen the two of you being at all sentimental," Teddy said in a teasing manner, then sobered. "I need to apologize as well."

Camille's brow rose. "Oh? Do you too have a younger sister you treated abominably in the past?"

"No, I don't have sisters, but . . ." Teddy blew a long breath. "Dee has been my dearest friend for much of my life. I must confess I have always resented the way you treated her."

"You have been a good, true friend to her." Camille studied the younger woman. "She was lucky to have you."

"And I was lucky to have her," Teddy said. "And, while I admit I was skeptical when she told me you and Beryl and she had agreed to be better sisters to one another, this time spent with both of you has shown me that I was wrong to doubt you."

"Thank you, Teddy." Camille paused. "So are we friends as well now?"

"I'd like that." Teddy smiled.

"Apparently, there's nothing like an exquisite, expensive Paris gown to bring sisters and friends together," Delilah said wryly.

Camille and Teddy stared at her for a moment then all three burst into laughter.

Mrs. Gilbert cleared her throat. "I beg your pardon, my lady, but we do need to make certain of a few more things and then we must take our leave if we are to return to London today."

"Yes, of course, my apologies. Besides . . ." Camille met her sister's gaze directly. "We have matters of a serious nature to attend to as well. Delilah, why don't you arrange for tea to be served in the parlor and Teddy and I will join you as soon as we're finished here."

"Excellent idea. I'm famished." It was amazing what having a plan, even one somewhat less than solid, could do for one's appetite. She took a step toward the door then paused. "Camille, you are positively glowing in that gown."

"That's what marrying the man you love does for you, dear." Camille grinned. "But an extravagantly expensive Paris gown helps a bit too."

Delilah laughed, bid Mrs. Gilbert and her assistant good day, then headed toward the stairs. It wasn't nearly late enough for tea, but biscuits and some of Mrs. Dooley's dainty sandwiches and perhaps tarts if they were available would be lovely.

It was hard not to envy Camille her happiness. She was at long last marrying her true love. For Camille love was the beginning of happily ever after.

Delilah heaved a heartfelt sigh. In her own case, love would surely destroy everything.

"Lady Hargate." William hurried toward her and met her on the stairs. "Mrs. Dooley needs some instruction as to dinner tonight."

"Yes, of course." Delilah started toward the kitchen. Camille had been managing the house but apparently she was only recovered enough to be the bride. She winced. Now that was rude. She really did have to try to be a better person. She'd always thought she was quite a nice person until recent months.

Until her blasted adventure!

Now, in one way or another, the man was going to ruin her life. Or she might ruin his. It scarcely mattered, she'd soon be rid of him. It would hurt but it would be over quickly. And she could continue with her life as planned. No reason why she shouldn't begin immediately. She raised her chin slightly. She used to be quite pleasant. She certainly could be again.

It took far longer than she'd anticipated to talk to Mrs. Dooley. In the course of recovering from the ill effects of the tainted food, the cook had had a dream that something dire was going to happen. Mrs. Dooley confided her vision in the dark and forbidding tone of a Shakespearean witch. Given what surely was some sort of premonition, she wanted to be prepared and go over any possibility. One could hardly fault her for that. Or stop her. Any number of disasters might well befall Millworth Manor but Mrs. Dooley's culinary offerings would not be one of them. Delilah resisted the temptation to mention the food poisoning.

By the time Delilah finally arrived at the small parlor, Teddy and Camille were already there. As were sandwiches and cakes and tea. They were gracious enough to keep their curiosity in check until she had eaten a biscuit.

"Well, here we are," Camille said in the manner of an older sister. "Now, how can we help you?"

"What kind of plan?" Teddy's eyes narrowed in suspicion.

"This is very difficult for me. I rarely have anything to confess and I hardly ever have, well, secrets." Delilah looked from her sister to her friend and back. "I'm going to tell you this story once. I don't want to be overwhelmed with curiosity and queries; this is hard enough as it is. Therefore, I will only answer one question from each of you. Do you understand?"

They nodded.

"Very well then." Delilah rose to her feet. This did seem the sort of thing one should stand for.

"Well?" Camille smiled encouragingly. "Go on."

Perhaps sitting was best after all. Delilah sat back down in one of the matching chairs that had been in this parlor for as long as she could remember. Camille and Teddy shared the settee and waited expectantly. Delilah drew a deep breath. "I did meet Sam in New York."

Teddy choked.

"I knew it," Camille said under her breath.

"He and I . . . well . . . we had . . . oh, I don't know . . . an adventure you might call it." She braced herself. "Of an amorous nature."

"You?" Camille stared. "Do remind me never to ask you to chaperone again."

Teddy's eyes widened. "Why didn't you tell me?"

"Are those your questions?" Delilah said sharply.

Teddy and Camille exchanged glances then shook their heads.

"No," Camille muttered.

"Not at the moment," Teddy said. "Please continue."

"I thought I would never see him again. Then, of course, he arrived here. Needless to say I didn't want a reminder of my adventure, which is why I wasn't as pleasant to him as I should have been." Entirely true as far as it went. "But the more I got to know him the more I realized he would break my heart if I let him." Because she realized as well that she loved him and probably had from the first. And he was so very wrong. "So I want you to help me get rid of him."

Camille crossed her arms over her chest. "What exactly do you mean by get rid of him? And that's not my question but part of the plan you have yet to explain."

"When we said we would do something illegal, neither of us meant murder," Teddy said.

Delilah stared. "Do you honestly think I would kill the man?"

"No, of course we don't. Do we, Teddy?"

"Absolutely not," Teddy said with scarcely any hesitation at all.

"Well, I wouldn't." Delilah sighed. "He's quite a wonderful man, really. He's just not the right man for me. And the longer he stays here the harder it is going to be to see him leave." She shook her head. "Make him leave I mean. And really, I wish him nothing but the best. But I also wish him gone."

Both her sister and her friend stared as if she had gone mad before their very eyes.

"Well?"

"I'm more than a little confused," Teddy said.

"*We're* more than a little confused." Camille frowned. "You think he's a wonderful man yet you want nothing to do with him?"

"Is that your question?"

Camille huffed.

"We have no common ground. We're entirely different people. We envision our lives, our futures, differently. How can I expect love to succeed between two people who have no commonality of background or desires or ambitions when love can fail between two people who are completely perfect for each other?"

Teddy stared and realization washed across her face. "Oh." She nodded. "I see."

"Well, I don't but I do have my question." Camille's gaze met her sister's. "Are you in love with him?"

"Oh, no." Delilah shook her head. "You had your question a moment ago."

"That wasn't my question! I didn't—"

"Never mind, I still have my question." Teddy's

gaze bored into hers. "Are you in love with him?"

"Does it matter?"

"I think so, yes," Camille said.

The door to the parlor flew open.

"What kind of family meeting could you possibly have without me?" Beryl stood in the doorway resplendent in an aubergine-colored traveling dress. A fashionable feathered hat perched on her head. As always her posture was perfect, her presence commanding, and there was a slightly wicked gleam in her eye.

"We didn't know when you were coming." A dry note sounded in Camille's voice. "If you would be so good as to give us some notice or indicate in a manner that wasn't as vague—"

"I said I'd be here before the wedding." Beryl pulled off her gloves. "And, unless I'm mistaken, it's still over a week away." She nodded at Teddy. "Lovely to see you again, Teddy."

Teddy smiled. "I'm delighted to see you as well."

"Delilah." Beryl's gaze met hers. "You look tired. How are you getting on?"

"Better than one might expect." Delilah cast her a grateful smile. "I'm glad to see you."

"I knew you would be." Beryl smiled in a satisfied manner and studied the other women. "You two look rather pale."

"It was something we ate," Teddy said.

"But we're fine now," Camille added.

"Good. Now that the pleasantries are out of the way . . ." Beryl took off her hat, tossed it onto a table, and seated herself in the chair beside Delilah's. "What is going on here? When Clement told me you were all in Mother's parlor I knew there was something afoot and I came directly upstairs." Her gaze skimmed the gathering. "Well?"

"Delilah needs our help," Camille began. "With Mr. Russell."

"Oh, does she?" Beryl's gaze shifted to Delilah. "Have you told them everything?"

Delilah nodded. "More or less."

"Very well then." Beryl considered her younger sister. "Are you keeping him or are you getting rid of him?"

"I'm not keeping him," Delilah said firmly.

Camille shook her head. "I still don't understand why not. Certainly, he's not what she had planned but he is something of a catch."

"Nonsense, Camille." Beryl sniffed. "He's not at all what she wants. He might well be handsome and obscenely wealthy—"

"And a good man," Delilah murmured in spite of herself.

"But the fact remains that he is all wrong for her."

"I don't see why." Camille huffed. "Yes, he's American and they don't see eye to eye on any number of—" Her eyes narrowed. "How do you know any of this?"

"I know everything," Beryl said smugly.

"I saw Beryl when I was in London," Delilah said quickly.

"And I was a great deal of help." Beryl cast her younger sister what appeared suspiciously like a look of affection.

"Were you?" Camille looked from one sister to the other. "Imagine that."

Beryl smirked.

Camille frowned and continued. "As I was saying, even though Delilah claims they have nothing in common, I'm fairly certain she's in love with the man. Are you going to deny it?"

"Yes," Delilah snapped.

"None of us believes you." Camille shrugged and turned her attention back to her twin. "So her desire to get rid of him makes no sense—"

"Come now, Camille." Beryl reached over and patted her younger sister's hand. "Delilah is simply protecting herself. It's entirely logical that she would wish to avoid love with a man who is all wrong. After all, she fell in love with Phillip who was an utterly perfect match and he broke her heart. One can't blame her for wanting to avoid heartbreak again."

Teddy grimaced.

Camille stared at her younger sister. "Is that true?"

"Which part?" Delilah asked weakly.

"Apparently, this is one detail she failed to mention, an oversight on her part, I might add, as this particular detail explains all the rest of it." Beryl shook her head. "She loved Phillip and he couldn't love her back."

"I never told you that." Delilah stared at her older sister. "I said he didn't share my feelings, not that he couldn't."

"My apologies, Delilah, if I extrapolated but that part was obvious. At least to me. I didn't especially know Phillip but I knew of him. How to say this?" Beryl thought for a moment. "When a gentleman in our world manages to get through his life before marriage without so much as a whiff of gossip associated with him—no failed love affairs, no broken engagements, no scandals with actresses or other women of a questionable reputation, nothing of that sort—and then he finally marries a young, lovely, unsullied girl from a good family only to then lead somewhat separate lives, the conclusion is that he's simply not especially interested in what else she has to offer." Her gaze locked with her younger sister's. "He wanted the perfect wife or at least a wife who would appear perfect to anyone who cared to look. He was not looking for love. And in any number of marriages, that's acceptable to both sides.

"He never expected love from you. It was not what he bargained for." Beryl's gaze met

Delilah's. "I for one don't blame you in the least for not being willing to risk your heart again. After all, the odds of you and Mr. Russell being able to overcome the differences between you are extremely slim." She shook her head slowly. "It's a wager I would never take."

"I don't blame you either," Teddy said staunchly. Of course, until recently Teddy was the only one who knew that Delilah had fallen in love with her husband. "And I am willing to do whatever you need from me to get rid of Sam."

"I think this is stupid." Camille glared at the others. "Love is entirely too rare to throw away." She pinned her younger sister with a hard look. "You said you and Sam had an *adventure*. It seems to me one of the necessary ingredients to any adventure is risk. Love, above all else, is worth the risk."

"You're looking at this through the starry eyes of someone who is finally about to marry her true love." Beryl's brow furrowed in annoyance. "You can't possibly see it logically. Delilah and Mr. Russell are entirely wrong for each other. Hearts are bound to be broken. Hers or his or, more likely, both. The sensible course is to avoid this match altogether."

"Sensible has nothing to do with love!" Camille glared at her twin.

Beryl glared back. "And therein lies the problem!"

"So what is your plan?" Teddy said in an obvious effort to stop the twins from coming to blows.

"Sam was engaged once, to a woman he was in love with. As it turned out, she was more interested in his position and his wealth than she was him. He has vowed to avoid fortune hunters." Delilah drew a deep breath. "I intend to prove to him I am exactly what he doesn't want."

"How very clever of you." Beryl favored her with an admiring smile.

"And how do you intend to do that?" Camille snapped.

"I don't know, which is precisely why I need your help." Delilah thought for a moment. "I had thought that I might, well, throw myself at the first wealthy, titled gentleman I saw. But as tonight's party has been cancelled, there is no one available to throw myself at. Although, there are any number of guests who will be staying at the manor and Mother made certain their number includes several eligible gentlemen."

Teddy shook her head. "But most of those won't be arriving until a few days before the wedding. I daresay you want to put your plan into effect as soon as possible."

"Actually, she has a bit of a reprieve." Camille sighed in surrender. "Grayson says he and Sam will be spending all their time at the carriage house until the motorwagon is repaired. So

Delilah should have no difficulties avoiding Sam." She glanced at her younger sister. "Which I assume you prefer."

Delilah nodded.

"What's a motorwagon?" Beryl asked.

"A horseless carriage," Teddy said.

"Really?" Beryl's eyes widened. "How very interesting."

"It's not at all easy to find an eligible gentleman when you need one, you know," Teddy pointed out. "Although, I suppose we could hire an actor."

All three sisters stared at her.

"No! Absolutely not." Horror shone in Camille's eyes. "Actors will not do. Actors are not at all dependable. There will be no actors."

"I don't know," Beryl said in an overly innocent manner. "That might be a possibility."

Camille leveled a scathing look at her sister. Beryl bit back a laugh.

"An actor won't do." Delilah sighed. "And this is the only plan I can think of."

"It shouldn't be discarded simply because there is a tiny problem," Beryl said. "It certainly isn't insurmountable."

"As much as I don't agree with what you're doing—I do like Sam after all—it is a clever idea," Camille said in a grudging manner.

"Then you will help me?" Delilah said to Camille.

"Of course I will," Camille said with a sigh.

"You're my sister and my first loyalty is to you."

"I knew you would come around." Beryl nodded smugly. "And aside from this one difficulty, I think it's a brilliant plan."

"How delightful." A familiar voice rang from the doorway. "I do so love it when one of you has come up with a brilliant plan."

Chapter Nineteen

"Mother!" Delilah jumped to her feet and greeted her mother.

The small parlor could barely contain the flurry of embraces and choruses of greetings.

"Travel must agree with you. You look wonderful!"

"Is Father with you? You haven't misplaced him again, have you?"

"What did you like best?"

"We have missed you!"

Lord and Lady Briston had been traveling since early spring and aside from an occasional letter—Mother had always been dreadful at keeping up with correspondence—Delilah wasn't certain at any given moment exactly where her wandering parents were on the map. Still, they were wandering together and there was much to be said for that.

"I can't tell you how good it is to be home." Mother settled in the chair Beryl had vacated for her. "Although I do find travel most stimulating. And let me say, there is nothing to bring a couple closer together than having to negotiate the deserts of Egypt sharing a camel or being forced to huddle together for warmth awaiting repairs on a sled somewhere in the Swiss Alps." She nodded at the cups on the table and Delilah obediently filled one for her.

Somewhere in the midst of greeting their returning parent, a nearly unnoticed footman had slipped in and added cups and another plate of sandwiches to the tray. It was good to have the servants back. Delilah vowed when she could rehire her staff, it would be at higher wages. There was nothing like being without servants to make one appreciate their worth.

"I had no idea extensive travel could be so enlightening," Mother continued. "Why, I feel much more intelligent now than when I left. But I must admit, there were times when I did long to understand what people were trying to say to me." She sighed. "It does seem rather odd that not everyone in the world speaks English. You would think, given the vast expanse of the empire, everyone would have mastered English by now. Still . . ." She beamed at the younger women. "All part and parcel of the adventure I would say."

Delilah smiled weakly.

"Oh, Camille dear." Mother turned to Camille. "We ran into Victor in London yesterday and it was quite awkward when the subject of your wedding came up. I gather you did not invite him?"

Camille's brows drew together in confusion. "Victor who?"

"Surely you don't mean Cousin Victor?" Beryl stared.

"Cousin Victor?" Teddy said in an aside to Delilah.

"Lord Charborough," Delilah said quietly. "He's a relation on my mother's side but so distant no one has any idea how we're related."

Camille frowned. "I can't even recall the last time I saw him."

"Neither could I. I feel quite badly about that." Mother shook her head. "I assured him his invitation must have gone astray. So . . ." She paused. "We brought him with us."

"You didn't." Camille stared although she shouldn't have been surprised. Mother had long had a tendency to collect strays, usually minor European royalty who had lost home or country. That she had now brought home a distant relative was veering perilously close to something a normal person might do.

"I most certainly did," Mother said in a no-nonsense tone. "It is my house, after all."

"Yes, of course." Camille heaved a resigned sigh. "Very well."

"The poor dear no longer has two shillings to rub together, thanks to his wastrel of a father and the fact that he pours whatever funds he manages to acquire into that estate of his. It's not easy supporting a crumbling castle, you know. Although I don't believe his financial difficulty is common knowledge."

"It's not a well-kept secret," Beryl said wryly.

"The best thing for the poor boy would be to find a wife with excellent connections and a sizable dowry. I thought, as there will be any number of suitable matches here for the wedding, this might be a good opportunity for him," Mother said. "Besides, one can always use another unattached gentleman about. Especially one as dashing as Victor. My goodness, he did turn out to be a handsome devil."

"He is, isn't he?" Beryl said thoughtfully and glanced at Delilah. "One might say he is very nearly perfect."

"Perhaps," Delilah said slowly. "But you just said everyone knows he has no money."

Teddy shook her head. "Sam wouldn't know that."

"Who is Sam?" Mother asked, eyes wide with confusion.

"An American friend of Grayson's, Mother," Camille said. "Grayson probably isn't aware of Victor's financial state either given that he's been out of the country for so many years."

"Still, it's one thing to throw oneself at a man who has a fortune and quite another to overtly pursue one who needs money." Teddy shook her head. "You wouldn't want to lead the poor man on and disappoint him."

"You're right. I hadn't considered that." Delilah sighed. "That would be wrong."

"You could certainly ask him to go along with

you." Camille shrugged. "As a favor, one distant cousin to another."

"Or you could pay him," Beryl said. "I daresay, given his financial straits he would be more than willing to play the role of perfect prospect."

"He would never take money for doing a favor for a relative, no matter how distant. He still has pride, after all. And I'm confident he will help without any compensation at all." Mother thought for a moment. "But you might offer him a loan, which would certainly encourage his cooperation. One never knows when it might come in handy to have a handsome gentleman indebted to you," she said to Teddy.

Teddy nodded, her eyes wide. But then Teddy had always found Lady Briston's views on life a little shocking and most amusing.

"That's that then." Delilah shook her head. "I have nothing to offer him at the moment. My funds are still unavailable and I doubt that problem will be completely resolved in the next few days."

"I can and I will." Beryl smiled at her younger sister. "And I'd be happy to do so."

"As would I," Camille added.

"Would you?" Beryl's brow rose. "And how would you explain that to Sam's dear friend, your future husband, should he find out?"

"We shall simply have to make certain he

doesn't find out," Camille said. "I know I can keep a secret."

"As can I. But before I can keep a secret, someone is going to have to reveal said secret to me." Mother's gaze slid from one sister to the next. "I have absolutely no idea what we are talking about, although an educated guess would indicate this has to do with the previously mentioned plan."

"Exactly." Beryl beamed. "And a brilliant plan at that."

"So you said. Very well then." Mother took a sip of tea then looked at her daughters expectantly. "Explain it to me."

"I will," Delilah said quickly. Far better for her to provide a somewhat abbreviated version of events thus far than for one of her sisters to attempt it. God knows what they might say inadvertently. Besides, there was no need for her mother to know every detail. "It all has to do with Mr. Russell, Samuel. . . ."

Delilah briefly explained nearly everything. That she and Sam did not suit, how a match between them would be disastrous and really, it was best for all concerned if they showed Sam how very wrong Delilah was for him. She did not feel it necessary to mention their shared adventures but, as Beryl had pointed out earlier, since it did seem to be at the crux of everything, Delilah did confess her feelings for Phillip and what a dreadful mistake that had been.

"My, my, you have been busy." Mother considered her youngest daughter for a long moment. "My poor dear girl. There is nothing worse in this world than loving someone who does not love you back."

"Yes, well . . ." Delilah shrugged. "That's in the past."

"Oh, come now, dear," Mother said. "It may be over but it certainly isn't in the past. Why, the risk of having your heart broken again is precisely why you don't want to entrust it to this American."

"And because we are wrong for each other," Delilah said. "It cannot end well."

"It can but the chances are exceptionally slim. Oh certainly, on occasion, one hears of a successful match in which the parties involved are obviously wrong for one another—a duke marrying a parlor maid and that sort of thing." Mother shrugged as if the very idea was too absurd to consider. "But usually such matches are doomed to failure. No." She nodded. "I think you're quite wise to put an end to this. Besides, making such an arrangement work would require a great deal of effort not to mention staggering compromise and that's really not a concept you embrace."

Delilah stared at her mother. "Are you saying I'm stubborn?"

"That's exactly what I'm saying." Mother

smiled. "I've never been anything less than honest with you or your sisters—"

"Except for that little matter about saying Father was dead when he wasn't," Beryl said under her breath.

Mother continued without pause. "And I don't intend to start now. So yes dear, you are stubborn. Beyond that, you have always been far too concerned with propriety and what you should do or who you should be for that matter. You have spent your entire life thus far doing exactly what you were expected to do and never treading from the path of proper behavior."

Delilah's eyes narrowed. "Goodness, Mother, I'm not certain if that was a compliment or a criticism."

"You are my youngest girl, my dear darling daughter." Mother smiled. "You've never given me a moment of trouble or so much as a single sleepless night. You have never created scandal or been the subject of gossip." She cast a pointed glance at Camille and Beryl then returned her attention to Delilah. "You are kind and generous, you have a good heart, you're clever and amusing and you're exceptionally lovely as well. Indeed, you look very much like I did at your age."

Someone snorted. Mother ignored it. "You made the very best of an awkward situation with Phillip. I long suspected something was awry but I do so hate to interfere so I kept my doubts to myself. I assumed you would tell me if you needed me."

Delilah nodded although she'd never considered confiding in her mother. It was hard to admit to anyone, let alone your mother, that your marriage was not what you wished it to be.

"I have always been proud of you and I always will be."

Delilah's throat tightened and she stared at her mother.

"You need to do what you think is right for you. Nothing and no one else really matters." Mother reached over and took her hand. "You have my complete and total support in however you want to handle this American. Although . . ." Amusement twinkled in her eyes. "If you wished to shoot the man, I do think that would be best left to your father."

"I don't." Delilah choked back a sob. "Thank you, Mother."

"Now that we have that settled I do have a another question." Mother's gaze narrowed. "What on earth did you mean when you said your funds were unavailable?"

Never in his life had Sam been at a loss over how to solve a dilemma. He stood outside the carriage house and stared unseeing off into the distance. Certainly, whatever problem he'd been faced with might be difficult, it might even appear impossible and yes, on occasion his solutions had been complete and utter failures but that was different. That was business. This was personal.

"Very well then," Gray said behind him. "I surrender."

"What do you mean, you surrender?" Sam turned toward his friend.

It was already late afternoon, a full day past the motorwagon's accident. He and Gray had practically taken up residence with Jim at the carriage house, only returning to the manor last night to sleep. They returned shortly after dawn this morning. All things considered, staying away from the manor was a wise move. It was all he could do to keep from knocking down Delilah's door and making her see how wrong she was. Making her admit that she did care for him and that, in spite of their differences, they were meant to be together. Sam needed distance between himself and that temptation but it wasn't easy. He could well understand where Sampson went wrong.

"I mean . . ." Gray handed him a cigar. "I give up."

Sam shook his head. "I have no idea what you're talking about." He aimed the cigar at his friend. "And where did you get these?"

"I had William bring them down with our last meal. I have one for Jim too." He struck a match and lit his cigar.

"Good." Sam lit his cigar. "He deserves it."

"The man is brilliant. You are lucky to have him."

"I know." Sam paused. "If we can get this motorwagon business running, I was thinking of offering him a new position."

Gray puffed on his cigar. "You want him to run the new company? I wouldn't be opposed to that."

"I don't think he'd like running the whole thing. It's not where his strength is. He's not much for sitting at a desk." Sam paused. "I'd like to put him in charge of development, that sort of thing. A position equal in importance to the head of the company. That's where the future lies. Benz's motorwagon is a first step, but this new engine of his is really the beginning and opens a world of possibilities. Jim's just the man to take that further."

"I agree." Gray nodded. "But the motorwagon isn't what I was referring to when I said I surrender."

"Then I have no idea what you mean."

"I mean, I have known you long enough to know when something is weighing on your mind."

"Any number of things are weighing on my mind. There's a lot of repair needed here."

"Yes, and I thought that was it initially but it's not. You've been distant and preoccupied since the accident. Usually I can tell what you're thinking, but I admit you have me stymied so I give up." Gray studied him closely. "Now, I'm asking. What is wrong with you?"

Sam considered the question, not that he needed to. What was wrong with him could be summed up in one word: Delilah. "It appears I may have fallen in love."

Gray stared. "With whom?"

Sam cast him a wry look.

"There's no one . . . ." Gray's eyes widened with surprise. "Delilah?"

"I'm afraid so." Sam nodded. "And I'm fairly certain she's in love with me as well."

"She doesn't even like you."

Sam shrugged.

"What are you not telling me?"

"For one thing, we did meet in New York."

"I knew it!" Gray paused. "And? Obviously there's more."

"And I haven't been able to get her out of my thoughts since then." Sam shook his head. "She's haunted me, Gray. Whether I'm awake or asleep, she's lingered, in my mind, in my dreams. I would have followed her back here long ago if she hadn't been so adamant about never seeing me again." He chuckled in a mirthless manner. "Almost rude about it, really."

"This explains so much," Gray murmured.

"I have never met a woman in my life who was more opposed to, well, love, than she is. I always thought love is ultimately what all women wanted, especially when it came to marriage."

"I thought Lenore would have awakened you to that fallacy."

"One would think. But it's not the same." He shook his head. "In ways too numerous to mention, Delilah is nothing like Lenore. Except that love is not on her list of requirements for marriage."

"You've asked her to marry you?" Shock rang in Gray's voice.

"I am not so stupid as to ask a question I already know the answer to, when the answer is one I don't want to hear."

"This is extremely confusing."

"Believe me, I am well aware of that."

"Let me see if I have this right." Gray puffed his cigar thoughtfully. "You love her. You think she loves you. But you won't ask her to marry you for fear she'll say no because she doesn't want to marry for love?"

"That's pretty much it." Sam stared at the glowing tip of his cigar. "If I live to be a thousand years, I will never understand the English. Or women for that matter."

"We can be a confusing lot but no man of any nationality understands women."

"Except the French and maybe the Italians."

"No, they just think they do."

"Delilah has this . . . this perfect match she's determined to marry."

"Ah yes." Gray nodded in a knowing manner. "A gentleman with a lofty title and an even greater bank account."

"Exactly."

"You have more money than she could spend in a lifetime."

"Yes, but it's new money. I'm nouveau riche, you know. Apparently, there is a stigma to that although I'm pretty sure it spends the same way. Plus, I'm American. An unforgivable sin in her eyes."

"Good God no." Gray heaved an overly dramatic sigh. "That will never do."

"And regardless of the position my family—mostly my mother—has clawed out in society we don't have titles in America." Sam puffed on his cigar. "There's more, of course. Basic differences between us. Delilah values tradition whereas I am aimed toward the future. As she has pointed out to me on more than one occasion, we have nothing in common."

"Except love."

"Which is not what Delilah wants. She thinks our differences are insurmountable. I don't." He paused. "She is protecting herself from heart-break. I can understand that. It's a most sensible position, really. Still . . ." He glanced at his friend. "What am I supposed to do, Gray?"

"I might not be the best person to give advice in this situation. It took me eleven years to accept that Camille was the only woman in the world for me."

"I'd prefer not to wait eleven years."

"Well, you do have a few choices." Gray drew on his cigar thoughtfully. "You could fight for her. Try to convince her she's wrong. Come up with a way to make her see that love is worth the risk of heartbreak. Although I should warn you." He grimaced. "I have known her all her life and she's fairly stubborn."

"Is she?" Sam's brow rose. "I hadn't noticed."

"Or you could bow to her wishes, I suppose." He paused. "You should probably consider that she might actually be right. The differences between you may be too great to overcome. Ultimately, you could both be miserable for the rest of your lives."

"Do you think she's right?"

"No, I don't." Gray puffed on his cigar. "I have been in love with Camille for much of my life. Even when I intended never to see her again, when she had married someone else, she was always with me. Somewhere, in the back of my mind or maybe in my heart, I don't know, but she was always there. I could no more forget about her than I could stop breathing. But it wasn't until I returned to England and saw her again that I realized, in spite of my best efforts, she was the love of my life." He aimed his cigar at Sam. "And life wasn't worth living without her."

"What are you saying?"

"I suppose I'm saying even if I knew marrying Camille would end in certain heartbreak, I would rather have a moment of happiness with her than a lifetime without her," he said slowly. "I'm saying the joys of love are worth the risks."

"Well, now that we have you convinced, how do I convince your future sister-in-law?"

"I have no idea. I wish I had some sage, sound, definitive advice for you but I don't." He shook his head. "Delilah is nothing like Camille. Of all three sisters, Delilah is the most practical and sensible. She is the one who has always done precisely what was expected of her in all matters. Up to and including the type of man she married." Gray thought for a moment. "I don't know that you can change that."

"I can try," Sam said grimly.

"It seems to me you are a risk she is not willing to take." He paused. "But then she's never taken risks before. She's never strayed from the path laid out for her. Never veered from the boundaries of proper and expected behavior. Delilah is not an adventurous sort."

"Probably not." Although for a few days in New York, she was.

"Answer me this," Gray said slowly. "If she was, oh, say, an investment, what would be your next step?"

"That's a ridiculous analogy."

418

"No, it's not. Just think about it for a moment." Gray's brow furrowed in thought. "If she were a company you wished to purchase, what would you do?"

"I don't know." He glared at his friend. "Evaluate its strengths and weaknesses, I suppose. Try to determine where it's vulnerable. Whether the plans for future operation and expansion are viable. Appraise its debts, assets, that sort of thing."

"So what are Delilah's strengths?"

"This is absurd." Sam sighed. "I don't know. She's intelligent. She's beautiful." He thought for a moment. "She's stronger than she thinks. I can't explain exactly how I know that but I do. It's an observation more than anything. She plays chess nearly as well as she plays tennis. She's passionate about her convictions. She's amusing. I enjoy her company. I enjoy just being with her."

"And her weaknesses?"

"She's intelligent. But she doesn't realize the value of that. She's stubborn, of course, but you know that. She absolutely refuses to see that she could possibly be wrong."

"Perhaps you have much in common after all." Gray puffed his cigar and stared into the distance. "So, does that make anything clearer? Do you see what you have to do now?"

"Not at all." Sam blew a perfect smoke ring. "Haven't a clue."

"Damn. Sorry, old man, that was the best I could do." Gray blew a ring to match his friend's. "Well, you have time to figure something out. Without access to her money she has nowhere else to go. She's essentially trapped here."

"That problem has been resolved, although I suspect it will be some time before everything is set to rights. Even if everything moves faster than expected, she'll be here at least through the wedding. So that gives me . . . what?" He glanced the other man. "Twelve days until the wedding?"

Gray nodded. "Plenty of time. You've accomplished more with less."

"You know, I think I could compete if this question of marriage involved a real suitor. If there was actually another man she had set her sights on."

"I'd wager on you in a heartbeat."

"But competing with an ideal, with a concept, regardless of how flawed it might be . . ." He shook his head. "There's nothing solid to fight."

"Hard to confront something that's little more than an idea."

"Exactly."

Both men fell silent. Beside him, Gray was lost in his own thoughts, his own problems.

Sam still had no idea how to reach Delilah, how to convince her love was worth the risk of heartbreak. He was willing to chance it and he had been hurt in the past. But then Delilah had never really taken risks until she'd allowed herself to fall in love with her husband. Gray was right from the beginning. Lord Hargate had been an idiot. Now, it was up to Sam to make her believe in love and magic and forever.

How was still the question.

When it came right down to it, maybe Delilah's only true weakness was that, even if she refused to admit it, she was in love with him.

Or maybe that was his.

Chapter Twenty

Eight days before the wedding . . .

Millworth Manor was fast filling up.

While Sam and Gray spent nearly all their time at the carriage house, whenever they did venture back to the manor someone new had arrived. Delilah's parents had finally returned home. Lord Briston seemed a good enough sort although Sam was still confused as to the details of his untimely death and subsequent resurrection. Lady Briston was lovely but a bit flighty. Still, one suspected there was steel beneath her capricious surface. She reminded him of his mother especially given the way she studied him like an insect under glass. It was more than a little unnerving. Lady Dunwell had also arrived although apparently her husband wouldn't join them until the day before the wedding. Then there was Lord Charborough, introduced as a friend of the family. He appeared pleasant enough although there was something about him that made Sam vaguely uneasy. Perhaps it was because no man had the right to be quite that handsome. Or perhaps it was because he was everything that Sam was not. Everything Delilah wanted.

After two full days of working at the carriage

house, he and Gray decided Sam and Jim would go into London to try to find parts they couldn't fix, or have parts fabricated to their specifications, as well as look for space to rent to repair the vehicle. It made sense to be closer to whatever supplies might still be needed. Besides, it might be necessary to telegraph Mr. Benz for advice. That would be much easier in London. If they could find an appropriate place, Jim and the motorwagon would move into the city. As London was so easily accessible, Sam and Gray would meet with Jim every few days to check on his progress.

Sam and Jim's foray into London served Gray well. Apparently, Camille was somewhat irritated at his constant absence from the manor. Not, as Gray pointed out, that his presence was necessary anyway. The groom, he confided, was nothing more than a theatrical prop. Necessary to the plot of the play but all in all a strictly minor character. Regardless, the bride was not happy especially given that her father had joined the men several times when he was expected to be elsewhere. Lord Briston was fascinated by the motorwagon but, as he always brought cigars and a decanter of good Scottish whisky with him, neither Sam nor Gray thought the vehicle was the primary attraction. Oddly enough, they didn't seem to get as much accomplished when Lord Briston was with them either.

"I didn't see you when you arrived back yesterday," Gray said when he met Sam at the carriage house. "I assume you came directly here. I would have joined you but . . ." He shuddered. "It appears the love of my life is insane."

Sam laughed. "Come now, Gray. It can't be that bad."

"You have no idea," Gray said darkly.

"I have five sisters. I have some idea."

"I have no sisters. I had no warning and no idea a wedding could turn a perfectly lovely woman into some kind of unrecognizable creature from the depths of hell. Frankenstein's creation pales in comparison."

"You're exaggerating." Sam chuckled.

"I wish I was." Gray shook his head. "If anything I'm being kind." He glanced from side to side as if afraid of being overheard and lowered his voice. "Did you know the wrong shoes can ruin an otherwise perfect wedding? And the shoes that Camille ordered from London are apparently wrong. Which seems to be part of a conspiracy to completely ruin her life. Did you know, if you point out in a manner designed to be helpful, that the shoes look fine to you, you will bring the wrath of a thousand furies down upon your head?"

"I would have guessed that one."

"Well, I am not so astute." Gray winced at the memory. "Did you know that if the dresses her sisters are wearing as her attendants are not the

424

right shade of peach they will clash with the satin flowers on her dress? Peach, Sam, peach!" He shook his head. "I thought it was a fruit."

Sam bit his lip to keep from laughing. Poor Gray was clearly out of his element.

"Did you know if some of the people coming to this wedding, people I've never met by the way, are forced to sit next to one another at dinner it could ignite the kind of feud that brings down nations?"

Sam choked back a laugh.

"Camille says it has to be perfect. Everything. Every detail, every aspect, every minuscule point. Perfect."

"But she's been through this before."

Gray waved off the comment. "She says this is different. She says this wedding is much more important because it's a miracle that we found our way back to each other. She says this is the beginning of the rest of our lives, therefore it has to be perfect. And woe be it to anyone who stands between her and perfection. I feel almost as sorry for Teddy as I do for myself. I never realized part and parcel of the work of the person planning the event was to keep the bride sane. Fortunately, Teddy is remarkably calm and seems to have everything well in hand." His eyes narrowed. "But Beryl keeps egging Camille on and delights in doing so."

In spite of his best efforts, Sam laughed.

"This is not amusing!" Gray had a look of panic about him.

"It will be over soon."

"Eight days and nine hours, more or less." Gray blew a long breath. "I'm not sure I can survive until then. Worst of all . . ."

He'd never seen his friend like this. Gray was right. He shouldn't be amused. But he couldn't help it. "I can't wait to hear what's worst of all."

"I can't stop thinking, I know it's absurd but, still, I can't get it out of my head. . . ."

"What?"

"What if she stays like this?" Genuine fear shone in Gray's eyes. "What if this is just the beginning? What if this wedding has pushed her over the edge into real insanity or revealed her true self?"

"Well," Sam said in an offhand manner. "You can always tell her you've changed your mind and call off the wedding."

"Now you're insane." Gray scoffed. "First of all, the murderous look in her eyes would then be directed at me. And if she didn't murder me, Beryl certainly would. She's wanted to do so for years. Beryl would jump at the chance to shoot me or, more likely, draw and quarter me. Slowly. And with a great deal of pleasure on her part. No, believe me, Sam, it's better to take my chances on life with a madwoman than to run afoul of Beryl."

"Good man." Sam clapped his friend on the

back. "Now, do you want me to tell you what happened in London?"

"Absolutely, but before we get into that . . ." Gray smiled in a wicked manner. "There's a price to be paid for your absence from the manor, even if we both know you're only trying to avoid Delilah."

"Not at all," Sam lied.

Avoiding Delilah until he could figure out exactly what to do about her had seemed like a good idea in the beginning. It had been four days since he'd so much as gotten a glimpse of her and he suspected she was avoiding him as well. Unfortunately, he was no closer to coming up with an answer for what to do and he couldn't avoid her forever. Nor did he really want to. Nights were the worst. He lay in his bed tossing and turning and thinking about how she was only steps away from him. Damn it all, he missed the woman. Missed talking to her and teasing her and even arguing with her. Still, he had only one idea and it might be worse than doing nothing at all.

"My thoughts are entirely engaged in trying to help Jim get this blasted machine back in perfect working condition. The fact that in doing so, I am also avoiding awkward encounters with Delilah, just happens to be an unexpected benefit."

"Then you won't mind joining us tonight for dinner although you really have no choice. Call it a command performance if you will."

"I'd be delighted."

"While you were gone yesterday, Lord Radnor, his wife, and his two daughters arrived. Lord Radnor is Lord Briston's second cousin I believe, or something like that. The daughters are relatively attractive and looking for husbands."

"Aren't they all?" Sam murmured.

"Also joining our ranks are Mr. Martin, his mother, and sister. She is in the market for a husband as well. No idea how they're related but they are. Or at least I think they are. Oh yes, and Lord Latimer and Lord Dantrey are expected this afternoon."

"That is quite a crowd."

"That's just the beginning. But it does appear that the hunt is on."

"The hunt?"

"The spouse hunt. There is nothing like a wedding to spur the forces of matchmaking into full-blown splendor." He grimaced. "Camille confided to me, before she went insane, that her mother had made certain there was a substantial number of eligible gentlemen about. Although I gather the very dashing Lord Charborough was a last-minute addition."

"Oh?" Sam raised a brow.

"Don't look at me like that. I have no idea why." He paused. "Although if one is hoping to encourage suitable matches . . ."

Sam's eyes narrowed. "He's perfect, isn't he?"

"I suppose that depends on how you define perfect." Gray shrugged. "He does have a castle I hear."

"Of course he does."

"But when you look at it, he's no more perfect than Latimer or Dantrey or Martin."

"I thought it was Mr. Martin?"

"It is, but he is the heir to an earldom."

"Imagine my surprise."

"So . . ." Gray adopted an overly nonchalant manner. "No queries about Delilah? No wondering if she is pining away without your presence?"

Sam raised a brow. "Is she?"

"It's hard to tell what with all the wedding anxiety in the air. She seems a bit on edge but then they all do." Gray studied him curiously. "I gather from your tone you have yet to decide what to do about the fair Delilah."

"You have always been perceptive." Sam paused. "I have given it some thought."

"Some?"

"All right, aside from the motorwagon I've thought of nothing but her."

"And?"

"I'm an intelligent man. I've built what some would call a small empire. You would think such a man would come up with some way to win the heart of the woman he loves."

"Love has nothing to do with intelligence."

"I accused her of falling in love with me. I never told her I had fallen in love with her." Sam shrugged. "Maybe I should tell her how I feel."

"That's it, that's the right attitude. Lay your heart out before her like a rug and hope she doesn't grind it into the ground."

"Do you have a better idea?"

"Not me." Gray shook his head. "I am too busy dealing with a lunatic bride to worry about what you are going to do. You are on your own."

"Always good to know where you stand."

"I do what I can." Gray paused. "You should probably do something though, even if it's wrong. You can't keep avoiding her and hope all will fall into place. It won't."

"I'm well aware of that."

"I know you have your own problems but do promise me you will be at dinner. That will be one less thing for Camille to be annoyed about."

Sam chuckled. "Believe me, I don't want to draw her ire."

"Yes, well, we would hate to distract her from the true villain of the piece, which is apparently imperfection in whatever form it might take. Be it in the wrong color or the wrong seating or the wrong shoes."

"At least it's not the wrong groom."

"There is that." Gray heaved a resigned sigh. "So tell me, how did things go in London?"

"Better than expected." Sam briefly explained

430

that they had found an ideal location to rent and Jim was even now making arrangements to transport the vehicle to London.

"That's one less thing to worry about." Gray stared apprehensively in the direction of the manor. "I suppose I should be getting back."

"Try not to sound so eager."

"I am eager for this to be over." He squared his shoulders. "Eight days and nine hours, more or less, and Camille will be my wife and either once again be the woman I love or . . ." He shuddered. "I can't even begin to think what *or* might be."

Sam chuckled. "She'll be fine. Someday you'll look back on this and—"

"What? Laugh?" Gray shook his head. "Only if we survive."

"You will." Sam cast him an encouraging smile. "Aren't you the man who told me love was worth the risk?"

"I didn't know I'd be taking my life in my hands when I said it."

"But you meant it."

"Of course I did." Gray drew a deep breath. "This is just a momentary aberration. It will all be over soon enough."

"And well worth it."

"I keep telling myself that," he said under his breath. "Dinner is at the usual time. Aside from the fact that Camille wants you there, I could use an ally."

"I wouldn't miss it."

"I would given half the chance." He cast his friend a half-hearted smile and headed toward the manor.

Gray was right, Sam had to do something. Declaring himself to Delilah didn't strike him as the best move but he had no other ideas.

It wasn't bad enough that the woman laid claim to his heart; she had turned him into an idiot as well.

Delilah greeted him politely enough when they gathered in the parlor before dinner and then pointedly turned her attention to Charborough. Sam was introduced to all the other members of the party and scarcely had any time at all to dwell on the way Delilah flirted with Charborough. He'd never in his life been jealous yet jealousy was surely what he was feeling now. Still, two could play that game and he turned his attentions toward the lovely Radnor sisters and the equally charming Miss Martin. None of whom seemed to find his being American to be anything other than delightful. Under other circumstances, he would have found the three young ladies most amusing and would have enjoyed their vying for his favor. But tonight, there was only one woman on his mind. Delilah, of course, was busy laughing at anything Charborough said or tapping her fan flirtatiously on his arm or even gazing into his eyes. Worst of all, Charborough seemed every bit as taken with her.

The conversation at dinner ebbed and flowed around the table with no less than half a dozen different discussions ongoing at any minute. Delilah was seated across from Sam and close to the head of the table between Gray and Charborough. Obviously, no accident. Lady Dunwell was on Sam's right, Miss Martin on his left. She seemed quite taken with Lord Latimer on her far side, giving Sam plenty of opportunity to watch Delilah engage Charborough in what appeared to be verging on intimate conversation.

"I must admit, Mr. Russell, I'm most intrigued by the idea of your motorwagon," Lady Dunwell said. "I should very much like to ride in it."

"It's not ready for a ride at the moment, I'm afraid." Sam shook his head. "And we're moving it to London tomorrow."

"I see." She paused. "But you will be back for the wedding, won't you, Mr. Russell?"

"Oh, I'm just accompanying the vehicle. I'll only be gone for the day." He smiled. "And it's Sam."

"Excellent, Sam, and you should call me Beryl." She leaned closer in a confidential manner. "I've always found it awkward when people sharing the same house stand on formalities. Tell me something, Sam."

"Yes?"

"Camille said you and Grayson might be seeking investors in your motorwagon company."

He nodded slowly. "That's one of the things we've discussed."

"Should you decide to pursue that course of action, I would be very interested."

"Would you?" His eyes narrowed. "Why?"

She laughed. "My goodness, Sam, you needn't look at me with quite that much suspicion."

"I am sorry." He grabbed his glass and took a quick swallow of wine. "You simply took me by surprise. You understand it is a risky venture."

"But what's worthwhile in life that isn't a risk?" Her direct gaze met his and it struck him that the motorwagon might not be the only thing she was talking about. "I'm always interested in something new and exciting."

"And your husband?"

"Oh, Lionel is quite a progressive sort. He'll be here a day or two before the wedding. Perhaps the two of you can talk then." She sipped her wine and studied him over the rim of her glass. "But you should know, I have my own funds. And while I would certainly discuss something like this with him, as I do value his opinion, I would as well do as I wished."

Sam chuckled. "That is progressive of him."

"I know." She cast him a smug smile. "It's one of his best features."

He laughed.

"Grayson, no doubt, has filled your head with all sorts of half-truths about me." Amusement twinkled in her blue eyes, the exact same shade as her younger sister's.

Sam chose his words with care. "He has mentioned you."

"He's wise to be wary of me."

"You don't like him."

"Goodness, Sam, I've known the man all of my life. I simply adore Grayson. But if you tell him that, I'll deny it and call you a lying lunatic."

Sam laughed. "I'll keep that in mind."

"See that you do." She paused. "I like Grayson, I always have but as much as I like him I love my sisters. He broke Camille's heart long ago and I suppose as she broke his heart as well, one could argue that they are on even footing."

"They seem to have gotten past that."

She nodded. "In truth, I'm delighted they have found each other again. She trusts him implicitly. I'm not sure I will until they have been married, happily mind you, some forty years or so."

He chuckled. "A bit long, don't you think?"

"Very well then." She heaved a resigned sigh. "Thirty years. But no less."

He laughed.

"I am very loyal, Sam."

"Remind me never to get on your bad side."

"You would be wise to remember that." Her tone hardened. "I only want what's best for my sisters. Both of them." She paused for a moment. "I've been remiss in that, in the past, when it comes to Delilah."

His gaze strayed down the table to Delilah. "I understand you've never been close."

"It's easy when one has a twin who is also your closest friend, to forget that she is not your only sister." She shook her head. "Oddly enough, as I rarely have regrets about anything, I do regret that. And I intend to do better." She paused. "He's perfect for her, you know."

"I have no idea what you're talking about," he said, his gaze still on Delilah.

"He's everything she wants. Or perhaps he's only everything she thinks she wants. Or thinks she should want."

"Perhaps?"

"I'm not a fool, Sam," Beryl said coolly. "As perfect as Charborough may be . . ." She leaned closer and lowered her voice. "She's in love with you."

"I know."

"Are you in love with her?"

His gaze snapped to Beryl's. "And if I am?"

"Then you should do something about it."

"Well, I hope you have some ideas as to what that might be because I do not," he said in a sharp tone. "My apologies. I didn't mean—"

"Think nothing of it." She waved off his apology. "But you might wish to smile and look as if we are discussing something no more significant than, oh, say, the weather."

"Of course." He smiled.

"And you have told me what I need to know."

"I suppose I have."

"It won't be easy," she warned.

"It hasn't been thus far. I don't expect that to change now."

"She is convinced that the differences between you are too great to overcome. I imagine that just makes it more of a challenge. And Sam." She laid her hand on his arm and gazed into his eyes. "You strike me as a man well suited to a challenge."

He nodded. "I am."

"And you rarely lose."

"Rarely."

"Oh, I do like it that you didn't say never. I don't think one should trust a man who doesn't acknowledge that he is not infallible. Now then." She glanced down the table at Delilah, who was paying them no notice whatsoever. No, she was entirely engrossed in whatever Charborough was saying. "What is your plan?"

"I don't really have a plan."

"Are you mad?" Her eyes widened in disbelief but her smile remained on her face. "One must always have a plan. Delilah is exceptionally fond of plans."

"I was thinking that I should just declare myself and ask her to marry me. . . ."

Beryl stared. "That's your plan?"

"It's all I've got," he said weakly.

"I must say it's not much of a plan. It's not especially original and I can't imagine it will work although it is a beginning, I suppose. But you should still try to think of another plan when this one fails." A vague hint of indecision flashed through her eyes. "You should probably know, Delilah does have a plan."

He studied her closely. "Are you going to tell me what it is?"

"Absolutely not." Her smile never faltered. "I promised Delilah my full support."

"And yet you're helping me."

"Nonsense, I really haven't done anything but ascertain your oh, worth if you will, for myself. Besides, my dear man, helping you *is* giving her my full support. Now then . . ." She cast him a brilliant smile. "Lovely weather for this time of year, don't you think?"

Chapter Twenty-One

Gray was right.

He was a minor player in the production that was his wedding. Camille was the star, the prima donna, the diva. While she appeared as gracious and charming as always to Sam, there was as well a glint of steel in her blue eyes. No man who valued his life would dare to confront her at the moment. Sam was safe enough. He had no reason to confront Camille. Her sister was a different matter.

While typically the gentlemen stayed in the dining room or retired to the billiards room for port and cigars, tonight Camille had quietly suggested to her parents and to Grayson that it would be lovely if the gentlemen limited their after-dinner ritual to no more than a quarter of an hour. As much as it was a suggestion, no one wanted to cross Camille and now the entire company was once again in the parlor.

The younger of the Radnor sisters, Jessamine, played the piano while Miss Martin turned the sheet music and Lord Dantrey teased both young ladies, which did not help the quality of Jessamine's musical skills. Around the room, the rest of the gathering broke into groups of two or three or more and stood or sat and chatted. Near the fireplace, Lord Briston and Lord Radnor engaged in a spirited discussion of Irish home rule although Sam wasn't clear which of the men was for it and who was against. He suspected the true enjoyment for the gentlemen was more in the debate than real passion for either side of the question. On the sofa, Lady Briston, Mrs. Martin, and Lady Radnor were trying to decide whether they should have tables set up for cards although they did do so last night and perhaps they should try something different tonight. By the window, Beryl and Teddy and Camille chatted with Lord Latimer, who appeared quite taken with Teddy although, from what Sam overheard, they had known each other for years so he might have been mistaken. Mr. Martin was in one corner of the room, flirting with the older Miss Radnor, Frances. Delilah and Lord Charborough were on the far side of the room, speaking in a low and intimate manner to each other punctuated by occasional laughter. She was obviously having a delightful time.

Sam and Gray stood near the open doorway, each with a glass of brandy in his hand.

"What's your opinion," Gray said in a low voice. "Is she mad?"

Delilah was gazing up at Charborough as if he were the sun and the stars and the entire universe wrapped up in one perfect package.

"Yes," Sam said in a hard tone.

"I was afraid of that." Gray sighed. "At least it will never be boring. Living with a lunatic, that is."

Sam's gaze snapped to his friend's. "What?"

"I see. We're back to your problems now, aren't we? You're not talking about Camille at all."

Sam shook his head in confusion. "Camille?"

"I asked if you thought she was mad."

"I'm beginning to suspect everyone in this family is a bit mad." Sam's gaze strayed back to Delilah. Did she actually just flutter her lashes at the man?

"At least the female members." Gray sipped his brandy. "Although I wouldn't want to rule out a certain element of madness when it comes to either Lord Briston or Colonel Channing."

"Colonel Channing?"

"Camille's Uncle Basil. Lord Briston's twin brother. He's an adventurous sort. Spent his life in travel and the odd bit of exploration. He has always been an interesting character."

"I can hardly wait to meet him."

Good Lord, if Delilah leaned any closer to Charborough she'd fall into his lap.

"Camille wants him here for the wedding. He'd better arrive soon or there will be hell to pay." Gray shuddered. "And I'll probably be the one paying it."

"Actually, I thought Camille seemed remarkably serene this evening."

"Don't let her fool you, Sam." Gray swirled his brandy in his glass and stared at his future wife. "She's a crafty sort. But then lunatics often are."

Sam laughed. Delilah glanced his way then immediately turned her attention back to Charborough. The laughter died in his throat.

"I don't know that anyone else has noticed but there seems to be steam coming out of your ears," Gray said mildly. "I've never seen you jealous before."

"I'm not . . ." Sam's jaw tightened. "Look at the way she's throwing herself at him."

Delilah laughed at something Charborough said.

Gray studied the couple. "She does seem to be taken with the man."

"But he'd never make her happy. Not really."

"Are you sure?"

"Yes."

"Because you're the only one who could truly make her happy?"

"Yes."

"But he is everything she wants."

"Everything she thinks she wants. Everything she's expected to want. Oh, she might well be content with him." Sam shook his head. "But she deserves more than merely content for the rest of her life."

"I gather you still haven't come up with a definitive plan."

"Not yet."

442

"Well, it seems to me you should probably do something and soon." Gray nodded at the couple. "Unless you intend to wait until she is walking down the aisle toward someone else."

Charborough's gaze locked with Delilah's and he leaned closer, as if he were about to kiss her. Surely, he wouldn't do that here? In front of everyone? Surely, she wouldn't allow it?

Beryl had said Delilah had a plan. What kind of plan could she possibly have? Did she plan to throw herself into Charborough's willing arms in front of her family and everyone else? She was entirely too concerned with proper behavior to do anything of the sort. She was—at once the truth struck him.

"You're right, Gray. And I've had quite enough of this."

He handed Gray his glass then crossed the room to Delilah and the dashing Lord Charborough. Sam smiled in as pleasant a manner as he could manage. It wasn't easy.

"Forgive me for interrupting, Lord Charborough, Delilah." His gaze met hers and it was all he could do to keep a pleasant note in his voice. "Could I have a word with you? Privately?"

"Goodness, Sam, Victor and I were just engaged in a most fascinating discussion about . . ."

"The weather?" Charborough suggested.

"Native birds," Delilah said at the same time.

"Surely both the weather and the birds can

wait." Sam glanced at the other man. "Do you mind if I borrow her for a few minutes?"

Charborough's gaze shifted from Sam to Delilah and back. "Of course not. As long as you bring her back."

Delilah laughed lightly and batted Charborough with her fan. "Why Victor, what a charming thing to say." Her smile stayed on her face but she cast a scathing look at Sam. "I'll only be a moment."

"Charborough." Sam nodded, took Delilah's elbow, and steered her toward the door, fairly dragging her into the hall. "You can't fool me, Dee. I know exactly what you're doing."

"I'm not trying to make you jealous if that's what you're thinking." She shook off his arm.

He glared down at her. "That's not what I was thinking. And I was not jealous."

"Really." Her brow rose. "Given the way you were watching us, it seemed rather obvious to me."

"You noticed?"

"It was hard to miss."

He clenched his teeth. "Making me jealous is simply an unexpected benefit."

"Nonsense, Sam. It doesn't matter to me if you're jealous or not," she said in a lofty manner. "An unexpected benefit of what?"

"Your plan." He fairly spit the words.

"My plan?" Her eyes narrowed slightly. "I don't know what you're talking about."

"I may be many things but I am not an idiot."

"I still don't—"

"You're trying to prove to me that you are no better than Lenore. You want me to think you are nothing more than a fortune hunter so that I'll leave. And you'll never face how you feel."

"Nonsense, Sam. I know exactly how I feel. Furthermore, I detest that phrase. *Fortune hunter.*" She practically spit the words. "Might I point out there is a vast difference between myself and a woman who marries for position and money because she has neither. I have both. Therefore, the term really isn't accurate."

"Close enough."

"Not at all. I'm not interested in a man's wealth and title because it will improve my lot in life. Although one certainly doesn't want to marry beneath oneself. I simply know what is appropriate in life. What is right. For me that is."

"What's expected you mean."

"Oh come now, just because it's what I am expected to do, what I want to do, doesn't mean it's not the right thing to do." She shrugged. "I have simply set my sights on a gentleman who meets all of my qualifications."

"Qualifications which do not include love."

"Exactly." She sighed. "We've had this discussion or one very much like it before. I have not changed my mind."

"There's a difference, Dee. Now we're talking about the two of us."

"Because you claim I'm in love with you?"

"Yes."

"That's nothing more than romantic rubbish and you know it." She paused. "And while I am not a fortune hunter as the term is correctly defined, while my motives are entirely different, I suppose, when you get to the core of it all, I am exactly like your former fiancée. We are both looking for benefits to marriage that have nothing to do with love. The only difference between us is that I'm not willing to lie about it. I'm not willing to let a man believe I love him to get what I want." She shook her head. "There is no two of us, Sam, and there never can be."

"Why not?"

"Good Lord, you're stubborn." She rolled her gaze toward the ceiling. "Because it's not right. Because it wouldn't work. Because we're too different from each other. Because we'll only cause each other pain in the end. You'll break my heart or I'll break yours. That's not a risk I'm willing to take."

He stared at her for a long moment. "I never imagined you to be a coward, Dee."

She sucked in a sharp breath and stared at him.

He shook his head. "Obviously, I was wrong."

"Yes, well, we're all wrong about something on occasion. I am sorry to disappoint you but there you have it. I'm not the woman you thought I was. I am narrow-minded and stubborn, I don't do the unexpected, and I am not one for adventure. And I don't take risks." She raised her chin. "Even you have to admit Victor is exactly the type of man I planned to marry."

"There's certainly no risk there."

"Exactly."

"That doesn't make it right."

"It's right for me. *He's* right for me."

"I don't give up easily, Dee," he warned. "In fact, I can't remember the last time I gave up at all."

"Then this will be a new experience for you. You've lost, Sam, and whether you want to face it or not, this is best for both of us." She turned to go back into the parlor. He grabbed her arm and pulled her back.

"Dee." He gazed into her blue eyes. "Don't turn your back on us."

"Oh, Sam." Her chin trembled and regret shone in her eyes. "There is no us."

Their gazes locked for a long moment. Words wouldn't come. He didn't know what to say, how to make her see that they belonged together. That regardless of what was practical and what made sense, no matter how many obstacles they had to overcome, they belonged together.

"Call it fate or magic or whatever you wish, this is right. I know you love me."

"I don't believe in fate or magic. Silly, foolish, romantic notions." She shook her head. "I've never said I loved you."

"It doesn't matter. I know." His gaze bored into hers. "I know, Dee, as surely as I have ever known anything in my life, as surely as I know the sun will come up tomorrow, I know I'm not wrong about that. And I—"

"May I be of assistance, Delilah?" Charborough stood in the doorway. His gaze shifted between Sam and Delilah.

"No, but thank you for the offer." She pulled out of Sam's grasp and cast Charborough a grateful smile. Sam's heart twisted at the sight. "There is nothing to be concerned about."

"No, there isn't," Sam said in a hard tone. "Nothing to be concerned about at all." He stared at her and she stared coolly back. "Simply a misunderstanding. But Lady Hargate has convinced me . . . I was wrong."

"Ah, well then." Charborough offered his arm to Delilah and she took it. "Shall we?"

She nodded. "Sam." She cast him a dismissive smile and accompanied Charborough back into the parlor.

He stood outside the doors to the parlor for a moment or perhaps it was forever. Maybe he was wrong. Maybe she didn't love him. Maybe she was right. Maybe this could only end in heartbreak for one of them, or for both of them.

He turned and started toward his rooms. He couldn't remember ever having given up on anything he'd wanted before. But this was a game he didn't know how to win. Damnation, he didn't even know how to play. But he did know he'd lost even if he wasn't entirely sure she had won.

He'd return to London with Jim and stay there until the wedding. It made perfect sense and was probably for the best. At least if he left, he could start putting her behind him, if that was possible.

No, there was no maybe about it. She was absolutely right about one part of it all.

His heart was already broken.

"My dear little cousin." Sympathy shone in Victor's eyes. "Are you sure this is what you want?"

"It's not at all what I want." She steeled herself and forced a smile. "But it is what's best for both of us."

He studied her closely. "As much as I hate to say this, I think you're wrong."

"You don't know anything about it."

"No, but I do know love when I see it." Victor shook his head. "You're breaking his heart and I suspect yours is broken as well."

"Better now than after we've failed to build a life together."

"Are you so sure it would fail?"

"We have nothing in common."

"Some might say that love in common is enough."

She shrugged. "Silly, romantic nonsense."

"I've always thought there is much to be said for silly, romantic nonsense."

"Then you're every bit the fool he is."

"Perhaps." He chuckled. "Delilah." He took her hand and gazed into her eyes. "If I am to salvage what's left of my family's heritage, I have no choice but to marry for financial considerations. But if a woman ever looked at me the way your American looks at you, I would abandon Charborough Castle and everything that goes along with it and spend the rest of my days thanking God for that rare and unique gift that so few of us find."

"You mean love?" She scoffed. "I've tried love. It doesn't always turn out the way one expects it to."

"Even so, Delilah, isn't it worth—"

"No, Victor. As much as I appreciate your help, this is the right thing to do."

"You're so very certain, Delilah." He studied her curiously. "There's no doubt in your mind? In your heart? No tiny part of you even now screaming that if there was so much of an iota of a chance that it is a chance worth taking?"

"No," she lied. "You see, a few minutes ago Sam called me a coward and he was right. I am terrified that I will give my heart away and it will be crushed." She shook her head. "I couldn't bear that."

"And you're not willing to take the risk."

She smiled. "I wish I was."

Still, she and Sam were both wrong. She wasn't a coward. Sending him away was the bravest thing she had ever done. And the hardest. And she needn't worry ever again about anyone breaking her heart.

It was already too late.

Chapter Twenty-Two

Two days before the wedding . . .

". . . and yes, I think it's an excellent idea and we should proceed." Gray sat across the table in the restaurant of Sam's hotel. "I'm glad moving to London has turned out to be so beneficial."

"I have managed to get a great deal accomplished." Sam nodded. "Aside from narrowing down properties that will work for a production site and meeting with several potential investors, Jim nearly has the motorwagon back in pristine condition. Oh, and did I tell you that Beryl has expressed interest in investing?"

"No, that must have slipped your mind," Gray said wryly. "I can't imagine why."

Sam shrugged. "She mentioned it at dinner the night before I left."

"I'm not surprised. She's very astute about investments. She did quite well financially when she was between husbands."

"You wouldn't have any objections?"

"Not at all. I like the idea of risking Beryl's money." Gray chuckled. "I would certainly never admit this to her and I would deny it to her face but I've always rather admired her. Even, on occasion, liked her."

"I'll take your secret to the grave."

"I knew you would." Gray studied his friend closely. "Speaking of the grave, I must say, you look—"

"I know how I look," Sam said sharply.

"Oh well, as long as you know." Gray paused for a long moment as if he had nothing of importance to say. Sam braced himself. "Delilah looks dreadful as well."

"Does she?" His brow rose. "Then I gather all is not going well with the perfect Lord Charborough?"

"Actually, the moment Delilah discovered you had left, she lost all interest in him. Which makes sense as he certainly isn't perfect."

"He looks perfect."

"Precisely why he was so suited to play the part of the perfect match. As it happens . . ." Gray grinned. "He's not only a distant cousin but an impoverished one at that."

Sam stared at his friend. "He was part of Delilah's plan, wasn't he?"

Gray's brow furrowed. "You know about her plan?"

"Not the details." He shook his head. "But it was fairly easy to figure out. She wanted to prove to me she was exactly the type of woman I had sworn to avoid. But I had no idea Charborough was nothing more than a prop."

"And did she prove that?"

"No. But she did make me realize my pursuit of her was doomed to failure."

"I see." Gray adopted a casual tone. "Well, she certainly is miserable in her triumph."

"Good."

Gray stared. "You don't mean that."

"Oh, but I do. I'm tired of being gallant, Gray. I gave Delilah what she wanted. She won, if you will. Although it did seem pointless to continue to argue a position I couldn't win. But I see no reason to be gracious about it. She got what she wanted, now she has to live with it. I'm out of her life, exactly as she wished. Good Lord, she'd been trying to get rid of me from the moment I stepped foot on the grounds of Millworth." He blew a long breath. "Admittedly, I would feel worse than I do now if I knew she wasn't feeling anything at all."

"Well, now that you know she is just as unhappy as you are, perhaps you should try again."

"Absolutely not."

"You're giving up?"

"Let's just say that I'm admitting defeat." He shook his head. "A smart man knows when he has lost. The woman refuses to admit her own feelings. She refuses as well to step so much as an inch off the road she has chosen. That's too much risk for her. She's afraid and there doesn't seem to be anything I can do to alleviate her fears."

"I've never seen you give up on anything."

"I prefer to think of it as admitting defeat." He

chuckled. "But regardless of what you call it, it is a new experience." He sobered and leaned toward his friend. "I appreciate your concern but I'm fine."

"She's not."

"Frankly, that's not my problem and not my choice." His tone hardened. "I have the motor-wagon to concern myself with and who knows what might be around the next corner. Besides"—he shrugged—"we had nothing in common."

Gray stared. "I've never seen you take this hard a stand, outside of matters of business that is."

"You were the one who told me to think of her as an investment. Eventually one realizes an investment doesn't have the potential you originally thought it did and you move on. I am moving on. But enough of that." Sam studied the other man. "How is your lovely bride?"

"Terrifying but it's almost over. You will be at Millworth for the wedding?"

"I wouldn't miss it." Sam smiled wryly. "You, old friend, are a beacon of hope in the wilderness."

"Good Lord, I hope not." Gray shuddered.

"Well, well, if it isn't the unholy alliance," a nearly forgotten female voice said. A voice Sam never thought he'd hear again and never especially wanted to.

He and Gray exchanged startled glances and rose to their feet.

"Mr. Elliott, Sam." Lenore Stanley cast him a brilliant smile and extended her hand. "Imagine running into you here of all places."

Sam hesitated then took her hand. "Lenore, what a surprise."

"I am nothing if not surprising." She turned to Gray. "And Mr. Elliott. I'm not surprised to see you here."

"I do live here, Miss Stanley," Gray said politely. He had never trusted Lenore and she had never liked him.

"Yes, of course." Her gaze turned to Sam. "Are you going to ask me to join you?"

The last person he expected to see, the last person he wanted to see right now, or ever, was Lenore. Regardless, she was here. "Please do."

Lenore took a seat at the table.

"Well, I must be getting back," Gray said. "I shall see you the day after tomorrow, then."

Sam nodded. "I'll be there."

Gray leaned close to Sam and lowered his voice for his friend's ears alone. "Just make certain moving on does not mean moving backward."

Sam smiled. "I have no intention of moving backward."

Gray nodded then turned his attention to Lenore. "Good day, Miss Stanley."

"Mr. Elliott." She smiled pleasantly. "Sam," she said as soon as he had taken his seat. "It's so very good to see you again."

"Is it?" He studied her coolly. The tall, statuesque blonde, as always in the latest Paris fashion, was as lovely as ever. "What are you doing here?"

Disappointment showed in her green eyes. "You're not glad to see me?"

"Not especially. What are you doing here?"

"Here as in London or here as in your hotel?"

"Both."

"Well, Mother thought London might be the perfect setting to, oh, relaunch her disappointment of a daughter on the seas of society." She pulled off her gloves and set them on the table. "And it wasn't at all difficult to discover where you were staying."

His eyes narrowed. "I thought you would be engaged or married by now."

"Goodness, Sam." She huffed. "I realized almost immediately he was an appalling error in judgment."

Sam raised a brow. "Not as wealthy as you thought?"

"Among other things." Her tone softened. "Haven't you ever made a dreadful mistake that you regret with all your heart?"

"Once," he said in a hard tone.

"Oh, don't look at me like that. I made a mistake. It's not as if I haven't apologized." She gazed at him in a pleading manner that almost hid the calculation in her eyes. "Can't you see your way clear to forgive me?"

There was a time when he couldn't so much as consider forgiving Lenore. Now, he really didn't care one way or the other. "All right." He shrugged. "You're forgiven."

"Wonderful." She beamed at him. "Mother will be so delighted and your mother as well. You know, it was your mother who told my mother that you were in London. I suspect she was every bit as eager as my mother to see us back together where we belong."

"Lenore." He drew his brows together. "We are not back together."

"We will be," she said confidently. "Now that I have apologized and you have forgiven me. Come now, Sam, even you have to admit we are perfect for each other. Our families, our backgrounds, what we want in life, there couldn't be a better-suited couple than the two of us. Why, everyone says so."

"Which doesn't make it right."

"It will be." She paused. "May I be honest with you?"

"Why start now?"

"Come now, Sam." She huffed. "That wasn't at all nice."

"My apologies. I do hate not being nice," he said dryly. As much as it really didn't matter what she had to say he was curious. "Go on."

"It wasn't until you broke off our engagement that I realized how very much I cared for you.

You may not believe me, and given all that's passed between us, I don't really blame you."

There was something about her confession that struck him as too perfect. Too well rehearsed.

She heaved an overly dramatic sigh. "I think about you all the time. Indeed, I can't seem to think of anyone but you. Why, I even dream about you."

"That's very flattering."

"It's not meant to be flattering." She pouted. "It's simply the truth. And it seems to me, when one finds someone they can't get out of their mind and their heart, someone they can't imagine living their life without, well, one shouldn't give up simply because the party in question is not inclined to be, oh, cooperative."

He stared at her for a long moment.

"It seems to me as well, when that happens, one would be a fool not to fight for what one knows, in one's heart, is truly right. For both parties," she added.

"I never thought I'd say this, Lenore, but you're absolutely right." He nodded slowly. "One would be a fool."

"I knew you would understand." She beamed, a gleam of triumph in her eyes.

"Lenore." He took her hand and met her gaze directly. "I want to thank you."

"Oh, Sam, you needn't thank me." She fluttered her lashes. "I'm just grateful you agree with me."

"I do." He nodded. "I agree completely. And I do want to thank you for helping me see things clearly." He shook his head. "You're absolutely right. I have been a fool."

Her lovely brow furrowed in concern. "I don't understand."

"Nor do I expect you to." He got to his feet and smiled down at her. "I wish you all the best, Lenore."

Her eyes widened. "You're not leaving, are you? Now?"

"I have business matters to take care of and then . . ." He grinned. "I have a wedding to attend."

"But you'll be back?"

"I'm afraid not."

She stared in disbelief. "But Sam, what about us?"

"My dear Lenore," he said in as kind a manner as he could manage. "There is no us, you made certain of that. And for that, you have my eternal gratitude."

"But Sam—"

"Enjoy your stay in London and give my best to your mother." He nodded and strolled away. He knew if he looked back she would be staring after him in shock and a fair amount of anger.

As much as he hadn't been pleased at her unexpected appearance, he was grateful to her for pointing out what he should have known. He would indeed be a fool not to fight for the one woman he couldn't get out of his mind. Or his heart.

Odd that today he could see Lenore so clearly when he hadn't been able to do so in the past. Then of course he'd been blinded by love or what he thought was love. Looking back, he realized he had been more angry at Lenore's betrayal than hurt. Certainly, he had thought his heart had broken but now he suspected it had merely cracked. And while it had seemed like forever at the time, upon reflection, it had healed quickly.

With Delilah, it would never heal.

Gray was right. Whether you called it admitting defeat or giving up, it wasn't what Sam did. Wasn't who he was. He'd lost sight of that for a moment. But this was a battle he couldn't abandon. This was for Delilah. This was for the rest of their lives.

He grinned.

And all he really needed was a plan.

The day before the wedding . . .

"They're not right." Camille stared at the roses Teddy, her sisters, and her mother were arranging in large baskets together with orchids, ferns, and other greenery. The baskets would go in the chapel. Large urns filled with the same flowers would decorate the ballroom along with swags of ivy and more blossoms. "You should have called me at once. The color is entirely wrong!"

The others traded wary glances. This was not the bride's first outburst of the day.

"Well?" Camille leveled an accusing glance at the others. "Just look at them."

"They look beautiful, dear," Mother said in a soothing tone. It didn't help.

"They look *wrong!*" Camille's voice rose. "Teddy, look at these. This isn't what we ordered." She waved in a frantic manner at the innocent roses. "They're entirely too, too peach! They're supposed to be a delicate, pale shade of peach to match Beryl and Delilah's dresses."

"They're exactly what we ordered, Camille," Teddy said calmly. "We thought the more intense color coupled with the white orchids would be the perfect accent for the dresses, remember?"

Suspicion narrowed Camille's eyes. "Did we?"

"Goodness, Camille." Beryl huffed. "She's not making that up simply to calm you down. Although I certainly would," she added under her breath.

"Yes." Teddy smiled. "We did."

With every hour closer to the wedding, Teddy grew more and more serene. She handled every difficulty from misunderstandings about the dinner menu to additional unexpected house-guests—all of which did seem fairly minor to Delilah—in a smooth, efficient fashion. Her demeanor was unruffled, her outlook optimistic, and her gentle but firm attitude was most impressive. Especially as she was the only one who seemed able to calm Camille, who grew more and more irrational with every passing hour.

Teddy took Camille's hands and gazed into her eyes. "The flowers are perfect. Everything will be perfect." She smiled. "Now then, do you recall what we talked about?"

Camille nodded. "When I begin to feel as if I wish to rip someone's heart out over what the rest of you think is an insignificant detail, even if I disagree, I am to breathe deeply."

"Very good, Camille." Teddy's tone was remarkably tranquil. "Now, take a deep breath."

Camille drew a deep breath then another. "Better?"

Camille sighed. "Much."

"One would think marrying Grayson after all this time would be perfect enough," Delilah muttered and turned back to the basket she'd been arranging.

"I heard that, Delilah," Camille said sharply. Apparently the benefits of a deep breath were as fleeting as the breath itself.

"Good!"

"It's because I'm marrying Grayson that I want it to be perfect." Camille's gaze locked with hers and Delilah could have sworn there were flames in her eyes. Straight from the fires of bridal hell no doubt. "And this is going to be perfect. Every detail, every aspect, every moment. Do you understand?"

"*We* are not the ones who have caused your problems, not that any of them were of any great importance," Delilah snapped. "We're doing all we can to help!"

"Deep breaths," Teddy said *sotto voce.*

"We would do anything to keep you from being quite so insane." Delilah glared at her older sister.

"We know it's your wedding," Beryl chimed in. "And while we do understand why you've become so irritating and vile—"

"Vile is rather harsh," Mother murmured.

"Harsh and yet *perfect,*" Beryl said. "Because *perfect* is what she wants. And God help anyone who stands in the way of perfection!"

"Breathe in . . ." Teddy murmured.

"Am I asking for so much?" Camille glared. "A bit of perfection on the happiest day of my bloody life!"

Teddy sighed. "Breathe out."

"You've gone mad, Camille." Delilah shot the bride a scathing look. "Quite, quite mad!"

"I know." Camille's voice rose again. "And I'm sorry!"

"We can all hear you, dear," Mother said in a chastising manner. "There's no need to scream."

"Well, I for one have had quite enough of it." Delilah tossed down the shears she'd been using to clip off thorns and pulled off the heavy gloves she'd donned. "You may call me when my lovely, pleasant older sister returns and the shrew who has taken over her body and soul has been vanquished." She stalked down the aisle and headed for the door.

"Come now, Delilah," Camille called after her. "You can't abandon me."

"Why not?" Beryl said. "You abandoned her."

"I have not! What on earth do you mean?"

Delilah turned on her heel and stared at her sisters. "What do you mean?"

"I don't mean physically, of course." Beryl shrugged. "It's not as if she has walked out on you when you needed her."

Camille cast her a smug look.

"What I mean is that Delilah has been miserable since she managed to get rid of Sam and no one has paid her the least bit of attention or even acknowledged how unhappy she is," Beryl said. "It's not at all nice of us if we are indeed trying to be better sisters to each other."

"I'm fine." Delilah's jaw clenched.

From her mother to her mad sister to her dearest friend, the expression was the same on everyone's face. Not one of them believed her.

"I am," she said again.

"Really, Dee?" Teddy said. "You've been very nearly as unpleasant as Camille. Honestly, I am enjoying Beryl's company more than any of the rest of you. And I certainly never expected that." Teddy glanced at Beryl. "My apologies. That sounded—"

Beryl waved off her comment. "Think nothing of it."

"You're absolutely right, Beryl." Camille blew a long breath. "I am sorry, Delilah. I've been so—"

"Crazy? Daft? Idiotic? Demanding? Rude? Insufferable?" Mother offered in a helpful tone. "I could continue if you like."

"That's quite all right but thank you, Mother." Camille sank down on a bench. "I do apologize. To all of you. I'm nervous, I suppose. Grayson and I have waited so long . . ." She cast a weak smile at the others. "I realize life together will not be perfect, which is fine. I think perfect would be dreadfully boring if there wasn't some sort of surprise or adventure or even misadventure along the way to bring a bit of excitement to your life. But it seems like something of a portent if your wedding isn't, well, perfect."

"What utter rubbish." Beryl stared at her twin. "What ever has happened to you? I know the weddings I remember the most fondly are the ones where minor disasters occurred. No, not the ones where the bride or the groom failed to appear but the ones where the bride fell in a duck pond or the groom was forced to wear an entirely inappropriate pair of trousers because his were misplaced. Furthermore, when I look at those marriages they are among the happiest I know."

"A wedding is simply a moment in what will be a lifetime of moments. You and Grayson are meant to be together and now you're going to be," Mother said. "My darling girl, nothing else really matters, does it?"

"No." Camille pulled a deep breath and looked at Delilah. "He will be coming to the wedding, you know."

"I should hope so." Indignation rang in Beryl's voice. "He is the groom, after all."

"No, not Grayson." Camille rolled her eyes. "Sam, of course. Grayson went into London yesterday to see him. I think it did him good to get away. Do you know he actually had the nerve the other day of accusing me of being ill-tempered and out of sorts?"

Beryl gasped. "No, not that."

Camille ignored her. "As I said, Sam will be here tomorrow."

"I assumed he would." And Delilah was prepared, as was Victor. Although he did seem to be somewhat taken with either Miss Martin or one of the Radnor sisters. Good, he was a very nice man and she certainly wished him the best. After the wedding. One more day and then she'd never see Sam again. That was for the best as well. Her life would go on exactly as planned. Exactly as she wanted. Still, it did make her stomach twist and her heart ache.

"Delilah." Her mother met her gaze directly. "I, or rather we, as we all agree, think you might have been too hasty in dismissing Mr. Russell. We think the only sensible, rational, practical thing to do is to reconsider."

Delilah stared. "No."

"Why not?" Camille asked.

"My reasons haven't changed." She shook her head. "We have no common ground. Sam and I are not Grayson and Camille. They belong together. They have everything in common. Sam and I are from entirely different worlds. The chances of us even being content with each other are slim. That's a risk I am not willing to take."

"Well, you should be." Beryl's gaze met her younger sister's. "Goodness, Delilah, if I have learned nothing else in life I have learned that the greater the risk, the greater the reward. The greater the adventure." She smiled. "Love, little sister, is a fabulous adventure."

"Love is not enough," Delilah said. "Mother loved Father and he chose to wander the world. And she chose not to let him come home and to tell the world he was dead."

"It was my finest hour," Mother said smugly, then paused. "Or perhaps my worst."

"In spite of love, in spite of the fact that you had everything in common, one would not call your lives together a great success."

"I have had a good time of it," Mother said more to herself than the others.

"For the most part without him," Beryl pointed out.

"Mother," Delilah said with a huff. "Do you think two people who are complete opposites can be happy together?"

"I would say it depends on the people. Regardless, it might be a great deal of fun to try." She thought for a moment. "Not trying is so much worse than failing. Most of my regrets in life are about those things I didn't attempt. It's wondering *what if* that will truly drive you mad, dear. Do keep in mind, Delilah, and all of you really, sometimes, even when one isn't completely wrong, one might not be entirely right either."

Camille frowned. "That makes no sense."

Mother scoffed. "Oh darling, it's not supposed to, it's life. We all make stupid mistakes, even when we're doing something for the absolutely right reasons."

"The right reasons?" Teddy said.

"Oh, you know. To protect ourselves or those we love. That sort of thing."

Delilah had no idea if Mother was speaking about Delilah and Sam or herself and Father. It really didn't matter. Her mind was made up, no matter how much it hurt.

She drew a deep breath. "As much as I do appreciate your advice and while I am grateful that you care enough to interfere, this is really none of your concern. Sam is no longer a topic of discussion and frankly, I'm tired of talking about him." Or thinking about him. Constantly.

"It seems to me we haven't talked about Sam at all up to now," Beryl said slowly. "I thought we were being extremely considerate not to so much as mention him. Especially given how unhappy you are at his absence."

"I'm fine," Delilah said through clenched teeth. She would simply have to get used to missing him and thinking about him and longing for him. He was not part of her plan and the sooner her, well, her heart apparently realized that the better off she would be. She drew a deep breath and glanced at Camille. "Now then, Camille, surely we can say something that will upset you."

"As odd as it may sound, I am now more concerned about you than I am the wedding. Although, as we are now speaking of the wedding . . ." Camille paused. "You should know that there's a possibility Sam will not be attending the wedding alone."

Delilah stared. "Oh?"

Camille nodded. "Grayson said they ran into Sam's former fiancée."

Delilah drew her brows together. "In London?"

Camille nodded.

"She broke his heart you know." Delilah's throat tightened at the thought of how badly that woman had hurt him. "And he's just the kind of foolish romantic who would be willing to overlook that sort of thing under the right circumstances."

"The right circumstances being that the woman he loves is unwilling to bend enough to accept his love?" Camille asked. "Grayson says Sam is every bit as unhappy as you are."

"He'll be fine." She squared her shoulders. "He'll return to America. He'll live his life exactly as he is supposed to, as will I."

"Well then," Mother said with a shrug. "There's nothing more to discuss. Delilah absolutely refuses to consider that she might possibly be wrong and making the greatest mistake of her life. And Mr. Russell might well be back in the arms of the woman who is no doubt much better suited for him than Delilah." She turned toward the bride. "Now then, Camille, I think these baskets would be better placed . . ."

Would he bring her? The woman who had broken his heart? Surely even an American would realize that was inappropriate. Unless he wanted to point out he was just as willing to move on as she was. She had Victor after all.

How had this become such an awful mess? All she'd wanted was one, tiny adventure. There was a lesson here but she had no idea what it was. Unless of course it had something to do with learning that love was unexpected and not the least bit sensible and, if allowed to do so, would ruin one's life. Of course, she had learned that long ago.

For the first time she wondered if she might indeed be wrong. Her family certainly thought so. Was she simply being stubborn, standing her ground when doing so was a dreadful mistake? Was she so afraid to risk love again that she didn't have the courage to follow her heart?

Would she spend the rest of her life wondering *what if?* Would regret haunt that perfect, expected life she had planned? Would Sam linger always in the back of her mind? In her dreams? In her soul?

Perhaps it wasn't love that had broken her heart but love with the wrong man. Perhaps with the right man . . .

It did seem that in her efforts to avoid heart-break by pushing him away, her heart had been broken just as surely. And one did wonder, if her heart was broken without him, maybe the risk of being with him was really no risk at all.

Maybe her adventure in New York hadn't been a dreadful mistake after all. Maybe it had been a beginning. And maybe, just maybe, what she really wanted wasn't never to see him again.

Maybe, what she really wanted from him was forever.

Chapter Twenty-Three

Camille's wedding day . . .

Even the most dull-witted of observers would admit Millworth Manor was a madhouse and Camille wasn't the only daft woman running about today. While Teddy managed to hang on to her usual serenity, Camille was once again crazed, Mother was frazzled, and even Beryl seemed to have lost her composure.

Add to that the fact that the number of house-guests had risen, including several of Grayson's friends from America. Fortunately, the number of new arrivals included Lionel—although Delilah was beginning to suspect Beryl's husband used his political responsibilities in London as a convenient excuse to avoid spending more time than was necessary with Beryl's family. Not that Delilah could blame the man. And Uncle Basil finally arrived late yesterday, alleviating at least one of Camille's concerns. But their father's twin did seem a bit more preoccupied than usual. He had mentioned there was a family matter of some importance he needed to discuss but, after gauging the level of insanity in the air, agreed it might well be best to wait until after the wedding. Thank God. The last thing any of them

473

needed was a family matter of some importance.

The wedding was just over an hour away. Delilah was ready except for the last-minute addition of her gown. Woe be it to anyone who dressed too early and then, God help them all, wrinkled the peach silk confections in any way.

The latest crisis had Delilah rummaging in the drawer of the ladies' desk in the sitting room for the brooch Camille had misplaced.

"I beg your pardon, Lady Hargate," Clement's voice sounded from the open door.

"Yes?" Delilah answered but didn't look up. How did such a small drawer fill up with so many odds and ends? Delilah suspected no one had tidied this drawer in years. Still, if the blasted brooch was here, she would find it.

"Lady Dunwell says the missing brooch has been found," Clement announced.

"Thank you, Clement." She breathed a sigh of relief and closed the desk drawer.

"And you have a—"

"I'll announce myself, Clement, but thank you."

Delilah's heart caught and she straightened. Sam strolled toward her in a casual manner, a rolled-up paper in his hand.

"What are you doing here?" He shouldn't be here. Not yet. She hadn't thought she'd see him until after the wedding. She still had no idea what she wanted to say. What she should say. Bloody hell, she still hadn't come up with a plan!

"I came for the wedding of course," he said smoothly.

"I don't mean here at Millworth." She pulled her wrapper tighter around her. "I mean here, in the sitting room."

"This is where you are, so this is where I wanted to be."

"Goodness, Sam." She drew her brows together. "This is entirely improper. The wedding is only an hour away and I am not quite dressed."

"I don't care."

She waved at the doorway. "You shouldn't be here."

"All right then." He turned and started toward the door.

"You said you'd never leave me," she said without thinking.

He paused in midstep. "I said all you had to do was ask."

"Very well then." She drew a deep breath. "I'm asking."

He again moved toward the door and she took a step toward him. "Blast it all, Sam, you're in love with me! Anyone can see that. Don't go!"

"I'm not." He closed the door then turned to face her. "I'm just closing the door." He started toward her. "I don't want to be interrupted."

She stared at him. "You don't?"

"We have a lot to discuss and we don't have much time in which to do it."

She swallowed hard. "We don't?"

"The wedding, remember?"

"Yes, of course." She smiled weakly. "The wedding."

"I have done a great deal of thinking since I left Millworth." He studied her for a moment. "You look beautiful, by the way. Gray said you looked as bad as I felt."

"I'm fine," she said with a shrug.

"So was I." He chuckled.

"How is Lenore," she asked casually.

"Lenore?" He shook his head. "I have no idea. Nor do I care." He adopted a somber expression. "As I said I have done a great deal of thinking. About us. And don't tell me there is no us."

"I wouldn't dare."

"Because whether you want to admit it or not there is an us. There has been from the first day Mrs. Hargate met an employee of Grayson's associate."

"Sam." She stepped toward him.

He held out his hand to stop her. "No, Dee, you need to listen to me. I was a fool to agree in New York that it would be best if we never saw each other again. I knew from the beginning, or I should have known, that you were the only woman in the world for me. I should have followed you back to England. I should have broken down the doors of Millworth Manor if necessary. I should never have let you go."

"I see." Her throat tightened.

"Furthermore, as you pride yourself on being practical and sensible, I thought the best way to lay my case before you was to come up with a list of reasons why we belong together. You have already laid out the reasons why we don't. Most of them having to do with the fact that we are entirely different people, from different countries, different backgrounds, and we have nothing in common."

She should stop him. Tell him none of that mattered anymore. All she wanted was him. But Delilah always did recognize a plan when she saw one. It would be, well, rude, to interrupt him now.

She crossed her arms over her chest. "Go on."

"Unfortunately, aside from the very real elements of fate and magic, which I am well aware you do not believe in—"

"I never have." Until now.

"The only thing I can put on that list is love. Oh, and you are right about one thing."

"I do so hate to be wrong about everything."

"As do I." His gaze met hers. "I do love you."

She bit back a smile. "I know."

"And you love me."

"I know that as well."

"As for the future . . ." He thrust the rolled-up paper at her.

"What is this?" She took it and unrolled it. She scanned the page then looked at him. "Is this a contract?"

"It is." He nodded. "I had my solicitors draw it up. Admittedly, it's not legally binding but it does carry a certain, oh, moral obligation I would say."

Her eyes narrowed. "What?"

"Go on, read it."

"Why don't you tell me what it says."

"All right." He adopted a businesslike attitude that would have annoyed her before now. Today, she found it rather endearing. "It says the party of the first part—"

She arched a brow. "The party of the first part?"

"That would be me." He started to pace then paused. "Unless you would prefer to be the party of the first part. I can have it changed."

"No." She gestured for him to continue. "Do go on."

"The party of the first part agrees, as the party of the second part's country and heritage is important to her, that both parties shall reside fully half the year in England and half the year in America. Unless, there are occasions of agreed upon importance that prevent said division of habitat." He glanced at her. "Business and the like. Family obligations, that sort of thing."

She nodded.

"In which case, there shall be suitable . . ." He paused in a significant manner. "Compensation."

"Oh, I do like compensation."

"I thought you would." He resumed pacing. "This provision shall not be construed so as to prohibit any additional, mutually agreed upon, visits to either country in any given year."

"Very sensible."

"I thought so." He nodded and continued. "Upon such time as there are children—"

"Children?"

"Children," he said firmly.

She glanced at the contract. "Does it say how many?"

"I don't think at this point that is a question for negotiation but I would suspect more than one and fewer than a herd."

"Very well then. Continue."

"Children are to be appropriately educated as to the heritage of the countries of origin of the party of the first part and the party of the second part. In addition, girls as well as boys will be encouraged to pursue higher forms of education."

"I like that." She nodded.

"And finally, the party of the second part will agree that, as we are nearing another century and whether she likes it or not progress is in the very air we breathe, to at least be amenable to the idea of heretofore unimagined inventions—"

"You mean motorwagons?"

"Among others." He pinned her with a firm look. "To be as amenable to other innovations as she is to the telephone."

She winced. "That's asking quite a lot, don't you think?"

"No." Certainty rang in his voice. "I don't. I think everything here is reasonable and fair to both sides. It's a compromise, Dee."

"Oh, dear." She shook her head in a mournful manner. "I've never been good at compromise."

He scoffed. "I hadn't noticed."

She studied him curiously. "What if I don't agree to this compromise or your contract?"

"Everything is negotiable but I warn you . . ." His eyes narrowed. "If this is not acceptable, then I will come up with another and another and another. I have no intention of giving up." He shook his head slowly. "I let you go once, I won't do it again."

"I see." She glanced at the contract. "Correct me if I'm mistaken but I see nothing here about marriage."

"Perhaps because I haven't asked you to marry me."

"It seems to me marriage is implied."

He frowned. "Are you sure?"

"Read it for yourself." She handed him the contract.

"Hm." He studied the document, his gaze stayed

on the paper. "Do you know why I haven't asked you to marry me?"

"Because you thought I would say no."

"Exactly." He raised his gaze to hers. "Was I right?"

"Yes." She paused. "I would have said no a few weeks ago, even a few days ago."

"Then it's a good thing I didn't ask."

"Absolutely. However, today . . ." She plucked the contract from his hands and waved it at him. "I not only accept your contract but I accept as well the concepts of magic and fate. It does seem to me that particular concession goes well beyond compromise and is more in the realm of—"

He pulled her into his arms and kissed her long and hard. Beryl was right. The reward was well worth the risk.

When at last he raised his head from hers she was hard-pressed to catch her breath. The man simply took her breath away and she suspected he always would.

"I haven't done that nearly enough."

"Perhaps that was your problem."

"I wouldn't be at all surprised."

"You are still extremely arrogant, you know."

"I know." He grinned. "You like it."

"Yes." She sighed. "I do." She chose her words with care. "You should know my funds have been restored. I can marry anyone I wish."

"You always could."

"And, as you still haven't proposed, you have lost the opportunity to do so." She braced herself, although if one was going to finally take a risk it might as well be a large one. "Therefore, Mr. Russell, Mrs. Hargate requests the honor of your hand in marriage."

"Does she?"

"She does indeed." She stared up at him. "You do realize it's terribly rude not to answer a question you've been asked."

"I would hate to be rude."

"As would we all. Well?"

"It was an oversight on my part, not to include marriage in the contract."

"Perhaps it could be rewritten?"

"I suspect it already has." He pulled her tighter against him and gazed down into her eyes. "I don't want to ever be without you."

"Good Lord, you are romantic."

He laughed. "I just want to be the last adventure you ever have."

"In spite of everything, I have come to believe our adventure only began in New York. Goodness, Sam." She shook her head. "For such a romantic man it's amazing the things you don't know."

"What might those be?"

"My dear darling American, don't you see . . ." She brushed her lips across his. "The very best adventures are the ones that never end."

Epilogue

"I am sorry to interrupt," Uncle Basil said in an apologetic manner. "I didn't think this could wait any longer. In truth, I shouldn't have waited this long. But it's rare that the entire family is together in one place and I didn't want to take the chance that some of you would scatter in the morning so I thought it best to do this now."

Basil had asked Mother, Father, and their daughters and husbands to join him in the dining room and Delilah had insisted Sam come as well. After all, he would soon be a member of the family and whatever Basil's *family matter of some importance* was, Sam should certainly be a part of it.

Basil nodded at Camille and Grayson. "But I do apologize for taking you away from the festivities."

"Nonsense, Uncle Basil," Camille said with a smile. "The ball is well underway and no one will miss us for a few minutes."

The ball was indeed in full swing and was as well as perfect as one could hope. As was the wedding itself. Although Delilah did think the true perfection was to be found in the love that shone in the eyes of the bride and groom. She glanced at Sam beside her and smiled. And was there really anything more perfect than that?

"I must confess, you have us all dying of curiosity," Beryl said.

"And a certain amount of apprehension." Father studied his twin closely. "It's not like you to be preoccupied and on edge but you have been since you arrived at Millworth."

"I will try to keep this as succinct as possible." Basil met his brother's gaze. "I know you have been concerned about the fate of Millworth as you have no sons. And upon our respective deaths, your title, the estate, and everything associated with it will be inherited by some distant relative we scarcely even know."

"It's the way of the world." Father shrugged. "I've made my peace with it."

"As have we all," Delilah added. "Admittedly, it will be rather sad to see Millworth pass into unfamiliar hands but it's not as if any of us will be left penniless."

"Thanks to appropriate first marriages," Mother said smugly.

Grayson and Lionel traded wry glances. As the second husbands of Briston daughters they were well aware of the nature of their wives' first marriages.

"That is one less thing to worry about," Basil said under his breath.

"I do wish you would tell us what this is all about." Impatience sounded in Mother's voice. "We do have a ball to return to, you know."

"Of course, I know," Basil snapped. "This isn't easy, Bernadette. I'm trying to think of the right way to say this."

"Just say it." Mother glared. "The more you dissemble, the more the rest of us think this is something truly dreadful."

"It's not dreadful," Basil said staunchly. "In many ways it's something of a miracle."

"Go on then." Father's brow furrowed. "Out with it, Basil."

"Very well." Basil paused. "It's a long story but I shall try to make it short."

"Too late," Beryl murmured.

"A very long time ago," Basil began, "I met a lovely young woman, the daughter of an American banker. We fancied ourselves in love and did what young people in love often do."

Bernadette's jaw clenched with impatience. "Do get on with it, Basil."

He ignored her. "We eloped."

A collective gasp washed around the room.

"Her parents were appalled and convinced the marriage was a terrible mistake. They convinced us of that as well."

Father stared. "You never told me any of this."

"It was not something I was particularly proud of," Basil said sharply. "At any rate, she returned to America and was to have the marriage annulled. Her father would see to that."

Beryl studied her uncle closely. "*Was* to have the marriage annulled?"

"Yes, well, that's apparently difficult to do if the bride is with child." Basil shook his head. "I only recently learned about this."

Camille's eyes widened. "Then you're still married?"

"And you have a child?" Shock rang in Delilah's voice.

"Basil," Father said in a hard tone. "What exactly are you trying to tell us?"

"I'm trying to tell you I have a son." Basil drew a deep breath. "I'm trying to tell you there is a new heir to Millworth Manor. And he's American."

The American Way
of Birth

JESSICA MITFORD

LONDON
VICTOR GOLLANCZ LTD
1992

First published in Great Britain 1992
by Victor Gollancz Ltd,
14 Henrietta Street, London WC2E 8QJ

© Jessica Mitford 1992

The right of Jessica Mitford to be identified as author
of this work has been asserted by her in accordance with
the Copyright, Designs and Patents Act, 1988

A CIP catalogue record for this book is available
from the British Library

ISBN 0 575 05430 1

Photoset in Great Britain by
Rowland Phototypesetting Ltd, Bury St Edmunds, Suffolk
and printed by St Edmundsbury Press Ltd,
Bury St Edmunds, Suffolk

To
Ted & Peewee Kalman
and their daughter
Janice

with profound gratitude
for their inestimable
help through
a long and difficult labour.